The Black Gondolier & Other Stories

The Black Gondolier & Other Stories

Fritz Leiber

Edited by
John Pelan & Steve Savile

OPEN ROAD

INTEGRATED MEDIA

NEW YORK

Edited by John Pelan & Steve Savile

Fritz & Me © 2000 John Pelan

Afterword: © 2000 Steve Savile

All Stories © The Estate of Fritz Leiber and are reprinted by permission of the Estate and The Richard Curtis Agency

ISBN 978-1-4976-4216-4

This edition published in 2014 by Open Road Integrated Media, Inc.

345 Hudson Street

New York, NY 10014

www.openroadmedia.com

The Black Gondolier & Other Stories

*"Before the mountains were brought forth,
Or ever Thou hadst formed the earth and
the world,
Even from everlasting to everlasting,
Thou art God. . . ."*

Psalm 90

Contents

Fritz and me

If you ask any long-time aficionado of fantastic literature to name his favorite authors, the fan of science fiction will likely name Fritz Leiber somewhere in his top five. So to, will the devotee of sword and sorcery mention the wonderful tales of Fafhrd and the Gray Mouser as among the very best that the genre has to offer. There have been many excellent writers of fantasy over the years, many excellent writers of science fiction, and many fine writers of horror stories. Arguably, the very best of them all was Fritz Leiber.

Leiber was the author that showed us what sword and sorcery fiction can and should be with his Lankhmar stories that spanned nearly fifty years. In the realm of science fiction, his Change War saga has stood the test of time and remains a classic in the genre. As far as horror fiction, most readers will place *Our Lady of Darkness* and *Conjure Wife* at or near the top of any list of great novels in the field. Then of course we have the socio-political satire of *A Specter is Haunting Texas* and the classic *X-files*-like paranoia of *You're All Alone*, written years before Chris Carpenter was a twinkle in his father's eye.

I'm afraid that I won't be able to fill this introduction with many personal anecdotes, I met the author on only a few occasions and our conversations often revolved around the malady of alcoholism and it's peculiar affinity for the creative sort. A subject that holds considerable fascination for those for whom it's a life or death issue, but to the average person it's a rather dull topic. I do treasure the fact that I was able to meet and chat with the man whose influence on my own reading and writing was so profound.

Like many of us who came on their first genre fiction at an early age in the sixties, I'd quickly discovered the works of Edgar Rice

Burroughs and Robert E. Howard; I was quite impressed, but when I stumbled on a book entitled *Swords Against Deviltry*, I was transported. . . . This was what I'd been looking for! I quickly used my meager allowance money to snap up every book that I could find that had the magical name of Leiber on it. This included some terrific science fiction, the novel *Gather, Darkness*, and finally a handful of anthologies where I discovered "Smoke Ghost", "The Dreams of Albert Moreland", and "Spider Mansion" for the first time.

Over the years I managed to accumulate as close to a complete collection of Leiber's work as you're likely to find. And for years I assumed that all his work was readily attainable, if not perpetually in print.

The book that you hold in your hands is a result of a curious serendipity, that there is no author living or dead that I would be more honored to pen an introduction about than Fritz Leiber goes without saying. That I would've thought this to be an unlikely occurrence is an understatement. After all, Leiber belongs to that pantheon of great writers that have shaped and molded the field of fantastic literature in the latter half of the twentieth century and the works of such individuals are perpetually kept in-print and readily accessible by one and all. Aren't they?

Apparently the answer to that question is in the negative. When Steve Savile first approached me to verify the appearances of several Leiber stories in conjunction with a chapbook that he was preparing for the British Fantasy Society I was amazed at just how much material was no longer available to modern readers. A few e-mails later and we were busily at work preparing two volumes that would bring the "lost Leiber" stories back into print. Even with the space of two volumes to work with it's been impossible to include everything that we would have liked to. We've chosen to focus on those stories that most modern readers would have the most difficult time locating with a couple of familiar tales included. Some stories we considered far too significant to be excluded and you will see some of these familiar tales interspersed in these two volumes. For the most part, our focus has been to restore to print the most significant of Leiber's weird tales that have been unavailable for twenty or more years.

The first thing that became apparent to me as we assembled this collection was just how early in his career Leiber had established himself as a master of the weird tale. While he did write a few stories that could be considered standard fare for the pulps, (such as "Spider Mansion" with its weird-menace excesses) as an example. From the very start his stories took on a modern attitude quite unlike that of his contemporaries in *Weird Tales*, who were busily scrambling to pen stories of improbably-named cosmic monstrosities and babbling aliens in a misguided homage to H.P. Lovecraft. . . .

While Leiber's earliest stories can be classified as updates of the tropes of earlier horror fiction, there is a decided modernity about them. A primary concern is that of the science fiction writer concerned about technologies gone horribly awry. In the early story "Spider Mansion", for all its classic gothic trappings it is at its core a tale of medical experiments gone wrong. The same can be said of the much later (1950) tale "The Dead Man" In both cases, it's not the *science* that is at fault for the dire consequences, but rather the fallible human element that manages to muck things up badly.

Both of these stories foreshadow Leiber's later work where he fuses the concerns of the twentieth century with the mold of the classic weird tale of decades past. In "The Girl with the Hungry Eyes" he considers the "vampirism" of advertising as a quite literal reality. In "The Black Gondolier", "The Man Who Made Friends with Electricity", and "Mr. Bauer and the Atoms" present our modern forms of energy in a new and terrifying light. Leiber's "mad" scientists are not mad in the sense of the old villains from the old Universal films from the 1930's, but rather they are often as not blinded by an arrogance and absolute certainty in their own wisdom that they fall afoul of their own inventions and concepts. In fact it could be said of Leiber that among his contemporaries only Philip K. Dick was his equal at writing science fiction that was truly horrifying.

The theme of humanity as but a bit player in the cosmic drama was an idea that Leiber often made use of in ways far more inventive than that of many of his contemporaries. Whereas H.P. Lovecraft took this idea in one direction, Leiber made the concept of an unknowable and hostile cosmos far more personal in stories such as "The Dreams of Albert Moreland". In this story a chess master is drawn into a game with frighteningly high stakes against an opponent reminiscent of one of Lovecraft's Great Old Ones. (Cthulhu as a galactic gamesmaster)? Not exactly, though in the hands of a lesser writer the story could easily have become that ludicrous. In Leiber's hands it's more about the all-consuming nature of the obsessive and the danger of actually getting what we want. Albert Moreland wants a suitable opponent to test his skill on and he gets exactly that.

Leiber's correspondence with Lovecraft is interesting in that of all of Lovecraft's correspondents only Leiber seemed immune to the desire to begin banging out slavish pastiches of the mythos created by the elder writer. In fact, it may well be that Leiber's correspondence led him to an early realization that the horrors of the past were just that, the past and would need a new and vital approach in the latter half of the century. It was not until considerably after Lovecraft's death that Leiber penned an actual mythos story. In this area as in other sub-genres, he excelled and his "The Terror from the Depths" is perhaps the standout piece in Edward Berglund's watershed anthology *Disciples of Cthulhu*.

Taken as a whole, this book chronicles Leiber's remarkable achievements in weird fiction, stories that are thoroughly modern examples of the horror story, tales such as "The Thirteenth Step" which uses the unlikely device of a speaker's "qualification" talk at an AA meeting to tales such as "Lie Still, Snow White", a masterpiece of erotic horror written years before the term had degenerated into a marketing label. There's a variety and richness here that could only have come from an author as gifted as Fritz Leiber.

John Pelan
Midnight House, 2000

The Black Gondolier

Daloway lived alone in a broken-down trailer beside an oil well on the bank of a canal in Venice near the café La Gondola Negra on the Grand Canal not five blocks from St. Mark's Plaza.

I mean, he lived there until after the fashion of intellectual lone wolves he got the wander-urge and took himself off, abruptly and irresponsibly, to parts unknown. That is the theory of the police, who refuse to take seriously my story of Daloway's strange dreads and my hints at the weird world-spanning power which was menacing him. The police even make light of the very material clues which I pointed out to them.

Or else Daloway was taken off, grimly and against his will, to parts utterly unknown and blackly horrible. That is my own theory, especially on lonely nights when I remember the dreams he told me of the Black Gondolier.

Of course the canal is a rather small one, showing much of its rough gravel bottom strewn with rusted cans and blackened paper, except when it is briefly filled by one of our big winter rains. But gondolas did travel it in the illusion-packed old days and it is still spanned by a little sharply humped concrete bridge wide enough for only one car. I used to cross that bridge coming to visit Daloway and I remember how I'd slow down and tap my horn to warn a possible car coming the other way, and the momentary roller-coaster illusion I'd get as my car heaved to the top and poised there and then hurtled down the opposite dusty slope for all of a breathless second. From the top of the little bridge I'd get my first glimpse of the crowded bungalows and Daloway's weed-footed trailer and close behind it the black hunch-shouldered oil well which figured so strangely in his dreads. *"Their* closest listening post," he sometimes called it during the final week, when he felt positively besieged.

And of course the Grand Canal is pretty dismal these days, with its several gracefully arching Bridges of Sighs raddled with holes showing their cement-shell construction and blocked off at either end by heavy wire barricades to keep off small boys, and with both its banks lined with oil wells, some still with their towering derricks and some — mostly those next to beach side houses — with their derricks dismantled , but all of them wearily pumping twenty-four hours a day with a soft slow syncopated thumping that the residents don't hear for its monotony, interminably sucking up the black petroleum that underlies Venice, lazily ducking and lifting their angularly oval metal heads like so many iron dinosaurs or donkeys forever drinking — donkeys moving in the somnambulistic rhythm of Ferde Grofe's Grand-Canyon donkey when it does its sleepy *hee . . . haw.* Daloway had a very weird theory about that — about the crude oil, I mean — a theory which became the core of his dreads and which for all its utter black wildness may still best explain his disappearance.

And La Gondola Negra is only a beatnik coffee house, successor to the fabulous Gashouse, though it did boast a rather interesting dirty drunken guitarist, whose face always had blacker smears on it than those of his stubbly beard and who wore a sweatshirt that looked like the working garment of a coal miner and whom Daloway and I would hear trailing off (I won't venture to say home) in the small hours of the morning, picking out on his twangy instrument his dinky "Texas Oilman Suite", which he'd composed very much in imitation of Ferde Grofe's one about the Grand Canyon, or raucously wailing his eerie beatnik ballad of the Black Gondola. He got very much on Daloway's nerves, especially towards the end, though I was rather amused by him and at the same time saw no harm in his caterwauling, except to would-be sleepers. Well, he's gone now, like Daloway, though not by the same route . . . I think. At least Daloway never suggested that the guitarist was one of *their* agents. No, as it turned out, *their* agent was a rather more formidable figure.

And they don't call the plaza St. Mark's, but it was obviously laid out to approximate that Adriatic-lapped area when it was created a half century ago. The porticos still shade the sidewalks in front of the two blocks of bars and grimy shops and there are still authentic

Venetian pillars, now painted salmon pink and turquoise blue — you may have seen them in a horror movie called *Delirium* where a beautiful crazy slim Mexican girl is chased round and round the deserted porticos by a car flashing its headlights between the pillars.

And of course the Venice isn't Venice, Italy, but Venice, USA — Venice, California — now just another district and postal address in the sprawling metropolis of Los Angeles, but once a proud little beach side city embodying the laughably charming if grotesque dream of creating Venice, Italy, scaled down but complete with canals and arched bridges and porticos, on the shores of the Pacific.

Yet for all the childish innocence of its bizarre glamor, Venice developed an atmosphere, or became the outpost of a sinister deep-rooted power, that did in Daloway. It is a place of dreams, not only the tinseled ones, but also the darker sort such as tormented and terrified my friend at the end.

For a while toward the beginning of this century the movie folk and real estate agents and retired farmers and the sailors from San Pedro went to spanking-new Venice to ride the gondolas — they had authentic ones poled by Italian types possibly hired from Central Casting — and eat exotic spaghetti and gambol romantically a bit with their wide-hatted long-skirted lady friends who also wore daring bathing suits with bare arms and rather short skirts and long black stockings — and gamble too with piled big yellow-backed green bills — and, with their caps turned front to rear, roar their wooden-spoked or wire-wheeled open touring cars along the Speedway, which is now a cramped one-way street that changes direction every block.

But then Redondo and Laguna and Malibu called away the film folk and the other people with fat pocketbooks, but as if to compensate for that they struck oil in Venice and built wells almost everywhere, yet despite this influx of money the gambling never regained its éclat, it became just bingo for housewives, and the Los Angeles police fought that homely extramural vice for a weary decade, until sprawling LA reached out a pseudopod one day and swallowed Venice up. Then the bingo stopped and Venice became very crowded indeed with a beach home or a beach apartment or a beach shack on every square yard that wasn't sidewalk or street — or oil well! — and with establishments as disparate as Bible Tabernacle and Colonic Irrigation Clinic and Mother Goldberg's Home for the Aged. It would have been going too far to have called Venice a beach slum, but it was trending in that direction.

And then, much later, the beats came, the gutter geniuses, the holy barbarians, migrating south in driblets from Big Sur and from North Beach in Frisco and from Disillusion, USA, everywhere, bringing their ratty art galleries and meager *avant garde* bookstalls and their black-trousered insolent women and their Zen and their guitars, including the one on which was strummed the Ballad of the Black Gondola.

And with the beats, but emphatically not of them, came the solitary oddballs and lone-wolf intellectuals like Daloway.

I met Daloway at a check-out desk of the excellent Los Angeles downtown public library, where our two stacks of books demonstrated so many shared interests — world history, geology, abnormal psychology, and psychic phenomena were some of them — that we paused outside to remark on it. This led to a conversation, in which I got some first intimations of his astonishing mentality, and eventually to my driving him home to save him a circuitous bus-trip, or, more likely, as I learned later, a weary hitch-hike.

Our conversation continued excitingly throughout most of the long drive, though even in that first exploratory confabulation Daloway made so many guarded references to a malefic power menacing us all and perhaps him in particular, that I wondered if he mightn't have a bee in this bonnet about World Communism or the Syndicate or the John Birch Society. But despite this possible paranoid obsession, he was clearly a most worthy partner for intellectual disputation and discourse.

Toward the end of the drive Daloway suddenly got nervous and didn't want me to take him the last few blocks. However, I overcame his reluctance. I remarked on the oil well next to his trailer — not to have done so would have implied I thought he was embarrassed by it — and he retorted sardonically, "My mechanical watchdog! Innocent-looking ugly beast, isn't it? But you've got to keep in mind that much more of it or of its domain is below the surface, like an iceberg. Which reminds me that I once ran across a seemingly well-authenticated report of a black iceberg — "

Thereafter I visited Daloway regularly in his trailer, often late at night, and we made our library trips together and even occasional brief expeditions to sleazily stimulating spots like La Gondola Negra.

At first I thought he had merely been ashamed of his battered aluminum-walled home, though it was neat enough inside, almost austere, but then I discovered that he hated to reveal to anyone where he lived, in part because he hesitated to expose anyone else to the great if shadowy danger he believed overhung him.

Daloway was a spare man yet muscular, with the watchful analytic gaze of an intellectual, but the hands of a mechanic. Like too many men of our times, he was amazingly learned and knowledgeable, yet unable to apply his abilities to his own advancement — for lack of connections and college degrees and because of nervous instabilities and emotional blockages. He had more facts at his fingertips than a Ph. D. candidate, but he used them to buttress off-trail theories and he dressed with the austere cleanly neatness and simplicity of a factory hand or a man newly released from prison.

He'd work for a while in a machine shop or garage and then live very thriftily on his savings while he fed his mind and pondered all the problems of the universe, or sometimes — this was before our meeting and the period of his dreads — organized maverick mental-therapy or para-psychology groups.

This unworldly and monetarily unprofitable pattern of existence at least made Daloway an exciting thinker. For him the world was a great conundrum or a series of puzzle boxes and he a disinterested yet childishly sensitive and enthusiastic observer trying to unriddle them. A scientist, or natural philosopher, rather, without the blinkered conformity of thought which sometimes characterizes men with professional or academic standing to lose, but rather with a fiercely romantic yet clear-headed and at times even cynical drive toward knowledge. Atoms, molecules, the stars, the unconscious mind, bizarre drugs and their effects, (he'd tried out LSD and mescaline), the play of consciousness, the insidious interweaving of reality and dream (as climatically in his dreams of the Black Gondola), the bafflingly twisted and folded strata of Earth's crust and man's cerebrum and all history, the subtle mysterious swings of world events and literature and sub-literature and politics — he was interested in all of them, and forever searching for some unifying purposeful power behind them, and sensitive to them to a preternatural degree.

Well, in the end he did discover the power, or at least convinced himself he did, and convinced me too for a time — and still does convince me, on lonely nights — but he got little enough satisfaction from his knowledge, that I know of, and it proved to be as deadly a discovery, to the discoverer, as finding out who is really back of Organized Crime or the Dope Traffic or American Fascism. Gunmen and poisoners and scientifically-coached bombers would be loosed against anyone making any of the last three discoveries; the agent who did away with Daloway was murkier-minded and deadlier even than the man who shot Kennedy.

But I mentioned sensitivity. In many ways, it was the hallmark of Daloway. He'd start at sounds I couldn't hear, or that were blanked out for me by the ceaseless ponderous low throb of the oil wells, especially the one a few yards beyond the thin wall of this trailer. He'd narrow his eyes at changes in illumination that didn't register on my retinas, or dart them at little movements I usually missed. He'd twitch his nostrils for special taints that to me were blanketed, at least in Venice, by the stench of the petroleum and the salt-fishy reek of the ocean. And he'd read meanings in newspaper articles and in paragraphs of books that I would never have seen except for his pointing them out, and I am not exactly unsubtle.

His sensitivity was almost invariably tinged with apprehension. For example, my arrivals seemed always to startle and briefly upset him, no matter how quiet or deliberately noisy I made them, and regardless of how much he seemed afterwards to enjoy my company — or at the very least the audience-of-one with which I provided him. Indeed this symptom — this jitteriness or jumpiness — was so strong in him that, taken together with his solitary fugitive mode of life and his unwillingness to have his dwelling known, it led me to speculate early in our relationship whether he might not be in flight from the law, or the criminal underworld, or some fearsomely ruthless political or sub-political organization, or from some less tangible mafia.

Well, considering the nature of the power Daloway really feared, its utter black inhumanity, its near-omnipresence and almost timeless antiquity, his great apprehension was most understandable — provided of course that you accepted his ideas, or at least were willing to consider them.

It was a long time before he would unequivocally identify the power to me — give me a specific name to his *They*. Perhaps he dreaded my disbelief, my skeptical laughter, even feared I would cut him off from me as a hopeless crank. Perhaps — and this I credit — he honestly believed that he would subject me to a very real danger by telling me, the same danger he was darkly shadowed by, or at least put me into its fringes — and only took the risk of doing so when the urge to share his suspicions, or rather convictions, with someone capable of comprehending them, became an overpowering compulsion.

He made several false starts and retreats. Once he began, "When you consider the source of the chemical fuels which alone make modern civilization possible, and modern warfare too, and the hope — or horror — of reaching other planets — " and then broke off.

Another time he launched off with, "If there is one single substance that has in it all of life and the potentiality for life, all past life by reason of its sources and all future life by the innumerable infinitely subtle compounds it provides — " and then shut tight his lips and opened them only to change the subject.

Another of these abortive revelations began with, "I firmly believe that there is no validity whatever in the distinction between the organic and the inorganic — I think it's every bit as false as that between the artificial and the natural. It's my absolute conviction that consciousness goes down to the level of the electrons — yes, and below that to the strata of the yet-undiscovered sub-particles. The substance which before all others convinces me that this is so, is — "

And once when I asked him without warning, "Daloway, what *is* it you're afraid of, anyhow?" he replied, "Why, the oil, of course," and then immediately insisted he was thinking of the possible role of hydrocarbons and coal tars — and their combustion products — in producing cancer.

I had better state as simply as possible Daloway's ideas about the power, as he finally revealed them to me.

Daloway's theory, based on his wide readings in world history, geology, and the occult, was that crude oil — petroleum — was more than figuratively the life-blood of industry and the modern world and modern lightning-war, that it truly had a dim life and will of its own, an inorganic consciousness or sub-consciousness, that we were all its puppets or creatures, and that its chemical mind had guided and even enforced the development of modern technological civilization. Created from the lush vegetation and animal fats of the Carboniferous and adjoining periods, holding in itself the black essence of all life that

11

had ever been, constituting in fact a great deep-digged black grave-yard of the ultimate eldritch past with blackest ghosts, oil had waited for hundreds of millions of years, dreaming its black dreams, slug-gishly pulsing beneath Earth's stony skin, quivering in lightless pools roofed with marsh gas and in top-filled rocky tanks and coursing through myriad channels and through spongy rocky bone, until a being evolved on the surface with whom it could realize and expend itself. When man had appeared and had attained the requisite sensi-tivity, and technical sophistication, then oil-like some black collective unconscious — had begun sending him its telepathic messages.

"Daloway, this is beyond belief!" I burst out here the first time he revealed to me his theory *in toto*. "Telepathy by itself is dubious enough, but telepathic communication between a lifeless substance and man — "

"Do you know that many companies hunting oil spend more money for dowsers than they do for geologists?" he shot back at me instantly. "For dowsers and for those psionic-electronic gadgets they call doodlebugs. The people whose money's at stake and who know the oil lands in a practical way believe in dowsing, even if most scien-tists don't. And what is dowsing but a man moving about on the sur-face until he gets a telepathic signal from . . . something below?"

In brief, Daloway's theory was that man hadn't discovered oil, but that oil had found man. Venice hadn't struck oil; oil had thrust up its vicious feelers like some vast blind monster, and finally made contact with Venice.

Everyone admits that oil is the lifeblood of modern technological culture — its automobiles and trucks and airplanes, its battleships and military tanks, its ballistic missiles and reekingly fueled space vehi-cles. In a sense Daloway only carried the argument one step further, positing behind the blood a heart — and behind the heart, a brain.

Surely in a great age-old oil pool with all its complex hydrocarbons — the paraffin series, the asphalt series, and many others — and with its subtle gradients of heat, viscosity, and electric charge, and with all its multiform microscopic vibrations echoing and re-echoing endless-ly from its lightless walls, there can be the chemical and physical equivalent of nerves and brain-cells; and if of brain-cells, then of thought. Some computers use pools of mercury for their memory units. The human brain is fantastically isolated, guarded by bony walls and by what they call the blood-brain barrier; how much more so subterranean oil, within its thick stony skull and earthen flesh.

Or consider it from another viewpoint. According to scientific materialism and anthropologic determinism, man's will is an illusion, his consciousness but an epiphenomenon — a useless mirroring of the atomic swirlings and molecular churnings that constitute ultimate reality. In any such world-picture, oil is a far more appropriate primal power than man.

Daloway even discovered the chief purpose animating oil's mentality, or thought he did. Once when we were discussing spaceflight, he said suddenly, "I've got it! Oil wants to get to other planets so that it can make contact with the oil there, converse with extraterrestrial pools — fatten on *their* millennial strength, absorb *their* wisdom . . ."

Of course a theory like that is something to laugh at or tell a psychiatrist. And of course Daloway may have been crazy or seeking a dark sort of laughter himself. I mean it is quite possible that Daloway was deceiving and mystifying me for his own amusement, that he elaborated his whole theory and repeatedly simulated his dreads simply as part of a long-drawn-out practical joke, that he noted a vein of credulity in me and found cruel delight in fooling me to the top of my bent, and that — as the police insist — even the starkly material evidence for the horror of his disappearance which I pointed out to them was only a final crude hoax on his part, a farewell jest.

Yet I knew the man for months, knew his dreads, saw him start and shiver and shake, heard him rehearse his arguments with fierce sincerity, witnessed the birth-quivers of many of his ideas — and I do not think so.

Oh, there were many times when I doubted Daloway, doubted his every word, but in the end his grotesque theory about the oil did not elicit from me the skepticism it might have from another hearing it elsewhere — perhaps, it occurs to me now, because it was advanced in a metropolis that is such a strange confirmation of it.

To the average tourist or the reader of travel brochures, Los Angeles is a gleaming city or vast glamorous suburb of movie studios and orange groves and ornate stucco homes and green-tiled long swimming pools and beaches and now great curving freeways and vast white civic centers and sleekly modern plants — aviation, missile, computer, research and development. What is overlooked here is that the City of the Angels, especially in its southern reaches stretching toward Long Beach, is almost half oil-field. These odorous grim industrial barrens interweave elaborately with airfields and showy tract housing developments — with an effect of savage irony. There is hardly a point from which one cannot see in the middle or farther distance, looming through the faintly bluish haze of the acrid smog, a hill densely studded with tall oil derricks. Long Beach herself is dominated by Signal Hill with oil towers thick as an army's spears and cruel as the murders which have been committed on its lonely slopes.

The first time I ever saw one of those hills — that near Culver City — I instantly thought of H. G. Wells' *War of the Worlds* and of his brainheavy Martians on their lofty metal tripods wherewith they strode ruthlessly about the British countryside. It seemed to me that I was seeing a congeries of such tower-high beings and that the next moment they might begin to stride lurchingly toward me, with something of the feeling, modernistically distorted, of Macbeth's Birnam Wood coming to Dunsinane.

And here and there along with the oil derricks, like their allies or reinforcements, one sees the gleaming distillation towers and the monstrous angular-shouldered cracking plants with muscles of knotted pipe, and the fields of dull silver oil tanks, livid in the smog, and the vaster gas tanks and the marching files of high-tension-wire towers, which look at a distance like oil derricks.

And as for Venice herself, with the oil's omnipresent reek, faint or heavy, and with her oil wells cheek-by-jowl with houses and shacks and eternally throbbing, as if pulsing the beat of a vast subterranean chemic heart — well, it was only too easy to believe something like Daloway's theory there. It was from the beach by Venice, in 1926, that Aimee Semple McPherson was mysteriously vanished, perhaps teleported, to the sinisterly-named Mexican town of Black Water — Agua Prieta. The coming of the illusioneers to Venice, and of the beatniks — and of the black oil, *aceite prieto* — all seemed alike mindless mechanic movements, or compulsive unconscious movements, whether of molecules or people, and in either case a buttressing of Daloway's wild theory — and at the very least an ironic picture of modern man's industrial predicament.

At all events the black savage sardonicism of that picture, along with Daloway's extreme sensitivity, made it easy to understand why his nerves were rasped acutely by the Ballad of the Black Gondola, as the black-smeared lurching beatnik guitarist came wailing it past the thin-walled trailer in the small hours of the night. I heard it only two or three times and the fellow's voice was thick to unintelligibility, though abominably raucous, so it was mostly from Daloway that I got the words of the few scattered lines I remember. They were a half-pla-giarized melange of ill-fitted cadences, but with a certain garishly eerie power:

> *Oh, the Black Gondola's gonna take you for a ride*
> *With a cargo of atom bombs and Atlases and nightmares . . .*
> *The Black Gondola's gonna stop at your door*
> *With a bow-wave of asphalt and a gravel spray . . .*
> *The Black Gondola'll . . . get . . . you . . . yet!*

Even of those five lines, the second comes — with a few changes of word — from a short poem by Yeats, the fifth derives from Vachel Lindsay's *The Congo*, while the Black Gondola itself sounds suspi-ciously like the nihilism-symbolizing Black Freighter in Brecht's and Weill's *The Three-Penny Opera*. Nevertheless, this crude artificial bal-lad, in which the Black Gondola seems to stand for our modern indus-trial civilization — and so, very easily, for petroleum too — may well have shaped or at least touched off Daloway's dreams, though his Black Gondola was of a rather different sort.

But before I describe Daloway's dreams, I had better round out his picture of the power which he believed dominated the modern world and, because he was coming to know too much about it, menaced his own existence.

According to Daloway, oil had intelligence, it had purpose . . .and it also had its agents. These beings, Daloway speculated, might be parts of itself, able to move independently man-shaped and man-sized for pur-poses of camouflage, composed of a sort of infernal black ectoplasm or something more material than that — a darkly oleaginous humanoid spawn. Or they might be, at least to begin with, living men who had become oil's worshipers and slaves, who had taken the Black Baptism or the Sable Consecration — as he put it with a strange facetiousness.

"The Black Man in the Witch-cult!" he once said to me abruptly. "I think he was a forerunner — spying out the ground, as it were. We have to remember too that oil was first discovered, so far as the modern world is concerned, in Pennsylvania, the hexing state, though in another corner than the Dutch territory — at Titusville, in fact, in 1859, just on the eve of a great and tragic war that made fullest use of new industrial technologies. It's important to keep in mind, incidentally, that the Black Man wasn't a Negro, which would have made him brown, but simply a man of Caucasian features with a dead-black complexion. Though there are dark brown petroleums, for that matter, and greenish ones. Of course many people used to equate the Black Man with the Devil, but Margaret Murray pretty well refuted that in her *God of the Witches* and elsewhere.

"Which is not to say that the Negro's not mixed up in it," Daloway continued on that occasion, his thoughts darting and twisting and back-tracking as rapidly as they always did. "I think that the racial question and — as with space flight — the fact that it's come to the front today, is of crucial significance. Oil's using the black as another sort of camouflage."

"What about atomic energy? You haven't brought that in yet," I demanded a little crossly, or more likely nervously.

Daloway gave me a strange penetrating look. "Nuclear energy is, I believe, an entirely separate subterranean mentality," he informed me. "Helium instead of marsh gas. Pitchblende instead of pitch. It's more introspective than oil, but it may soon become more active. Perhaps the conflict of these two vampiristic mentalities will be man's salvation! — though more likely, I'm afraid, only a further insurance of his immediate destruction."

Oil's dark agents not only spied, according to Daloway, but also dispersed clues leading to the discovery of new oil fields and new uses for oil, and on occasion removed interfering and overly perceptive human beings.

"There was Rudolf Diesel for one, inventor of the all-important engine," Daloway asserted. "What snatched him off that little North Sea steamer back in 1913? — just before the first war to prove the supremacy of petro-powered tanks and armored cars and zeppelins and planes. No one has ever begun to explain that mystery. People didn't realize so well then that oil is as much a thing of the salt water — especially the shallows above the continental shelves — as it is of the shores. I say that Diesel knew too much — and was snatched because he did! The same may have been true of Ambrose Bierce, who disappeared at almost the same time down in the oil lands between Mexico and Texas, though I don't insist on that. The history of the oil industry is studded with what some call legends, but I believe are mostly true accounts, of men who invented new fuels, or made other key discoveries, and then dropped out of existence without another word spoken. And the oil millionaires aren't exactly famous for humanitarianism and civilized cosmopolitan outlook. And every oil field has its tales of savagery and its black ghosts — the fields of Southern California as much as the rest."

I found it difficult — or, more truthfully, uncomfortable — to adjust to Daloway's new mood of piled revelations and wild sudden guesses, in contrast to his previous tight-lipped secrecy, and especially to these last assertions about a black lurking infernal host — here, in the ultramodern, garishly new American Southwest. But not too difficult. I have never been one to be dogmatically skeptical about preternatural agencies, or to say that Southern California cannot have ghosts because its cities are young and philistine and raw that sprawl across so much of the inhospitable desert coast and because the preceding Amerind and Mission cultures were rather meager — the Indians dull and submissive, the padres austere and cruel. Ghostliness is a matter of atmosphere, not age. I have seen an unsuccessful subdivision in Hollywood that was to me more ghostly than the hoariest building I ever viewed in New England. Only thirty years ago they had scythed and sawed down the underbrush and laid out a few streets and put in sidewalks and a water pipe and a few hydrants. But then the lot-buyers and home-builders never materialized and now the place is a wilderness of towering weeds and brush, with the thin-topped streets eroded so that at some points they are a dozen feet below the hanging under-eaten sidewalks, and the water pipe is exposed and rusting and each hydrant is in the midst of a yellow thicket and the only living things to be seen are the tiny darting lizards and an occasional swift sinuous snake or velvet dark shifty tarantula and whatever else it is that rustles the dry near-impassable vegetation.

Southern California is full of such ghost-districts and ghost-towns despite the spate of new building and hill-chopping and swamp-draining that has come with the rocket plants and television and the oil refineries and the sanatoria and the think-factories and all the other institutions contributing to the area's exploding population.

Or I could let you look down into Potrero Canyon, an eroded earth-quake crack which cuts through populous Pacific Palisades, another postal address in Los Angeles. But I could hardly lead you down into it, because its sides are everywhere too steep and choked with manzanita and sumac and scrub oak, where they don't fall away altogether to the clay notch of its bottom. Trackless and almost impenetrable, Potrero Canyon dreams there mysteriously, the home of black foxes and coyotes and silently-soaring sinister hawks, oblivious to the bright costly modern dwellings at its top —"that deep romantic chasm . . . a savage place . . . holy and enchanted," to borrow the words of Coleridge.

Or I could invite you on any clear day to look out across the Pacific at the mysterious, romantically crested Santa Barbara Islands — all of their 218,000 acres, save for Santa Catalina's 55,000, forbidden territory by Government ukase or private whim.

Even the earth of Southern California, sedimentary, lacking a strongly knit rocky skeleton, seems instinct with strange energies hardly known in geologically stabler areas and lending a weird plausibility to Daloway's theory of sentient, seeking, secretive oil. Every year there are unforeseen earth-falls — and falls of houses too — and mud-slides that drown dwellings and engulf cars. Only in 1958 one of them sent half of a hundred-foot-high hill slumping forward to bury the Pacific Coast Highway; they were more than six months filling in beach, trucks running rock night and day, to get a bed on which to lay the road around it.

Once, not too long ago, they called that road Roosevelt Highway, but now it is Cabrillo Highway or even El Camino Real. Just as the street names, straining for glamor, have progressed from Spanish to British to Italian and back to Spanish again, and the favorite subdivision names from Palisades to Heights to Knolls to Acres to Rivieras to Mesas to Condominiums. In Southern California, seemingly, history can run backwards, with an unconscious fierce sardonicism.

And then there are all the theosophists and mystics and occultists, genuine and sham, who came swarming to Southern California in the early decades of the century. A good many of those were sensitive to the uncanny forces here, I think, and were drawn by them — as well as by the lavish gypsy camp of the movie-makers, the bankrolls of the retired and the elderly, and a health-addict's climate, the last somewhat marred by chilly damp western winds and by burningly dry Santa Anas, threatening vast brush fires, and now by smog. And the occultists keep swarming here — the I Am folk with their mysterious mountain saints and glittering meetings in evening dress; the barefoot followers of Krishna Venta and the mysterious errand-of-mercy appearances they made at local disasters and finally their own great Box Canyon mystery-explosion of December 7, 1958, which claimed ten lives, including — possibly — their leader's; the Rosicrucians and Theosophists; Katherine Tingley and Annie Besant; the latter's World Master, Krishnamurti, still living quietly in Ojai Valley; the high-minded Self-Realization movement, the dead body of whose founder Paramhansa Yogananda resisted corruption for at least twenty days, as testified by Forest Lawn morticians; Edgar Rice Burroughs, who fictionalized the fabulous worlds of theosophy on Mars and is immortalized in Tarzana; the flying-saucer cultists with their great desert conventions; beautiful Gloria Lee listening raptly to her man on Jupiter — there is no end to them.

So when Daloway began to rehearse to me his fearful suspicions, or beliefs rather, about oil's black ghosts — or acolytes, or agents, or budded-off black ameboid humanoid creatures, or whatever they exactly might be — I was uneasily sympathetic to the idea if not consciously credulous. Good Lord, if there could be such things as ghosts, it would be easy to imagine them in Venice — ghosts of the Channel Indians and those whom the Indians called "the Ancient Ones," ghosts of Cabrillo's men when he discovered this coast in 1592 before he died on windswept forbidden San Miguel, westernmost of the Santa Barbara Islands; ghosts from the harsh theocratic Mission days and the lawless Mexican years that followed, ghosts of the Spanish and Yankee Dons, ghosts of gold-seekers and vigilantes, anarchists and strike-breakers, and ghosts of the gamblers and gondoliers and the other folk from the illusion-packed years. Especially now that the illusions are edging back again: in the swampy south end of Venice they've just built a great marina or small-boat harbor, with fingers of sea interlocking fingers of low-lying land and with all sorts of facilities for luxurious dockside apartments and homes — if the buyers materialize and if they fully subdue the strange tidal waves which first troubled the marina. There is even talk of linking the marina to the old canal system and cleaning that up and filling it all year round and perhaps bringing back the gondolas. Though at the same time, by a cackling irony, a battle goes on in the courts as to whether or not industry may be licensed to drill for offshore oil, setting up its derricks in the shallows off the Pacific, just beyond the breakers that beat against the beaches of Venice — Wells' Martians submerged to their chests in waves. In our modern world, illusion and greed generally walk hand in hand.

So it was by no means with complete skepticism about his wild theory of black buried oil and its creatures that I listened to Daloway's accounts of his dreams of the Black Gondola, or rather his dream, since it was always basically the same, with minor variations. I will tell it one time in his words, as he most fully told it, remembering too how I heard it — in his cramped trailer, late at night, perhaps just after the passing of the wailing drunken guitarist, no other sound but the faint distant rattle of the breaking waves and the slow throb of the oil pump a few yards beyond the thin metal wall with the small half-curtained window in it, the edges of my mind crawling with thoughts of the black preternatural creatures that might be on watch outside that same wall and pressing even closer.

"I'm always sitting in the Black Gondola when the dream begins," Daloway said. "I'm facing the prow and my hands grip the gunwales to either side. Apparently I've just left the trailer and got aboard her, though I never remember that part, for we're in the canal outside, which is full to the top of its banks, and we're headed down the middle of it toward the Grand Canyon. There's oil on my clothes, I can feel it, but I don't know how it got there.

"It's night, of course, dark night. The street lights are all out. There's just enough glow in the sky to silhouette the houses. No light shows in any of their windows, only the glimmer coming between them — a glimmer no brighter than the phosphorescence that paints the breakers some summer nights when the sewage breeds too big an algae crop and there's a fish-kill. Yet the glimmer and glow are enough to show the tiny ripples angling out from the gondola's prow as we move along.

"It's a conventional gondola, narrow and with a high prow, but it's black — sooty black — no highlights reflect from it. You know, gondola also means coal car, those black open-topped cars on the railroads. I've ridden the freights often enough — perhaps there's a connection there.

"I can hear the swish and the faint fluid-muffled thump of the gondolier's pole against the bottom as he drives us along. It's thudding in the same slow rhythm as the pumping of the oil wells. But I cannot look around at him — I daren't! The fact is, I'm frozen with terror, both of the voiceless gondolier standing behind me and of our destination, though I cannot yet conceive or name that. My grip on the gunwales tightens convulsively.

"Sometimes I try to visualize what the gondolier looks like — never in my dreams, but at times like this — what his appearance would be if I had the courage to turn my head, or if the dream changed so that I was forced to look at him. And then I get a glimpse of a thin figure about seven feet tall. His shoulders are twisted and his head, bent forward, is hooded. The rest of his clothing is tight-fitting, down to his long narrow sharply pointed shoes. His big long-fingered hands grip the black pole strongly. And everywhere he himself is black, not dull black like the gondola, but gleaming black as if he were thickly coated with black oil which had just the faintest greenish sheen to it — as if he were some infernal merman newly swum up from the depths of a great oil ocean.

"But in my dream I dare not look or even think of him. We turn into the Grand Canal and head toward the marina, but there are no lights there or on the heights of Playa del Rey beyond. There are no stars in the sky, only that exceedingly faint shimmer. I watch for the lights of a plane mounting from the International Airport. Even one tiny red-green pair moving across the sky out to sea so far away would be a great comfort to me. But none comes.

"The reek of the oil is strong. (In how many dreams do we experience odors? This is the only one where it's happened to me.) We pass under two of the bridges. The glimmer shows me their curving ruin-notched outlines and one or two ragged fragments of cement dangling by the wires imbedded in them.

"The reek grows stronger. And now at last I notice a change in our movement, although the bow ripples have the same angles and the muffled thud of the pole has the same slow rhythm. The change is simply that the gondola has settled a little deeper in the water, not more than two or three inches.

"I ponder the problem. Nothing has entered the boat — nothing before me that I have seen or behind me that I have felt. I scrape my feet against the bottom — it is dry, no water has entered. Yet the gondola is riding deeper. Why?

"The reek grows stronger still — suffocatingly so, almost. The gondola settles still deeper in the water, so deep that the ends of my fingers on the outside of the gunwales are immersed. And now the problem is solved. Touch tells me that the gondola is riding not in water, but in oil. Or rather in an ever-thickening layer of oil floating on top of the water. The thicker the layer gets, the deeper the boat sinks."

Daloway stared at me sharply. "That would actually be true, you know," he interjected. "A boat would ride very high in a sea of mercury, because the stuff is heavier than lead, but low in a sea of gasoline or petroleum — sink, in fact, if it hadn't enough freeboard — because the stuff is light. Petroleum may have as little as seven-tenths the weight of water. Which is odd considering the thick greases we get out of it. Yet thick greases like Vaseline float.

"And it would be true, too, that a boat riding in a layer of oil floating atop water — an oil-layer thinner than the boat's draught — would sink proportionately deeper as the layer got thicker, until it was riding wholly in oil. Then it would steady — or sink for good.

"The layer of oil in which my gondola is riding is getting thicker, at all events," he went on, resuming the narration of his dream.

"I get the impression that we are reaching a length of the Grand Canal in which there is nothing but oil. The black stuff begins to pour over the gunwales in a thin sleek waterfall. Yet the Black Gondola is moving ahead as steadily and strongly as ever and even more swiftly. We are like an airplane taking off — downward. Or like a submarine diving.

"I nerve myself to loosen my grip on the gunwales and make a wild plunge toward the bank, although I fear I will drown in even that short distance. But at that instant the gondolier's pole comes down firmly on my right shoulder, projecting perhaps a yard ahead of me and pinning me to my seat. Though its injunction not to move is more hypnotic, or magical, than physical, it is absolute. I cannot stir, or break my grip on the submerging gondola.

"I know this is Death. I peer yearningly one last time for the lights of a mounting airplane. Then as the oil, moving past me in an unending sleep caress, mounts to my face, I shut my lips, I hold my breath, I close my eyes.

"The oil covers me. I am aware in those last paralyzed seconds that we are moving still more swiftly through the black stuff. Yet the solid oil rushing past does not unseat me from the gondola, or even tug at me. The effect is always of a great unending caress.

"Death and Agony do not come. I wait for the urge to breathe to become overpowering. There is no urge. The straining muscles of my chest and jaw and face relax.

"I open my eyes. I can see through the oil. It has become my medium of vision. By a darkly green shimmering I can see that, still descending and even more swiftly now, we are traversing a great rocky cavern filled with oil. Evidently we plunged into it from the Grand Canal, by way of some unsuspected gate or lock, while I waited with closed eyes for my death-spasm.

"During the same period of blindness, the Black Gondolier has moved from behind me and taken up a position below and a little ahead of the Black Gondola, dragging it along like some mythic slim long dolphin or infernal merman. Now and again past the forward gunwales I glimpse, greenly outlined in midkick, the black soles of his long narrow sharply pointed feet — or bifid narrow tail-fin.

"I say to myself, 'I have received the Black Baptism. I have partaken of the Black Communion.'

"Our speed ever increasing, we pass through weird grottos, we twist and turn through narrow passageways whose irregular walls flash with precious gems and nuggets of gold and copper, we soar across great vaults domed with crusty salt crystals glittering like thick-packed diamonds.

"I know, even in my dream, that this picture of underground oil in vast interconnected lakes and tanks is false by all geology — that untapped oil is mixed with earth and porous rocks and shales and sand, not free — but the picture and experience remain the same and exquisitely real. Perhaps I have suffered a size-change, become microscopic. Perhaps I have suffered a sense-change and see things symbolically. Perhaps geology is false.

"Our speed becomes impossible. We flash about like a single black corpuscle in the oil plasma of the great world-creature. I know, intuitively, that one instant we are beneath Caracas; the next Ploesti; then

Baku, Iraq, Iran, India, Indonesia, Argentina, Columbia, Oklahoma, Algeria, Antarctica, Atlantis . . .

"It is more as if we were flashing through black outer space, softly gleaming with galaxies, than through earth's depths.

"There is a feeling of nightmare-ride now . . . wild whirlings and spiralings . . . a blurred glitter . . . a blessed sense of fatigue . . .

"Yet at the same time I become aware that the white-green sinuous gleamings I see are the nerves of oil, which stretch everywhere to every tiniest well; that I am approaching the great brain; that I will soon see God.

"And I never, even in this nightmare phase, lose the awareness of the close presence of my conductor. From time to time I still glimpse, in frozen instants, standing out sharply against the glistening green, the black shapes of his long narrow sharply pointed lower extremities.

"There the dream ends. I can no longer endure its flashing transitions. I am out wearied. I awake sweating and groaning or fall into a deeper dreamless sleep from which I slowly arouse hours later, lethargic and spent."

As he finished his narrative he would generally give me a tired questioning look, smiling thinly as if at the extravagance of it all, but with a loneliness in his eyes that made me think of him looking hopelessly in his dream for the lights of a distant plane as the Black Gondola went under.

That was Daloway's dream. To describe my reactions to it is more difficult. Remember that he did not tell it to me all at once, but only sketchily at first with an air of, "Here's a ridiculous dream;" later much more seriously, putting in the details, building the picture. Also remembering that he dreamed it about six times during the period of our friendship, and that each time the dream was somewhat fuller and he told me more of it — and between times revealed to me more of his wild theory of world oil, bit by bit, and revealed, bit by bit, too, how deeply he believed or at least felt this theory. Remember finally that his nerves were in pretty good shape when he first told me the dream, but pretty bad toward the last.

I seem to recall that the first time or two, we both poked at the dream psychoanalytically. There were obvious birth and death and sex symbols in it: trips through fluid, return to the womb, the caress of oil, the gondolier's punting pole, passage under bridges, twisting tunnels, difficulties in breathing, flying sensations, all the usual stuff. I think he advanced the rather farfetched notion that his disappearing into strangling darkness with an unknown menacing male indicated unconscious fears of homosexuality, while I championed the prosier explanation that the whole horror of oil might merely stand for his resentment at having to work as a mechanic to earn a living. We speculated as to whether the racial question might not be tied up in it — Daloway had a touch of Indian blood — and tried to identify the person in his early life whom the Black Gondolier might represent.

But the last time he told it to me, we just looked at each other for a long while and I went over stoopingly and drew the curtain fully across the little window in the side of the low-ceilinged trailer toward the oil well and the night, and we began to talk about something else, something trivial.

By that time, you see, he'd had the first of his outbursts of more active fear. It had been touched off by a rumor or report that petroleum was leaking into the Grand Canal through some underground fissure, perhaps from a defective well. He wanted us to walk over to the spot and have a look, but the sun set before we got there and we couldn't see any lights indicating men at work or hunting for the leak, and he suddenly decided it would be too much trouble and we turned back. The dark comes quite quickly in Venice — Los Angeles is near enough to the Tropic of Cancer so you can see all of Scorpius and the Southern Crown too, while Fomalhaut rides high in the southern sky. And Venice's narrow streets, half of them only pedestrian passageways blocked off to cars, swiftly grow gloomy. I remember that going back we hurried a bit, stumbling through sand and around rubbish, but hardly enough to account for the way Daloway was gasping by the time we reached his trailer.

Once during that unconfessed flight, while we were crossing an empty lot by the Grand Canal, he stopped me by catching hold of my elbow and then he led us in a circle around a slightly darker stretch of ground — almost as if he feared it were a scummed-over dust-camouflaged oil pool which might engulf us. You do run into such things in oil fields, though I've never heard of them in Venice.

And two or three times, later that night, Daloway made excuses to go out and scan the light-patched darkness toward the Grand Canal, almost as if he expected to see tongues of petroleum running toward us across the low ground, or other shapes approaching.

To quiet his nerves and put the thing on a more rational basis, I pointed out that, as he himself had told me, natural oil leakages are by no means uncommon in the Pacific Southland. Ocean bathers are apt to get bits of tar on their feet and they usually blame it on modern industry and its poorly-disposed wastes, seldom discovering that it is asphalt from undersea leakages which were recurring regularly long before Cabrillo's time. Another example, this one in the heart of western Los Angeles, is La Brea tar pits, which trapped many saber-toothed tigers and their prey, as the asphalt-impregnated bones testify. (There's a tautology there: *brea* means tar. Other glamorous-sounding old Los Angeles street names have equally ugly or homely meanings: Las Pulas means "the fleas," Temescal means "sweat house," while La Ciénega, street of the wonder-restaurants, means "the swamp.")

My effort was ill-considered. Daloway's nerves were not quieted. He muttered, "Damned oil killing animals too! Well, at least it got the exploiters as well as the exploited," and he stepped out again to scan the night, the growl of the pump growing suddenly louder as he opened the door.

The report of the petroleum leakage turned out to have been much exaggerated. I don't recall hearing how they fixed it up, if they ever did. But it gave me an uncomfortable insight into the state of Daloway's nerves — and didn't do my own any good, either.

Then there was the disastrous business of Daloway's car. He bought an old jalopy for almost nothing at about this time and put it in good shape, expending most of his dwindling cash reserve buying essential replacements at second hand. I inwardly applauded — I thought the manual work would be therapeutic. Incidentally, Daloway repeatedly refused my offers of a small loan.

Then one evening I dropped over to find the car gone and Daloway just returned from a long, half hitch-hiked trudge and pitifully strained and shaky. It seemed he'd been driving the car along the San Bernadino Freeway when a huge kerosene truck just ahead of him had jack knifed in an underpass and split its tank and spilled its load and caught afire. I'd heard about the accident on the radio a few hours earlier — it tied up the freeway for almost half a day. Daloway had managed to bring his car to a swerving stop in the swift-shooting oil. Two other cars, also skidding askew, crashed him lightly from behind, preventing his car's escape. He managed to leap out and run away before the fire got to it — the truck driver escaped too, miraculously — but Daloway's car, uninsured of course, was burned to a shriveled black ruin along with several others.

Daloway never admitted to me straight out that he had been escaping from Venice and LA, leaving them for good, when that catastrophe on the San Bernardino Freeway thwarted him. I suppose he was ashamed to admit he would go away without telling me his plans or even saying goodby. (I would have understood, I think: some partings have to be made with ruthless suddenness, before the fire of decision burns out.) But a big old suitcase that had used to stand inside the door of the trailer was gone and I imagine it burned with the car.

Later the police neatly turned all this into an argument for their theory that Daloway's ultimate departure from Venice was voluntary. He'd once started to leave without informing me, they pointed out — and would have, except for the accident. His money was running out. (There was a month's rent owing on the trailer at the end.) He had a history of briefly-held jobs alternating with periods of roving or dropping out of sight — or so they claimed. What more natural than that he should have seized on some sudden opportunity or inspiration to decamp?

I had to admit they had a point, of sorts. It turned out that the police had an old grudge against Daloway: they'd once suspected him of being mixed up in the marijuana traffic. Well, that may have been true, I suppose; he admitted to me having smoked hemp a few times, years before.

I used to carp at horror stories in which the protagonist could at any time have departed from the focus of horror — generally some lonely dismal spot, like Daloway's trailer — but instead insisted on staying there, though shaking with fear, until he was engulfed. Since my experience with Daloway, I've changed my mind. Daloway did try to leave. He made that one big effort with the car and it was foiled. He lacked the energy to make another. He became fatalistic. And perhaps the urge to stay and see what would happen — always strong, I imagine, curiosity being a fundamental human trait — at that point became somewhat stronger than the opposing urge to flee.

That evening after the freeway accident I stayed with him a long time, trying to cheer him up and get him to look at the accident as a chance occurrence, not some cat-and-mousing malignancy aimed directly and solely at him. After a while I thought I was succeeding.

"You know, I hung back of that truck for fully ten minutes, afraid to pass, though I had enough speed," he admitted. "I kept thinking something would happen while I was passing it."

"You see," I said. "If you'd passed it right off, you wouldn't have been involved in the accident. You courted danger by sticking close behind a vehicle that you probably knew, at least subconsciously, was behaving dangerously. We can all have accidents that way."

"No," Daloway replied, shaking his head. "Then the accident would have come earlier. Don't you understand? — it was an *oil* truck! And if I had got by it, the oil would have stopped me some way, I'm convinced of that now — even if it had to burst out in a spontaneous gusher beside the highway and skid my car into a wreck! Remember how the oil burst out of Signal Hill in the 1933 Long Beach earthquake and flowed inches thick down the streets?"

"Well, at any rate you escaped with your life," I pointed out, trying to salvage a little of my imagined advantage.

"It didn't want to kill me there," Daloway countered gloomily. "It just wanted to herd me back. It's got something else in store for me."

"Now look here, Daloway," I burst out, a little angry and trying to sound more so, "if we all argued that way, there wouldn't be any trifling mischance that couldn't be twisted into a murder-attempt by some weird power. Just this morning I found a little gas-leak in my kitchen. Am I to suppose — ?"

"It's after you too now!" he interrupted me, paling and starting to his feet. "Natural gas — petroleum — the same thing — siblings. Keep off me, it's not safe! I've warned you before. You better get out now."

I wouldn't agree to that, of course, but the couple hours more I stayed with Daloway didn't improve his mood, or mine either. He set himself to analyzing last year's Los Angeles catastrophe, when a three hundred million gallon water reservoir broke its thick earthen wall in the Baldwin Hills and did tens of millions of dollars worth of damage, floating and tumbling cars and flooding thousands of homes and smashing hundreds of buildings with a deluge of water and mud —

though only a few lives were lost because of efficient warning by motorcycle police and a helicopter cruising with a bullhorn.

"There were oil wells by the reservoir," he said. "Even the purblind officials admit that soil subsidence from oil drilling may have started the leaks. But do you remember the east west bounds of the flood? From La Brea to La Ciénega — the tar to the swamp! And what was the substance lining the reservoir? What was the stuff that craftily weakened from point to point and then gave way at the crucial moment, triggering the thing? Asphalt!"

"Men did the drilling, Daloway," I argued wearily. "Asphalt is inert . . ."

"Inert!" he almost snarled back at me. "Yes, like the uranium atom! What moves the dowsers' wands? Do you still think that men run things up here?"

By the time I left I was glad to be gone and disgusted with myself for wasting too much time, and very irked at Daloway too and glad I had an engagement the next evening that would prevent me from visiting him.

For the first time in weeks, going home that night, I wondered if Daloway mightn't be an all-out psychopath. At the same time I found myself so nervous about the very faint stench of oil in my car that I opened all the windows, though there was a chilly fog, and even then I kept worrying about the motor and the oil in it, as it heated. Damn it, the man was poisoning my life with his paranoid suspicions and dreads! He was right, I'd better keep off him.

But the next night a thunder stroke woke me about two; there was rain sizzling and rattling on the roof and gurgling loudly in the resonating metal drain pipes, and right away I was thinking how much louder it must be pounding on Daloway's trailer and wondering how apt lightning striking an oil well was to cause a fire — things like that. It was our first big downpour of the season, rather early in the fall too, and it kept on and on, a regular cloudburst, and the lightning too. I must have listened to them for a couple of hours, thinking about Daloway and his wild ideas, which didn't seem so wild now with the storm going, and picturing Venice with its canals filling fast and with its low crowded houses and oil wells and derricks under the fist of the rain and the lightning's shining spear.

I think it was chiefly the thought of the canals being full that finally got me up and dressed around five and off in the dark to see how Daloway was faring. The rain had stopped by now and of course the thunder too, but there were signs of the storm everywhere — my headlights showed me falling branches, fans of eroded mud and gravel crossing the street, gutters still brimming, a few intersections still shallowly flooded, and a couple of wide buttons of water still pouring up from manholes whose heavy tops had been displaced by the pressure from brim-filled flumes.

Hardly any private automobiles were abroad yet, but I met a couple of fire trucks and light-and-power trucks and cars off on emergency errands, and when I got to Venice, Daloway's end was dark — there'd evidently been a major power failure there. I kept on, a bit cautious now that my headlights were just about the only illumination there was. Venice seemed like a battered city of the dead — a storm-bombed ruin — I hardly saw a soul or a light, only a candle back of a window here and there. But the streets weren't flooded too deep anywhere along my usual route and just as I sensed the eastern sky paling a little I crossed the narrow high-humped bridge — no need to tap my horn this time! — and swung into my usual parking place and stopped my car and switched off the lights and got out.

I must be very careful to get things right now.

My first impression, which the motor of my car had masked up to now, was of the great general silence. All the sounds of the storm were gone except for the tiny occasional drip of the last drop off a leaf or a roof.

The oil well by Daloway's trailer was still pumping though. But there was an odd wheezy hiss in it I'd never heard before, and after each hiss a faint tinkly spatter, as of drops hitting sheet metal.

I walked over to the edge of the canal. There was just enough light for me to manage that safely. I stooped beside it. Just as I'd imagined, it was full to the brim.

Then I heard the other sounds: a faint rhythmic swish and, spaced about three seconds apart, the faint muffled thuds that would be made by a gondolier's pole.

I stared down the black canal, my heart suddenly pounding and my neck cold. For a moment I thought I saw, in murkiest silhouette, the outlines of a gondola, with gondolier and passenger, going away from me, but I simply couldn't be sure.

Fences blocked the canal for me that way, even if I'd had the courage to follow, and I ran back to my car for my flashlight. Halfway back with it, I hesitated, wondering if I shouldn't drive the car to the canal edge and use my high headlight beams, but I wasn't sure I could position it right.

I kept onto the canal and directed my flashlight beam down it.

In the first flare of light and vision, I again thought I saw the Black Gondola, much smaller now, near the turn into the Grand Canal.

But the beam wavered and when I got it properly directed again — a matter of a fraction of a second — the canal seemed empty. I kept swinging my flashlight a little, up and down, side to side, for quite a few seconds and studying the canal, but it stayed empty.

I was half inclined to jump into my car and take the long swing around to the road paralleling the Grand Canal. I did do that, somewhat later on, but now I decided to go to the trailer first. After all, I hadn't made any noise to speak of and Daloway might well be there asleep — it would take only seconds to check. Everything I had heard and seen so far might conceivably be imagination, the auditory and visual impressions had both been very faint, though they still seemed damnably real.

There was a hint of pink in the east now. I heard again that unfamiliar hissing wheeze from the oil well, with subsequent faint splatter, and I paused to direct my light at it and then, after a bit, at the wall of Daloway's trailer.

Something had gone wrong with the pump so that it had sprung a leak and with every groaning stroke a narrow stream of petroleum was sprayed against the wall of Daloway's trailer, blotching it darkly, and through the little window, which stood open.

It was never afterwards established whether a lightning stroke had something to do with this failure of the valves of the pump, though several people living around there later assured me that two of the lightning strokes had been terrific, seeming to hit their roofs. Personally I've always had the feeling that the lightning unlocked *something*.

The door to the trailer was shut, but not locked. I opened it and flashed my light around the walls. Daloway wasn't anywhere there, nobody was.

The first thing I flashed my light steadily on was Daloway's bunk under the little open window. At that moment there came the hissing wheeze and oil rattled against the wall of the trailer and some came through the window, pattering softly on the rough brown blankets, adding a little to the great black stain on them. The oil stank.

Then I directed my flashlight another way . . . and was frozen by horror.

What I'd heard and seen by the bank of the canal might have been imagination. One has to admit he can always be fooled along the faint borderlines of sensation.

But this that I saw now was starkly and incontrovertibly real and material.

The accident to the oil pump, no matter how sardonically grim and suggestive in view of Daloway's theories, could be . . . merely an accident.

But this that I saw now could be no accident. It was either evidence of a premeditated supernormal malignancy, or — as the police insist — of a carefully planned and executed hoax. Incidentally, the police looked at me speculatively as they made this last suggestion.

After a while I got control of myself to the point where I could trace what I saw to its ending and then back again, still using my flashlight to supplement the gathering dawn.

A little later I made the round-about car trip I mentioned earlier to the Grand Canal and searched furiously along it, running down to its bank at several spots and venturing out on a couple of the ruined bridges.

I saw no signs of any boat or body at all, or of any oil either, for that matter, though the odor is always strong there.

Then I went to the police. Almost at once, a little to my shame, I found myself resorting to the subterfuge of emphasizing the one point that my friend Daloway had an almost crazily obsessive fear of drowning in the Grand Canal and that this might be a clue to his disappearance.

I guess I had to take that line. The police were at least willing to give some serious attention to the possibility of a demented suicide, whereas they could hardly have been expected to give any to the hypothesis of a black inanimate, ancient, almost ubiquitous liquid engineering a diabolical kidnaping.

Later they assured me that they had inspected the canal and found no evidence of bodies or sunken boats in it. They didn't drag it, at least not all of it.

That ended the investigation for them. As for the real and material evidence back at the trailer, well, as I've said at least twice before, the police insist that was a hoax, perpetuated either by Daloway or myself.

And now the investigation is ended for me too. I dare not torture my mind any longer with a theory that endows with purposeful life the deepest buried darkness, that makes man and his most vaunted technological achievements the sardonic whim of that darkness and invests it with a hellish light visible only to its servitors, or to those about to become its slaves. No, I dare no longer think in this direction, no matter how conclusive the evidence I saw with my own eyes. I almost flipped when I saw it, and I *will* flip if I go on thinking about it.

What that evidence was — what I saw back at the trailer when I directed my flash another way, froze in horror, and later traced the thing from end to end — was simply this: a yard-long black straight indentation in the bank of the canal by Daloway's trailer, as if cut by one end of the keel of an oil-drenched boat, and then, leading from that point to Daloway's oil-soaked bunk and back again — a little wider and more closely spaced on the way back, as if something were being carried — *the long narrow sharply pointed footprints, marked in blackest thickest oil, of the Black Gondolier.*

The Dreams of Albert Moreland

I think of the autumn of 1939, not as the beginning of the Second World War, but as the period in which Albert Moreland dreamed the dream. The two events — the war and the dream — are not, however, divorced in my mind. Indeed, I sometimes fear that there is a connection between them, but it is a connection which no sane person will consider seriously, if he is wise.

Albert Moreland was, and perhaps still is, a professional chess player. That fact has an important bearing on the dream, or dreams. He made most of his scant income at a games arcade in Lower Manhattan, taking on all comers — the enthusiast who gets a kick out of trying to beat an expert, the lonely man who turns to chess as to a drug, or the down-and-outer tempted into purchasing a half hour of intellectual dignity for a quarter.

After I got to know Moreland, I often wandered into the arcade and watched him playing as many as three or four games simultaneously, oblivious to the clicking and whirring of the pinball games and the intermittent reports from the shooting gallery. He got fifteen cents for every win; the house took the extra dime. When he lost, neither got anything.

Eventually I found out that he was a much better player than he needed to be for his arcade job. He had won casual games from internationally famous masters. A couple of Manhattan clubs had wanted to groom him for the big tournaments, but lack of ambition kept him drifting along in obscurity. I got the impression that he thought chess too trivial a business to warrant serious consideration, although he was perfectly willing to dribble his life away at the arcade, waiting for something really important to come along, if it ever did. Once in a

34

while he eked out his income by playing on a club team, getting as much as five dollars.

I met him at the old brownstone house where we both had rooms on the same floor, and it was there that he first told me about the dream.

We had just finished a game of chess, and I was idly watching the battle-scarred pieces slide off the board and pike up in a fold of the blanket on his cot. Outside, a fretful wind eddied the dry grit. There was a surge of traffic noises, and the buzz of a defective neon sign. I had just lost, but I was glad that Moreland never let me win, as he occasionally did with the players at the arcade, to encourage them. Indeed, I thought myself fortunate in being able to play with Moreland at all, not knowing then that I was probably the best friend he had.

I was saying something obvious about chess.

"You think it a complicated game?" he inquired, peering at me with quizzical intentness, his dark eyes like round windows pushed up under heavy eaves. "Well, perhaps it is. But I play a game a thousand times more complex every night in my dreams. And the queer thing is that the game goes on night after night. The same game. I never really sleep. Only dream about the game."

Then he told me, speaking with a mixture of facetious jest and uncomfortable seriousness that was to characterize many of our conversations.

The images of his dream, as he described the, were impressively simple, without any of the usual merging and incongruity. A board so vast he sometimes had to walk out on it to move his pieces. A great many more squares than in chess and arranged in patches of different colors, the power of the pieces varying according to the color of the square on which they stood. Above and to each side of the board only blackness, but a blackness that suggested starless infinity, as if, as he put it, the scene were laid on the very top of the universe.

When he was awake he could not quite remember all the rules of the game, although he recalled a great many isolated points, including the interesting fact that — quite unlike chess — his pieces and those of his adversary did not duplicate each other. Yet he was convinced that he not only understood the game perfectly while dreaming, but also was able to play it in the highly strategic manner of the master chess player. It was, he said, as though his night mind had many more dimensions of thought than his waking mind, and were able to grasp intuitively complex series of moves that would ordinarily have to be reasoned out step by step.

"A feeling of increased mental power is a very ordinary dream-delusion, isn't it?" he added, peering at me sharply. "And so I suppose you might say it's a very ordinary dream."

I did not know quite how to take that last remark, so I prodded him with a question.

"What do the pieces look like?"

It turned out that they were similar to those of chess in that they were considerably stylized and yet suggested the original forms — architectural, animal, ornamental — which had served as their inspiration. But there the similarity ended. The inspiring forms, so far as he could guess at them, were grotesque in the extreme. There were terraced towers subtly distorted out of the perpendicular, strangely asymmetric polygons that made him think of temples and tombs, vegetable-animal shapes which defied classification and whose formalized limbs and external organs suggested a variety of unknown functions. The more powerful pieces seemed to be modeled after life forms, for they carried stylized weapons and other implements, and wore things similar to crowns and tiaras — a little like the king, queen and bishop in chess — while the carving indicated voluminous robes and hoods. But they were in no other sense anthropomorphic. Moreland sought in vain for earthly analogies, mentioning Hindu idols, prehistoric reptiles, futurist sculpture, squids bearing daggers in their tentacles, and huge ants and mantis and other insects with fantastically adapted end-organs.

"I think you would have to search the whole universe — every planet and every dead sun — before you could find the original models," he said, frowning. "Remember, there is nothing cloudy or vague about the pieces themselves in my dream. They are as tangible as this rook." He picked up the piece, clenched his fist around it for a moment, and then held it out toward me on his open palm. "It is only in what they suggest that the vagueness lies."

It was strange, but his words seemed to open some dream-eye in my own mind, so that I could almost see the things he described. I asked him if he experienced fear during his dream.

He replied that the pieces one and all filled him with repugnance — those based on higher life forms usually to a greater degree than the architectural ones. He hated to have to touch or handle them. There was one piece in particular which had an intensely morbid fascination for his dream-self. He identified it as "the archer" because the stylized weapon it bore gave the impression of being able to hurt at a distance; but like the rest it was quite inhuman. He described it as representing a kind of intermediate, warped life form which had achieved more than human intellectual power without losing — but rather gaining — in brute cruelty and malignity. It was one of the opposing pieces for which there was no duplicate among his own. The mingled fear and loathing it inspired in him sometimes became so great that they interfered with his strategic grasp of the whole dream-game, and he was afraid his feeling toward it would sometime rise to such a pitch that he would be forced to capture it just to get it off the board, even though such a capture might compromise his whole position.

"God knows how my mind ever cooked up such a hideous entity," he finished, with a quick grin. "Five hundred years ago I'd have said the Devil put it there."

"Speaking of the Devil," I asked, immediately feeling my flippancy was silly, "whom do you play against in your dream?"

Again he frowned. "I don't know. The opposing pieces move by themselves. I will have made a move, and then, after waiting for what seems like an eon, all on edge as in chess, one of the opposing pieces will begin to shake a little and then to wobble back and forth. Gradually the movement increases in extent until the piece gets off balance and begins to rock and career across the board, like a water tumbler on a pitching ship, until it reaches the proper square. Then, slowly as it began, the movement subsides. I don't know, but it always makes me think of some huge, invisible, senile creature — crafty, selfish, cruel. You've watched that trembly old man at the arcade? The one who always drags the pieces across the board without lifting them, his hand constantly shaking? It's a little like that."

I nodded. His description made it very vivid. For the first time I began to think of how unpleasant such a dream might be.

"And it goes on night after night?" I asked.

"Night after night!" he affirmed with sudden fierceness. "And always the same game. It has been more than a month now, and my forces are just beginning to grapple with the enemy. It's draining off my mental energy. I wish it would stop. I'm getting so that I hate to go to sleep." He paused and turned away. "It seems queer," he said after a moment in a softer voice, smiling apologetically, "it seems queer to get so worked up over a dream. But if you've had bad ones, you know how they can cloud your thoughts all day. And I haven't really managed to get over to you the sort of feeling that grips me while I'm dreaming, and while my brain is working at the game and plotting move-sequence after move-sequence and weighing a thousand complex possibilities. There's repugnance, yes, and fear. I've told you that. But the dominant feeling is one of responsibility. I must not lose the game. More than my own personal welfare depends on it. There are some terrible stakes involved, though I am never quite sure what they are.

"When you were a little child, did you ever worry tremendously about something, with that complete lack of proportion characteristic of childhood? Did you ever feel that everything, literally everything, depended upon your performing some trivial action, some unimportant duty, in just the right way? Well, while I dream, I have the feeling that I'm playing for some stake as big as the fate of mankind. One wrong move may plunge the universe into unending night. Sometimes, in my dream, I feel sure of it."

His voice trailed off and he stared at the chessmen. I made some remarks and started to tell about an air-raid nightmare I had just had, but it didn't seem very important. And I gave him some vague advice about changing his sleeping habits, which did not seem very important either, although he accepted it with good grace. As I started back to my room he said, "Amusing to think, isn't it, that I'll be playing the game again as soon as my head hits the pillow?" He grinned and added lightly, "Perhaps it will be over sooner than I expect. Lately I've had the feeling that my adversary is about to unleash a surprise attack, although he pretends to be on the defensive." He grinned again and shut the door.

As I waited for sleep, staring at the wavy churning darkness that is more in the eyes than outside them, I began to wonder whether Moreland did not stand in greater need of psychiatric treatment than most chess players. Certainly a person without family, friends, or proper occupation is liable to mental aberrations. Yet he seemed sane enough. Perhaps the dream was a compensation for his failure to use anything like the full potentialities of his highly talented mind, even at chess playing. Certainly it was a satisfyingly grandiose vision, with its unearthly background and its implications of stupendous mental skill.

There floated into my mind the lines from the *Rubaiyat* about the cosmic chess player who, "Hither and thither moves and checks, and slays, And one by one back in the Closet lays."

Then I thought of the emotional atmosphere of his dreams, and the feelings of terror and boundless responsibility, of tremendous duties and cataclysmic consequences — feelings I recognized from my own dreams — and I compared them with the mad, dismal state of the world (for it was October, and sense of utter catastrophe had not yet been dulled) and I thought of the million drifting Morelands suddenly shocked into a realization of the desperate plight of things and of priceless chances lost forever in the past and of their own ill-defined but certain complicity in the disaster. I began to see Moreland's dream as the symbol of a last-ditch, too-late struggle against the implacable forces of fate and chance. And my night thoughts began to revolve around the fancy that some cosmic beings, neither gods nor men, had created human life long ago as a jest or experiment or artistic form, and had now decided to base the fate of their creation on the result of a game of skill played against one of their creatures.

Suddenly I realized that I was wide awake and that the darkness was no longer restful. I snapped on the light and impulsively decided to see if Moreland was still up.

The hall was as shadowy and funereal as that of most boarding houses late at night, and I tried to minimize the inevitable dry creakings. I waited for a few moments in front of Moreland's door, but heard nothing, so instead of knocking, I presumed upon our familiarity and edged open the door, quietly, in order not to disturb him if he were abed.

It was then that I heard his voice, and so certain was my impression that the sound came from a considerable distance that I immediately walked back to the stair-well and called, "Moreland, are you down there?"

Only then did I realize what he had said. Perhaps it was the peculiarity of the words that caused them first to register on my mind as merely a series of sounds.

The words were, "My spider-thing seizes your armor-bearer. I threaten."

It instantly occurred to me that the words were similar in general form to any one of a number of conventional expressions in chess, such as, "My rook captures your bishop. I give check." But there are no such pieces as "spider-things" or "armor-bearers" in chess or any other game I know of.

I automatically waled back towards his room, though I still doubted he was there. The voice had sounded much too far away — outside the building or at least in a remote section of it.

But he was lying on the cot, his upturned face revealed by the light of a distant electric advertisement, which blinked on and off at regular intervals. The traffic sounds, which had been almost inaudible in the hall, made the half-darkness restless and irritably alive. The defective neon sign still buzzed and droned insect like as it had earlier in the evening.

I tiptoed over and looked down at him. His face, more pale than it should have been because of some quality of the intermittent light, was set in an expression of painfully intense concentration — forehead vertically furrowed, muscles around the eye contracted, lips pursed to a line. I wondered if I ought to awaken him. I was acutely aware of the impersonally murmuring city all around us — block on block of shuttling, routine, aloof existence — and the contrast made his sleeping face seem all the more sensitive and vividly individual and unguarded, like some soft though purposefully tense organism which has lost its protective shell.

As I waited uncertainly, the tight lips opened a little without losing any of their tautness. He spoke, and for a second time the impression of distance was so compelling that I involuntarily looked over my shoulder and out the dustily glowing window. Then I began to tremble.

"My coiled-thing writhes to the thirteenth square of the green ruler's domain," was what he said, but I can only suggest the quality of the voice. Some inconceivable sort of distance had drained it of all richness and throatiness and overtones so that it was hollow and flat and faint and disturbingly mournful, as voices sometimes sound in open country, or from up on a high roof, or when there is a bad telephone connection. I felt I was the victim of some gruesome deception, and yet I knew that ventriloquism is a matter of motionless lips and clever suggestion rather than any really convincing change in the quality of the voice itself. Without volition there rose in my mind visions of infinite space, unending darkness. I felt as if I were being wrenched up and away from the world, so that Manhattan lay below me like a black asymmetric spearhead outlined by leaden waters, and then still farther outward at increasing speed until earth and sun and stars and galaxies were all lost and I was beyond the universe. To such a degree did the quality of Moreland's voice affect me.

I do not know how long I stood there waiting for him to speak again, with the noises of Manhattan flowing around yet not quite touching me, and the electric sign blinking on and off unalterably like the ticking of a clock. I could only think about the game that was being played, and wonder whether Moreland's adversary had yet made an answering move, and whether things were going for or against Moreland. There was no telling from his face; its intensity of concentration did not change. During those moments or minutes I stood there, I believed implicitly in the reality of the game. As if I myself were somehow dreaming, I could not question the rationality of my belief or break the spell which bound me.

When finally his lips parted a little and I experienced again that impression of impossible, eerie ventriloquism — the words this time being, "My horned-creature vaults over the twisted tower, challenging the archer," — my fear broke loose from whatever controlled it and I stumbled toward the door.

Then came what was, in an oblique way, the strangest part of the whole episode. In the time it took me to walk the length of the corridor back to my room, most of my fear and most of the feeling of complete alienage and other-worldliness which had dominated me while I was watching Moreland's face, receded so swiftly that I even forgot, for the time being, how great they had been. I do not know why that happened. Perhaps it was because the unwholesome realm of Moreland's dream was so grotesquely dissimilar to anything in the real world. Whatever the cause, by the time I opened the door to my room I was thinking, "Such nightmares can't be wholesome. Perhaps he should see a psychiatrist. Yet it's only a dream," and so on. I felt tired and stupid. Very soon I was asleep.

But some wraith of the original emotions must have lingered, for I awoke next morning with the fear that something had happened to

Moreland. Dressing hurriedly, I knocked at his door, but found the room empty, the bedclothes still rumpled. I inquired of the landlady, and she said he had gone out at eight-fifteen as usual. The bald statement did not quite satisfy my vague anxiety. But since my job-hunting that day happened to lie in the direction of the arcade, I had an excuse to wander in. Moreland was stolidly pushing pieces around with an abstracted, tousle-haired fellow of Slavic features, and casually conducting two rapid-fire checker games on the side. Reassured, I went on without bothering him.

That evening we had a long talk about dreams in general, and I found him surprisingly well-read on the subject and scientifically cautious in his attitudes. Rather to my chagrin, it was I who introduced such dubious topics as clairvoyance, mental telepathy, and the possibility of strange telescopings and other distortions of time and space during dream states. Some foolish reticence about admitting I had pushed my way into his room last night kept me from telling him what I had heard and seen, but he freely told me he had another installment of the usual dream. He seemed to take a more philosophical attitude now that he had shared his experiences with someone. Together we speculated as to the possible daytime sources of his dream. It was after twelve when we said goodnight.

I went away with the feeling of having been let down — vaguely unsatisfied. I think the fear I had experienced the previous night and then almost forgotten must have been gnawing at me obscurely.

And the following evening it found an avenue of return. Thinking Moreland must be tired of talking about dreams, I coaxed him into a game of chess. But in the middle of the game he put back a piece he was about to move, and said, "You know, that damned dream of mine is getting very bothersome."

It turned out that his dream adversary had finally loosed the long-threatened attack, and that the dream itself had turned into a kind of nightmare. "It's very much like what happens to you in a game of chess," he explained. "You go along confident that you have a strong position and that the game is taking the right direction. Every move your opponent makes is one you have foreseen. You get to feeling almost omniscient. Suddenly he makes a totally unexpected attacking move. For a moment you think it must be a stupid blunder on his part. Then you look a little more closely and realize that you have totally overlooked something and that his attack is a sound one. Then you begin to sweat.

"Of course, I've always experienced fear and anxiety and a sense of overpowering responsibility during the dream. But my pieces were like a wall, protecting me. Now I can see only the cracks in that wall. At any one of a hundred weak points it might conceivably be broken. Whenever one of the opposing pieces begins to wobble and shake, I wonder whether, when its move is completed, there will flash into my mind the unalterable and unavoidable combination of moves leading to my defeat. Last night I thought I saw such a move, and the terror was so great that everything swirled and I seemed to drop through millions of miles of emptiness in an instant. Yet just in that instant of waking I realized I had miscalculated, and that my position, though perilous, was still secure. It was so vivid that I almost carried with me into my waking thoughts the reason why, but then some of the steps in the train of dream-reasoning dropped out, as if my waking mind were not big enough to hold them all."

He also told me that his fixation on "the archer" was becoming increasingly troublesome. It filled him with a special kind of terror, different in quality, but perhaps higher in pitch than that engendered in him by the dream as a whole: a crazy morbid terror, characterized by intense repugnance, nerve-twisting exasperation, and reckless suicidal impulses.

"I can't get rid of the feeling," he said, "that the beastly thing will in some unfair and underhanded manner be the means of my defeat."

He looked very tired to me, although his face was of the compact, tough-skinned sort that does not readily show fatigue, and I felt concern for his physical and nervous welfare. I suggested that he consult a doctor (I did not like to say psychiatrist) and pointed out that sleeping tablets might be of some help.

"But in a deeper sleep the dream might be even more vivid and real," he answered, grimacing sardonically. "No, I'd rather play out the game under the present conditions."

I was glad to find that he still viewed the dream as an interesting and temporary psychological phenomenon (what else he could have viewed it as, I did not stop to analyze). Even while admitting to me the exceptional intensity of his emotions, he maintained something of a jesting air. Once he compared his dream to a paranoid's delusions of persecution, and asked whether I didn't think it was good enough to get him admitted to an asylum.

"Then I could forget the arcade and devote all my time to dream-chess," he said, laughingly sharply as soon as he saw I was beginning to wonder whether he had not meant the remark half-seriously.

But some part of my mind was not convinced by his protestations, and when later I tossed in the dark, my imagination perversely kept picturing the universe as a great arena in which each creature is doomed to engage in a losing game of skill against demoniac mentalities which, however long they may play cat and mouse, are always assured of final mastery — or almost assured, so that it would be a miracle if they were beaten. I found myself comparing them to certain chess players, who if they cannot beat an opponent by superior skill, will capitalize on unpleasant personal mannerisms in order to exasperate him and break down the lucidity of his thinking.

This mood colored my own nebulous dreams and persisted into the next day. As I walked the streets I felt myself inundated by an omnipresent anxiety, and I sensed taut, nervous misery in each passing face. For once I seemed able to look behind the mask which every person wears and which is so characteristically pronounced in a congested city, and see what lay behind — the egotistical sensitivity, the smouldering irritation, the thwarted longing, the defeat ... and, above all, the anxiety, too ill-defined and lacking in definite object to be called fear, but nonetheless infecting every thought and action, and making trivial things terrible. And it seemed to me that social, economic, and physiological factors, even Death and the War, were insufficient to explain such anxiety, and that it was in reality an up-welling from something dubious and horrible in the very constitution of the universe.

That evening I found myself at the arcade. Here too I sensed a difference in things, for Moreland's abstraction was not the calculating boredom with which I was familiar, and his tiredness was shockingly apparent. One of his three opponents, after shifting around restlessly, called his attention to a move, and Moreland jerked his head as if he had been dozing. He immediately made an answering move, and quickly lost his queen and the game by a trap that was very obvious even to me. A little later he lost another game by an equally elementary oversight. The boss of the arcade, a big beefy man, ambled over and stood behind Moreland, his heavy-jowled face impassive, seeming to study the position of the pieces in the last game. Moreland lost that too.

"Who won?" asked the boss.

Moreland indicated his opponent. The boss grunted noncommittally and walked off.

No one else sat down to play. It was near closing time. I was not sure whether Moreland had noticed me, but after a while he stood up and nodded at me, and got his hat and coat. We walked the long stretch back to the rooming house. He hardly spoke a word, and my sensation of morbid insight into the world around persisted and kept me silent. He walked as usual with long, slightly stiff-kneed strides, hands in his pockets, hat pulled low, frowning at the pavement a dozen feet ahead.

When we reached the room he sat down without taking off his coat and said, "Of course, it was the dream made me lose those games. When I woke this morning it was terribly vivid, and I almost remembered the exact position and all the rules. I started to make a diagram . . ."

He indicated a piece of wrapping paper on the table. Hasty crisscrossed lines, incomplete, represented what seemed to be the corner of an indefinitely larger pattern. There were about five hundred squares. On various squares were marks and names standing for pieces, and there were arrows radiating out from the pieces to show their power of movement.

"I got that far. Then I began to forget," he said tiredly, staring at the floor. "But I'm still very close to it. Like a mathematical puzzle you've not quite solved. Parts of the board kept flashing into my mind all day, so that I felt with a little more effort I would be able to grasp the whole. Yet I can't."

His voice changed. "I'm going to lose, you know. It's that piece I call "the archer". Last night I couldn't concentrate on the board; it kept drawing my eyes. The worst thing is that it's the spearhead of my adversary's attack. I ache to capture it. But I must not, for it's a kind of catspaw too, the bait of the strategic trap my adversary is laying. If I capture it, I will expose myself to defeat. So I must watch it coming closer and closer — it has an ugly, double-angled sort of hopping move — knowing that my only chance is to sit tight until my adversary overreaches himself and I can counterattack. But I won't be able to. Soon, perhaps tonight, my nerve will crack and I will capture it."

I was studying the diagram with great interest, and only half heard the rest — a description of the actual appearance of "the archer." I heard him say something about "a five-lobed head . . . the head almost hidden by a hood . . . appendages, each with four joints, appearing from under the robe . . . an eight-pronged weapon with wheels and levers about it, and little bag-shaped receptacles, as though for poison . . . posture suggesting it is lifting the weapon to aim it . . . all intricately carved in some lustrous red stone, speckled with violet . . . an expression of bestial, supernatural malevolence . . ."

Just then all my attention focused suddenly on the diagram, and I felt a tightening shiver of excitement, for I recognized two familiar names, which I had never heard Moreland mention while awake. "Spider-thing" and "green ruler."

Without pausing to think, I told him of how I had listened to his sleep-talking three nights before, and about the peculiar phrases he had spoken which tallied so well with the entries on the diagram. I poured out my account with melodramatic haste. My discovery of the entries on the diagram, nothing exceptionally amazing in itself, probably made such a great impression on me because I had hitherto strangely forgotten or repressed the intense fear I had experienced when I had watched Moreland sleeping.

Before I was finished, however, I noticed the growing anxiety of his expression, and abruptly realized that what I was saying might not have the best effect on him. So I minimized my recollection of the unwholesome quality of his voice — the overpowering impression of distance — and the fear it engendered in me.

Even so, it was obvious that he had received a severe shock. For a little while he seemed to be on the verge of some serious nervous derangement, walking up and down with fierce, jerky movements, throwing out crazy statements, coming back again and again to the diabolical convincingness of the dream — which my revelation seemed to have intensified for him — and finally breaking down into vague appeals for help.

Those appeals had an immediate effect on me, making me forget any wild thoughts of my own and putting everything on a personal level. All my instincts were now to aid Moreland, and I once again saw the whole matter as something for a psychiatrist to handle. Our roles had changed. I was no longer the half-awed listener, but the steadying friend to whom he turned for advice. That, more than anything, gave me a feeling of confidence and made my previous speculations seem childish and unhealthy. I felt contemptuous of myself for having encouraged his delusive trains of imagination, and I did as much as I could to make up for it.

After a while my repeated assurances seemed to take effect. He grew calm and our talk became reasonable once more, though every now and then he would appeal to me about some particular point that worried him. I discovered for the first time the extent to which he had taken the dream seriously. During his lonely brooding, he told me, he had sometimes become convinced that his mind left his body while he slept and traveled immeasurable distances to some transcosmic realm where the game was played. He had the illusion, he said, of getting perilously close to the innermost secrets of the universe and finding they were rotten and evil and sardonic. At times he had been terribly afraid that the pathway between his mind and the realm of the game would "open up" to such a degree that he would be "sucked up bodily from the world," as he put it. His belief that loss of the game would doom the world itself had been much stronger than he had ever admitted to me previously. He had traced a frightening relationship between the progress of the game and of the War, and had begun to believe that the ultimate issue of the War — though not necessarily the victory of either side — hung on the outcome of the game.

At times it had got so bad, he revealed, that his only relief had been in the thought that, no matter what happened, he could never convince others of the reality of his dream. They would always be able to view it as a manifestation of insanity or overwrought imagination. No matter how vivid it became to him he would never have concrete, objective proof.

"It's this way," he said. "You saw me sleeping, didn't you? Right here on this cot. You heard me talk in my sleep, didn't you? About the game. Well, that absolutely proves to you that it's all just a dream, doesn't it? You couldn't rightly believe anything else, could you?"

I do not know why those last ambiguous questions of his should have had such a reassuring effect on me of all people, who had only three nights ago trembled at the indescribable quality of his voice as he talked from his dream. But they did. They seemed like the final seal on an agreement between us to the effect that the dream was only a dream and meant nothing. I began to feel rather buoyant and self-satisfied, like a doctor who has just pulled his patient through a dangerous crisis. I talked to Moreland in what I now realize was almost a pompously sympathetic way, without noticing how dispirited were his obedient nods of agreement. He said little after those last questions.

I even persuaded him to go out to a nearby lunchroom for a midnight snack, as if — God help me! — I were celebrating my victory over the dream. As we sat at the not-too-dirty counter, smoking our cigarettes and sipping burningly hot coffee, I noticed that he had begun to smile again, which added to my satisfaction. I was blind to the ultimate dejection and submissive hopelessness that lay behind those smiles. As I left him at the door of his room, he suddenly caught hold of my hand and said, "I want to tell you how grateful I am for the way you've worked to pull me out of this mess." I made a deprecating gesture. "No, wait," he continued. "It does mean a lot. Well, anyway, thanks."

I went away with a contended, almost virtuous feeling. I had no apprehension whatever. I only mused, in a heavily philosophic way, over the strange forms fear and anxiety can assume in our pitiably tangled civilization.

As soon as I was dressed next morning, I rapped briskly at his door and impulsively pushed in without waiting for an answer. For once sunlight was pouring through the dusty window.

Then I saw it, and everything else receded.

It was lying on the crumpled bedclothes, half hidden by a fold of blanket, a thing perhaps ten inches high, as solid as any statuette, and as undeniably real. But from the first glance I knew that its form bore no relation to any earthly creature. This fact would have been apparent to someone who knew nothing of art as to an expert. I also knew that the red, violet-flecked substance from which it had been carved or cast had no classification among the earthly gems and minerals. Every detail was there. The five-lobed head, almost hidden by a hood. The appendages, each with four joints, appearing from under the robe. The eight-pronged weapon with wheels and levers about it, and the little bag-shaped receptacles, as though for poison. Posture suggesting it was lifting the weapon to aim it. An expression of bestial, supernatural malevolence.

Beyond doubting, it was the thing of which Moreland had dreamed. The thing which had horrified and fascinated him, as it now did me, which had rasped unendurably on his nerves, as it now began to rasp on mine. The thing which had been the spearhead and catspaw of his adversary's attack, and whose capture — and it now seemed evident that it had been captured — meant the probable loss of the game. The thing which had somehow been sucked back along an ever-opening path across the unimaginable distances from a realm of madness ruling the universe.

Beyond doubting, it was "the archer."

Hardly knowing what moved me, save fear, or what my purpose was, I fled from the room. Then I realized that I must find Moreland. No one had seen him leaving the house. I searched for him all day. The arcade. Chess clubs. Libraries.

It was evening when I went back and forced myself to enter his room. The figure was no longer there. No one at the house professed to know anything about it when I questioned them, but some of the denials were too angry, and I know that "the archer," being obviously a thing of value and having no overly great terrors for those who do not know its history, has most probably found its way into the hands of some wealthy and eccentric collector. Other things have vanished by a similar route in the past.

Or it may be that Moreland returned secretly and took it away with him.

But I am certain that it was not made on earth.

And although there are reasons to fear the contrary, I feel that somewhere — in some cheap boarding house or lodging place, or in some madhouse — Albert Moreland, if the game is not already lost and the forfeiture begun, is still playing that unbelievable game for stakes it is unwholesome to contemplate.

Game for Motel Room

Sonya moved around the warm, deeply carpeted motel room in the first gray trickle of dawn as if to demonstrate how endlessly beautiful a body can be if its owner will only let it. Even the body of a woman in, well, perhaps, her forties, Burton judged, smiling at himself in lazy reproof for having thought that grudging word "even." It occurred to him that bodies do not automatically grow less beautiful with age, but that a lot of bodies are neglected, abused and even hated by their owners: women in particular are apt to grow contemptuous and ashamed of their flesh, and this always shows. They start thinking old and ugly and pretty soon they look it. Like a car, a body needs tender constant care, regular tuneups, an occasional small repair and above all it needs to be intimately loved by its owner and from time to time by an admiring second party, and then it never loses beauty and dignity, even when it corrupts in the end and dies.

Oh, the dawn's a cold hour for philosophy, Burton told himself, and somehow philosophy always gets around to cold topics, just as lovemaking and all the rest of the best of life make one remember death and even worse things. His lean arm snaked out to a bedside table, came back with a cigarette and an empty folder of matches.

Sonya noticed. She rummaged in her pale ivory traveling case and tossed him a black, pear-shaped lighter. Burton caught the thing, lit his cigarette, and then studied it. It seemed to be made of black ivory and shaped rather like the grip of a revolver, while the striking mechanism was of blued steel. The effect was sinister.

"Like it?" Sonya asked from across the room.

"Frankly, no. Doesn't suit you."

"You show good taste — or sound instinct. It's a vacation present from my husband."

"He has bad taste? But he married you."

"He has bad everything. Hush, Baby,"

Burton didn't mind. Not talking let him concentrate on watching Sonya. Slim and crop-haired, she looked as trimly beautiful as her classic cream-colored, hard-topped Italian sports car, in which she had driven him to this cozy hideaway from the bar where they'd picked each other up. Her movements now, stooping to retrieve a smoke-blue stocking and trail it across a chair, momentarily teasing apart two ribs in the upward-slanting Venetian blinds to peer at the cold gray world outside, executing a fraction of a dance figure, stopping to smile at emptiness . . .these movements added up to nothing but the rhythms and symbolisms of a dream, yet it was the sort of dream in which actor and onlooker might float forever. In the morning twilight she looked now like a schoolgirl, now like a witch, now like an age-outwitting ballerina out for her twenty-fifth season but still in every way the *premiere danseuse*. As she moved she hummed in a deep contralto voice a tune that Burton didn't recognize, and as she hummed the dim air in front of her lower face seemed to change color very faintly, the deep purple and blues and browns matching the tones of the melody. Pure illusion, Burton was sure, like that which some hashish-eaters and weed-smokers experience during their ecstasy when they hear words as colors, but most enjoyable.

To exercise his mind, now that his body had its fill and while his eyes were satisfyingly occupied, Burton began to set in order the reasons why a mature lover is preferable to one within yoohooing distance of twenty in either direction. Reason One: she does quite as much of the approach work as you do. Sonya had been both heartwarmingly straightforward and remarkably intuitive at the bar last night. Reason Two: she is generally well-equipped for adventure. Sonya had provided both sports car and motel room. Reason Three: she does not go into an emotional tailspin after the act of love even if her thoughts trend toward death then, like yours do. Sonya seemed both lovely and sensible — the sort of woman it was good to think of getting married to and having children by.

Sonya turned to him with a smile, saying in her husky voice that still had a trace of the hum in it, "Sorry, Baby, but it's quite impossible. Especially your second notion."

"Did you really read my mind?" Burton demanded. "Why couldn't we have children?"

Sonya's smile deepened. She said, "I think I will take a little chance and tell you why." She came over and sat on the bed beside him and bent down and kissed him on the forehead.

"That was nice," Burton said lazily. "Did it mean something special?"

She nodded gravely. "It was to make you forget everything I'm going to tell you."

"How — if I'm to understand what you tell?" he asked.

"After a while I will kiss you again on the forehead and then you will forget everything I have told you in between. Or if you're very good, I'll kiss you on the nose and then you'll remember — but be unable to tell anyone else."

"If you say so," Burton smiled. "But what is it you're going to tell me?"

"Oh," she said, "just that I'm from another planet in a distant star cluster. I belong to a totally different species. We could no more start a child than a Chihauhau and a cat or a giraffe and a rhinoceros. Unlike the mare and the donkey we could not even get a cute little sterile mule with glossy fur and blue bows on his ears."

Burton grinned. He had just thought of Reason Four: a really grown-up lover plays the most delightfully childish nonsense games.

"Go on," he said.

"Well," she said, "superficially of course I'm very like an Earth woman. I have two arms and two legs and *this* and *these* . . ."

"For which I am eternally grateful," he said.

"You like them, eh?"

"Oh yes — especially *these*."

"Well, watch out — they don't even give milk, they're used in espying. You see, inside I'm very different," she said. "My mind is different too. It can do mathematics faster and better than one of your electric calculating machines — "

"What's two and two?" Burton wanted to know.

"Twenty-two," she told him, "and also one hundred in the binary system and eleven in the trinary and four in duodecimal. I have perfect recall — I can remember every least thing I've ever done and every word of every book I've leafed through. I can read unshielded minds — in fact anything up to triple shielding — and hum in colors.

I can direct my body heat so that I never really need clothes to keep me warm at temperatures above freezing. I can walk on water if I concentrate, and even fly — though I don't do it here because it would make me conspicuous."

"Especially at the present moment," Burton agreed, "though it would be a grand sight. Why *are* you here, by the way, and not behaving yourself on your home planet?"

"I'm on vacation," she grinned. "Oh yes, we use your rather primitive planet for vacations — like you do Africa and the Canadian forests. A little machine teaches us during one night's sleep several of your languages and implants in our brains the necessary background information. My husband surprised me by giving me the money for this vacation — same time he gave me the lighter. Usually he's very stingy. But perhaps he had some little plot — an affair with his chief nuclear chemist, I'd guess — of his own in mind and wanted me out of the way. I can't be sure though, because he always keeps his mind quadruple-shielded, even from me."

"So you have husbands on your planet," Burton observed.

"Yes indeed! Very jealous and possessive ones, too, so watch your step, Baby. Yes, although my planet is much more advanced than yours we still have husbands and wives and a very stuffy system of monogamy — *that* seems to go on forever and everywhere — oh yes, and on my planet we have death and taxes and life insurance and wars and all the rest of the universal idiocy!"

She stopped suddenly. "I don't want to talk about that any more," she said. "Or about my husband. Let's talk about you. Let's play truths, deep-down truths. What's the thing you're most afraid of in the whole world?"

Burton chuckled — and then frowned. "You really want me to give you the honest answer?" he asked.

"Of course," she said. "It's the first rule of the game."

"Well," he said, "I'm most afraid of something going wrong with my brain. *Growing* wrong, really. Having a brain tumor. That's it." He had become rather pale.

"Oh Poor Baby," Sonya said. "Just you wait a minute."

Still uneasy from his confession, Burton started nervously to pick up Sonya's black lighter, but its black pistol-look repelled him.

Sonya came bustling back with something else in her right hand. "Sit up," she said, putting her left arm around him. "No, none of *that*

53

— this is serious. Pretend I'm a very proper lady doctor who forgot to get dressed."

Burton could see her slim back and his own face over her right shoulder in the wide mirror of the dresser. She slipped her right hand and the small object it held behind his head. There was a click.

"No," said Sonya cheerily. "I can't see a sign of anything wrong in your brain or likely to grow wrong. It's as healthy as an infant's. *What's the matter, Baby?*"

Burton was shaking. "Look," he gasped reproachfully, "it's wonderful to play nonsense games, but when you use magic tricks or hypnotism to back them up, that's cheating."

"What do you mean?"

"When you clicked that thing," he said with difficulty, "I saw my head turn for a moment into a pinkish skull and then into just a pulsing blob with folds in it."

"Oh, I'd forgotten the mirror," she said, glancing over her shoulder. "But you were really just imagining things. Or having a mild optical spasm and seeing colors."

"No," she added as he reached out a hand, "I won't let you see my little XYZ-ray machine." She tossed it across the room into her traveling case. "It would spoil our nonsense game."

As his breathing and thoughts quieted, Burton decided she was possibly right — or at least that he'd best pretend she was right. It was safest and sanest to think of what he'd glimpsed in the mirror as an illusion, like the faint colors he'd fancied forming in front of her humming lips. Perhaps Sonya had an effect on him like hashish or some super-marijuana — a plausible enough idea considering how much more powerful drug a beautiful woman is than any opiate or resin. Nevertheless —

"All right, Sonya," he said, "what's *your* deepest fear?"

She frowned. "I don't want to tell you."

"*I* stuck to the rules."

"Very well," she nodded, "it's that my husband will go crazy and kill me. That's a much more dreadful fear on my planet than yours, because we've conquered all diseases and we each of us can live forever (though it's customary to disintegrate after forty or fifty thousand years) and we each of us have tremendous physical and mental powers — so that the mere thought of any genuine insanity is dreadfully shocking. Insanity is so nearly unknown to us that even our advanced intuition doesn't work on it — and what is unknown is always most frightening. By insanity I don't mean minor irrationalities. We have those, all right — my husband for instance, is bugged on the number 33, he won't begin any important venture except on the thirty-third day of the month — and me, I have a weakness for black-haired babies from primitive planets."

"Hey, wait a minute," Burton objected, "you said the thirty-third day of the month."

"On my planet the months are longer. Nights too. You'd love them — more time for demonstrating affection and empathy."

Burton looked at her broodingly. "You play this nonsense game pretty seriously," he said. "Like you'd read nothing but science fiction all your life."

Sonya shrugged her lovely shoulders. "Maybe there's more in science fiction than you realize. But now we've had enough of that game. Come on, Black-Haired Baby, let's play — "

"Wait a minute," Burton said sharply. She drew back, making a sulky mouth at him. He made his own grim, or perhaps his half-emerged thoughts did that for him.

"So you've got a husband on your planet," he said, "and he's got tremendous powers and you're deathly afraid he'll go crazy and try to kill you. And now he does an out-of-character thing by giving you vacation money and — "

"Oh yes!" she interrupted agitatedly, "and he's such a dreadful mixed-up superman and he always keeps up that permissible but uncustomary quadruple shield and he looks at me with such a secret gloating viciousness when we're alone that I'm choke-full of fear day and night and I've wished and wished I could really get something on him so that I could run to an officer of public safety and have the maniac put away, but I can't, I can't, he never makes a slip, and I begin to feel *I'm* going crazy — *I*, with my supremely trained and guarded mind — and I just *have* to get away to vacation planets and forget him in loving someone else. Come on, Baby, let's — "

"*Wait a minute!*" Burton commanded. "You say you've insurance on your planet. Are you insured for much?"

"A very great deal. Perfect health and a life-expectancy of fifty thousand years makes the premiums cheap."

"And your husband is the beneficiary?"

"Yes, he is. Come on, Burton, let's not talk about him. Let's — "

"No!" Burton said, pushing her back. "Sonya, what does your husband do? What's his work?"

Sonya shrugged. "He manages a bomb factory," she said listlessly and rapidly. "I work there too. I told you we had wars — they're between the league our planet belongs to and another star cluster. You've just started to discover the super-bombs on Earth — the fission bomb, the fusion bomb. The bombs my husband's factory manufactures can each of them destroy a planet. They're really fuses for starting the matter of the planet disintegrating spontaneously so that it flashes into a little star. Yet the bombs are so tiny you can hold one in your hand. In fact, this cigarette lighter is an exact model of one of them. The models were for Cosmos Day presents to top officials. My husband gave me his along with the vacation money. Burton, reach me one of your foul Earth cigarettes, will you? If you're going to refuse the other excitements, I've got to have something."

Burton automatically shook some cigarettes from his pack. "Tell me one more thing, Sonya," he rapped out. "You say you have a perfect memory. How many times have you struck that cigarette lighter since your husband gave it to you?"

"Thirty-one times," she answered promptly. "Counting the one time you used it."

She flicked it on and touched the tiny blue flame to her cigarette, inhaled deeply, then let the tiny snuffer snap down the flame. Twin plumes of faint smoke wreathed from her nostrils. "Thirty-two now." She held the black pear-shaped object towards him, her thumb on the knurled steel-blue trigger. "Shall I give you a light?"

"NO!" Burton shouted. "Sonya, as you value your life and mine — and the lives of three billion other primitives — don't work that lighter again. Put it down."

"All right, all right, Baby," she said smiling nervously and dropping the black thing on the white sheet. "Why's Baby so excited?"

"Sonya," Burton said, "Maybe *I'm* crazy, or maybe you *are* only playing a nonsense game backed up with hypnotism — but . . ."

Sonya stopped smiling. "What is it, Baby?"

Burton said, "If you really do come from another planet where there is almost no insanity, homicidal or otherwise, what I'm going to tell you will be news. Sonya, we've just lately had several murders on Earth where a man plants a time-bomb on a big commercial airplane to explode it in the air and kill all its passengers and crew just to do away with one single person — generally for the sake of collecting a big life-insurance policy. Now if an Earth-murderer could be cold-blooded or mad enough to do that, why mightn't a super-murderer — "

"On no," Sonya said slowly, "not blow up a whole planet to get rid of just one person– "

She started to tremble.

"Why not?" Burton demanded. "Your husband is crazy, only you can't prove it. He hates you. He stands to collect a fortune if you die in an accident — such as a primitive vacation planet exploding. He presents you with money for a vacation on such a planet and at the same time he gives you a cigarette lighter that is an exact model of — "

"I can't believe it," Sonya said very faintly, still shaking, her eyes far away. "Not a whole planet . . ."

"But that's the sort of thing insanity can be, Sonya. What's more, you can check it," Burton rapped out flatly. "Use that XYZ-ray gadget of yours to look through the lighter."

"But he *couldn't*," Sonya murmured, her eyes still far away. "Not even *he* could . . ."

"Look through the lighter," Burton repeated.

Sonya picked up the black thing by its base and carried it over to the traveling case.

"Remember not to flick it," Burton warned her sharply. "You'd told me he was bugged on the number thirty-three, and I imagine that would be about the right number to allow to make sure you were settled on your vacation planet before anything happened."

He saw the shiver travel down her back as he said that and suddenly Burton was shaking so much himself he couldn't possibly have moved. Sonya's hands were on the other side of her body from him, busy above her traveling case. There was a click and her pinkish skeleton showed through her. It was not quite the same as the skeleton of an Earth human — there were *two* long bones in the upper arms and upper legs, fewer ribs, but what looked like two tiny skulls in the chest.

She turned around, not looking at him.

"*You were right,*" she said.

She said, *"Now I've got the evidence to put my husband away forever! I can't wait!"*

She whirled into action, snatching articles of clothing from the floor, chairs and dresser, whipping them into her traveling case. The whole frantic little dance took less than ten seconds. Her hand was on the outside door before she paused.

She looked at Burton. She put down her traveling case and came over to the bed and sat down beside him.

"Poor Baby," she said. "I'm going to have to wipe out your memory and yet you were so very clever — I really mean that, Burton."

He wanted to object, but he felt paralyzed. She put her arm around him and moved her lips towards his forehead. Suddenly she said, "No, I can't do that. There's got to be some reward for you."

She bent her head and kissed him pertly on the nose. Then she disengaged herself, hurried to her bag, picked it up, and opened the door.

"Besides," she called back. "I'd hate you to forget any part of me."

"Hey," Burton yelled, coming to life, "You can't go out like that!"

"Why not?" she demanded.

"Because you haven't a stitch of clothes on!"

"On my planet we don't wear them!"

The door slammed behind her. Burton sprang out of bed and threw it open again.

He was just in time to see the sports car take off — straight up.

Burton stood in the open door for half a minute, stark naked himself, looking around at the unexploded Earth. He started to say aloud, "Gosh, I didn't even get the name of her planet," but his lips were sealed.

The Phantom Slayer

[EXT]His ghastly shadow hung over block upon block of dingy city buildings — and his theme song was the nervous surge of traffic along infrequent boulevards . . .[/EXT]

"So this is the room?" I said, setting down my cardboard suitcase. The landlord nodded.

"Nothing been changed in it since your uncle died." It was small and dingy, but pretty clean. I took it in. The imitation oak dresser. The cupboard, the bare table. The green-shaded drop light. The easy chair. The kitchen chair. The cast-iron bed. "Except the sheets and stuff," the landlord added. "They been washed."

"He died unexpectedly, didn't he?" I said in a sort of apologetic voice.

"Yeah. In his sleep. You know, his heart."

I nodded vaguely and, on an impulse, walked over and opened the cupboard door. Two of the shelves were filled with canned stuff and other supplies. There was an old coffee pot and two saucepans, and some worn china covered with a fine network of brownish cracks.

"Your uncle had cooking privileges," the landlord said. "Of course you can have them, too, if you want."

I went over and looked down three stories at the dirty street. Some boys were pitching pennies. I studied the names of the stores. When I turned around I thought maybe the landlord would be going, but he was still watching me. The whites of his eyes looked discolored.

"There's twenty-five cents for the washing I told you about." I dug in my pocket for a quarter. That left me forty-seven cents.

He laboriously wrote me a receipt. "There's your key on the table," he remarked, "and the one for the outside door. Well, Mister, the place is yours for the next three months an' two weeks."

He walked out, shutting the door behind him. From below came the rackety surge of a passing street car. I dropped down into the easy chair.

People can inherit some pretty queer things. I had inherited some canned goods and the rent of a room, just because my Uncle David, whom I never remembered seeing, paid for things in advance. The court had been decent about it, especially after my telling them I was broke. The landlord had refused to make a refund, but you could hardly blame him for that. Of course, after hitch-hiking all the way to the city, I'd been disappointed to hear there was no real money involved. The policeman's pension had stopped with my uncle's death, and funeral expenses had eaten up the rest. Still, I was thankful I had a place to sleep.

They said my uncle must have made his will just a little while after I was born. I don't think my father and mother knew about it, or they'd have mentioned it — at least when they died. I never heard much about him except that he was my father's elder brother.

I vaguely knew he was a policeman, that was all. You know how it is; families split up, and only the old folks keep in touch, and they don't talk to the young folks about it, and pretty soon the whole connection is forgotten, unless something special happens. I guess that sort of thing has been going on since the world began. Forces are at work that break up people, and scatter them, and make them lonely. You feel it most of all in a big city.

They say there's no law against being a failure, but there is, as I'd found out. After a childhood in easy circumstances, things got harder and harder. The depression. Family dying. Friends going off. Jobs uncertain and difficult to find. Delays and uncertainties about government assistance. I'd tried my hand at bumming around, but found I lacked the right temperament. Even being a tramp or a sponger or a scavenger takes special ability. Hitch-hiking to the city had left me feeling nervous and unwell. And my feet hurt. I'm one of those people who aren't much good at taking it.

* * *

Sitting there in my dead uncle's worn, old, easy chair with night coming on I felt the full impact of my loneliness. Through the walls I heard people moving around and talking faintly, but they weren't people I knew or had ever seen. From outside came the mixed-up rumbling and murmuring of a big city. Far away I could hear a steam-engine grunting heavily; nearer, the monotonous buzz of a defective neon sign. There was a steady thumping from some machinery I couldn't identify, and I thought I heard the whine of a sewing machine. Lonely unfriendly sounds, all of them. The dusty square of window kept getting darker, but it was more like heavy smoke settling than a regular evening.

Some trivial thing was bothering me. Something unconnected with the general gloominess. I tried to figure out what it was, and after a while it came to me suddenly. It was very simple. Although I usually slump to one side when I sit in an easy chair, I was now leaning straight back, because the upholstery was deeply indented toward the center. And that, as I immediately realized, must have been because my uncle had always leaned straight back. The sensation was a little frightening, as if he had somehow taken hold of me. But I resisted the impulse to jump up. Instead I found myself wondering what sort of man he'd been and how he'd lived, and I began to picture him moving around and sitting down and sleeping in the bed, and occasionally having some friend from the police force in to visit with him. I wondered how he passed the time after he was retired.

There weren't any books in sight. I didn't notice any ash-trays, and there wasn't a tobacco smell. It had probably been pretty lonely for the old man, without family or anything. And here I was inheriting his loneliness.

Then I did get up, and started to walk around aimlessly. It struck me that the furniture looked sort of uncomfortable all stuck back against the walls, so I pulled some of it out. I went over to the dresser. There was a framed picture on it, lying face down. I took it over to the window. Yes, it was my uncle, all right, for "David Rhode, Lieutenant of Police, retired July 1, 1927," was inscribed on it in small, careful handwriting. He had on his policeman's cap, and his cheeks were thin, and his eyes were more intelligent and penetrating than I'd expected. He didn't look so old. I put it back on the dresser and then changed my mind and propped it up on top of the cupboard. I still felt too nervous and sickish to want anything to eat. I knew I should have gone to bed and tried to get a good rest, but I was on edge after the day at court. I was lonely, yet I didn't want to take a walk or be near people.

So I decided to put in some time looking through my inheritance in detail. It was the obvious thing to do, but a sort of embarrassment had been holding me back. Once I started, I became quite curious. I didn't expect to find anything of value. I was mostly interested in learning more about my uncle. I began by taking another look at the cupboard. There was canned stuff and coffee enough for maybe a month. That was fortunate. It would give me time to rest up and hunt for a job. On the bottom shelf were a few old tools, screws, wire and other junk.

When I opened the closet door I got a momentary shock. Hanging against the wall was a policeman's uniform, with a blue cap on the hook above and two heavy shoes jutting out underneath, and a night stick hung alongside on a nail. It looked lifelike in the shadows. I realized it was getting dark and switched on the green-shaded drop light. I found a regular suit and an overcoat and some other clothes in the closet — not many. On the shelf was a box containing a service revolver and a belt with some cartridges stuck in the leather loops. I wondered if I ought to do anything about it. I was puzzled by the uniform, until I realized he must have had two, one for summer, the other for winter. They had buried him in the other one.

This far I hadn't found much, so I started on the dresser. The two top drawers contained shirts and handkerchiefs and socks and underwear, all washed and neatly folded but frayed a little at the edges. They were mine now. If they fitted me, I had a right to wear them. It was an unpleasant thought, but there was no getting away from it.

The third drawer was filled with newspaper clippings, carefully arranged into separate piles and bundles. I glanced at the top ones. They all seemed to be concerned with police cases, two of them fairly recent. Here I figured, was a clue to what my uncle did after his retirement. He kept up an interest in his old job.

The bottom drawer contained a heterogeneous assortment of stuff. A pair of spectacles, a curiously short, silver-headed cane, an empty briefcase, some green ribbon, a toy wooden horse that looked very old (I wondered idly, if he had bought if for me when I was a baby and then forgotten to send it) and other things.

Quickly I shoved in the drawer and walked away. This business wasn't as interesting as I'd expected. I got a picture of things all right, but it made me think of death and feel shivery and lost. Here I was in the midst of a big city, and the only person I felt at all close to was three weeks buried. The personality of the room was getting a tighter hold on me all the time.

Still, I figured I'd better finish the job, so I pulled out the shallow drawer under the table top. I found two recent newspaper, a pair of scissors and a pencil, a small bundle of receipts in the landlord's laborious hand, and a detective story from a lending library. Would they want me to pay the rental on it? I guess they would not insist.

That was all I could find. And, as I thought it over, it seemed very little. Didn't he use to get any letters? The general neatness had led me to expect a couple of boxes of them, carefully tied in packets. And weren't there any photographs or other mementoes? Or magazines or notebooks? Why, I hadn't even come across that jumble of advertisements and folders and cards and other worthless stuff you find somewhere in almost every home. It suddenly struck me that his last years must have been awfully empty and barren, in spite of the clippings and the detective story.

There wasn't any knock, but the door opened and the landlord stepped inside, moving softly in big, loose slippers. It startled me and made me a trifle angry — a jumpy sort of anger.

"I just wanted to tell you," he said, "that we don't like to have any noise after eleven o'clock. Oh, and your uncle used to cook at eight-thirty and five."

"Okay. Okay," I said quickly and was about to add something sarcastic when a thought struck me.

"Did my uncle keep a trunk or box in the basement, or anything like that?" I asked. I was thinking of letters, photographs.

He looked at me stupidly for a moment, then shook his head. "No. Everything he had is right here," and he indicated the room with a sideways movement of his big, thick-fingered hand.

"Did he have many visitors?" I asked. I thought the landlord hadn't heard this question but after a while he came to and shook his head.

"Thank you," I said, moving off. "Well, good-night."

When I turned back he was still standing in the doorway, staring sleepily around the room. Again I noticed how the whites of his eyes were discolored.

"Say," he remarked. "I see you've moved the furniture back the way your uncle had it."

"Yes, it was all up against the walls, and I pulled it out."

"You put his picture back on the top of the cupboard."

"That's where it used to be?" I asked. He nodded, looked around again, yawned and turned to go.

"Well — " he said, "sleep well."

The last two words sounded unnatural as if dragged out with prodigious effort. He closed the door noiselessly behind him. Immediately I had snatched the key from the table and was locking it. I wasn't going to stand for him prying around without knocking, not if I could help it. Again loneliness closed in on me.

So I had rearranged the furniture in the old pattern, and put the picture back in its proper place, had I? The thought frightened me a little. Made me think I was getting too near the dead policeman and his habits. I wished I didn't have to sleep in that ugly cast-iron bed. But where else could I go with my forty-seven cents and my lack of gumption?

I realized suddenly, that I was being foolish. It was perfectly natural that I should feel a little uneasy. Anyone would in such queer circumstances. But I mustn't let it get me down. I would have to live in this room for some time. The thing to do was to get used to it. So I got out some of the newspaper clippings that were in the dresser and began to go through them. They covered a period of twenty years or so. The older ones were yellow and stiff, and cracked easily. They were mostly about murders. I kept turning them over, looking at the headlines and here and there reading a little. After a while I found myself plunged into accounts of a "Phantom Slayer": who killed wantonly and for no apparent motive. His crimes were similar to those with which the uncaught "Jack the Ripper" horrified London in 1888, except that men and children, as well as women, were numbered among his victims. I vaguely remembered hearing about two of the cases years ago — there were seven or eight altogether. Now I read the details. They were not conducive to pleasant thought. My uncle's name was mentioned among the investigators in some of the earlier cases.

That was by far the biggest pile of clippings. All the piles were carefully arranged, but I couldn't find any notes or comments, except a tiny scrap of paper with an address on it, 2318 Robey Street. It puzzled me. Just that solitary address without any explanation. I planned to look it up some day.

It was night outside now, and the upward slanting light from the street lamp made it easier to see the dust on the window-pane. There weren't so many noises coming through the walls, just the low, sharp drone of some radio voices. I could still hear the buzz of the defective neon sign, and another engine puffing in the distant yards. To my relief, I found I was getting sleepy. As I undressed and hung my clothes on the kitchen chair, I found myself wondering if my uncle had arranged his in the same way: coat over the back, trousers over the seat, shoes underneath with the socks tucked inside them, shirt and tie draped on top of the coat.

I opened the window three inches from the top and bottom, then remembered that I seldom opened my bedroom window from the top. Was I conforming to my uncle's custom here, too? I was thankful I still felt sleepy, and able to conquer the faint desire I had to keep glancing over my shoulder. I pulled back the covers of the bed, switched off the drop light, and quickly jumped in.

My first thought was, "Here his head lay." I wondered if he died in his sleep like they told me, or if he waked paralyzed, an old man alone in the dark. That wouldn't do, I told myself, and tried to think of how tired and tense my muscles were, of how good it was to rest my feet and be able to stretch and relax. That helped a little. As my eyes became accustomed to the semi-darkness, I noted the dim outlines of the objects in the room. The chair piled with my clothes. The table. A queer little highlight reflected from my uncle's picture on top of the cupboard. The walls seemed to press in close.

Gradually my imagination went to work picturing the great city beyond the walls, the city I hardly knew. I visualized block after block of dingy buildings, with here and there clusters of higher structures, where the stores and the street-car lines lay. The great looming masses of warehouses and factories. The dismal expanse of track and cinders in the railroad yards, with the rank and file of empty cars. Lightless alleys, and the nervous surge of traffic along infrequent boulevards. Row after row of ugly two story frame houses, crowded close together. Human forms that , in my imagination, never walked upright, but slunk through the shadows close to the walls. Criminals. Murderers.

Abruptly I broke off this train of thought, a little frightened at its vividness. It was almost as if my mind had been outside my body, spying and peering. I tried to laugh at the idea, so obviously a result of my tiredness and tension as I told myself. No matter how alien the city seemed, I was here in my little room with the door locked. A policeman's room. David Rhode, Lieutenant of Police, retired July 1, 1927. I dozed and fell asleep.

My dream was simple, vivid, and singularly realistic. I seemed to be standing in a cobblestoned alley. There was an unpainted fence with a board fallen from it, and beyond it the dark brick wall of an apartment building with out jutting back porches of wooden framework painted gray. It was the hour of dawn, when life is at low ebb and sleep clings everywhere like a chilly mist. Formless clouds hid the sky. I could see a yellow shade flapping out of a window on the first floor, yet I could not hear the sound. That was all. But the feeling of cold fear that got hold of me was difficult to describe. I seemed to be looking for something and yet afraid to move.

The scene changed, although my emotions remained the same. It was night, and an empty lot, with a great billboard shutting off the harsh light of the street lamp from most of it. Dimly I could see the things in the lot: a pile of bricks and old bottles, some broken barrels, and the stripped wrecks of two automobiles, their fenders rusted and broken away. Weeds and rank grass grew in the sprawling clumps. Then I noticed there was a narrow, bumpy path crossing the lot diagonally and along it a little boy was moving slowly, as if he had come back to look for something he had lost earlier in the evening. The horror brooding over the place was directed at him, and I felt terribly afraid for him. I tried to warn him, to shout and tell him to run home. But I could not speak or move.

Again the scene changed. Again it was the hour of dawn. I was standing in front of a two-story stucco house, set back a little from the street. There was a neat lawn and two flower beds. A block away I could see a policeman slowly walking his beat. Then a force seemed to take hold of me and move me toward the house. I could not resist the force. I saw a cement walk and a coil of hose and then, in a kind of little nook of trees, a huddled form. The force bent me down toward it and I saw it was a young woman, that her skull was beaten in and her face splotched with blood. Then I struggled and tried to cry out, and I made a great effort and came awake.

For what seemed a long time I lay tense and afraid to move, feeling my heart pounding in my throat. The dim room swam around me, and figures moved about, and for a while the window wasn't where it should be. Gradually I got control of my panic, and forced things to return to their normal forms by looking at them closely. Then I sat up, still shivering. It was one of the worst nightmares I could remember having. I reached for a cigarette and lit it shakily, and pulled the bedclothes around me.

Suddenly I remembered something. That stucco house, I'd seen it before, very recently, and I thought I knew where. I got out of bed, switched on the light, and riffled through the newspaper clippings. I found the photograph, all right. The house was the same as the one in my dream. I read the caption. "Where Girl Victim of Phantom Slayer Was Found." So that was what had caused my nightmare. I might have known it.

I thought I heard a noise in the hall outside, and I jumped to the door to make sure it was still locked. As I returned to the table I realized I was trembling. That wouldn't do. I had to conquer that silly fear, that feeling that someone was trying to get at me. I sat down and puffed at my cigarette. I looked at the clippings on the table. Had my uncle used to set them out in that way, study them, ponder over them? Did he ever wake in the middle of the night and sit up, waiting for sleepiness to return? Strongly I felt his presence in the personality of the room. I didn't want to feel it.

Abruptly I got to my feet, swept the clippings into one big pile, and returned them to the dresser. By mistake I opened the bottom drawer and saw again that queer conglomeration of objects. The spectacles, the silver-headed cane, the empty briefcase, the green ribbon, the toy horse, the tortoise-shell comb, and the rest. As I shut the clippings away, I again thought I heard a faint noise, and whirled around quickly. This time I didn't go to the door, since I could still see my key in it, unmoved. But I couldn't resist the temptation to look inside the closet. There hung the blue uniform, the cap above, the shoes below, the night stick at one side. David Rhode, Lieutenant of Police, retired July 1, 1927. I shut the door.

I knew I had to get hold of myself. I rehearsed in my mind the obvious and logical reasons for my mood and those unnerving dreams. I was tired and unwell. I hadn't had much sleep for two nights. I was in a strange city. I was sleeping in the room of an uncle whom I had never seen or remembered seeing anyway, and who had been dead for three weeks. I was surrounded by that man's belongings, by the aura of his habits. I had been reading about some particularly gruesome murders. Reasons enough, surely!

If only I could get rid of the conviction that someone was trying to get at me! What could anyone want with me? I had no money. I was a stranger. If only I could get rid of the feeling that my dead uncle was trying to warn me about something, trying to tell me something, make me do something!

I stopped pacing up and down. My glance caught the table top, worn and covered with scratches, but bright under the drop light. It was not quite bare though. I hadn't forgotten any of the clippings, but near one corner lay the scrap of paper I had discovered earlier in the evening. I reached for it and again read the penciled address, 2318 Robey Street.

I can only explain the strange feeling that gripped me by saying it was as if I had for an instant been plunged back into the atmosphere of my dreams. In dreams, perfectly commonplace objects can be invested with an inexplicable horrible significance. It was that way with the slip of paper. I had no idea what the address meant, yet it stared at me like some sentence of doom, like some secret too terrible for a man to know. With a single, quick clutch of my fingers I crumpled it into a ball, dropped it to the floor, and sank down onto the edge of the bed. God help me, I thought, if I went reacting to things is this way. The beginnings of insanity must be like that.

Presently my heart stopped pounding and things got a little clearer in my mind. My senseless terror was subdued, but I realized it might come back at any moment. The thing to do was to get to sleep again before that happened, and take a chance on the dreams.

Once again as I lay in bed, I felt the pressure and the presence of the room. Once again I saw the whole city around me. I had a sensation of a breaking down of walls and of floating over an alien expanse of dingy buildings. It was stronger this time.

And then the dream returned. I seemed to be at a meeting of two streets. On my right hand loomed tall structures with many windows, none of which showed a light. On my left hand flowed a broad, ugly river. In its oily, slow moving surface were dimly reflected the street lamps on the opposite side. I could see the outlines of a moored barge. One of the streets followed the river and, a little way beyond, ducked under the approach of a bridge made of great steel girders. It was very dark under the bridge. The other street went off at right angles. The sidewalk was littered with old newspapers, swirled there by the wind. I could not hear their rustling, nor could I smell the chemical stench I knew the river must be exuding. A sick horror seemed to hang over the whole scene.

A small elderly man was approaching along the side street. I knew I must cry out to him, warn him, but I was powerless. He was looking around uncertainly, but I could tell that had nothing to do with my presence. He was carrying a briefcase, and he tapped the torn newspapers out of his way with a silver-headed cane. As he reached the intersection, another figure stepped out from behind me. It was a dark indistinct figure. I couldn't make out the face. It seemed to be wrapped in shadows. The elderly man's first look of frightened apprehension turned to one of unmixed relief. He seemed to be asking questions and the other, the dark figure, to be making replies. I could not hear the voices.

The dark figure pointed down the street that led under the bridge. The other smiled and nodded as if he were expressing thanks. Fright and terror held me in a vise. I exerted all my will power, but could neither speak nor move closer. Slowly the two figures began to move along the river's edge, side by side. I was like a man frozen. Finally they disappeared in the darkness under the bridge.

There was a long wait. Then the dark figure returned alone. It seemed to see me and move toward me. Terror gripped me and I made a violent effort to escape from the spell that held me.

Then, abruptly, I was free. I seemed to shoot upward at a fantastic speed. In an instant I was so high above the city that I could see the checkerboard of blocks, like a map through smoked glass. The river was no more than a leaden streak. Off to one side I observed tiny chimneys spurting ghostly fire — mills working a night shift. A feeling of terrible and frantic loneliness assailed me. I forgot the scene I had just witnessed on the river bank. My sole desire was to flee from the limitless emptiness in which I was poised. To flee, and find a place of refuge.

At this point my dream became both more and less realistic. Less, because of my impossible swimming and swooping through space, and my sensation of being disembodied. More realistic, because I knew where I was and wanted to get back to my uncle's room, in which my body lay sleeping.

Downward I shot like a stone, until I was only a hundred feet above the city. Then my motion changed and I skimmed over what seemed to be miles of rooftops. I noted the soot-covered chimneys and oddly shaped ventilator, the ragged tar-paper, the rain-streaked corrugated iron. Larger buildings — offices and factories — loomed up ahead of me like cliffs. I plunged straight through them without retardation, glimpsing flashes of metal and machinery, corridors and partitions. At one time I seemed to be racing a street car and beating it. At another I hurtled across several brightly lighted streets, in which many people and automobiles were moving. Finally my speed began to lessen and I swerved. A dark wall came into view, moved closer, engulfed me, and I was inside my uncle's room.

The most terrible phase of a nightmare is often that in which the dreamer believes himself to be in the very room in which he is sleeping. He recognizes each object but it is subtly distorted. Hideous shapes peer from the darker corners. If he then chances to waken, the dream room is for a time superimposed on the real room. That was the way in my case, except the dream refused to come to an end. I seemed to be hovering near the ceiling, looking down. Most of the objects were as I had last seen them. The table, the cupboard, the dresser, the chairs. But both doors, the one to the closet and the one to the hall, were ajar. And my body was not in the bed. I could see the crumpled sheets, the indented pillow, the blankets flung back. Yet my body was not in the bed.

Immediately my feelings of terror and loneliness rose to a new pitch. I knew that something was dreadfully wrong. I knew that I must find myself quickly. As I hovered, I became aware of an insistent tugging, like the pull a magnetic field exerts on a piece of iron.

Instinctively I gave way to it and was immediately drawn out through the walls into the night.

Again I sped across the darkened city. And now the strangest thoughts were whirling through my mind. They were not dream thoughts but waking thoughts. Horrible suspicions and accusations. Wild trains of deductive reasoning. Buy my emotions were dream emotions — helpless panic and mounting fear. The house tops over which I skimmed became dingier, grimier and more decrepit. Two-story houses gave way to sagging huddles of shacks. Coal dust choked the clumps of sickly grass. What ground showed was bare or heaped with refuse. My speed lessened and simultaneously my fear mounted.

I noted a dirty sign. "Robey Street," it read. I noted a number. I was in the 2300 block.

"2318 Robey Street."

The address written on the slip of paper in my uncle's dresser.

It was a ramshackle cottage, but neater than its neighbors. I turned off back of the house, where the muddy alley was and the dim shapes of packing cases.

It was at this time I began to realize I wasn't dreaming.

There was a light in the back of the house. The door opened and a little girl stepped out, carrying a small tin pail with a cover on it. She wore a short dress and her legs were thin and her hair was straight and smoky yellow. She turned back for a moment in the doorway and I heard a coarse female voice say, "Now mind you, get over there fast. Your Pa likes to have his food hot. And don't stop on the way and don't let nobody see you." I could hear again.

The little girl nodded meekly and started toward the dark alley. Then I saw the other figure, the one crouching in the shadows at a spot that she must pass. At first I saw only a dark form. Then I came nearer. I saw the face.

It was my own face.

I hope to heaven no one ever sees me as I looked then. The indolent mouth twisted up into something between a grin and a snarl. Nostrils twitching. The nondescript eyes bulging from their sockets so that the white showed all around the pupils. More animal than human.

The little girl was coming nearer. Waves of blackness seemed to oppose me, driving me back, but with one last despairing effort I threw myself at the distorted face I recognized as my own. There was

71

one supreme moment of pain and terror, and then I realized I was looking down at the little girl and she was looking up at me. She was saying, "My, but you scared me. I didn't know who you were at first."

I was in my own body and I knew I wasn't dreaming. Ill-fitting clothes cramped my waist and shoulders, pulled at my wrists. I looked down at the lead-weighted night stick I held in my hand. I reached up and felt for the stiff visored cap on my head, then downward, where in the dim light I could see that I was wearing the dark blue uniform of a policeman.

I do not know what my reaction would have been, if I hadn't realized that the little girl was still staring up at me, puzzled, half-smiling, but frightened. I forced my lips to smile. I said, "It's all right, little girl. I'm sorry I scared you. Where does your pa work? I'll see that you get there safely and I'll bring you home again."

And I did that.

Mercifully, my emotions were exhausted, paralyzed, for the next few hours. By questioning the little girl cautiously, I found out the way to the section of the city in which my uncle's rooming house was situated. Afterwards I managed to return there undetected and strip off those hateful clothes, hang them in the closet from which I had taken them.

Next morning I went to the police. I told them nothing of my dreams, my uncanny experience. I only said that the queer assortment of objects in the bottom dresser drawer, in conjunction with the things mentioned in the clippings had awakened certain ghastly suspicions in my mind. They were unwilling to believe, and obviously skeptical, but consented to a routine investigation, which had startling and conclusive results. Most of the objects in the bottom drawer, the silver-headed cane and the rest, were identified as having been in the personal possession of the victims of the "Phantom Slayer," and as having disappeared at the time of the murders. For example, the cane and briefcase had been carried by an old man found dead under a viaduct near the river; the toy horse had belonged to a boy murdered in an empty lot; the tortoise-shell comb was similar to one missing from the battered head of a woman whose dead body was found in a residential district; the green ribbon had come from another battered head. A close examination of my uncle's assignments and beats completed the damning evidence by showing that in almost every case he had been patrolling or stationed near the scene of the murder.

For many reasons this horrible discovery was not made public in its entirety. There had been at least eight murders, all told. They had begun while my uncle was still on the force, and continued after his retirement.

But apparently he had always worn his uniform to lull his victim's suspicions. The collection of newspaper clippings was attributed to his vanity. The incriminating objects he had kept by him were explained as "symbols" of his crimes — ghastly mementoes. "Fetishes" one man called them.

There is no need to describe the degree to which my nerves were shaken by this confirmation of my dreams and my fearful sleep-walking experience. Most of all I was terrified by the notion that some murderous taint in the blood of our family had been communicated to me as well as my uncle. I was only slightly relieved when the passing weeks brought no further horrors.

A considerable time afterwards I related the whole matter, in strict confidence, to a doctor whom I trust. He did not question my sanity, as I feared he might. He took my story at face value. But he attributed it to the workings of my unconscious mind. He said that, during my perusal of the clippings, my unconscious mind had realized that my uncle was a murderer, but that my conscious mind had refused to accept the idea. This resulted in a kind of mental turmoil, magnified by my distraught and highly suggestible state. The "will to murder" in my own mind was wakened without my knowing it. The slip of paper with the address written on it somehow focused that force. In my sleep I had got up, dressed myself in my uncle's uniform and walked to the address. While I was sleep-walking my mind imagined it was on all sorts of wild journeys through space and into the past.

The doctor has told me of some very remarkable actions performed by other sleep-walkers. And, as he says, I have no way of proving my uncle was really planning to commit that last murder.

I hope his explanation is correct.

Lie Still, Snow White

I tiptoed into Vivian's bedroom and softly closed the door behind me. She was lying outside the covers, wrapped in a white silk kimono. She had a little sleeping mask on — a narrow black oval without eye holes, but it had sequin eyes stitched on it with black velvet pupils staring at the ceiling.

Her legs were stretched out straight and close together, her arms were at her side, her head was thrown back on a little silk pillow, emphasizing her cameo-perfect profile and the long swan-line of her throat.

The moon was chilly and the blue lights were all on, making the white coverlet and the kimono and Vivian's flesh one pale blue marble. It would only have taken a sleeping wolfhound at her feet, his back against their soles, to have perfected the illusion of a medieval tomb statue.

"Lie still, my darling," I called gently on a sudden impulse. "I'll be with you in a moment. Don't say a word. You're so beautiful just as you are."

I am a man of very odd impulses. But following all faint cues from the unknown is the only way I know of wresting a little beauty from life. And beauty is everything.

I have a great instinct for beauty. I can see subtle possibilities for it where the average intelligent person beholds a blank. For instance, I don't think I'd have gotten the inspiration for this midnight rendezvous if it hadn't been for Vivian's strange penchant for blue-tinted electric light bulbs — a penchant which she told me annoyed her female friends quite a bit. Vivian has always been most imaginative, but sly with it.

True, blue light is cold and does disastrous things to a normal complexion or makeup job. But it can cover up things too. By turning everything blue, it can disguise a blue skin. There are persons with blue skin, you know. Some of them got that way by taking patent medicines containing silver nitrate. The chemical circulates through the body and sunlight striking it breaks it up and precipitates the silver as a fine powder throughout the cells just under the skin. Harmless, but the person turns a slate blue color if he keeps it up. Most such blue people got that way fifty years ago, when patent medicines were uncontrolled. There also was almost no sunbathing then, so I suppose such oldsters are only blue on their faces, throats and arms, though I really don't know. But now, especially with sunlamps, a person can easily be blue all over from silver nitrate.

Then there are the ancient Britons with their woad, though you don't see any of those these days — at least I never have.

And then there are heart conditions that give a person a blue tinge. And there are other reasons — or perhaps I'm only thinking of *extreme* heart conditions.

My dear Vivian, I knew, had a bluish skin, but the blue light disguised, or shall I say *tempered* the fact, harmonized it with the background.

The blue light also gave an uncanny, enchanted underwater feeling to the bedroom as I slowly circled around to the bedside table. I didn't look at Vivian steadily but only stole glances at her from time to time. It seemed more fun that way, more of a game, and perhaps I was still suffering a little from my old shyness — the terrified, guilty shyness that always locks me up tight as soon as I get within kissing distance of a woman or just alone in the same room or landscape with her.

"Don't take any notice of me, dear Sleeping Beauty," I said with a tender chuckle. "It's just me, just Arch the Warch, the distinguished-looking but harmless gaffer who's your older friend and who talks insightful-sympathetic with you, especially about your problems with younger men, and who takes you to museums and parks and restaurants and theaters and does half your office work and helps you work off your head of imaginative steam for you — and who gets tongue-tied and involuntarily jerks back whenever you give him that speculative smile.

75

"Don't let Arch disturb you. Please just lie there and go on dreaming or meditating or uniting with the cosmic all or savoring the delights of Heaven or suffering the pains of Hell, or whatever it is you're doing now."

You know, it's a funny thing. I hadn't intended to say a word when I came into the bedroom, but here I was talking and talking. I guess that sex or the sure prospect of sex opens a man up. I decided to experiment a little more.

"The trouble with everything is sex repression," I hadn't known I was going to say all *that*, or so loudly. "I know this is supposed to be an age of sexual freedom," I continued, "but that's a big lie. How can sex be free if they still bend every effort to make you scared of it? How can it be free if it's still surrounded with taboos and crazy complexes and awful warnings and the dread of ridicule and disapproval and even legal penalties and all sorts of other stop signs?

"How can sex be free if they make as much a secret and a shame of it as they do of death these aseptic days? — rating the goat-odor as vile as the corpse-odor.

"How can sex be free if the priests still want the privilege of doling it out like medicine, happy if they convince you it tastes nasty? And if the social workers and counselors give it to you like a wonder drug that must only be taken under their supervision, according to their rules. As if your sex urge didn't belong to you, but to society — meaning whoever currently rules society.

"How can a thing be free if nine-tenths of the people are really against it *for anyone else* and self-appoint themselves a secret police and spy constantly to make sure that nobody gets more than the legal maximum, which is a stale and uncertain minimum at best and sometimes completely unavailable. They say out of one side of their mouths that sex is okay and beautiful, but out of the other side they say that any real enthusiasm for sex is a sign of immaturity, Don Juanism, nymphomania, satyriasis, and social irresponsibility.

"Go ahead and enjoy sex, they say, if you're willing to make everybody else murderously jealous and maybe drive them crazy and if you're willing to degrade the girl and deal with the leering motel proprietress and the abortionist and the police. Go ahead and enjoy it, and then boast about it and snicker and sneer at it for the dirty thing it is. (*They* lie when they say it's beautiful, though not I.) Go ahead and enjoy it, they say, if you're willing to pay the price. But remember there's always a price. My God, the price you sometimes have to pay!"

I shut my mouth. The breath whistled through my nose for a while. I was standing by the bedside table now. The drinking glass had a half inch of water left in it and a lipstick print that looked purple in the blue light. The pillbox I'd given Vivian that morning was sitting beside it, open and empty. I was glad of that because I'd been afraid all along she might have taken only one of the two capsules and one might not have worked so completely or so cleanly.

I let myself look at Vivian now for several seconds. She hadn't vomited at all or been sick in any way that I could see. I'd somehow guessed all along that the effects of the cyanide wouldn't be as unpleasantly violent as the books described — they always exaggerate those things and try to throw an extra scare into you, about death as well as sex! — though I had been prepared to clean Vivian up if that had been necessary, clean her up in all tenderness and reverence.

I lightly touched the hand nearest me. It rocked a little, as though there were something under it liquid and gurgling. And it was icy cold.

Somehow the fact that her hand was cold shocked me and I quicky drew back my fingers. Naive of me, I suppose, but really except for her pale blue complexion, which was justified by the blue light, and the cold of her hand, and of course the empty pillbox, there was no way of knowing she was dead.

Then, gaining in boldness, I leaned closer to her and for the first time I caught the sweet musky rotten odor of corruption.

That jarred, I didn't want it, and I started for the bathroom, but before I got there I saw the slim fanciful bottles on her dressing table. I selected a lilac spray cologne and passed it back and forth at arm's length above her, from feet to head, several times.

Then, as the floral alcoholic mist settled, I plunged my hands through it and reverently parted the white silk kimono above her waist and drew back a little and looked at her breasts.

At that moment I experienced ecstasy, awe, and a kind of stubborn astonishment. Why, *why*, is it that two curving cones of flesh should exercise such a fiendish hold on man's imagination? They must mean something, be something; they can't be just a meaningless arbitrary target for man's fixation. I do not buy that theory about remembering mother's good milk and being cuddled into mother's warm protective bosom. Grown men aren't milk maniacs. Surely giving milk and pillowing a squirming brat are only subordinate functions of a woman's breasts, the sort of work they can do when they're broken down and good for nothing else. No, a woman's breasts must be designed for something fundamentally much more important. They're organs for voiceless communication, dear helpless hands, lovely mouthless snouts. They're trying to say or do something. They're like soft-nosed velvet creatures pushing out of a woman's body, wanting to feel and sense intensely — maybe Shelley was getting at something deep when he thought of a woman's breasts with each nipple replaced by a peering eye. Breasts are sacraments — an outward sign of some mysterious hidden glory. They're beautiful, beautiful, beautiful — and I don't understand it at all.

Once I saw some pornographic movies of what I suppose are the ordinary sort — at any rate, men and live women doing it together — and after the first second or so I didn't feel any of the ususal delightful hot excitement (such as comes to me when I have someone undress a woman in my imagination or as used to come to me at burlesque shows) but only a cold intense awe like watching live birth or death might awaken or observing some completely inorganic phenomenon on a grand scale, such as the creep of a glacier or the surging of the sea in storm or the implacable rush and leap of a forest fire and the flight of large animals before it, or the slow wheeling of the stars.

"No, Vivian, I don't understand it at all," I heard myself say, quite loudly. It hit me that I could freely talk to Vivian now, talk to her about all the things I'd never been able to hint at before, talk to her about the things *beyond* those things — the things you couldn't even think of until you'd talked about the others first — why, there was no end to it.. What's more, I realized I wouldn't have minded if Vivian had been able to listen to me, yes, and answer me too, comment on what I said, show me her view of things and maybe bring new light into my own brain that way; in fact, I even wished she would.

It hit me hard, let me tell you, it struck me all in a heap as our country cousins say, to realize that in one way I was sorry now I had killed Vivian. I decided that I would have to get this thing straightened out, I would have to explain myself to myself, before I did anything else.

Don't get me wrong, I didn't want to go back and change what I'd done. I was still delighted that I had Vivian in a situation where I could enjoy her just as I wanted to. My gaze kept licking back every few seconds to her naked breasts and every time it did I re-experienced that same mixed ecstasy. But I was secure in the knowledge that I could find fulfillment with Vivian whenever I wanted: I had all the night ahead of me. It was just that it was beginning to seem a necessary or at least a desirable part of my fulfillment that I explain myself first. And if I talked to Vivian while doing it, that wasn't because I really wanted her alive or had any superstitious notions about a listening spirit, but just because it made the words come out of me easier. It was for the same general reason that I didn't take off, though I'd been going to, her black sleeping mask with its velvet-pupiled sequin eyes staring at the ceiling. It was easier for me to talk to her with her real eyes covered, whether they were open or closed underneath. (And the mask did add to my excitement.)

"I had to kill you, Vivian, didn't you see?" I began. "I've fought against this warped and cowardly urge of mine most of my life, and I was beginning to think I had it licked, that the delights of art and knowledge would be enough for me as I grew older and finally faded away. But then you came along, Vivian, and you fascinated me so, you were so fearfully lovely and dreadfully desirable, and you had an imagination that innocently teetered so close to the verge of my dirtiest most delightful inner pits — like the night you wondered what Persephone thought when she was stolen by Hades — that all my old dreams reawakened and I simply had to possess you. And the only way I could possess you was to kill you. Each man kills the thing he loves — a great poet said that, Vivian, Oscar Wilde. Man has always killed his gods — the least study of anthropology shows you that, Vivian. The god has to be sacrificed so that there can be that great release, that great fulfillment. And the same is true of the goddess.

"It's not altogether my fault I'm the way I am, though I do like to take a little credit for the things I do," I continued. I had begun to pace now, back and forth past the foot of the bed, glancing at Vivian at the turns. "But I have to admit that my family background and some chance circumstances were largely responsible. I was a lonely and yearning child and pretty much unloved. I had a couple of parents who were very severe with me and with themselves, but who also drank too much. You know, Vivian, I sometimes think America is inhabited solely by a race of puritanical drunks — some of whom admittedly never take a drink all their lives. I also had a sister two years older named Beatrice.

"I've told you about Beatrice, Vivian, and especially about her tragic death from flu when I was only thirteen, how she died while I was alone in the house with her, my mother being alcoholically occupied. I often tell that anecdote to get a little sympathy. What I never tell was that Beatrice was a big prig and a tattletale and a tease — I call her big because she was two years older than me. As soon as she realized that I, her brother, was curious about her body, she started to make a great show of modesty and propriety. 'Ma, Archie tried to come into the bathroom while I was taking my bath;' 'Ma, Archie climbed on the top of the porch and peeked in my bedroom' — that sort of thing. Naturally it made my curiosity wilder. She also deliberately created situations to tease and frustrate and shame me and get me punished. One hot summer afternoon she pretended to be taking a nap — I swear she was just pretending — and her door was open and I couldn't help myself, I just had to tiptoe in and slowly, very slowly, frightened half to death, draw back the sheet. I was just starting to ease open the buttons of her pyjamas when she jerked up and let off an awful scream. I said I had just been going to tickle her, but it was no good; I got a severe whipping, an unnecessarily severe one by any standards, but then Beatrice was just an age for my father to be deeply in love with her — unconsciously, no doubt! — in that disgustingly pontifical, possessive, sentimental, self-satisfied way that hairy-chested fathers always seem to feel about their nubile daughters.

"After that I stayed strictly away from Beatrice and wouldn't bite on any of her traps — until the afternoon I came home from school and found mother snoring on the floor in the living room and Beatrice dead in bed upstairs. I satisfied my curiosity then — oh, I knew she was my sister and in a way I sincerely loved and respected her, and I knew what incest meant and that it was supposed to be very terrible, and I was very frightened of death and the dead and I was really scared of catching the flu, but I simply had to. Or maybe I wasn't entirely frightened of death. I mean, maybe I was frightened of death in the same way I was of sex — because they'd both been made horror-mysteries for me — and maybe I wanted to penetrate both mysteries at the same time.

"Anyway, I satisfied my curiosity, and it went further than that, further than I'd expected.

"You know, sex is a funny thing, Vivian. You start out just being overpoweringly curious and you end up getting hooked. You do something once and it can set a pattern forever. Why? How? I get the strangest feeling of reality-unreality whenever I think back to that cold bleak bedroom and the smoky twilight closing down and the burnt-linen stink of flu coming through the smell of mother's lilac toilet water — "

I got the damndest scare just then. I thought Vivian moved. I thought her body moved just a little. But I decided right away that it was because I'd been frightening myself remembering that afternoon with Beatrice so long ago.

"That was how I got hooked, Vivian. The fixation might have gradually faded, or it might not, but I was slow in getting social and starting to go with the girls and then about four or five years later there came the fiendish wonderful coincidence of moving to the city and discovering that my uncle there had the job of night attendant at the morgue. He had the family weakness for liquor; I hung around and played up to him. Pretty soon he took to leaving me to answer the phone while he sneaked out to get a drink. I won't go into that much, it didn't last long, but for a few evenings I inhabited a temple of Edgar Allan Poe — Poe had my weakness, Vivian, or at least he understood it damned well, just read 'Premature Burial,' 'The Oblong Box,' 'Usher,' 'Berenice,' and 'Ligeia.' Yes, for a brief space I had my dark-faned shrine, my Ulalumes and Annabel Lees. Most of the bodies were horrible, but not all.

"It only lasted three nights. On the fourth someone came checking up. I wasn't suspected, I got things hidden in time, but my uncle was reprimanded both for being away and for leaving me in charge, and he was transferred to another job.

"Right then I realized I was up against a big choice. I could go into the undertaking business and find a spot where I'd be able to fulfill myself from time to time — someday even in my own parlor! — or I could turn my back on the whole thing for the childish disgusting obsession I sometimes knew it was. I could try to fight it.

"I stewed around for quite a while making my decision. I once even contemplated trying to work my way through medical school and become a doctor, but it occurred to me in time that the temptations I'd be subjected to then would be too dreadful. I've never wanted to hurt society, Vivian, believe me! What little I've done, I've been driven to by overpowering urges.

"I finally decided I would try to fight it, and for the next twenty years I must say I made a pretty good job of the battle. I even went so far as to achieve relations of a sort with a couple of women — it wasn't so much completely successful as dull and troublesome. It never led anywhere. I found more satisfaction in certain aspects of art and literature and fantasies.

"I'm no dunce, Vivian. I know there are some women who are supposed to enjoy playing dead, but neither of mine did. One of them laughed at my suggestion, the other tried but was no good at it. Or maybe the pretense meant nothing to me, like some people can't enjoy sex with mechanical contraceptives, or even achieve it.

"I also seriously tried out a number of different churches, figuring they'd help me control myself and achieve some serenity, but I eventually discovered that most religions put so much emphasis on death and on sex as an evil or dangerous thing that they contributed to my urge instead of dissipating it. I stayed away from the church then and did a better job of keeping myself in line.

"But you know how it is with men in their forties, Vivian — or maybe you don't — anyway, they wake up one morning and realize that things they've always told themselves they'd do some day, in some sweet never-never land of success, are suddenly a matter of now-or-never.

"And then you came along, Vivian dear, and you were so damnably attractive that all my old urges awakened at a bound. You looked like a Poe heroine, a Pre-Raphaelite sorceress, a Bronte-Hepburn type; your eyes were dark-circled, you were delightfully thin, so that I was always conscious of your lovely skeleton, as if it were trying to burst out and join in a dance of death. And you were obviously neurotic, restless, easily frightened, very nervous, habitually melancholy and depressed, so that from the very start I thought of you as the Little Sister of Death. And then I finally got to know you, I found that you were very intelligent, sensitive, charming, and compassionate, full of little insights that hovered around the out-skirts of my secret. You liked to walk in cemeteries and romance about the old gravestones.

You liked to hear about the pastel tombs of Mexico, the narrow vaults of New Orleans, the Aztec maidens thrown in the well, and the nuns who died in their cells a-fever with love of Christ. And once you imagined you were Persephone, Queen of the Dead, and I stopped you quick, because I knew I couldn't keep my secret for long if you went on like that.

"You know, Vivian, I think that if I ever could have really loved a living woman, it would have been you. With you it could have happened, Vivian.

"You know why it never happened, Vivian, why it never had a chance of happening? It was because during those first months I only watched you from a distance — remember how long I was in saying more than two words? — and during that time I built you up into a symbol, I watched you die and I handled your dead body in my fantasies every night, so that by the time I got to know you better the pattern was set and only some impossible explosion of the mind could have changed it. I could only go on seeing as much of you as I dared, enduring the bittersweet torture of your presence, having my fantasies get more complex and unsatisfactory, and imperious every night, feeling the pressure build up, fighting to hold myself in check.

"I've always thought you were at least partly aware of what was going on those two times I almost killed you on impulse. First, there was the night I almost threw you into the lagoon in the park. I was going to go in with you and hold you under. There was a faint blue light around us from the distant boulevard lamps, remember? You always have been my Blue Girl, Vivian, moody and pale, though now you're painted by electricity rather than Gainsborough. Yes, there was a blue light around us and we were talking about suicide and there was nobody near — "

Again I thought Vivian moved! Just as though she'd shuddered and I'd caught the end of the shudder as my eyes turned to her. I was certain that once again I'd been scaring myself remembering eerie things, but this time I had more difficulty putting what I thought I'd seen out of my mind. I watched her motionless chest for several seconds before I went on.

"The second time was when I almost brained you with the stone ashtray out there in the living room. You suddenly turned round and caught me holding it back over my shoulder and I had to do a ridiculous pirouette to pass it off as a jape. You know why I checked myself that time, Vivian? It was solely because I had thought : 'I don't want her all bloodied up, I don't want even the back of her skull crushed, I'll do it a better way.'

"Once I'd thought of that I had no choice. It was just a matter of moving efficiently with a minimum waste of time, of stealing the cyanide from the photoengraving department and refilling the two Nembutal capsules, of getting a duplicate set of keys to this apartment the noon you let me come here from the office to fetch the homework you'd forgotten, of waiting for the time in your mood-cycle when you'd make the big complaint about not being able to sleep and, when it came this morning, taking you aside and offering you my two yellow capsules with much insistence that you take them both tonight and with repeated warnings that you tell no one — because, I said, most people these days are so irrationally critical of sleeping pills and especially of anyone not a doctor handing them out.

"I was afraid afterwards that I'd overdone it. You know, Vivian, I've often wondered during this last month of preparation whether you hadn't caught on, at least in some nebulous way, to what I was up to. I've been behaving in such a flighty, abstracted way, or at least it's seemed so to me. I'm no actor, you know. I never could play it cool. My repressions don't make me restrained, only tongue-tied and jumpy. So I've often wondered whether you hadn't caught on as to what I had in mind and were letting me go ahead with it because you yourself wanted it that way. Oh, not that you've asked me to kill you in so many words, but you've liked talking about suicide and you thought the Mexican candy skull I bought you was charming and you've told me how you keep coming back to the line in Keats' 'Nightingale' about being 'half in love with easeful death' and after all you are my Blue Girl, my Dancing Skeleton, my Sleeping Beauty, my Snow White, my Little Sister of Death . . .

"Yes, I really thought you knew the cyanide or some swift death was in the capsules when you took them from me. But if you did know that, Vivian, I wonder now if you really had to take them. If you were so much in love with death, I might have been able to love you alive. I'm actually beginning to think I could. My God, Vivian, if that was the way you felt, why didn't you tell me? Why didn't you open my eyes blinded by my mania-habits and my fears? Vivian, why — "

For a third time I thought that Vivian moved! Only this time it was I who shuddered. What if she should get up now, I asked myself, and come at me grinding her teeth and tear off the sleeping mask, and open her eyes to show just the whites and throw her arms around my neck stranglingly? I've never believed in the supernatural, though I've had an aesthetic taste for the weird, but now in that blue-litten room the whole impossible universe of vampires and zombies and werewolves suddenly came alive for me. What if the dead did come back . . . in the body?

No, no, I told myself, it was clearly an illusion born of my nervousness and self-dramatizing. And even if Vivian's body actually had twitched a little, there were natural causes. I mustn't forget rigor mortis — my uncle told me the ususal horrendous stories and I had done enough reading on the subject.

Besides, in all my rather absurd oratory I had lost sight temporarily of my chief purpose in coming here tonight. Thinking of that, I almost laughed. I moved toward the bed. Once again I caught the sweet foul odor of corruption — upsetting but reassuring too. Once again I sprayed the lilac cologne.

And then — you know, it's hard to believe this, but it's true — I discovered that I had lost my desire, or rather the hot, male intensity of it. Either my somewhat ridiculous spouting and melodramatic self-justification had sublimated it, or that moment of supernatural dread had chilled it. At any rate, there was Vivian lying there, more beautiful than I've ever seen her, infinitely desirable, all ready for me, and here I was worse than a eunuch. It was a scene for the gods to snicker at as they watched our painful antics from their lecherous couches on Olympus.

But I wasn't going to be cheated that way, no, I told myself, I'd murdered to get Vivian and I was going to have her. So I rang up the red curtain that had been closed ever since I met Vivian, and my girls came out of the wings and began to put on their thousandth performance, or something like that, of Lesbian Gang, Miss Satan's School, Sisters of the Whip, Hell's Sorority House, and the other little dramas I have concocted over the years. I don't know why it's so exciting to imagine girls torturing girls, but it is for me and I gather from pornographic books and photographs that my taste is not unique.

I must say my girls never seemed such cheap and sleazy creatures as they did tonight, even Miss Satan herself and poor frightened

Lovey-Dovey. Or maybe they put on a brilliant performance and it was just me that felt cheap, having to use them that way.

At any rate, they eventually had the desired effect on me. They always do. I turned once more to the bed.

And then — oh, I didn't lose my ardor, quite the contrary, but Vivian looked so very beautiful and lovely and loving, as if she were somehow making an effort to make herself nice for me in death, that I wished her alive with that understanding of me and I felt lonely and sad to my core, though still loving, and I knelt down beside the bed at her feet to kiss, not her icy hand, but the sleeve of her white silk kimono, begging for forgiveness, yearning for her pardon.

As I did so, I noticed that the white bedclothes were wet at that point, so wet that droplets were forming at the hanging edge of the white coverlet and dripping noiselessly onto the thick carpet. The liquid was absolutely colorless and odorless too — I touched my nose to it. And it was very cold.

It had to be ice water — as if a rubber sheet full of ice water under the bedclothes were leaking.

I didn't move. I didn't breathe.

Then I got the odor of corruption, stronger than ever, but clearly *not* from the ice water. I stooped lower then on my knees, still holding the hem of Vivian's kimono to my lips, and looked under the bed.

Not two feet away from me was a dishpan full of garbage. A purple-gray hunk of meat was the main part of it, flanked by crescents of mold-spotted cantaloupe rind, and scattered over with gardenia blossoms. Beyond it was a little, gray, grill-faced microphone lying on its back with thin wires going from it toward the head of the bed.

Still holding the hem of her kimono and kneeling and bending so that my face almost touched the carpet, I followed the inconspicuous wires with my eyes. They traveled around the foot of the baseboard and disappeared under the bathroom door.

I instantly realized exactly what had happened — there was no reasoning to it, no deduction; one moment ten thousand facts and ideas weren't in my head, the next moment they were.

Just as I'd guessed, Vivian had suspected me all along. She'd gone to the police — maybe not for the first time — as soon as I gave her the capsules — during lunch hour, of course. The powder in the capsules had been easily identified as cyanide, but because they only had Vivian's word that I'd given her the capsules and because in any case they wanted to nail me — and because policemen have as hot nasty tastes as other men — they'd laid this little trap for me with Vivian's cooperation. Maybe the blue lights had helped give them the idea, though if the lights hadn't been blue they'd have simply turned them off.

Yes, it must have been the police who had planted this microphone, and maybe the police who had hit on the point about the blue lights, but it must have been Vivian who had thought of concealing her eyes, which no one can keep from blinking, with the black sleeping mask. As for her breathing, she'd have kept it shallow and I hadn't even looked at her five consecutive seconds.

And I was somehow certain that it was Vivian who had thought of the rubber sheet full of ice cubes and the dishpan full of garbage. I could imagine the police chuckling enthusiastically as she suggested those items. The police are our guardians, but they like their pornography as much as the next chap.

Yes, I was curiously sure they'd enjoyed my little performance, even been thrilled by it, both Vivian and the police — and I rather wished I'd gotten the bit about Miss Satan's School on the tape, and Lovey-Dovey's last torments.

Yes, Archie, I told myself, Vivian will have nightmares about it, or maybe pleasant dreams, all the rest of her life. And those crooked-brained, blue-coated voyeurs will keep the tape in their secret black museum and play it for kicks for the next fifty years. But after all, you did put the cyanide in those capsules, Archie old boy, and for killing the thing you love there's no pardon to the end of time, or at least until the end of you.

I knew exactly what was going to happen next, but just the same I stood up and quietly started for the door to the living room.

Before I was halfway there it began to open. I stopped where I was.

Vivian sat up in bed with a jerk. Jill-in-the-box. The mask stared at me.

Through both doors the cops came into the bedroom. One of them switched on the big yellow ceiling light. Under it, Vivian's skin was pinkly flushed.

The cops came toward me, but I stood there aloof, looking at Vivian. Now I could see her eyes through the mask.

She jerked the sheet up to her neck, but kept staring at me.

A hand grabbed my shoulder and jerked me one way, but almost immediately another hand jerked me the other. My coat tore. It was comic. I pretended not to notice, and really I hardly did.

Vivian's face was contorted with fury, but whether at me — and why — or at the cops — and why — I couldn't tell. Maybe if she'd taken the mask off, baring all her expression, I'd have been able to. For instance, was the flush merely anger?

It was an interesting problem. I still ponder it when the bare globe turns out in the concrete ceiling overhead and I wait for sleep.

Mr. Bauer and The Atoms

Dr. Jacobson beamed at him through the thick glasses. "I'm happy to tell you there is no sign whatever of cancer."

Mr. Bauer nodded thoughtfully. "Then I won't need any of those radium treatments?"

"Absolutely not." Dr. Jacobson removed his glasses, wiped them with a bit of rice paper, then mopped his forehead with a handkerchief. Mr. Bauer lingered.

He looked at the X-ray machine bolted down by the window. It still looked as solid and mysterious as when he had first glimpsed a corner of it from Myna's bedroom. He hadn't gotten any farther.

Dr. Jacobson replaced his glasses.

"It's funny, you know, but I've been thinking . . ." Mr. Bauer plunged. "Yes?"

"I guess all this atomic stuff got me started, but I've been thinking about all the energy that's in the atoms of my body. When you start to figure it out on paper — well, two hundred million electron volts, they say, from just splitting one atom, and that's only a tiny part of it." He grinned. "Enough energy in my body, I guess, to blow up, maybe . . . the world."

Dr. Jacobson nodded. "Almost. But all safely locked up."

Mr. Bauer nodded. "They're finding out how to unlock it."

Dr. Jacobson smiled. "Only in the case of two rare radioactive elements."

Mr. Bauer agreed, then gathered all his courage. "I've been wondering about that too," he said. "Whether a person could somehow make himself . . . I mean, become . . . radioactive?"

Dr. Jacobson chuckled in the friendliest way. "See that box at your elbow?" He reached out and turned something on it. The box ticked. Mr. Bauer jerked.

"That's a Geiger-Müller counter," Dr. Jacobson explained. "Notice how the ticks come every second or so? Each tick indicates a high-frequency wave. If you were radioactive, it would tick a lot oftener."

Mr. Bauer laughed. "Interesting." He got up. "Well, thanks about the cancer."

Dr. Jacobson watched him fumble for his panama hat and duck out. So that was it. He'd sensed all along something peculiar about Bauer. He'd even felt it while looking over the X-ray and lab reports — something intangibly wrong. Though he hadn't thought until now of paranoia, or, for that matter, any other mental ailment, beyond the almost normal cancer-fear of a man in his fifties.

Frank Bauer hesitated at the corridor leading to Myna's apartment, then went on. His heart hammered enragedly. There he'd gone chicken again, when he knew very well that if he could ever bring himself to state his fear coldly and completely — that crazy fear that a man's thoughts could do to the atoms of his body what the scientists had managed to do with uranium 235 and that other element — why, he'd be rid of the fear in a minute.

But a man just didn't go around admitting childish things like that. A human bomb exploded by thought! It was too much like his wife Grace and her mysticism.

Going crazy wouldn't be so bad, he thought, if only it weren't so humiliating.

Frank Bauer lived in a world where everything had been exploded. He scented confidence games, hoaxes, faddish self-deception, and especially (for it was his province) advertising copy exaggerations behind every faintly unusual event and every intimation of the unknown. He had the American's nose for leg-pulling, the German's contempt for the non-factual. Mention of such topics as telepathy, hypnotism, or the occult — and his wife managed to mention them fairly often — sent him into a scoffing rage. The way he looked at it, a real man had three legitimate interests — business, bars and blondes. Everything else was for cranks, artists, and women.

But now an explosion had occurred which made all other explosions, even of the greatest fakeries, seem like a snap of the fingers.

By the time he reached the street, he thought he was beginning to feel a bit better. After all, he had told the doctor practically everything, and the doctor had disposed of his fears with that little box. That was that.

He swabbed his neck and thought about a drink, but decided to go back to the office. Criminal to lose a minute these days, when everybody was fighting tooth and nail to get the jump. He'd be wanting money pretty soon, the bigger the better. All the things that Grace would be nagging for now, and something special for Myna — and then there was a chance he and Myna could get away together for a vacation, when he'd got those campaigns lined out.

The office was cool and dusky and pleasantly suggestive of a non-atomic solidity. Every bit of stalwart ugliness, every worn spot in the dark varnish, made him feel better. He even managed to get off a joke to ease Miss Minter's boredom. Then he went inside.

An hour later he rushed out. This time he had no joke for Miss Minter. As she looked after him, there was something in her expression that had been in Dr. Jacobson's.

It hadn't been so bad at first when he'd got out paper and black pencil. After all, any advertising copy had to make Atomic Age its keynote these days. But when you sat there, and thought and thought, and whatever you thought, you always found afterwards that you'd written:

INSIDE YOU . . . TRILLIONS OF VOLTS!

You wouldn't think to look at them, that there was much resemblance between John Jones and the atom bomb . . .

UNLOCKED!
THE WORLD IN YOUR HANDS
JUST A THOUGHT —

Frank Bauer looked around at the grimy street, the windows dusty or dazzlingly golden where the low sun struck, the people wilted a little by the baking pavement — and he saw walls turned to gray powder, their steel skeletons vaporized, the people became fumes, or, if they were far enough away, mere great single blisters. But they'd have to be very far away.

He *was* going crazy — and it was horribly humiliating. He hurried into the bar.

After his second bourbon and water he began to think about the scientists. They should have suppressed the thing, like that one fellow who wanted to. They shouldn't ever have told people. So long as people didn't know, maybe it would have been all right . . . But once you'd been told . . .

Thought was the most powerful force in the world. It had discovered the atom bomb. And yet nobody knew what thought was, how it worked inside your nerves, what it couldn't manage.

And you couldn't stop thinking. Whatever your thoughts decided to do, you couldn't stop them.

It was insanity, of course.

It had better be insanity!

The man beside him said, "He saw a lot of those Jap suicide flyers. CRAZY as loons. Human bombs."

Human bombs! Firecrackers. He put down his drink.

As he hurried through the thinning crowd, retracing the course he had taken early in the afternoon, he wondered why there should be so much deadly force locked up in such innocent-seeming, inert things. The whole universe was a booby trap. There must be a reason. Who had planned it that way, with the planets far enough apart so they wouldn't hurt each other when they popped?

He thought he began to feel sharp pains shooting through his nerves, as the radioactivity began, and after he had rushed up the steps the pain became so strong that he hesitated at the intersection of the corridors before he went on to Myna's.

He closed the door and leaned back against it, sweating. Myna was drinking and she had her hair down. There was a pint of bourbon on the table, and some ice. She jumped up, pulling at her dressing gown.

"What's wrong? Grace?"

He shook his head, kept staring at her, at her long curling hair, at her breasts, as if in that small hillocky, yellow entwined patch of reality lay his sole hope of salvation, his last refuge.

"But my God, what is it!"

He felt the pains mercifully begin to fade, the dangerous thoughts break ranks and retreat. He began to say to himself, "It must have hit a lot of people the same way it hit me. It's just so staggering. That must be it. That must be it."

Myna was tugging at him. "It's nothing," he told her. "I don't know. Maybe my heart. No, I don't need a doctor."

She wandered into the bedroom and came back with a large waffle-creased metal egg which she held out to him, as if it were a toy to cajole an ailing child.

"My cousin just landed in San Francisco," she told him. "Look at the souvenir he smuggled in for me."

He got up carefully and took it from her.

"Must be your dumb cousin, the one from downstate."

"Why?"

"Because, unless I'm very much mistaken, this is a live hand grenade. Look, you'd just have to pull this pin — "

"Give it to me!"

But he fended her off, grinning, holding the grenade in the air.

"Don't be frightened," he told her, "this is nothing. It's just a flash in the pan, a match head. Haven't you heard of the atom bomb? That's all that counts from now on."

He enjoyed her fear so much that he kept up his teasing for some time, but after a while he yielded and laid the grenade gingerly away in the back of the closet.

Afterwards he found he could talk to her more easily than ever before. He told her about the Atomic Age, how they'd be driving around in an airplane with a fuel-tank no bigger than a peanut, how they'd whisk to Europe and back on a glass of water. He even told her a little about his crazy fears. Finally he got philosophical.

"See, we always thought everything was so solid. Money, automobiles, mines, dirt. We thought they were so solid that we could handle them, hold on to them, do things with them. And now we find they're just a lot of little bits of deadly electricity, whirling around at God knows what speed, by some miracle frozen for a moment. But any time now — " He looked across at her and then reached for her. "Except you," he said. "There aren't any atoms in you."

"Look," he said, "there's enough energy inside you to blow up the world — well, maybe not inside you, but inside any other person. This whole city would go pouf!"

"Stop it."

"The only problem is, how to touch it off. Do you know how cancer works?"

"Oh shut up."

"The cells run wild. They grow any way they want to. Now suppose your thoughts should run wild, eh? Suppose they'd decide to go to work on your body, on the atoms of your body."

"For God's sake."

"They'd start on your nervous system first, of course, because that's where they are. They'd begin to split the atoms of your nervous system, make them, you know, radioactive. Then — "

"Frank!"

He glanced out of the window, noticed the light was still in Dr. Jacobson's office. He was feeling extraordinarily good, as if there were nothing he could not do. He felt an exciting rush of energy through him. He turned and reached for Myna.

Myna screamed.

He grabbed at her.

"What's the matter?"

She pulled away and screamed again.

He followed her. She huddled against the far wall, still screaming. Then he saw it.

Of course, it was too dark in the room to see anything plainly. Flesh was just a dim white smudge. But this thing beside Myna glowed greenishly. A blob of green about as high off the floor as his head. A green stalk coming down from it part way. Fainter greenish filaments going off from it, especially from near the top and bottom of the stalk.

It was his reflection in the mirror.

Then the pains began to come, horrible pains sweeping up and down his nerves, building a fire in his skull.

He ran out of the bedroom. Myna followed him, saw him come out of the closet, bending, holding something to his stomach. About seconds after he'd gotten through the hall door, the blast came.

Dr. Jacobson ran out of his office. The corridor was filled with acrid fumes. He saw a woman in a dressing gown trying to haul a naked man whose abdomen and legs were tattered and dripping red. Together they carried him into the office and laid him down.

Dr. Jacobson recognized his patient.

"He went crazy," the woman yelped at him. "He thought he was going to explode like an atom, and something horrible happened to him, and he killed himself."

Dr. Jacobson, seeing the other was beyond help, started to calm her. Then he heard it.

His thick glasses, half dislodged during his exertions, fell off. His red-rimmed naked eyes looked purblind, terrified.

He could tell that she heard it too, although she didn't know its meaning. A sound like the rattle of a pygmy machine gun.

The Geiger-Müller counter was ticking like a clock gone mad.

In the X-Ray

"Do the dead come back?" Dr. Ballard repeated the question puzzledly. "What's that got to do with your ankle?"

"I didn't say that," Nancy Sawyer answered sharply. "I said: 'I tried an ice pack.' You must have misheard me."

"But . . ." Dr. Ballard began. Then, "Of course I must have," he said quickly. "Go on, Miss Sawyer."

The girl hesitated. Her glance strayed to the large, gleaming window and the graying sky beyond. She was a young woman with prominent eyes, a narrow chin, strong white teeth, reddish hair, and a beautiful, doe-like figure which included legs long and slim — except for the ankle of the one outstretched stockingless on the chair before her. That was encircled by a hard, white, somewhat irregular swelling.

Dr. Ballard was a man of middle age and size, with strong, soft-skinned hands. He looked intelligent and as successful as his sleekly-furnished office.

"Well, there isn't much more to it," the girl said finally. "I tried the ice pack but the swelling wouldn't go down. So Marge made me call you."

"I see. Tell me, Miss Sawyer, hadn't your ankle bothered you before last night?"

"No. I just woke up from a nightmare, frightened because something had grabbed my foot, and I reached down and touched my ankle — and there it was."

"Your ankle didn't feel or look any different the day before?"

"No."

"Yet when you woke up the swelling was there?"

"Just as it is now."

"Do you think you might have twisted your foot while you were asleep?"

"No."

"And you don't feel any pain in it now?"

"No, except a feeling of something hard clasped snugly around it and every once in a while squeezing a bit tighter."

"Ever do any sleepwalking?"

"No."

"Any allergies?"

"No."

"Can you think of anything else — anything at all — that might have a bearing on this trouble?"

Again Nancy looked out the window. "I have a twin sister," she said after a moment, in a different voice. "Or rather, I had. She died more than a year ago." She looked back quickly at Dr. Ballard. "But I don't know why I should mention that," she said hurriedly. "It couldn't possibly have any bearing on this. She died of apoplexy."

There was a pause.

"I suppose the X-ray will show what's the matter?" she continued.

The doctor nodded. "We'll have it soon. Miss Snyder's getting it now."

Nancy started to get up, asked, "Is it all right for me to move around?" Dr. Ballard nodded. She went over to the window, limping just a little, and looked down.

"You have a nice view, you can see half the city," she said. "We have the river at our apartment. I think we're higher, though."

"This is the twentieth floor," Dr. Ballard said.

"We're twenty-three," she told him. "I like high buildings. It's a little like being in an airplane. With the river right under our window I can imagine I'm flying over water."

There was a soft knock at the door. Nancy looked around inquiringly. "The X-ray?" He shook his head. He went to the door and opened it.

"It's your friend Miss Hudson."

"Hi, Marge," Nancy called. "Come on in."

The stocky, sandy-haired girl hung in the doorway. "I'll stay out here," she said. "I thought we could go home together though."

"Darling, how nice of you. But I'll be a bit longer, I'm afraid."

"That's all right. How are you feeling, Nancy?"

"Wonderful, dear. Especially now that your doctor has taken a picture that'll show him what's inside this bump of mine."

"Well, I'll be out here," the other girl said and turned back into the waiting room. She passed a woman in white who came in, shut the door, and handed the doctor a large, brown envelope.

He turned to Nancy. "I'll look at this and be back right away."

"Dr. Myers is on the phone," the nurse told him as they started out. "Wants to know about tonight. Can he come here and drive over with you?"

"How soon can he get here?"

"About half an hour, he says."

"Tell him that will be fine, Miss Snyder."

The door closed behind them. Nancy sat still for perhaps two minutes. Then she jerked, as if at a twinge of pain. She looked at her ankle. Bending over, she clasped her hand around her good ankle and squeezed experimentally. She shuddered.

The door banged open. Dr. Ballard hurried in and immediately began to reexamine the swelling, swiftly exploring each detail of its outlines with gentle fingers, at the same time firing questions.

"Are you absolutely sure, Miss Sawyer, that you hadn't noticed anything of this swelling before last night? Perhaps just some slight change in shape or feeling, or a tendency to favor that ankle, or just a disinclination to look at it? Cast your mind back."

Nancy hesitated uneasily, but when she spoke it was with certainty. "No, I'm absolutely sure."

He shook his head. "Very well. And now, Miss Sawyer, that twin of yours. Was she identical?"

Nancy looked at him. "Why are you interested in that? Doctor, what does the X-ray show?"

"I have a very good reason, which I'll explain to you later. I'll go into the details about the X-ray then, too. You can set your mind at rest on one point, though, if it's been worrying you. This swelling is in no sense malignant."

"Thank goodness, Doctor."

"But now about the twin."

"You really want to know?"

"I do."

Nancy's manner and voice showed some signs of agitation. "Why, yes," she said, "we were identical. People were always mistaking us for each other. We looked exactly alike, but underneath . . ." Her voice trailed off. There was a change hard to define. Abruptly she continued, "Dr. Ballard, I'd like to tell you about her, tell you things I've hardly told anyone else. You know, it was she I was dreaming about last night. In fact, I thought it was she who had grabbed me in my nightmare. What's the matter, Dr. Ballard?"

It did seem that Dr. Ballard had changed color, though it was hard to tell in the failing light. What he said, a little jerkily, was: "Nothing, Miss Sawyer. Please go ahead." He leaned forward a little, resting his elbows on the desk, and watched her.

"You know, Dr. Ballard," she began slowly, "most people think that twins are very affectionate. They think stories of twins hating each other are invented by writers looking for morbid plots.

"But in my case the morbid plot happened to be the simple truth. Beth tyrannized me, hated me, and . . . wasn't above expressing her hate in a physical way." She took a deep breath.

"It started when we were little girls. As far back as I can remember, I was always the slave and she was the mistress. And if I didn't carry out her orders faithfully, and sometimes if I did, there was always a slap or a pinch. Not a little-girl pinch. Beth had peculiarly strong fingers. I was very afraid of them.

"There's something terrible, Dr. Ballard, about the way one human being can intimidate another, crush their will power, reduce to mush their ability to fight back. You'd think the victim could escape so easily — look, there are people all around, teachers and friends to confide in, your father and mother — but it's as if you were bound by invisible chains, your mouth shut by an invisible gag. And it grows and grows, like the horrors of a concentration camp. A whole inner world of pain and fright. And yet on the surface — why, there seems to be nothing at all.

"For of course no one else had the faintest idea what was going on between us. Everyone thought we loved each other very much. Beth especially was always being praised for her 'sunny gaiety.' I was supposed to be a little 'subdued.' Oh, how she used to fuss and coo over me when there were people around. Though even then there would be pinches on the sly — hard ones I never winced at. And more than that, for . . ."

Nancy broke off. "But I really don't think I should be wasting your time with all these childhood gripes, Dr. Ballard. Especially since I know you have an engagement for this evening."

"That's just an informal dinner with a few old cronies. I have lots of time. Go right ahead. I'm interested."

Nancy paused, frowning a little. "The funny thing is," she continued, "I never understood why Beth hated me. It was as if she were intensely jealous. She was the successful one, the one who won the prizes and played the leads in the school shows and got the nicest presents and all the boys. But somehow each success made her worse. I've sometimes thought, Dr. Ballard, that only cruel people can be successful, that success is really a reward for cruelty . . . to someone."

Dr. Ballard knit his brows, might have nodded.

"The only thing I ever read that helped explain it to me," she went on, "was something in psychoanalysis. The idea that each of us has an equal dose of love and hate, and that it's our business to balance them off, to act in such a way that both have expression and yet so that the hate is always under the control of the love.

"But perhaps when the two people are very close together, as it is with twins, the balancing works out differently. Perhaps all the softness and love begins to gather in the one person and all the hardness and hate in the other. And then the hate takes the lead, because it's an emotion of violence and power and action — a concentrated emotion, not misty like love. And it keeps on and on, getting worse all the time, until it's so strong you feel it will never stop, not even with death.

"For it did keep on, Dr. Ballard, and it did get worse." Nancy looked at him closely. "Oh, I know that what I've been telling you isn't supposed to be so unusual among children. 'Little barbarians,' people say, quite confident that they'll outgrow it. Quite convinced that wrist-twisting and pinching are things that will automatically stop when children begin to grow up."

Nancy smiled thinly at him. "Well, they don't stop, Dr. Ballard. You know, it's very hard for most people to associate actual cruelty with an adolescent girl, maybe because of the way girls have been glorified in advertising. Yet I could write you a pretty chapter on just that topic. Of course a lot of it that happened in my case was what you'd call mental cruelty. I was shy and Beth had a hundred ways of embarrassing me. And if a boy became interested in me, she'd always take him away."

"I'd hardly have thought she'd have been able to," remarked Dr. Ballard.

"You think I'm good-looking? But I'm only good-looking in an odd way, and in any case it never seemed to count then. It's true, though, that twice there were boys who wouldn't respond to her invitations. Then both times she played a trick that only she could, because we were identical twins. She would pretend to be me — she could always imitate my manner and voice, even my reactions, precisely, though I couldn't possibly have imitated her — and then she would . . . do something that would make the boy drop me cold."

"Do something?"

Nancy looked down. "Oh, insult the boy cruelly, pretending to be me. Or else make some foul, boastful confession, pretending it was mine. If you knew how those boys loathed me afterwards . . .

"But as I said, it wasn't only mental cruelty or indecent tricks. I remember nights when I'd done something to displease her and I'd gone to bed before her and she'd come in and I'd pretend to be asleep and after a while she'd say — oh, I know, Dr. Ballard, it sounds like something a silly little girl would say, but it didn't sound like that then, with my head under the sheet, pressed into the pillow, and her footsteps moving slowly around the bed — she'd say: 'I'm thinking of how to punish you.' And then there'd be a long wait, while I still pretended to be asleep, and then the touch . . . oh, Dr. Ballard, her hands! I was so afraid of her hands! But. . . what it is, Dr. Ballard?"

"Nothing. Go on."

"There's nothing much more to say. Except that Beth's cruelty and my fear went on until a year ago, when she died suddenly — I suppose you'd say tragically — of a blood clot on the brain. I've often wondered since then whether her hatred of me, so long and cleverly concealed, mightn't have had something to do with it. Apoplexy's what haters die of, isn't it, doctor?"

"I remember leaning over her bed the day she died, lying there paralyzed, with her beautiful face white and stiff as a fish's and one eye bigger than the other. I felt pity for her (you realize, doctor, don't you, that I always loved her?) but just then her hand flopped a little way across the blanket and touched mine, although they said she was completely paralyzed, and her big eye twitched around a little until it was looking almost at me and her lips moved and I thought I heard her say: 'I'll come back and punish you for this,' and then I felt her fingers moving, just a little, on my skin, as if they were trying to close on my wrist, and I jerked back with a cry.

"Mother was very angry with me for that. She thought I was just a little selfish, thoughtless girl, afraid of death and unable to repress my fear even for my dying sister's sake. Of course I could never tell her the real reason. I've never really told that to anyone, except you. And now that I've told you I hardly know why I've done it."

She smiled nervously, quite unhumorously.

"Wasn't there something about a dream you had last night?" Dr. Ballard asked softly.

"Oh yes!" The listlessness snapped out of her. "I dreamed I was walking in an old graveyard with gnarly grey trees, and overhead the sky was grey and low and threatening, and everything was weird and dreadful. But somehow I was very happy. But then I felt a faint movement under my feet and I looked down at the grave I was passing and I saw the earth falling away into it. Just a little cone-shaped pit at first, with the dark sandy earth sliding down its sides, and a small black hole at the bottom. I knew I must run away quickly, but I couldn't move an inch. Then the pit grew larger and the earth tumbled down its sides in chunks and the black hole grew. And still I was rooted there. I looked at the gravestone beyond and it said 'Elizabeth Sawyer, 1926-48.' Then out of the hole came a hand and arm, only there were just shreds of dark flesh clinging to the bone, and it began to feel around with an awful, snatching swiftness. Then suddenly the earth heaved and opened, and a figure came swiftly hitching itself up out of the hole. And although the flesh was green and shrunken and eaten and the eyes just holes, I recognized Beth — there was still the beautiful reddish hair. And then the ragged hand touched my ankle and instantly closed on it and the other hand came groping upward, higher, higher, and I screamed . . . and then I woke up."

* * *

Nancy was leaning forward, her eyes fixed on the doctor. Suddenly her hair seemed to bush out, just a trifle. Perhaps it had 'stood on end.' At any rate, she said, "Dr. Ballard, I'm frightened."

"I'm sorry if I've made you distress yourself," he said. The words were more reassuring than the tone of voice. He suddenly took her hand in his and for a few moments they sat there silently. Then she smiled and moved a little and said, "It's gone now. I've been very silly. I don't know why I told you all I did about Beth. It couldn't help you with my ankle."

"No, of course not," he said after a moment.

"Why did you ask if she was identical?"

He leaned back. His voice became brisker again. "I'll tell you about that right now — and about what the X-ray shows. I think there's a connection. As you probably know, Miss Sawyer, identical twins look so nearly alike because they come from the same gene cell. Before it starts to develop, it splits in two. Instead of one individual, two develop. That was what happened in the case of you and your sister." He paused. "But," he continued, "sometimes, especially if there's a strong tendency to twin births in the family, the splitting doesn't stop there. One of the two cells splits again. The result — triplets. I believe that also happened in your case."

Nancy looked at him puzzledly. "But, then what happened to the third child?"

"The third sister," he amplified. "There can't be identical boy-and-girl twins or triplets, you know, since sex is determined in the original gene cell. There, Miss Sawyer, we come to my second point. Not all twins develop and are actually born. Some start to develop and then stop."

"What happens to them?"

"Sometimes what there is of them is engulfed in the child that does develop completely — little fragments of a body, bits of this and that, all buried in the flesh of the child that is actually born. I think that happened in your case."

Nancy looked at him oddly. "You mean I have in me bits of another twin sister, a triplet sister, who didn't develop?"

"Exactly."

"And that all this is connected with my ankle?"

"Yes."

"But then how — ?"

"Sometimes nothing happens to the engulfed fragments. But sometimes, perhaps many years later, they begin to grow — in a natural way rather than malignantly. There are well-authenticated cases of this happening — as recently as 1890 a Mexican boy in this way 'gave birth' to his own twin brother, completely developed though of course dead. There's nothing nearly as extensive as that in your case, but I'm sure there is a pocket of engulfed materials around your ankle and that it recently started to grow, so gradually that you didn't notice it until the growth became so extensive as to be irritating."

Nancy eyed him closely. "What sort of materials? I mean the engulfed fragments."

He hesitated. "I'm not quite sure," he said. "The X-ray was . . .oh, such things are apt to be odd, though harmless stuff — teeth, hair, nails, you never can tell. We'll know better later."

"Could I see the X-ray?"

He hesitated again. "I'm afraid it couldn't mean anything to you. Just a lot of shadows."

"Could there be . . . other pockets of fragments?"

"It's not likely. And if there are, it's improbable they'll ever bother you."

There was a pause.

Nancy said, "I don't like it."

"I don't like it," she repeated. "It's as if Beth had come back. Inside me."

"The fragments have no connection with your dead sister," Dr. Ballard assured her. "They're not part of Beth, but of a third sister, if you can call such fragments a person."

"But those fragments only began to grow after Beth died. As if Beth's soul . . . and was it my original cell that split a second time? — or was it Beth's? — so that it was the fragments of half her cell that I absorbed, so

that . . ." She stopped. "I'm afraid I'm being silly again."

He looked at her for a while, then, with the air of someone snapping to attention, quickly nodded.

"But doctor," she said, also like someone snatching at practicality, "what's to happen now?"

"Well," he replied, "in order to get rid of this disfigurement to your ankle, a relatively minor operation will be necessary. You see, this sort of foreign body can't be reduced in size by heat or X-ray or injections. Surgery is needed, though probably only under local anaesthetic. Could you arrange to enter a hospital tomorrow? Then I could operate the next morning. You'd have to stay about four days."

She thought for a moment, then said, "Yes, I think I could manage that." She looked distastefully at her ankle. "In fact, I'd like to do it as soon as possible."

"Good. We'll ask Miss Snyder to arrange things."

When the nurse entered, she said, "Dr. Myers is outside."

"Tell him I'll be right along," Dr. Ballard said. "And then I'd like you to call Central Hospital. Miss Sawyer will take the reservation we got for Mrs. Phipps and were about to cancel." And they discussed details while Nancy pulled on stocking and shoe.

Nancy said goodbye and started for the waiting room, favoring her bad leg. Dr. Ballard watched her. The nurse opened the door. Beyond, Nancy's friend got up with a smile. There was now, besides her, a dark, oldish man in the waiting room.

As the nurse was about to close the door, Dr. Ballard said, "Miss Sawyer."

She turned. "Yes?"

"If your ankle should start to trouble you tonight — or anything else — please call me."

"Thank you, doctor, I will."

Dr. Ballard nodded. Then he called to his friend, "Be right with you." The dark, oldish man flapped an arm at him.

The door closed. Dr. Ballard went to his desk, took the X-ray photograph out of its brown envelope, switched on the light, and studied the photograph incredulously.

He put it back in its envelope and on the desk. He got his hat and overcoat from the closet. He turned out the light. Then suddenly he went back and got the envelope, stuffed it in his pocket, and went out.

The dinner with Dr. Myers and three other professional friends proved if anything more enjoyable than Dr. Ballard had anticipated. It led to relaxation, gossip, a leisurely evening stroll, a drink together, a few final yarns. At one point Dr. Ballard felt a fleeting impulse to get the X-ray out of his overcoat pocket and show it to them and tell his little yarn about it, but something made him hesitate, and he forgot the idea. He felt very easy in his mind as he drove home about midnight. He even hummed a little. This mood was not disturbed until he saw the face of Miss Willis, his resident secretary.

"What is it?" he asked crisply.

"Miss Nancy Sawyer. She . . ." For once the imperturbable, greying blonde seemed to have difficulty speaking.

"Yes?"

"She called up first about an hour and a half ago."

"Her ankle had begun to pain her?"

"She didn't say anything about her ankle. She said she was getting a sore throat."

"What!"

"It seemed unimportant to me, too, though of course I told her I'd inform you when you got in. But she seemed rather frightened, kept complaining of this tightness she felt in her throat . . ."

"Yes? Yes?"

"So I agreed to get in touch with you immediately. She hung up. I called the restaurant, but you'd just left. Then I called Dr. Myers' home, but didn't get any answer. I told the operator to keep trying.

"About a half hour ago Miss Sawyer's friend, a Marge Hudson, called. She said Miss Sawyer had gone to bed and was apparently asleep, but she didn't like the way she was tossing around, as if she were having a particularly bad dream, and especially she didn't like the noises she was making in her throat, as if she were having difficulty breathing. She said she had looked closely at Miss Sawyer's throat as she lay sleeping, and it seemed swollen. I told her I was making every effort to get in touch with you and we left it at that."

"That wasn't all?"

"No." Miss Willis' agitation returned. "Just two minutes before you arrived, the phone rang again. At first the line seemed to be dead. I was about to hang up. Then I began to hear a clicking, gargling sound. Low at first, but then it grew louder. Then suddenly it broke free and whooped out in what I think was Miss Sawyer's voice. There were only two words, I think, but I couldn't catch them because they were so loud they stopped the phone. After that, nothing, although I listened and listened and kept saying 'hello' over and over. But, Dr.

Ballard, that gargling sound! It was as if I were listening to someone being strangled, very slowly, very, very . . ."

Dr. Ballard had grabbed his surgical bag and was racing for his car. He drove rather well for a doctor and, tonight, very fast. He was about three blocks from the river when he heard a siren, ahead of him.

Nancy Sawyer's apartment hotel was at the end of a short street terminated by a high concrete curb and metal fence and, directly below, the river. Now there was a fire engine drawn up to the fence and playing a searchlight down over the edge through the faintly misty air. Dr. Ballard could see a couple of figures in shiny black coats beside the searchlight. As he jumped out of his car he could hear shouts and what sounded like the motor of a launch. He hesitated for a moment, then ran into the hotel.

The lobby was empty. There was no one behind the counter. He ran to the open elevator. It was an automatic. He punched the twenty-three button.

On that floor there was one open door in the short corridor. Marge Hudson met him inside it.

"She jumped?"

The girl nodded. "They're hunting for her body. I've been watching. Come on."

She led him to a dark bedroom. There was a studio couch, its covers disordered, and beside it a phone. River air was pouring in through a large, hinged window, open wide. They went to it and looked down. The circling launch looked like a toy boat. Its searchlight and that from the fire engine roved across the dark water. Shouts and chugging came up faintly.

"How did it happen?" he asked the girl at the window.

"I was watching her as she lay in bed," Marge Hudson answered without looking around.

"About twenty minutes after I called your home, she seemed to be getting worse. She had more trouble breathing. I tried to wake her, but couldn't. I went to the kitchen to make an ice pack. It took longer than I'd thought. I heard a noise that at first I didn't connect with Nancy. Then I realized that she was strangling. I rushed back. Just then she screamed out horribly. I heard something fall — I think it was the phone — and footsteps and the window opening. When I came in she

107

was standing on the sill in her nightdress, clawing at her throat. Before I could get to her, she jumped."

"Earlier in the evening she'd complained of a sore throat?"

"Yes. She said, jokingly, that the trouble with her ankle must be spreading to her throat. After she called your home and couldn't get you, she took some aspirin and went to bed."

Dr. Ballard switched on the lamp by the bed. He pulled the brown envelope from his coat pocket, took out the X-ray and held it up against the light.

"You say she screamed at the end," he said in a not very steady voice. "Were there any definite words?"

The girl at the window hesitated. "I'm not sure," she said slowly. "They were suddenly choked off, exactly as if a hand had tightened around her throat. But I think there were two words. 'Hand' and 'Beth.'"

Dr. Ballard's gaze flickered toward the mocking face in the photograph on the chest of drawers, then back to the ghostly black and whites of the one in his hands. His arms were shaking.

"They haven't found her yet," Marge said, still looking down at the river and the circling launch.

Dr. Ballard was staring incredulously at the X-ray, as if by staring he could make what he saw go away. But that was impossible. It was a perfectly defined and unambiguous exposure.

There, in the X-ray's black and greys, he could see the bones of Nancy Sawyer's ankle and, tightly clenched around them, deep under the skin and flesh, the slender bones of a human hand.

Spider Mansion

A TREMENDOUS splash of lightning gave us our first glimpse of the pillared front of the Old Orne House — a pale Colonial mask framed by wildly whipping leaves. Then, even before the lightning faded, it was blotted out by a solid sheet of muddy water sloshing up against the windshield.

"But I still don't like midgets," Helen said for the third time, "and besides — " Close thunder, like thick metal ripping drowned out the rest.

"It's gotten beyond a question of your or my personal taste in heights," I argued, squinting for a sight of the road between mud splashes. "Sure Malcolm Orne's a midget, but you don't know how slippery the road is ahead or how deep those Jersey salt marshes are on either side of it. And no garages or even houses for miles. Too risky, in this storm. Anyway, we figured all along we might visit him on the way. That's why we took this road."

"Yes, this lonely, god-forsaken road." Helen's voice was as strained and uneasy as her face, pallidly revealed by another lightning flash. "Oh, I know it's silly of me, but I still feel that — "

Again cracking thunder blanketed her words. Our coupe was progressing by heaves, as if through a gelatinous sea. I spotted the high white posts a little ahead, and swung out for the turn-in.

"Still really want to go on?" I asked.

Maybe it was the third blast of thunder, loudest of the lot, that decided her against further argument. She gave me a "You win" look, and even grinned a little, being a much better sport that I probably deserved for a wife.

The coupe slithered between the posts, lurched around squishily on a sharp slippery rise, made it on the last gasp, and lunged toward the house through a flail of lasting, untrimmed branches.

The windows in front were dark and those to the right were tightly shuttered, but light flickered faintly through the antique white fan-light above the six-paneled Colonial door. Helen hugged my arm tight as we ducked through the drenching rain up onto the huge porch, with its two-story pillars. I reached for the knocker.

Just at that moment there came one of those brief hushes in the storm. The lightning held off, and the wind stopped. I felt Helen jump at the ugly rustling, scraping sound of a branch which, released from the wind's pressure, brushed against a pillar as it swung back into place. I remembered noting that the paint was half-peeled away from the pillar.

Then things happened fast. Groping for the knocker, I felt the door give inward. There was a deafening blast from *inside* the house. A ragged semi-circle of wood disappeared from the jamb about a foot from the ground. Splinters flew from a point in the floor eight inches from my shoe. The door continued to swing slowly open from the first push I had given it, revealing a Negro with grizzled hair and fear-wide eyes, clad in the threadbare black of an out-dated servant's costume. Despite his slouching posture he still topped six feet. Smoke wreathed from the muzzle of the shotgun held loosely in his huge pink-palmed hands.

"Oh, Lordy," he breathed in quaking tones. "Dat rustlin' soun' — I t'ought it was — "

Something, then, checked my angry retort and the lunge I was about to make forward for the weapon. It was the appearance of another face — a white man's — over the Negro's shoulder. A saturnine face with aristocratic features and bulging forehead. Judging from the way he towered over the gigantic Negro, the second man could hardly be more than a few inches short of seven feet. But that wasn't what froze me dead in my tracks. It was that the face was unmistakably that of Malcolm Orne, the midget.

The Negro was grasped and swung aside as if he were a piece of furniture. The gun was lifted from his nerveless fingers as if it were a child's toy. Then the giant bowed low and said, "A thousand pardons! Welcome to Orne House!"

Helen's scream, long delayed, turned to hysterical laughter. Then the storm, recommencing with redoubled fury, shattered the hush and sent us hurrying into the hall.

The giant's teeth flashed in a smile. "One moment, please," he murmured to us, then turned and seized the cowering Negro by the slack of the coat, slapped his face twice, hard.

"You are never to touch that gun, Buford!" Again the Negro's head was buffeted by a solid blow. "You almost killed my guests. They would be well within their rights if they demanded your arrest."

But what caught my attention was the fact that the Negro hardly seemed to notice either the words or the stinging blows. His eyes were fixed in a peculiarly terrified way on the open door, seemingly staring at a point about a foot from the floor. Only when a back-draft slammed it shut, did he begin to grovel and whine.

The giant cut him short with a curt, "Send Milly to show my guests their room. Then stay in the kitchen." The Negro hurriedly shambled off without a backward glance.

The giant turned to us again. He looked very much in place in this darkly wainscoted hall. On the wall behind him were a pair of crossed sabers of Civil War vintage.

"Ah, Mrs. Egan, I am glad to see that you are taking this deplorable affair so calmly." His smile flashed at Helen. "And I am delighted to make your acquaintance, though just now you have every reason to be angry with me." He took her hand with a courtly gesture. His face grew grave. "Almost — a hideous accident occurred. I can explain, though not excuse it. Poor Buford lives in abnormal terror of a large mastiff I keep chained outside — an animal quite harmless to myself or my guests, I hasten to add. A little while ago it broke loose. Evidently Buford thought it was attempting to force its way in. His fear is irrational and without bounds — though otherwise he is a perfect servant. I only hope you will let my hospitality serve as an apology."

He turned to me. "Your wife is charming," he said. "You're a very lucky man, Tom."

Then he seemed to become aware of my dumbfounded look, and the way my gaze was stupidly traveling up and down his tremendous though well-proportioned form. A note of secret amusement was added to his smile.

Helen broke the silence with a little laugh, puzzled but not unpleased.

"But, excuse me, who are *you?*" she asked.

The wavering candlelight made queer highlights, emphasizing the massive forehead and the saturnine features.

"Malcolm Orne, Madam!" he answered with a little bow.

"But I thought," said Helen, "that Malcolm Orne was . . ." An involuntary expression of disgust crossed her face.

"A midget?" His voice was silky. "Ah, yes. I can understand your distaste." Then he turned slowly toward me. "I know what's bothering you, Tom," he said. "But *that* is a long and very strange story, which can best wait until after dinner. Milly will take you up to your room. Your luggage will be brought up. Dinner in about three-quarters of an hour? Good!"

An impassive-faced Negress had appeared silently from the back of the hall, bearing in her ebony hands a branched candlestick. There were a dozen questions hammering at my brain, but instead of asking them I found myself following the Negress up the curving stairs, Helen at my side, watching the fantastic shadows cast by the candles.

As soon as we were alone, Helen bombarded me with a dozen incredulous questions of her own. I did my best to convince her that the giant downstairs was really Malcolm Orne — there was the birthmark below his left ear and curious thin scar on his forehead to back up the rest of the evidence — and that Malcolm Orne had been, when I last saw him, a midget who missed four feet by several inches.

I wasn't very successful and no wonder, since I could hardly believe it myself. Helen seemed to think I was mixing him up with someone else.

"You mentioned a brother — " she said.

I shook my head doggedly. "No possibility there," I told her. "Malcolm Orne did have an elder brother, but he died a year ago."

"And you're sure it's only a year and a half since you last saw Malcolm?" she persisted. "What was the brother like?"

"He was short, though no midget. About five feet. So don't go getting any wild theories of murder and impersonation. Marvin Orne was his name. A doctor. Made quite a reputation in New York, then came down here to start a country clinic in connection with research he was doing. Some of his work was supposed to be very important. Embryology. Cellular development. Hormones. Obscure vitamin factors. Growth processes."

There I stopped, suddenly realizing the implications of what I was saying. It was farfetched, of course, but —

"Go on, dear!" Helen prodded. "You've thought of something! Don't keep me in suspense." She looked interested and eager now, her uneasiness completely departed.

"I know it sounds awfully pseudo-scientific," I began cautiously, "but I suppose it's barely possible that, before his death, Marvin Orne discovered some serum or extract or whatever you call it, something to stimulate growth, and used it on — "

"Wonderful!" Helen interrupted, catching my idea. "That's the first sensible thing you've said tonight. I could believe that."

"It's only a wild theory," I hedged quickly. "The kind I warned you against. Better wait. Remember he hinted he'd tell us about it after dinner."

"Oh, but what a wonderful theory!" Helen cut in. "Just think what it would mean to a man to be changed from a pygmy into a giant almost overnight. The psychological implications — why, it opens up all sorts of vistas. He seems to be a very charming man, you know."

The last remark had a trace of impishness in it. I nodded though I didn't quite agree.

When we went down to dinner, she was still flushed with excitement, and I realized for the thousandth time what a thoroughly charming woman I had married. As if in response to a challenge emanating from the high courtly halls and rich though dusty woodwork, she wore her formal black evening gown with silver trimmings. And of course she had wheedled me into putting on a somewhat travel-crumpled dinner jacket.

There was no one in the hall, so we waited at the bottom of the stairs. The storm had died away and it was very quiet. I tried the high double doors to what was surely the living room, but they were stuck or locked. A faint but sharply nauseous stench rose to my nostrils. I noticed that Helen wrinkled her nose, and I took the opportunity to whisper, "There are some drawbacks, it seems to ancient grandeur. Ancient plumbing, for one."

Then we became aware of the Negro Buford standing uneasily at the very far end of the hall. As soon as he saw that we were looking at him, he bowed and motioned to us, then quickly turned and went out. We followed after. There was something very ridiculous about his long-distance courtesy. "I suppose he's embarrassed because of what happened, and afraid we're still going to have him arrested," Helen speculated lightly. "The poor superstitious savage."

"Just the same, it was a narrow squeak," I reminded her. "But if Malcolm keeps the firearms safely locked up hereafter, I'll forgive the villain."

The dining room, where antique cut glass chandeliers glittered softly with candle-light, held another surprise.

"Tom . . . and Mrs. Egan," said our host, "I wish to present my wife, Cynthia."

She was literally one of the most lavishly beautiful women I have ever seen. Really creamy skin. Masses of warmly golden hair. A Classic face, but with the Classic angularity alluringly softened and the Classic strength missing. The strapless evening gown of red velvet emphasized a narrow waist, a richly molded bosom and perfectly rounded, almost plump shoulders. Lavish was the only word for her. More like one of Titian's or Renoir's models than a modern or a Greek. She was Venus to Helen's slim Diana. There was a gleam of old gold from her hands and the pendant at her neck. Like a picture on exhibition.

She seemed a singularly reserved woman for one so gorgeous, acknowledging the introduction with a smile and a little nod. Helen too for some reason did not break into the lively if artificial feminine chatter one expects at dinner parties, and the meal began in silence, with Buford pouring the white wine and serving the seafood in crystal hemispheres set in silver. The seafood was not iced, however, and as the meal progressed other deficiencies became apparent. The grizzled Negro avoided looking at Helen or myself, as he moved softly around the table.

While the seafood was being replaced by a thick meaty soup, Malcolm Orne leaned back sipping his wine, and said to me, "Quite a surprise to find that I was married? Well, there was a time when we too would have found it surprising, eh, dear?" The last remark was directed at his wife. She smiled and nodded quickly. I thought her throat moved as if she swallowed hard. His gaze lingered on her, his own smile becoming more expansive. "Yet things have a way of changing, or being changed, eh dear? But that's part of the mystery which must wait until coffee."

From then on conversation picked up, though one peculiar feature of it soon became obvious. Cynthia Orne did not join in at all, except for the most voiceless of polite murmurings — more gesture than word. Moreover, Malcolm Orne deliberately answered any questions directed at her. He did it with a casual cleverness, but it was none the less apparent. For a while what was almost a verbal duel developed between Helen and him, she directing one remark after another at our hostess, he deftly or bluntly interposing. Helen was responding with mounting excitement to the atmosphere of mystery and tension.

After the soup the culinary pretensions of Buford and Milly rapidly collapsed. There followed a peppery stew, float — with fat, which sought to make up in quantity what it lacked in quality. It made a disagreeable contrast with the thick silver service and rich damask. And then I began to notice the other false notes; the great blotches of damp on the ceiling, the peeling wall-paper, the thumb-marks on the crystal, the not-quite-eradicated stains on the thick, hand-embroidered linen.

With the stew was served — inappropriately enough — a sugary port wine. Helen and I, our appetites satisfied, toyed with the meat. Cynthia Orne hardly touched a thing; she'd grow thin soon enough on this diet, I thought. But Malcolm ate enormously, voraciously, knife and fork moving with a perfectly correct yet machinelike rapidity.

Gradually I found myself loathing the man. I think his attitude toward his wife was chiefly responsible, at first. He so obviously gloated in possessing her and dominating her, so that she dared not speak a word for herself. He was showing her off, drinking in our admiration. And he gloated in his mystification of us, too; his veiled references to coming revelations, his unwillingness to discuss even the lesser mystery of Buford and the mastiff. Oh, I was still devilishly curious to know the explanation of the baffling phenomenon with which we were faced — a phenomenon which had changed a midget into a giant — but my curiosity was dulled, and I felt that the solution would somehow be sickening. Again and again I studied his face, racking my memory for the exact appearance of Malcolm Orne the midget, comparing, contrasting. Even the head seemed larger, the forehead more swollen, though these features had been characteristic of the midget too. I tried hard to pretend that this was a different man — and I failed. The identity was too apparent. I went over in my mind the manner of Malcolm Orne the midget. Sardonic he had been, I recalled, and at times overly in love with his own cleverness.

A not very pleasant or kindly person. One expects such behavior in an individual seeking to compensate for marked physical deficiencies. Malcolm Orne the giant retained all these qualities, but there was added to them supreme self-satisfaction along with a wanton delight in exercising power. His sense of inferiority , which had been the balance wheel in his nature, was now gone, and the result was not very nice. And beyond all this I sensed something else — some unguessed, almost inhuman power or some equally unguessed, equally inhuman striving. Unwholesome force emanated from him. I recalled Helen's words: ". . . changed from a pygmy into a giant almost overnight. The psychological implications . . . why it opens us all sort of vistas." I did not like the look of those vistas.

Buford splashed stew, a great puddle of it, on the tablecloth. I looked at him. His face was muddy with fear. It was the sound from outside that was affecting him — an excited growling and yapping, growing louder every moment. Malcolm Orne, frowning, half rose. I expected him to strike Buford, but he did not. He was listening too.

"Sounds as if your mastiff's caught something," I remarked. Malcolm Orne impatiently motioned me to be silent.

Suddenly the sound changed in character, became a wail of terror, one vast horrid squeal that rose and fell without ever ceasing, like a siren. Moving with startling rapidity for so tall a man, Malcolm Orne darted toward the door. I rose to follow. He turned and rapped out a peremptory command, "None of you are to leave this room until I return." Then, seeing my angry look, he added with obvious effort, "If you please, Tom. I can best handle this alone." The door slammed behind him.

The wailing decreased in volume, though becoming more pitifully agonized. With a shrug I sat down. The Negress Milly had come in from the kitchen, and she and Buford were clinging together in abject terror, though he if anything seemed the more frightened.

"Caught another dog, I suppose — " ventured Helen. Her voice trailed off.

"Very likely," I replied. But I was thinking that if there were a second dog involved he had a very similar voice.

"Well, I'm sure your husband knows just how to handle him, Mrs. Orne," Helen remarked with an attempt at reassurance.

Mrs. Orne did not reply. I looked at her more closely. Her lips were moving wordlessly, as though she were seeking to reply and unable to. Beads of sweat stood out on her white forehead, and trickled from the line of her golden hair. Her whole body was trembling, so slightly that you hardly noticed it at first, but continuously. Gradually it was borne in on me that this was no mere anxiety for her husband. She was in the grip of ultimate panic.

The wailing sank to a coughing moan, then mercifully ceased. And now we heard the voice of Malcolm Orne, in sharp accents of command.

Again Mrs. Orne seemed to be attempting unsuccessfully to speak. Her eyes were fixed on Helen's beseechingly. Then, with rapid nervous movements, she spread out her tiny handkerchief on the tablecloth and began to write something on it in lipstick with shaking hand. We watched her, fascinated. There came the sound of slamming doors, and then, during one moment of stillness, a rustling, so very faint that I could hardly be sure I had heard, yet it wrung from Buford a pitiful groan of horror. I recalled the first words we had heard him speak, "Dat rustlin' soun' — " Hardly a noise that one would associate with a mastiff.

Another door slammed. There were footsteps in the hall. In frantic haste, Mrs. Orne wadded up the handkerchief and held it out to Helen, who quickly tucked it in the bosom of her dress. Then the door opened, and Malcolm Orne stood regarding us. His shoes and trouser legs were muddied.

"A dangerous beast — to outsiders," he remarked, breathing a little heavily. "A stray hound wandered in, and he tore it to ribbons before I could interfere." He looked around as if challenging us to say that what we had heard hadn't sounded like a dog-fight.

"I shouldn't think you'd want to have such a brute around," said Helen rapidly.

He seemed about to reply when his gaze lighted on Buford and Milly. "What do you mean coming in here?" he snarled at the Negress. "Get out! Buford, we will take coffee now."

His urbane manner returned when he had settled himself again at the table. "Sorry I can't offer you coffee in the living room. But I've shut it up. It's a great barn of a place two stories high, very hard to heat. Besides, before his death, my brother had begun to use it as a sort of laboratory, for his experiments." Again the gloating, secretive smile.

Night-black coffee, in fragile eggshell china, was something I welcomed. Malcolm Orne drained his cup, refilled it and began abruptly to speak.

"I'm hardly the right one to tell this story, since I'm no scientist. But I'm the only one who knows it all. So bear with me if I fumble for words." His manner belied what he said. He was obviously supremely self-confident, savoring the dramatic quality of his introduction. "Well, you may have heard something of my brother's work on growth processes. His early investigating created quite a stir. But first I should try to explain something.

"Growth, as I understand it, is not a process that has any absolutely fixed stopping point. It may stop early in the teens, or continue on well into the twenties. It may seem to stop, and then start again. Moreover, there are well authenticated cases of growth during middle age. Though usually in such cases the growth is of an unbalanced or localized sort, as in acromegaly, where the bones of the hands or jaw become abnormally enlarged. Factors of heredity, diet, and climate are all of importance. Scientists today are of course able to exert some control over growth by influencing glandular secretions. If they knew enough, their control would become complete. They would know how to start growth when it had seemed to stop forever.

"Perhaps my being a midget turned my brother's mind to this problem. But once he had begun, he pursued it with a single-mindedness that crowded out all other interests. Not that he had a narrow range of thought — he was a genius! — but he saw in every phenomenon some aspect of the process of growth. His country clinic here was a part of it — he made extensive statistical studies of the sizes and growth rates of country and city people.

"Growth Factor One — that was what he called the thing he was looking for. The hormone or sub-vitamin that influenced all others. The ultimate physiological catalyst. The master-switch to turn on or shut off the whole process of growth."

Helen and I were leaning forward now, hanging on his words. He waited for a moment, relishing the suspense, then said lazily, "Well, that's about all there is to the story. Except that eventually he found it. Found Growth Factor One." He rolled the words on his tongue.

"What was it, you ask? That's something I'd like to know too, now. But I'm no scientist. It was . . . something that was injected. That much I know, since after the preliminary experiments on animals and insects, I insisted on being his first human subject. You can readily guess why."

His gloating smile and his air of utter superiority were fast becoming insufferable, but you just had to listen.

"Yes," he repeated. "I think you can all readily imagine why a midget should want to grow. No one loves a midget, eh dear?" His words caressed his wife cruelly, like a whip dragged slowly across the naked skin. "And a midget loves no one. Or at least that midget didn't."

He seemed then to become lost in reverie, but I felt sure he was only taking time to let his words sink in, and to absorb our unwilling interest. Helen gripped my hand under the table and I could feel her shivering.

Then, staring past us, he continued in a low dreamy voice, "An interesting thing, the way this Growth Factor One works. It doesn't merely increase the size of and number of body cells already existing. After the fashion of true growth, it develops new *kinds* of cells. I have, for example, in my brain, neurons of a sort that probably have never existed before. Very likely they have — new powers. The same holds for muscular cells. I could demonstrate. But it would be rather melodramatic, wouldn't it, if I crumpled this coffee urn in one hand? Incidentally, the growth process would work in the same way with animals. By careful use of Growth Factor One you might make an animal, as intelligent, almost, as a man."

He broke off and looked around at us, patronizingly. "Well, now you've heard it. A year ago my brother died. His work was turned over to a group of distinguished scientists. But his notes were inadequate and very confusing. I don't think they'll ever be able to learn much from them. I remain the sole product of his labors. The other creatures he experimented with were all destroyed."

Helen gave a little squeal of fright and jerked away from the table. A tiny black spider was scuttling among the silverware. Malcolm Orne calmly reached out the gravy ladle left from the stew, and crashed it with a little thwack. Then, as Helen began to apologize for being so startled, we noticed that Cynthia Orne had fainted.

Her husband made no movement. For a moment I stared at him, then hurried around and did what I could to revive her, chafing her temples with a wet napkin, lowering her head to bring the blood back. Finally her lips twitched and her eyes shuddered open. Leaning over her, close to her face, I seemed to hear her murmur over and over again a peculiar phrase: "Not the web again. Not the web." Mechanically, almost inaudibly, but with an accent of extreme fear. Then she realized where she was and quickly sat up. She seemed embarrassed by my attempts to help her.

Malcolm Orne sipped the last of his coffee, and stood up. "It's time we were all in bed," he remarked. "Our guests must be tired from their trip. Come, dear."

She struggled to her feet, swaying a little, and took his arm. Helen and I followed silently, though angry words were on the tip of my tongue.

Right then and there I suppose I ought to have had it out with him, but after all it was his house, so I held myself in.

In the hall the unpleasant odor that I had ascribed to defective plumbing was more noticeable, and as we passed the high double doors of the living room I fancied I heard a faint sibilant rustling. Up the stairs we followed them, Cynthia Orne leaning heavily on her husband's arm. He did not look down at her. At the first door at the head of the stairs he paused, "Good night, dear. I'll be coming considerably later," he said. She unlinked her arm from his, nodded at us with the specter of a smile, and went in.

At the door of our bedroom he said good night, adding, "If you want anything, there's the bell-pull. Please don't consider stirring out of this room. The servants or I can attend to all your wants."

The door closed and his footsteps moved away. Helen drew out Cynthia Orne's handkerchief, spread it out on the table. We read it together. The lipstick had smudged, and the printing was hurried, but there was no question as to what the words were.

"Get out. For your lives."

Half an hour later I was tiptoeing in my stockinged feet down the almost pitch-black hall toward Cynthia Orne's bedroom. I felt slightly ridiculous and not altogether sure of myself. Meddling with the affairs of a married couple is undiplomatic to say the least. But Helen and I had decided there was nothing else we could do. Malcolm Orne certainly gave the impression of being vindictive, cruel, and dangerous. For her own sake as well as our own, it seemed imperative that one of us talk with her alone and find out what it was all about.

I had successfully negotiated the turn in the hall and was approaching the head of the stairs when the noise of talking from below brought me to a stop. It sounded like Malcolm Orne. After a few moments I inched forward past the bedroom door and peered over the ornately carved balustrade down the well of the stairs. There were no candles below, but the storm had blown over and moonlight shone through the fanlight — enough to illuminate vaguely the face of our host. An oblong of darkness showed me that the door of the living room was open, and there mounted to my nostrils that now-familiar stench, stronger than before. Somehow that odor, more than anything else, cut through my conscious mind to the hidden levels of fear below.

Orne was looking in that open doorway. At first I thought he was talking to someone, but afterward I became certain that he was conducting a wild moody monologue. At least, one does not expect a sane man to talk with the dead.

"You'll rot forever, eternally embalmed in hell," were the first words I heard. He intoned them like a malign indignation. "Yes, dear brother, you're well taken care of. You who always felt so 'sorry' for me and wanted to make a 'real' man out of me, yet were so contemptuous of my intelligence that you treated me as a child. You with your babbling about 'humanity' and your moralizing lectures. Well, you succeeded all right. You made a man — or perhaps more than a man — out of me. But you found out too late what the consequences are. I wish you comfort, dear brother. I hope you like my wife's company. She's not been behaving well of late. Again good night, brother."

A mocking laugh ended this murderous confession. Then he whistled and snapped his fingers impatiently, as if calling a dog, and moved off toward the dining room.

It is not pleasant to confess that one has ever been literally paralyzed by fear, but what happened then did just that to me. I *saw* nothing. The moonlight struck too high to illuminate what issued from the living room and hurried down the hall after him. But there was a rustling, clicking sound — Merciful heavens, how I tried to convince myself a dog might make such a sound! — and it carried an indescribable impression of *swift* scurrying movement. With it came a sharp increase in the fetid stench.

I am not certain how long I crouched there with the cold sweat of terror breaking out from my forehead. Hardly a minute probably. Then my mind began to work again, returning automatically to the problem with which it had previously been engaged — the urgent need of conferring with Cynthia Orne.

Cautious rapping at her door brought no response. I tried it and found it locked. Then I risked a little louder rapping, and, with my lips close to the keyhole, softly called her name. Still no response. Memory of Orne's fantastic words rose in my numbed mind, "I hope you like my wife's company." And with those words the chilling possibility of murder rose in my mind.

Then, as I stepped back from the door, I heard again that abominable rustling, but this time behind me, in the direction of our bedroom. And then I heard Helen scream. That stung me into instant action. But in my reckless haste I misjudged the turn in the corridor and crashed against the wall. Half stunned, I staggered onward and wrenched open the bedroom door. The flickering light from the branched candelabrum revealed an undisturbed empty room. Helen was gone.

My first move was toward the open window. Below, rapidly crossing the moon-silvered unkempt lawn, I saw two figures. But they were not the ones I expected. Burdened with an ancient carpetbag and several ragged bundles, Buford and Milly were hurrying away from Orne House.

My next move, after quickly rummaging in my suitcase for the flashlight, was back toward the stair. I had remembered the crossed sabers on the wall in the hall below, and it seemed to me essential that I procure a weapon of some sort before I start my search. But I was stopped short at the head of the stairs, for again Malcolm Orne was standing at the library door. Only this time the front door was open too and this time his words were brief.

"After 'em boy. Get 'em boy," he called, snapping his fingers and then pointing outside. There was a momentary pause. Then something scuttled like a shadow across the path of moonlight, moving with such rapidity that I could make out nothing of its shape except that it was squat but not small. Malcolm Orne gave a low laugh and followed it, closing the door behind him. With a sickening heart I realized that the desperately fleeing figures I had seen crossing the lawn were to be hunted down.

But at least I was momentarily safe to pursue my search. I switched on the flashlight, hurried down the stairs and lifted one of the sabers from the wall. It was a heavy yet well-balanced weapon. Then I entered the living room.

The stench was nauseously thick here, the very air a sea of decay. My flashlight, directed at random, fell twice on moldering tapestries and then on something so incredible that I believed I must be going mad. Suspended in midair at the far end of the room, still clad in that red velvet evening gown, was the body of Cynthia Orne.

The head, its golden hair disarranged, lolled backward. The arms stretched taut to either side. Then I began to see the thin opalescently grayish strands that twined around her wrists and arms, and wrapped around her skirt, drawing it tight against her legs. The strands seemed to radiate off in all directions. My flashlight roved outward across the glimmering net-work. Horror and revulsion rooted me to the spot where I stood. The thing was a gigantic spiderweb.

I saw that there were other victims. Here and there, thickest at the corners of the web, were forms suggestive of small animals, each wrapped in a shimmering cocoon. Shudderingly I recalled the eating habits of spiders, how they preserve their prey for the future. In the lower right hand corner was the shape of a large dog, his silken wrappings only half completed. This, I told myself, must be the mastiff which had howled so horribly in the night.

And then I saw the man. He was suspended close to the wall; a drab fearfully emaciated thing whose shrunken face awoke groping, incredulous thoughts in my mind.

Filled with a mad desire to destroy that loathsome web, I stepped forward with upraised sword.

And then my staggered senses reeled at another blow directed at the seat of sanity itself. For the man, whom I thought could be nothing else but dead, spoke. His voice was a thin cracked whisper, but it carried a note of terrible urgency.

"Back, for your life! One touch of these strands, and you would be trapped forever, like a fly. Your sword would be entangled by the very strands it cut. Get that can of heavy grease behind you. There, by the table! Smear your hands and the swordblade with it. And bring the hooked pole that stands in the corner, and those things that look like fire tongs. Smear them with grease too."

I do not like to think of the next half hour. I have never done work one-tenth as ugly and revolting — and always behind me the threat of the creature's return. Choking on the fetid air and with that fiendish webwork often only a few inches from my body, I hooked and sliced, dodged the flicking ends of cut strands, like a damned soul performing some endless task in hell. I think it was the voice of the man that kept me sane, directing me, warning me, sometimes rambling off, but never ceasing, like the voice of a hypnotist.

"First cut the strands above her head — the inside of the hook is sharp as a sickle. That will bring her down a good three feet. Now the strands below, and then those to either side, one by one. Carefully, man! And watch that loose one swinging by your neck. Flip it to one side so it catches! That's right. Oh, I know how to do this thing backward. A dozen times I've watched him and the beast hang her up there and then hours later, take her down. It's his way of punishing her because she once laughed when Malcolm Orne the midget asked her to marry him. Her mistake was that she fell in love with him after he grew tall, and let him marry her. Through her, he seeks to revenge himself on all womankind. I tell you, to watch that man and beast work together is the most hideous sight in existence. He hasn't let it poison her yet. That distinction is reserved for me. A slight bite produces paralysis — you know the habits of spiders? How they preserve their prey? I was last bitten a month ago. The creature was loose for a while tonight, killed the dog. But he lets it range around pretty freely. Boasts of his power over it.

"Gently now! Mind those strands to the left. There, that's done it. Now pull her away from it. Don't try to lift her. Slowly. Slowly."

I turned to the task of releasing the man, his voice still directing me. But now it rambled more often on to sidetracks.

"It must be a year I've hung here. And all because I was fool enough to change him from a midget into a giant — and a devil. He's literally no longer human. His schemes are those of a mad malign god. Do you know what he wants to make me do, besides tell him the secret of growth? He wants to force me to search for a *Negative* Growth Factor One, a degenerative hormone, something that will make living things *decrease* evenly in size so that he can infect all mankind with it, in order that he may ultimately rule over a race of pygmies. But I won't! I tell you I won't!" His voice rose in a thin scream of defiance. But his next words were sane again. "More grease on your sword. It's sticking. And now sever that strand to the left, so I swing away from the main web."

Finally I got him down. He tried to stand, but his wasted limbs would not support him, and with a groan he sank to his knees. I saw that Cynthia Orne had recovered consciousness, and was pushing herself up from the floor. My mind, gradually emerging from the half-hour nightmare of frantic action, was beginning to function under its own power. I realized the danger that remained, and I remembered that Helen was still to be found. Perhaps she had been confined somewhere at the back of the house. I started for the door.

But through that door strode the towering form of Malcolm Orne. In his right hand was a flickering candelabrum. Slung effortlessly over his left arm like a bundle of cloth was a limp form — Helen's. Acting instinctively, I directed the flashlight at his face. It seemed hardly to startle him.

"So the fly has obligingly walked into the spider's parlor," he murmured, with a laugh. "Most convenient. First the charming Mrs. Egan, who does not like midgets, brought to join my dear brother and wife. Then those black fools finished off for good. And last but not least my dear friend Tom, who used to pity me so much in the old days."

But now his eyes, despite the dazzling beam of the flashlight, perceived that something was wrong with the web. Helen slipped from his arm as he placed the candelabrum on the table and called peremptorily, "Boy! Boy!"

In that instant I flung the tongs. They struck him full across the forehead, and he swayed like a great tree and crashed headlong to the floor. I snatched up the sword and directed the flashlight at the open door. Then, before I could move to close it, there came a rustling and scurrying, and the horror was upon us.

Big as the dog it had killed, it regarded us from the doorway, its eight reddish eyes glowing evilly. I could see the swollen black abdomen and the black poison-dripping chelicerae, fangs that projected inches forward from its ugly little mouth. Then it struck with a rush, one spring sufficing to carry it across Helen's supine silk-clad form. With instinctive cunning it had chosen me as the most active opponent and therefore the one first to dispose of. Blindly I thrust out my sword, and, as it swerved away from the point, slashed out toward it. The wound it received was only slight, but it scuttled away to the shadows.

Someone was standing beside me. It was Cynthia Orne. Without a word she took the flashlight from me. I never expected such courage from her, but during all that hideous duel she kept the light fixed on the creature, leaving me free to wield the sword alone. The beam never once wavered, nor did the creature manage to escape from the circle of light.

And then I noted that Marvin Orne was painfully crawling straight toward his prostrate brother, unmindful of the scuttling monster. Death was in Marvin Orne's sere face!

When my sword found its black body for a second time, the spider changed its tactics, ran with incredible rapidity up the tapestry, and launched itself down at me. I sidestepped. It only missed my sword by an inch!

And Malcolm Orne had risen dizzily to his knees, but simultaneously his brother was upon him, clawing at his throat. It was an unequal contest, but for a moment Marvin Orne had the advantage. They rolled against the table, knocking off the candelabrum, whose flames began to lick at the bone-dry tapestry.

The glance I spared on this other conflict nearly cost me my life. A sticky strand whipped around the hilt of my sword, almost wrenching it from my hand.

I tore at the sword to free it. Malcolm Orne, I saw, had warded off his brother's feeble attack. And now for the first time I realized the full strength of the giant. His fist rose and fell, again and again, smashing in the skull of Marvin Orne as if it were an eggshell. Flame was roaring up the tapestry now, and the whole room was illuminated by a wild reddish glow.

The monster swooped down at me like a nightmare. I threw myself down, thrusting upward with the sword. This time it went home, thick blood oozing from the wound. I scrambled to my feet, raising my weapon for a second blow. But the monster, badly hurt, was moving away from me now toward Malcolm Orne. What the giant saw in those eight evil eyes I do not know — perhaps some long-nurtured hate for its master — but he threw up his hands and screamed horribly. The dying monster ran up his body. I followed it thrusting again at the black abdomen. But the chelicerae had done their work. Malcolm Orne screamed once again, a tortured bellow of anguish. Then Cynthia Orne was pulling me backward, out of the path of the falling tapestries, which collapsed with a roar, wrapping the monster and its master — and the dead body of Marvin Orne — in a flaming shroud.

It missed Helen by inches. But before the flames could reach out across the carpet, I had dragged her aside. As I raised her in my arms I saw her eyes blinking wonderingly open, and felt her hand tighten on my shoulder.

Then, like lost souls escaping from some hell, we fled from that house of monstrous growth and forbidden secrets, lost to science. As I sent the coupe roaring down the drive, I spared time for one glance over my shoulder. Flames were already eating through the shutters below the pillared facade. Soon, I knew, the whole white mask of Orne House would be one roaring holocaust.

The Secret Songs

Promptly after supper, before Gwen had cleared away the dishes, Donnie began the Sleep Ritual. He got a can of beer from the refrigerator, selected a science-fiction magazine, and shut off the TV sound.

"The picture too?" he asked, "Might as well."

Gwen smiled at him as she shook her head. With the gesture of one who eats peanuts she threw her right hand to her mouth swallowed, then dropped her hand with the tiny bottle it held back to the pocket of her smock.

Donnie sighed, shrugged his shoulders, settled himself in the easy chair, opened his magazine, and began to read and sip rapidly.

Gwen, who had been ignoring the TV, now began to study the screen. A kindly old rancher and a tall young cowpoke, father and son, were gazing out across broad acres framed by distant mountains. Gwen turned her ears and after a bit she could faintly hear what they were saying.

THE OLD RANCHER: *Aim to plant her to hemp and opium poppy, Son, with benzedrine bushes between the rows.*

THE YOUNG COWPOKE: *Yeah, but what legal crop you fixin' to raise, Dad?*

THE OLD RANCHER: (smiling like God) *Gonna raise babies, Son.*

Gwen looked away quickly from the screen. It never paid to try to hear too much too soon.

Donnie was studying her with a teasing grin.

"I bet you imagine all sorts of crazy things while you watch it," he said. "Those terrible bennies get your mind all roiled up."

Gwen shrugged. "You won't allow any noise while you're putting yourself to sleep. I have to have something," she said reasonably.

"Besides," she added, "you're having orgies out in space with those girls in fluorescent bikinis."

"That shows how little you know about science fiction," Donnie said. "They dropped the sex angle years ago. Now it's all philosophy and stuff. See this old guy?"

He held up the magazine, keeping his place with his forefinger. On the cover was a nicely drawn picture of a smiling intelligent-looking young man in a form-fitting futuristic uniform and standing beside him, topping him by a long head, a lean green-scaled monster with a large silver purse slung over his crested shoulder. The monster had a tentacle resting in comradely fashion across the young man's back and curling lightly past his feather epaulet.

"You mean that walking crocodile?" Gwen asked.

Donnie sniffed. "That walking crocodile," he said, "happens to be a very wise member of a civilization that's far advanced beyond man's." He lifted his other hand with two fingers pressed together. "Him and me are like that. He tells me all sorts of things. He even tells me things about you."

"Science fiction doesn't interest me," Gwen said lightly, looking back to the TV. There was a commercial on now, first a white-on-black diagram of the human body with explosions of bubbles occurring in sequence at various points, then a beautiful princess in a vast bathroom, then a handsome policeman. Gwen expertly retuned her ears.

VOICE OF MEDICAL EXPERT: *Benzedrine strikes at hidden sleepiness! Tones muscles! Strengthens the heart! Activates sluggish wake centers . . .One . . . Two . . . Three!*

THE BEAUTIFUL PRINCESS: (looking depressed) *Yesterday I was overweight, listless, intensely unhappy. Mother called me The Ugly Dumpling. Now* (becoming radiant) *I build beauty with benzedrine!*

THE HANDSOME POLICEMAN: (flashing badge with huge "N" for Narcotic Squad) *You're all under arrest! Grrr . . . aarrarrgghhh!*

Gwen quickly looked away. It was the only thing you could do when you got static or the wrong voice channel. She began to carry the supper dishes to the sink.

Donnie winced violently without putting down his beer can or looking up from his page. "Don't clank them," he said. Gwen removed her shoes and began to do the dishes as if she were a diver in the silent world under the surface of the sea, ghosting between table, sink and cupboard.

She was still lost in this rather fascinating operation and even beginning to embroider it with little arabesques when Donnie continued the Sleep Ritual by opening his second can of beer, this time a warm one by choice. Before taking the first sip he swallowed a blue capsule of amytal. At the kerzing! of the opener Gwen stopped to watch him. She carefully dried the suds off her right hand, popped onto her tongue another benzedrine tablet from the bottle in her smock pocket, and still watching him thoughtfully, rinsed a glass, ran an inch of water into it and drank it.

If Donnie had his Sleep Ritual, she told herself in not exactly those words, she had her Vigil.

Donnie stood shaking her head at her.

"I suppose now you'll be wandering around all night," he said, "making all sorts of noise and disturbing me."

"I don't make any more noise than a snowflake," Gwen countered. "Not one-tenth as much as the autos and streetcars and planes. Almost every night the people next door have their TV on high."

"Yes, but those noises are outside," Donnie said. "It's your noises that bother me — the inside noises." He looked at Gwen speculatively. "Why don't you try a sleeping pill just for once?" he said with insidious appeal.

"No," Gwen answered instantly.

"A three-grain amytal," Donnie persisted, "would cancel those bennies and still have enough left over to make you nice and dozy. We'd go to sleep together and I wouldn't worry about noises."

"You don't want to go to sleep until you know everyone else is asleep," Gwen said. "Just like my mother. If I took one of your pills, you'd watch me sleep and you'd gloat."

"Well, isn't that what you do to me?"

"No, I do other things. By myself."

Donnie shrugged resignedly and went back to his chair and magazine.

Gwen wiped the itchy suds off her left hand, and leaving the rest of the dishes soaking, sat down opposite the TV. A curly-haired disk jockey was looking out thoughtfully across a record he was holding:

THE DISK JOCKEY: *Some might think it strange that with such divergent tastes in drugs Donnie and Gwen Martin should seek happiness together and in their fashion find it . . . but life holds many mysteries, my friends. I could mention Jack Sprat and wife. We'll all hope the Hubbard . . . oops! . . . Martin medicine cupboard is never bare. And now we will hear, by the joint request of Mr. and Mrs. Martin — are you out there, Don and Gwennie? — that popular old favorite* (glancing down at record) The Insane Asylum Blues!

The music was real gone.

Donnie leaned back from his magazine and looked up at the ceiling. Gwen wondered if he were watching one of the glittering stars he'd named and pointed out to her on one of the rare Saturday nights they got outdoors. But after a while he said, "Benzedrine is an utterly evil drug, worse than coffee. Other drugs soothe and heal, but benzedrine only creates tension and confusion. I'll bet if I ask the Wise Old Crocodile he'll tell me the Devil invented it."

Gwen said, "If we ever went out nights and did anything, maybe I wouldn't need so much benzedrine. Besides, you have your sleeping pills and things."

"You don't need less benzedrine when you go out, you need more," Donnie asserted unalterably. "And if I ever went out on week nights, I'd get excited and start to drink and you know what would happen. How often do I have to tell you, Woman, that the only reason I take my barbiturates and 'things' as you call them, is to keep calm and get enough sleep. If I didn't get enough sleep, I wouldn't be able to stand my job. If I couldn't stand my job, I'd start to drink. And if I started to drink, I'd be back in the Booby Hatch. And since the only reason you're outside is that I'm outside, holding a job, why you'd be back in the Booby Hatch too and they'd put you on tranquilizers and you wouldn't like it at all. So don't criticize my sleeping medicines, Woman. They're a mater of pure necessity whatever the doctors and psychologists say. Whereas your bennies and dexies — "

"We've been through all this before," Gwen interrupted without rancor.

Donnie nodded owlishly. "Show me half," he agreed, his words blurring for the first time.

"Besides," Gwen said, "you're behind schedule."

Donnie squinted at the clock and snapped his fingers. The sound was dull but there was no unsteadiness in his walk as he went to the refrigerator and poured himself two fingers of grape juice. Then he reached down from the top shelf of the cupboard the bottle of paraldehyde and poured himself a glistening tablespoonful. Swift almost as though the intense odor, midway between gasoline and banana oil, leaped to the corners of the half-merged living room and kitchen. Gwen momentarily wrinkled her nose.

Donnie mixed the paraldehyde with the grape juice and licked the spoon. "Here's to the druggists and the one understanding doctor in ten," he said and took a sip.

Gwen nodded solemnly and swallowed another benzedrine tablet.

Donnie transported his cocktail back to the armchair with great care and did not take his eye off the purple drink until he felt himself firmly anchored. He found his place in the science-fiction lead novelette, but the print began to slip sideways and so as he sipped his stinging drink, he began to imagine the secrets the Wise Old Crock might tell him if he were the young man on the cover.

THE WISE OLD CROCK: *Got a hot tip shaping for tonight, son. Three new novas flaring in the next galaxy southeast-by-up and dust cloud billowing out of Andromeda like black lace underwear.* (Dips in his purse.) *Drop this silver sphere in your pocket, son. It's a universal TV pickup on the old crystal-ball principle. It lets you tune in on any scene in the universe. Use it wisely, son, for character building as well as delight. Don't use it to spy on your wife.* (Dips again.) *Now I want to give you this small black cylinder. Keep it always on your person. It's a psychic whistle by which you can summon me at all times. All you have to do is concentrate on me, son. Concentrate . . .*

There was a courtroom scene on the TV screen. A lawyer with friendly eyes but a serious brow was talking quietly to the jury, resting his hand on the rail of the box. Gwen had her ears fine-tuned by now and his voice synchronized perfectly with the movements of his lips.

THE FRIENDLY LAWYER: *I have no wish to conceal the circumstance that my client met her husband-to-be while they were both patients in a mental hospital. Believe me, folks, some of life's sweetest romances begin in the nut house. Gwen's affection inspired Don to win his release, obtain employment as a precision machinist, offer my client marriage upon her release, and shower her with love and the yellow health-tablets, so necessary to her exis-*

tence, which you have watched her consume during these weary days in court. Needless to remark, this was before Don Martin began traveling in space, where he came under the influence of (sudden scowls) *a certain green crocodile, who shall be referred to hereinafter as Exhibit A. Enter it, clerk.*

Donnie rose up slowly from the armchair. His drink was finished. He was glaring at the TV.

"The Old Crock wouldn't be seen dead looking at junk like that," he cried thickly. "He's wired for real-life experience."

Donnie was half of a mind to kick in the picture tube when he looked toward the bedroom doorway and saw the Wise Old Crocodile standing in it, stooping low, his silver purse swinging as it dangled from his crested shoulder. Donnie knew it wasn't an hallucination, only a friendly faint green film on the darkness.

Fixing his huge kindly eyes on Donnie, the Wise Old Crock impatiently uncurled a long tentacle toward the darkness beyond him, as if to say, "Away! Away!" and then faded into it. Donnie followed him in a slow motion like Gwen's underwater ballet, shedding his shoes and shirt on the way. He was pulling his belt from the trouser loops with the air of drawing a sword as he closed the door behind him.

Gwen gave a sigh of pure joy and for a moment even closed her eyes. This was the loveliest time of all the night, the time of the Safe Freedom, the time of the Vigil. She started to roam.

First she thought she'd brush the bread crumbs from the supper table, but she got to studying their pattern and ended by picking them up one by one — she thought of it as a problem in subtraction. The pattern of the crumbs had been like that of the stars Donnie had showed her, she decided afterwards, and she was rather sorry she'd disturbed them. She carried them tenderly to the sink and delicately dusted them onto the cold gray dishwater, around which a few suds still lifted stubbornly, like old foam on an ocean beach. She saw the water glass and it reminded her to take another benzedrine tablet.

Four bright spoons caught her eye. She lifted them one by one, turning them over slowly to find all the highlights. Then she looked through the calendar on the wall, studying the months ahead and all the numbers of the days.

Every least thing was enormously fascinating! She could lose herself in one object for minutes or let her interest dart about and effortlessly follow it.

And it was easy to think good thoughts. She could think of every person she knew and wish them each well and do all kinds of wonderful things for them in her mind. A kind of girl Jesus, that's what I am, she told herself with a smile.

She drifted back into the living room. On the TV a bright blonde housewife was leading a dull brunette housewife over to a long couch. Gwen gave a small cry of pleasure and sat down on the floor. This show was always good.

THE BRIGHT BLONDE: *What do you feed your husband when he comes home miserable?*

THE DULL BRUNETTE: *Poison.*

THE BRIGHT BLONDE: *What do you feed yourself?*

THE DULL BRUNETTE: *Sorrow.*

THE BRIGHT BLONDE: *I keep my spirits bright with benzedrine. Oh happy junior high!*

THE DULL BRUNETTE: *What was happy about it? I had acne.*

THE BRIGHT BLONDE: (bouncing as they sit on the couch) *You mean to say I never told you how I got started on benzedrine? I was in junior high and unhappy. My mother sent me to the doctor because I was fat and at the foot of my class. He gave me some cute little pills and* zowie! — *I was getting slim, smart and giddy. But pretty soon they found I was going back for an extra refill between refills. They cut me off. I struck. Uh-huh, little old me called a lie-down strike. No more school, I said, unless I had my pills. If the doctor wouldn't give them to me, I'd forage for them — and I did. Two years later my mother had me committed. If I hadn't become a TV start I'd still be in the Loony Bin.*

THE DULL BRUNETTE: *Did they give you electroshock?*

THE BRIGHT BLONDE: *Think happy thoughts. What do you do for kicks? Are you on bennies too?*

THE DULL BRUNETTE: *No.* (Her face grows slack and subtly ugly.) *I practice witchcraft.*

Gwen switched off her ears and looked away from the screen. She did not like the thought that had come to her: that she had somehow planted that idea about witchcraft in the brunette's mind. It was months since Gwen had let herself think about witchcraft, either white or black.

There came a long low groan from the bedroom, adding to Gwen's troubled feeling because it seemed too much of a coincidence that it should have come just after the word witchcraft had been spoken.

DONNIE was twisting on the bed, going through hell in his dreams. The Wise Old Crock had abandoned him in a cluster of dead stars and cosmic dust on the far side of the Andromeda Galaxy, first blindfolding him, turning him around three times, and giving him a mighty shove that had sent him out of sight of whatever asteroid they had been standing on. Floating in space, Donnie went through his pockets and found only a Scout knife and a small silver sphere and black cylinder, the purpose of which he had forgotten. A cameo-small image of Gwen's face smiled at him from the sphere. He looked up. Worms twenty feet long and glowing dull red were undulating toward him through the dusty dark. He had an intense sensation of the vast distance of the Earth. He made swimming movements only to discover that a cold paralysis was creeping through his limbs. Eternities passed.

GWEN had got out her glue and glitter and sequins and had spread newspapers on the table and was making a design on a soup plate that she hoped would catch something of the remembered pattern of the bread crumbs. The idea was to paint with glue the design for one color of glitter and then sprinkle the glitter on it, knocking off the excess by tapping the edge of the plate on the table. Sprinkling the glitter was fun, but the design was not developing quite the way she wanted it to. Besides she had just discovered that she didn't have any red or gold glitter, though there were three bottles of green. Some of the green glitter stuck to the back of her finger where she had got glue on it.

She stole a look over her shoulder at the TV. The two women had been replaced by a large map of the United States and a rugged young man wearing glasses and holding a pointer. The first word she heard told her she wasn't going to like it, but she hitched her chair around just the same, deciding that in the long run it would be best to know the worst.

THE THINGS FORECASTER: *A witchcraft high is moving down from Western Canada. Werewolf warnings have been posted in three states. Government planes are battling the black front with white radio rays, but they're being forced back. Old folks who ought to know say it's the end of the world.* (Scans sheet handed him by page girl.) *Flash from outer space! Don Martin, famed astronaut, is facing nameless perils in the Lesser Magellanic Cloud!*

DONNIE had just blown the psychic whistle, having remembered its use only as the red worms began to spiral in around him, and the

Wise Old Crock had appeared at once, putting the worms to flight with a shower of green sparks flicked from the tip of his right-hand tentacle.

THE WISE OLD CROCK: *You passed the test, son but don't pride yourself on it. Some night we're going to give it to you without paraldehyde. Now it's time you returned to Terra. Think of your home planet, son, think of the Earth. Concentrate* . . . (They are suddenly in orbit a thousand miles above North America. The larger cities gleam dully, the moon is reflected in the Great Lakes. Donnie has become a green-scaled being a head shorter than the Wise Old Crock, who weaves a tentacle majestically downward.) *Observe the cities of men, my Son. Think of the millions sleeping and dreaming there, lonely as death in their apartment dwellings and all hating their jobs. The outward appearance of these men-beings may horrify you a little at first, but you have my word that they're not fiends, only creatures like you and me, trying to control themselves with drugs, dreads, incantations, ideals, self hypnosis and surrender, so that they may lead happy lives and show forth beauty.*

GWEN was looking intently in the living-room mirror, painting evenly-spaced bands of glue on her face. The bands curved under her eyes and outward, following the line of her jaw. She painted another band down the middle of her forehead and continued it straight down her nose. Then she closed her eyes, held her breath, lifted her face and shook green glitter on it for a long time. At last she lowered her face with a jerk, shook it from side to side, puffed out through her nostrils what breath she had left, and inhaled very slowly. Then she looked at herself again in the mirror and smiled. The green glitter clung to her face just as it had to her finger.

A feeling of deadly fatigue struck her then, the first of the night, and the room momentarily swam. When it came to rest she was looking at a flashing-eyed priest in a gorgeous cloak who was weaving across the TV screen.

THE GORGEOUS PRIEST: *The psychology of Donnie and Gwen must be clear to you by now. Each wants the other to sleep so that he may stand guard over her, or she over him, while yet adventuring alone. They have found a formula for this. But what of the future? What of their souls? Drugs are no permanent solution, I can assure them. What if the bars of the Safe Freedom should blow away? What if one night one of them should go out and never come in?*

DONNIE and the Wise Old Crock were hovering just outside the bedroom window three stories up. Friendly trees shaded them from the street lights below.

THE WISE OLD CROCK: *Goodby, my Son, for another night. Use your Earthly tenement well. Do not abuse your powers. And go easy on the barbiturates.*

DONNIE: *I will, Father, believe me.*

THE WISE OLD CROCK: *Hold. There is one further secret of great consequence that I must impart to you tonight. It concerns your wife.*

DONNIE: *Yes, Father?*

THE WISE OLD CROCK: *She is one of us!*

DONNIE flowed through the four-inch gap at the bottom of the bedroom window. He saw his body lying on its back on the bed and he surged toward it through the air, paddling gently with his tentacle tips. His body opened from crotch to chin like a purse and he flowed inside and the lips of the purse closed over his back with a soft *click*. Then he squirmed around gently, as if in a sleeping bag, and looked through the two holes in the front of his head and thrust his tentacles down into his arms and lifted his hands above his eyes and wriggled his fingers. It felt very strange to have finger-tipped arms with bones in them instead of tentacles. Just then he heard laughter from the living room.

GWEN was laughing admiringly at the reflection of her breasts. She had taken off her smock and brassiere and painted circles of glue around the nipples and sprinkled on more green glitter.

Although her ears were switched off, she thought she heard the priest call from behind her, "Gwen Martin, you ought to be ashamed of yourself!" and she called back to the TV, "You shouldn't peek, Father!" and she turned around, haughtily shielding her breasts with a forearm held crosswise.

The bedroom door was open and Donnie was standing in it, swaying and staring. Gwen felt another surge of deadly fatigue but she steadied herself and stared back at her husband.

Woman, the Cave Keeper, the Weaver of Words, faced Man, the Bread Winner, the Far Ranger.

They moved together slowly, dragging their feet, until they were leaning against each other. Then more slowly, still, as if they were supporting each other through quicksands, they moved toward the bedroom.

"Do you like me, Donnie?" Gwen asked.

Donnie's gaze brushed across her glittering green-striped face and breasts. His hand tightened on her shoulder and he nodded.

"You're one of us," he said.

The Man Who Made
Friends With Electricity

When Mr. Scott showed Peak House to Mr. Leverett, he hoped he wouldn't notice the high-tension pole outside the bedroom window, because it had twice before queered promising rentals — so many elderly people were foolishly nervous about electricity. There was nothing to be done about the pole except try to draw prospective tenants' attention away from it — electricity follows the hilltops and these lines supplied more than half of the juice used in Pacific Knolls.

But Mr. Scott's prayers and suave misdirections were in vain — Mr. Leverett's sharp eyes lit on the "negative feature" that instant they stepped out on the patio. The old New Englander studied the rather short thick wooden column, the 18-inch ridged glass insulators, the black transformer box that stepped down voltage for this house and a few others lower on the slope. His gaze next followed the heavy wires swinging off rhythmically four abreast across the empty gray-green hills. Then he cocked his head as his ears caught the low but steady frying sound, varying from a crackle to a buzz, of electrons leaking off the wires through the air.

"Listen to that!" Mr. Leverett said, his dry voice betraying excitement for the first time in the tour. "Fifty thousand volts if there's five! A power of power!"

"Must be unusual atmospheric conditions today — normally you can't hear a thing," Mr. Scott responded lightly, twisting the truth a little.

"You don't say?" Mr. Leverett commented, his voice dry again, but Mr. Scott knew better than to encourage conversation about a negative feature. "I want you to notice this lawn," he launched out heartily. "When the Pacific Knolls Golf Course was subdivided, the original owner of Peak House bought the entire eighteenth green and — "

For the rest of the tour Mr. Scott did his state-certified real estate broker's best, which in Southern California is no mean performance, but Mr. Leverett seemed a shade perfunctory in the attention he accorded it. Inwardly Mr. Scott chalked up another defeat by the damn pole.

On the quick retrace, however, Mr. Leverett insisted on their lingering on the patio. "Still holding out," he remarked about the buzz with an odd satisfaction. "You know, Mr. Scott, that's a restful sound to me. I hate the clatter of machinery — that's the *other* reason I left New England — but this is like the sound of nature. Downright soothing. But you say it comes seldom?"

Mr. Scott was flexible — it was one of his great virtues as a salesman.

"Mr. Leverett," he confessed simply, "I've never stood on this patio when I didn't hear that sound. Sometimes it's softer, sometimes louder, but it's always there. I play it down, though, because most people don't care for it."

"Don't blame you," Mr. Leverett said. "Most people are a pack of fools or worse. Mr. Scott, are any of the people in the neighboring houses Communists to your knowledge?"

"No, Sir!" Mr. Scott responded without an instant's hesitation. "There's not a Communist in Pacific Knolls. And that's something, believe me, I'd never shade the truth on."

"Believe you," Mr. Leverett said. "The east's packed with Communists. Seem scarcer out here. Mr. Scott, you've made yourself a deal. I'm taking a year's lease on Peak House as furnished and at the figure we last mentioned."

"Shake on it!" Mr. Scott boomed. "Mr. Leverett, you're the kind of person Pacific Knolls wants."

They shook. Mr. Leverett rocked on his heels, smiling up at the softly crackling wires with a satisfaction that was already a shade possessive.

"Fascinating thing, electricity," he said. "No end to the tricks it can do or you can do with it. For instance, if a man wanted to take off for elsewhere in an elegant flash, he'd only have to wet down the lawn good and take twenty-five foot of heavy copper wire in his two bare hands and whip the other end of it over those lines. Whango! Every bit as good as Sing Sing and a lot more satisfying to a man's inner needs."

Mr. Scott experienced a severe though momentary sinking of heart and even for one wildly frivolous moment considered welshing on the verbal agreement he'd just made. He remembered the red-haired lady who'd rented an apartment from him solely to have a quiet place in which to take an overdose of barbiturates. Then he reminded himself that Southern California is, according to a wise old saw, the home (actual or aimed-at) of the peach, the nut and the prune; and while he'd had few dealings with real or would-be starlets, he'd had enough with crackpots and retired grouches. Even if you piled fanciful death wishes and a passion for electricity atop rabid anti-communist and anti-machine manias, Mr. Leverett's personality was no more than par for the S. Cal. course.

Mr. Leverett said shrewdly, "You're worrying now, aren't you, I might be a suicider? Don't. Just like to think my thoughts. Speak them out too, however peculiar."

Mr. Scott's last fears melted and he became once more his pushingly congenial self as he invited Mr. Leverett down to the office to sign the papers.

Three days later he dropped by to see how the new tenant was making out and found him in the patio ensconced under the buzzing pole in the old rocker.

"Take a chair and sit," Mr. Leverett said, indicating one of the tubular modern pieces. "Mr. Scott, I want to tell you I'm finding Peak House every bit as restful as I hoped. I listen to the electricity and let my thoughts roam. Sometimes I hear voices in the electricity — the wires talking, as they say. You've heard of people who hear voices in the wind?"

"Yes, I have," Mr. Scott admitted a bit uncomfortably and then, recalling that Mr. Leverett's check for the first quarter's rent was safely cleared, was emboldened to speak his own thoughts. "But wind is a sound that varies a lot. That buzz is pretty monotonous to hear voices in."

"Pshaw," Mr. Leverett said with a little grin that made it impossible to tell how seriously he meant to be taken. "Bees are highly intelligent insects, entomologists say they even have a language, yet they do nothing but buzz. I hear voices in the electricity."

He rocked silently for a while after that and Mr. Scott sat.

"Yep, I hear voices in the electricity," Mr. Leverett said dreamily. "Electricity tells me how it roams the forty-eight states — even the forty-ninth by way of Canadian power lines. It's sort of pioneer-like:

141

the power wires are its trails, the hydro-stations are its water holes. Electricity goes everywhere today — into our homes, every room of them, into our offices, into government buildings and military posts. And what it doesn't learn that way it overhears by the trace of it that trickles through our phone lines and over our air waves. Phone electricity's the little sister of power electricity, you might say, and little pitchers have big ears. Yep, electricity knows everything about us, our every last secret. Only it wouldn't think of telling most people what it knows, because they believe electricity is a cold mechanical force. It isn't — it's warm and pulsing and sensitive and friendly underneath, like any other live thing."

Mr. Scott, feeling a bit dreamy himself now, thought what good advertising copy that would make — imaginative stuff, folksy but poetic.

"And electricity's got a mite of viciousness too," Mr. Leverett continued. "You got to tame it. Know its ways, speak it fair, show no fear — make friends with it. Well now, Mr. Scott," he said in a brisker voice, standing up, "I know you've come here to check up on how I'm caring for Peak House. So let me give you the tour."

And in spite of Mr. Scott's protests that he had no such inquisitive intention, Mr. Leverett did just that.

Once he paused for an explanation: "I've put away the electric blanket and the toaster. Don't feel right about using electricity for menial jobs."

As far as Mr. Scott could see, he had added nothing to the furnishings of Peak House beyond the rocking chair and a large collection of Indian arrow heads.

Mr. Scott must have talked about the latter when he got home, for a week later his 9-year-old son said to him, "Hey, Dad, you know that old guy you unloaded Peak House onto?"

"Rented is the proper expression, Bobby."

"Well, I went up to see his arrow heads. Dad, it turns out he's a snake-charmer!"

Dear God, thought Mr. Scott, *I knew there was going to be something really impossible about Leverett. Probably likes hilltops because they draw snakes in hot weather.*

"He didn't charm a real snake, though, Dad, just an old extension cord. He squatted down on the floor — this was after he showed me those crumby arrow heads — and waved his hands back and forth over it and pretty soon the end with the little box on it started to move around on the floor and all of a sudden it lifted up, like a cobra out of a basket. It was real spooky!"

"I've seen that sort of trick," Mr. Scott told Bobby. "There was a fine thread attached to the end of the cord pulling it up."

"I'd have seen a thread, Dad."

"Not if it were the same color as the background," Mr. Scott explained. Then he had a thought. "By the way, Bobby, was the other end of the cord plugged in?"

"Oh it was, Dad! He said he couldn't work the trick unless there was electricity in the cord. Because you see, Dad, he's really an electricity-charmer. I just said snake-charmer to make it more exciting. Afterwards we went outside and he charmed electricity down out of the wires and made it crawl all over his body. You could see it crawl from part to part."

"But how could you see that?" Mr. Scott demanded, struggling to keep his voice casual. He had a vision of Mr. Leverett standing dry and sedate, entwined by glimmering blue serpents with flashing diamond eyes and fangs that sparked.

"By the way it would make his hair stand on end, Dad. First on one side of his head, then on the other. Then he said, 'Electricity, crawl down my chest,' and a silk handkerchief hanging out of his top pocket stood out stiff and sharp. Dad, it was almost as good as the Museum of Science and Industry!"

Next day Mr. Scott dropped by Peak House, but he got no chance to ask his carefully thought-out questions, for Mr. Leverett greeted him with, "Reckon your boy told you about the little magic show I put on for him yesterday. I like children, Mr. Scott. Good Republican children like yours, that is."

"Why yes, he did," Mr. Scott admitted, disarmed and a bit flustered by the other's openness.

"I only showed him the simplest tricks, of course. Kid stuff."

"Of course," Mr. Scott echoed. "I guess you must have used a fine thread to make the extension cord dance."

"Reckon you know all the answers, Mr. Scott," the other said, his eyes flashing. "But come across to the patio and sit for a while."

The buzzing was quite loud that day, yet after a bit Mr. Scott had to admit to himself that it *was* a restful sound. And it had more variety than he'd realized — mounting crackles, fading sizzles, hisses, hums, clicks, sighs. If you listened to it long enough, you probably would begin to hear voices.

Mr. Leverett, silently rocking, said, "Electricity tells me about all the work it does and all the fun it has — dances, singing, big crackling band concerts, trips to the stars, foot races that make rockets seem like snails. Worries, too. You know that electric breakdown they had in New York? Electricity told me why. Some of its folks went crazy — overwork, I guess — and just froze. It was a while before they could send others in from outside New York and heal the crazy ones and start them moving again through the big copper web. Electricity tells me its fearful the same thing's going to happen in Chicago and San Francisco. Too much pressure.

"Electricity doesn't *mind* working for us. It's generous-hearted and it loves its job. But it would be grateful for a little more consideration — a little more recognition of its special problems.

"It's got its savage brothers to contend with, you see — the wild electricity that rages in storms and haunts the mountaintops and comes down to hunt and kill. Not civilized like the electricity in the wires, though it will be some day.

"For civilized electricity's a great teacher. Shows us how to live clean and in unity and brother-love. Power fails one place, electricity's rushing in from everywhere to fill the gap. Serves Georgia same as Vermont, Los Angeles same as Boston. Patriotic too — only revealed its greatest secrets to true-blue Americans like Edison and Franklin. Did you know it killed a Swede when he tried that kite trick? Yep, electricity's the greatest power for good in all the U.S.A."

Mr. Scott thought sleepily of what a neat little electricity cult Mr. Leverett could set up, every bit as good as Mind Science or the swami that got blown up with dynamite. He could imagine the patio full of earnest seekers while Krishna Leverett — or maybe High Electro Leverett — dispensed wisdom from his rocker, interpreting the words of the humming wires. Better not suggest it, though — in Southern California such things sometimes had a way of coming true.

Mr. Scott felt quite easy at heart as he went down the hill, though he did make a point of telling Bobby not to bother Mr. Leverett any more. The old man seemed harmless enough, still...

But the prohibition didn't apply to himself. During the next months Mr. Scott made a point of dropping in at Peak House from time to time for a dose of "electric wisdom." He came to look forward to these restful, amusingly screwy breaks in the hectic round. Mr. Leverett appeared to do nothing whatever except sit in his rocker in the patio, yet stayed happy and serene. There was a lesson for anybody in that, if you thought about it.

Occasionally Mr. Scott spotted amusing side effects of Mr. Leverett's eccentricity. For instance, although he sometimes let the gas and water bills go, he always paid up phone and electricity on the dot.

And the newspapers eventually did report short but severe electric breakdowns in Chicago and San Francisco. Smiling a little frowningly at the coincidences, Mr. Scott decided he could add fortune-telling to the electricity cult he'd imaged for Mr. Leverett. "Your life's story foretold in the wires!" — more novel, anyway than crystal balls or Talking with God.

Only once did the touch of the gruesome, that had troubled Mr. Scott in his first conversation with Mr. Leverett, come briefly back, when the old man chuckled and observed, "Recall what I told you about whipping a copper wire up there? I've thought of a simpler way, just squirt the hose at those H-T lines in a hard stream, gripping the metal nozzle. Might be best to use the hot water and throw a box of salt in the heater first." When Mr. Scott heard that he was glad that he'd warned Bobby against coming around.

But for the most part Mr. Leverett maintained his mood of happy serenity.

When the break in that mood came, it was suddenly, though afterwards Mr. Scott realized there had been one warning note sounded when Mr. Leverett had added onto a rambling discourse, "By the way, I've learned that U.S. power electricity goes all over the world, just like the ghost electricity in radios and phones. It travels to foreign shores in batteries and condensers. Roams the lines in Europe and Asia. Some of it even slips over into Soviet territory. Wants to keep tab on the Communists, I guess. Electric freedom-fighters."

On his next visit Mr. Scott found a great change. Mr. Leverett had deserted his rocking chair to pace the patio on the side away from the pole, though every now and then he would give a quick funny look up over his shoulder at the dark muttering wires.

"Glad to see you, Mr. Scott. I'm real shook up. Reckon I better tell someone about it so if something happens to me they'll be able to tell the FBI. Though I don't know what *they'll* be able to do.

"Electricity just told me this morning it's got a world government — it had the nerve to call it that — and that there's Russian electricity in our wires and American electricity in the Soviet's — it shifts back and forth with never a quiver of shame. It doesn't have a spark of feeling for the U.S.A. *or* for Russia. It thinks only of itself.

"When I heard that you could have knocked me down with a paper dart.

"What's more, electricity's determined to stop any big war that may come, no matter how rightful that war be or how much in defense of America. It doesn't care a snap about us — it just doesn't want its webs and water holes destroyed. If the buttons are pushed for the atomic missiles — here *or* in Russia — it'll flash out and kill anybody who tries to set them of another way.

"I pleaded with electricity, I told it I'd always thought of it as American and true — reminded it of Franklin and Edison — finally I commanded it to change its ways and behave decent, but it just chuckled.

"Then it threatened me back! It told me if I tried to stop it, if I revealed its plans, it would summon down its savage brothers from the mountains and with their help it would seek me out and kill me! Mr. Scott, I'm all alone up here with electricity on my window sill. What am I going to do?"

Mr. Scott had considerable difficulty soothing Mr. Leverett enough to make his escape. In the end he had to promise to come back in the morning bright and early — silently vowing to himself that he'd be damned if he would.

His task was not made easier when the electricity overhead, which had been especially noisy this day, rose in a growl and Mr. Leverett turned and said harshly, "Yes, I hear!"

That night the Los Angeles area had one of its rare thunderstorms, accompanied by gales of wind and torrents of rain. Palms and pines and eucalyptus were torn down, earth cliffs crumbled and sloshed, and the great square concrete spill-ways ran brimful from the hills to the sea.

The lightning was especially fierce. Several score Angelinos, to whom such a display was a novelty, phoned civil defense numbers to report or inquire fearfully about atomic attacks.

Numerous freak accidents occurred. To the scene of one of these Mr. Scott was summoned next morning bright and early by the police, because it had occurred on a property he rented and because he was the only person known to be acquainted with the deceased.

The previous night Mr. Scott had awakened at the height of the storm when the lightning had been blinding as a photoflash and the thunder had cracked like a mile long whip just above the roof. At that time he had remembered vividly what Mr. Leverett had said about electricity threatening to summon its wild giant brothers from the hills. But now, in the bright morning, he decided not to tell the police about that or say anything to them at all about Mr. Leverett's electricity mania — it would only complicate things to no purpose and perhaps make the fear at his heart more crazily real.

Mr. Scott saw the scene of the freak accident before anything was moved, even the body — except there was now, of course, no power in the heavy corroded wire wrapped tight as a bullwhip around the skinny shanks with only the browned and blackened fabric of cotton pajamas between.

The police and the power-and-light men reconstructed the accident this way: At the height of the storm one of the high-tension lines had snapped a hundred feet away from the house and the near end, whipped by the wind and its own tension, had struck back freakishly through the open bedroom window of Peak House and curled once around the legs of Mr. Leverett, who had likely been on his feet at the time. He had been killed instantly.

One had to strain that reconstruction, though, to explain the additional freakish elements in the accident — the fact that the high-tension wire had struck not only through the bedroom window, but then through the bedroom door to catch the old man in the hall, and that the black shiny cord of the phone was wrapped like a vine twice around the old man's right arm, as if to hold him back from escaping until the big wire had struck.

The Dead Man

Professor Max Redford opened the frosted glass door of the reception room and beckoned to me. I followed him eagerly. When the most newsworthy doctor at one of America's foremost medical schools phones a popular-science writer and asks him to drop over, but won't tell him why, there is cause for excitement. Especially when that doctor's researches, though always well-founded, have tended towards the sensational. I remembered the rabbits so allergic to light that an open shade raised blisters on their shaved skins, the hypnotized heart patient whose blood-pressure slowly changed, the mold that fed on blood clots in a living animal's brain. Fully half my best articles with a medical slant came from Max. We had been close friends for several years.

As we hurried along the hushed corridor, he suddenly asked me, "What is death?"

That wasn't the sort of question I was expecting. I gave him a quick look. His bullet-shaped head, with its shock of close-cropped grizzled hair, was hunched forward. The eyes behind the thick lenses were bright, almost mischievous. He was smiling.

I shrugged.

"I have something to show you," he said.

"What, Max?"

"You'll see."

"A story?"

He shook his head. "At present I don't want a word released to the public or the profession."

"But some day — ?" I suggested.

"Maybe one of the biggest."

148

We entered his office. On the examination table lay a man, the lower half of his body covered by a white sheet. He seemed to be asleep.

Right there I got a shock. For although I hadn't the faintest idea who the man was, I did recognize him. I was certain that I had seen that handsome face once before — through the French windows of the living room of Max's home, some weeks ago. It had been pressed passionately to the face of Velda, Max's attractive young wife, and those arms had been cradling her back. Max and I had just arrived at his lonely suburban place after a long evening session at the laboratory, and he had been locking the car when I glanced through the window. When we had got inside, the man had been gone, and Max had greeted Velda with his usual tenderness. I had been bothered by the incident, but of course there had been nothing I could do about it.

I turned from the examination table, trying to hide my surprise. Max sat down at his desk and began to rap on it with a pencil. Nervous excitement, I supposed.

From the man on the examination table, now behind me, came a dry, hacking cough.

"Take a look at him," said Max, "and tell me what disease he's suffering from."

"I'm no doctor," I protested.

"I know that, but there are some symptoms that should have an obvious meaning even to a layman."

"But I didn't even notice he was ill," I said.

Max goggled his eyes at me, "You didn't?"

Shrugging my shoulders, I turned — and wondered how in the world I could have missed it at the first glance. I supposed I had been so flustered at recognizing the man that I hadn't noticed anything about him — I had been seeing the memory image more than the actual person. For Max was right. Anyone could have hazarded a diagnosis of this case. The general pallor, the hectic spots of color over the cheek bones, the emaciated wrists, the prominent ribs, the deep depressions around the collar bones, and above all the continued racking cough that even as I watched brought a bit of blood specked mucous to the lips — all pointed at an advanced stage of chronic tuberculosis. I told Max so.

Max stared at me thoughtfully, rapping again on the table. I wondered if he sensed what I was trying to hide from him. Certainly I felt very uncomfortable. The presence of that man, presumably Velda's lover, in Max's office, unconscious and suffering from a deadly disease, and Max so sardonic-seeming and full of suppressed excitement, and then that queer question he had asked me about death — taken all together, they made a peculiarly nasty picture.

What Max said next didn't help either.

"You're quite sure it's tuberculosis?"

"Naturally I could be wrong," I admitted uneasily. "It might be some other disease with the same symptoms or — " I had been about to say "or the effects of some poison," but I checked myself. "But the symptoms are there, unmistakably," I finished.

"You're positive?" He seemed to enjoy drawing it out.

"Of course!"

He smiled. "Take another look."

"I don't need to," I protested. For the first time in our relationship I was wondering if there wasn't something extremely unpleasant about Max.

"Take one, just the same."

Unwillingly I turned — and for several moments there was room in my mind for nothing but astonishment.

"What kind of trick is this?" I finally asked Max, shakily.

For the man on the examination table had changed. Unmistakably the same man, though for a moment I questioned even that, for now instead of the cadaverous spectre of tuberculosis, a totally different picture presented itself. The wrist, so thin a minute ago, was now swollen, the chest had become so unhealthily puffy that the ribs and collar bones were lost to view, the skin had a bluish tinge, and from between the sagging lips came a labored, wheeze breathing.

I still had a sense of horror, but now it was overlaid with an emotion that can be even stronger, an emotion that can outweigh all considerations of human personality and morals: the excitement of scientific discovery. Whoever this man was, whatever Max's motives might be, whatever unsuspected strain of evil there might exist deep in his nature, he had *hit* on something here, something revolutionary. I didn't know what it was, but my heart pounded and little chills of excitement chased over my skin.

Max refused to answer any of the questions I bombarded him with. All he would do was sit back and smile at me and say, "And now, after your second look, what do you think's wrong with him?"

He finally badgered me into making a statement.

"Well of course there's something fishy about it, but if you insist, here's my idea: Heart disease, perhaps caused by kidney trouble. In any case, something badly out of order with his pump."

Max's smile was infuriatingly bland. Again he rapped with his pencil, like some supercilious teacher.

"You're sure of that?" he prodded.

"Just as sure as I was the first time that it was tuberculosis."

"Well, take another look . . . and meet John Fearing."

I turned, and almost before I realized it, my hand had been firmly clasped and was being vigorously shaken by that of one of the finest physical specimens I have ever seen. I remember thinking dazedly, "Yes, he's as incredibly handsome and beautifully built as he seemed to me when I glimpsed him kissing Velda. And along with it a strange sort of smoothness, like you felt in Rudolf Valentino. No wonder a woman might find him irresistible."

"I could have introduced you to John long ago," Max was saying. "He lives right near us, with his mother and often drops over. But, well . . ." he chuckled, ". . . I've been a little jealous about John. I haven't introduced him to anyone connected with the profession. I've wanted to keep him to myself until we got a little further along with our experiments.

"And John," Max went on, "this is Fred Alexander, the writer. He's one science popularizer who never strays a hairs-breadth into sensationalism and who takes infinite pains to make his reporting accurate. We can trust him not to breathe a word about our experiments until we tell him to. I've been thinking for some time now that we ought to let a third person in on our work, and I didn't want it to be a scientist or yet an ordinary layman. Fred here struck me as having just the right sort of general knowledge and sympathetic approach. So I rang him up — and I believe we've succeeded in giving him quite a surprise."

"You certainly have," I agreed fervently.

John Fearing dropped my hand and stepped back. I was still running my eyes over his marvelously proportioned athletic body. I couldn't spot a trace of the symptoms of the two dreadful diseases that had seemed to be wracking it minutes ago, or of any other sort of ill health. As he stood there so cooly, with the sheet loosely caught around his waist and falling in easy folds, it seemed to me that he might well be the model for one of the great classical Greek statues. His eyes had something of the same tranquil, ox-like "all-body" look.

Turning towards Max, I was conscious of a minor shock. I had never thought of Max as ugly. If I'd ever thought of him at all in regard to looks, it had been as a man rather youthful for his middle age, stalwart, and with pleasingly rugged features.

Now, compared to Fearing, Max seemed a humped and dark-browned dwarf.

But this feeling of mine was immediately swallowed up in my excited curiosity.

Fearing looked at Max. "What diseases did I do this time?" he asked casually.

"Tuberculosis and nephritis," Max told him. They both acted pleased. In fact, mutual trust and affection showed so plainly in their manner toward each other that I was inclined to dismiss my suspicions of some sinister underlying hatred.

After all, I told myself, the embrace I had witnessed might have been merely momentary physical intoxication on the part of the two young and lovely people, if it had been even that much. Certainly what Max had said about his desire to keep Fearing a secret from his friends and colleagues might very well explain why Fearing had disappeared that night. On the other hand, if a deeper and less fleeting feeling did exist between Max's pretty wife and protege, Max might very well be aware of it and inclined to condone it. I knew him to be a remarkably tolerant man in some respects. In any case, I had probably exaggerated the importance of the matter.

And I certainly didn't want any such speculations distracting my thoughts now, when I was bending all my mental efforts to comprehend the amazing experiment that had just been conducted before my eyes.

Suddenly I got a glimmer of part of it.

"Hypnotism?" I asked Max.

He nodded, beaming.

"And the pencil-rappings were 'cues?' I mean, signals for him to carry out instructions given to him in an earlier stage of the trance?"

"That's right."

"I seem to recall now," I said, "that the raps were different in each case. I suppose each combination of raps was hooked up with a special set of instructions you'd given him."

"Exactly," said Max. "John won't respond until he gets the right signal. It seems a rather complicated way of going about it, but it isn't really. You know how a sergeant will give his men a set of orders and then bark out 'March!'? Well, the raps are John's marching signals. It works out better than giving him the instructions at the same time he's supposed to be carrying them out. Besides," and he looked at me roguishly, "it's a lot more dramatic."

"I'll say it is!" I assured him. "Max, let's get to the important point. How in the world did John fake those symptoms?"

Max raised his hands. "I'll explain everything. I didn't call you in just to mystify you. Sit down."

I hurriedly complied. Fearing effortlessly lifted himself onto the edge of the examination table and sat there placidly attentive, forearms loosely dropped along his thighs.

"As you know," Max began, "it's a well-established fact that the human mind can create all sorts of tangible symptoms of disease, without the disease itself being present in any way. Statistics show that about half the people who consult doctors are suffering from such imaginary ailments."

"Yes," I protested, "but the symptoms are never so extreme, or created with such swiftness. Why, there was even blood in the mucus. And those swollen wrists — "

Again Max raised his hands. "The difference is only one of degree. Please hear me out."

"Now John here," he continued, "is a very well adjusted, healthy-minded person, but a few years ago he was anything but that." He looked at Fearing, who nodded his agreement. "No, our John was a regular bad boy of the hospitals. Rather his subconscious mind was, for of course there is no question of faking in these matters, the individual sincerely believes that he is sick. At all events, our John seemed to go through an unbelievable series of dangerous illnesses that frightened his mother to distraction and baffled his doctors, until it was realized that the illnesses were of emotional origin. That discovery wasn't made for a long time because of the very reason you mentioned — the unusual severity of the symptoms.

"However in the end it was the extraordinary power of John's subconscious to fake symptoms that gave the show away. It began to fake the symptoms of too many diseases, the onsets and recoveries were too fast, it jumped around too much. And then it made the mistake of faking the symptoms of germ diseases, when laboratory tests showed that the germs in question weren't present.

"The truth having been recognized, John was put in the hands of a competent psychiatrist, who eventually succeeded in straightening out the personality difficulties that had caused him to seek refuge in sickness. They turned out to be quite simple ones — an overprotective and emotionally demanding mother and a jealous and unaffectionate father, whose death a few years back had burdened John with guilt feelings.

"It was at that time — just after the brilliant success of the psychiatrist's treatment — that I ran across the case. It happened through Velda. She became friends with the Fearings, mother and son, when they moved into our neighborhood, and she visited with them a lot."

As he said that, I couldn't resist shooting a quick glance at Fearing, but I couldn't see any signs of uneasiness or smugness. I felt rather abashed.

"One evening when John was over at our place, he mentioned his amazing history of imaginary illnesses, and pretty soon I wormed the whole story out of him. I was immediately struck with something about his case that the other doctors had missed. Or if they had noticed it, they hadn't seen the implications — or the possibilities.

"Here was a person whose body was fantastically obedient to the dictates of his subconscious mind. All people are to some degree psychosomatic, to give it its technical name— you know, *psyche* and *soma*, mind and body. But our John was psychosomatic to a vastly greater degree. One in a million. Perhaps unique.

"Very likely some rare hereditary strain was responsible for this. I don't believe John will be angry with me if I tell you that his mother used to be — she's really changed herself a great deal under the psychiatrist's guidance — but that she used to be an excessively hysterical and emotionally tempestuous person, with all sorts of imaginary ailments herself, though not as extreme as John's, of course. And his father was almost exactly the same type."

"That's quite right, Dr. Redford," Fearing said earnestly.

Max nodded. "Apparently the combination of these two hereditary strains in John produced far more than a doubling of his parents' sensitivities.

"Just as the chameleon inherits a color-changing ability that other animals lack, so John had inherited a degree of psychosomatic control that is not apparent in other people — at least not without some kind of psychological training of which at present I have only a glimmering.

"All this was borne in on me as I absorbed John's story, hanging on every word. You know, I think both John and Velda were quite startled at the intensity of my interest." Max chuckled. "But they didn't realize that I was on to something. Here, right in my hands, was a person with, to put it popularly, only the most tenuous of boundaries between his mental and material atoms — for of course, as you know, both mind and matter are ultimately electrical in nature. Our John's subconscious mind had perfect control of his heartbeat and circulatory system. It could flood his tissue with fluids, producing instant swellings, or dehydrate them, giving the effect of emaciation. It could play on his internal organs and ductless glands as if they were musical instruments, creating any life-time it wanted. It could produce horrible discords, turn John into an idiot, say, or an invalid, as it tried to do, or perhaps an acromegalic monster, with gigantic hands and head, by stimulating bone-growth after maturity.

"Or his subconscious mind could keep all his organs in perfect tune, making him the magnificently healthy creature you see today."

I looked at John Fearing and realized that my earlier impression of the excellence of his physique had, if anything, fallen short of the mark. It wasn't just that he was a clear-eyed, unblemished, athletically-built young man. There was more to it than that — something intangible. It occurred to me that if any man could be said to radiate health, in the literal meaning of that ridiculous cliche, it was John Fearing. I knew it was just my imagination, but I seemed to see a pulsating, faintly golden aura about him.

And his mind appeared to be in as perfect balance as his body. He was wonderfully poised as he sat there with just the sheet pulled around him.. Not the faintest suggestion of nerves. Completely alive, yet in a sense completely impassive.

It was only too easy to imagine such a man making love successfully, with complete naturalness and confidence, without any of the little haltings and clumsiness, the jarrings of rhythm, the cowardices of body, the treacheries of mind that betray the average neurotic — which is to say, the average person. Suddenly it hit me, right between the eyes as they say, that Velda *must* love John, that no woman could avoid becoming infatuated with such a man. Not just a football star or a muscle maniac, but a creature infinitely subtler.

And yet, in spite of all this, I was conscious of something a shade repellent about Fearing. Perhaps it was that he seemed too well-balanced, too smooth-running, like a gleaming dynamo say, or a beautiful painting without that little touch of ugliness or clashing contrast which creates individuality. In most people, too, one senses the eternal conflict between the weak and indecisive tyrant Mind and the stubborn and rebellious slave Body, but in Fearing the conflict seemed completely absent, which struck me as unpleasant. There was a kind of deep-seated toughness about him, a suggestion of indestructibility. One might have said, "He'd make a nasty ghost."

Of course all this may just have been envy on my part for Fearing's poise and physique, or some sort of jealousy I felt on Max's account.

But whatever the sources of my feeling of revulsion, I now began to believe that Max shared it. Not that Max had slackened in his genial, affectionate, almost fatherly manner toward John, but that he was so effortful about it. Those elephantine "our Johns," for example. I didn't get the feeling that he was concealing a jealous hatred, however, but that he was earnestly fighting an irrational inward aversion.

As for Fearing, he seemed completely unaware of any hostile feeling on Max's part. His manner was completely open and amiable.

For that matter, I wondered if Max himself were aware of his own feeling. All these thoughts didn't take much time. I was intent on Max's story.

Max leaned across the desk. He was blinking excitedly, which, with his glasses, gave an odd effect of flashing eyes.

"My imagination was stirred," he went on. "There was no end to the things that might be learned from such a super-psychosomatic individual. We could study disease symptoms under perfect conditions, by producing them in controlled amounts in a healthy individual. All sorts of physiological mysteries could be explored. We could trace out the exact patterns of all the nervous processes that are normally beyond the mind's reach. Then if we could learn to impart John's ability to other people — but that's getting a bit ahead of my story.

"I talked to John. He saw my point, realized the service he m render mankind, and gladly agreed to undergo some experiments.

"But at the first attempt a snag appeared. John could not produce any symptoms by a conscious effort, no matter how hard he tried. As I said before, you can't consciously fake a psychosomatic illness, and that was what I was asking John to do. And since he'd undergone psychiatric treatment his subconscious mind was so well behaved that it wouldn't yield to any ordinary blandishments.

"At that point we almost gave up the project. But then I thought of a way we might be able to get around the snag: suggestions given directly to the subconscious mind through hypnotism.

"John proved a good hypnotic subject. We tried it — and it worked!"

Max's eyes looked bright as stars as he said that.

"That's about how matters stand today," he finished off, sinking back in his chair. "We've started a little special work on arterial tension, the lymphatic glands and their nerve supply, one or two other things. But mainly we've been perfecting our setup, getting used to the hypnotic relationship. The important work still lies ahead."

I exhaled appreciatively. Then an unpleasant thought struck me. I wasn't going to voice it, but Max asked, "What is it, Fred?" and I couldn't think of anything else to say, and after all it was a thought that would have occurred to anyone.

"Well, with all this creation of extreme symptoms," I began, "isn't there a certain amount of — "

Max supplied the word. "Danger?" He shook his head. "We are always very careful."

"And in any case," Fearing's bell-like voice broke in, "the possibilities being what they are, I would consider almost any risks worth running." He smiled cheerfully.

The double meaning I momentarily fancied in his words nettled me. I went on impulsively, "But surely some people would be apt to consider it extremely dangerous. Your mother, for instance, or Velda."

Max looked at me sharply.

"Neither my mother nor Mrs. Redford know anything of the extent of our experiments," Fearing assured me.

There was a pause. Unexpectedly, Max grinned at me, stretched, and said to Fearing, "How do you feel now?"

r little demonstration?"

...at reminds me, Max," I said abruptly, "out in the corridor you mentioned something about — "

He shot me a warning glance.

"We'll go into that some other time," he said.

"What disease are you going to have me do this time?" Fearing queried.

Max wagged his finger. "You know you're never told that. Can't have your conscious mind messing things up. We'll have some new signals, though. And, Fred, I hope you won't mind waiting outside while I put John under and give him his instructions — acquaint him with the new signals. I'm afraid we still haven't gotten far along enough to risk the possibly disturbing presence of a third person during the early stages of an experiment. One or two more sessions and it should be all right, though. Understand, Fred, this is just the first of a large number of experiments I want you to witness. I'm asking a great deal of you, you see. The only tangible compensation I can offer you is exclusive rights to break the story to the public when we feel the time is ripe."

"Believe me, I consider it a great honor," I assured him sincerely as I went out.

In the corridor I lit a cigarette, puffed it a moment, and then the tremendous implications of Max's experiments really hit me.

Suppose, as Max had hinted, that it proved possible to impart Fearing's ability to other people?

The benefits would be incalculable. People would be able to help their bodies in the fight against disease and degenerative processes. For instance, they could cut down the flow of blood from a wound, or even stop it completely. They could marshal all the body's resources to fight local infections and stop disease germs before they ever got started. Conceivably, they could heal sick organs, get them working in the right rhythm, unharden arteries, avert or stifle cancers.

It might be possible to prevent disease, even aging, altogether.

We might look forward to a race of immortals, immune to time and decay.

A happy race, untroubled by those conflicts of body and mind, of instinct and conscience, that sap Mankind's best energies and are at the root of all discords and wars.

There was literally no limit to the possibilities.

I hardly felt I'd been in the corridor a minute, my mind was soaring so, when Max softly opened the door and beckoned to me.

Again Fearing lay stretched on the table. His eyes were closed, but he still looked every whit as vibrantly healthy as before. His chest rose and fell rhythmically with his breathing. I almost fancied I could see the blood coursing under the fair skin.

I was aware of a tremendous suppressed excitement in Max.

"We can talk, of course," he said. "Best keep it low, though."

"He's hypnotized?" I asked.

"Yes."

"And you've given him the instructions?"

"Yes. Watch."

"What are they this time, Max?"

Max's lips jerked oddly.

"Just watch."

He rapped with the pencil.

I watched. For five, ten seconds nothing seemed to happen.

Fearing's chest stopped moving.

His skin was growing pale.

There was a weak convulsive shudder. His eyelids fell open, showing only the whites. Then there was no further movement whatever.

"Approach him," Max ordered, his voice thick. "Take his pulse."

Almost shaking with excitement, I complied.

To my fumbling fingers, Fearing's wrist felt cold. I could not find a pulse.

"Fetch that mirror," Max's finger stabbed at a nearby shelf. "Hold it to his lips and nostrils."

The polished surface remained unclouded.

I backed away. Wonder gave place to fear. All my worst suspicions returned intensified. Once again I seemed to sense a strain of submerged evil in my friend.

"I told you I would show you something with a bearing on the question, 'What is death?'" Max was saying huskily. "Here you see death perfectly counterfeited — death-in-life. I would defy any doctor in the world to prove this man alive." There was a note of triumph in his voice.

My own was uneven with horror. "You instructed him to be dead?"

"Yes."

"And he didn't know it ahead of time?"

"Of course not."

For an interminable period — perhaps three or four seconds — I stared at the blanched form of Fearing. Then I turned to Max.

"I don't like this," I said. "Get him out of it."

There was something sneering about the smile he gave me.

"Watch!" He commanded fiercely, and rapped again.

It was only some change in the light, I told myself, that was giving Fearing's flesh a greenish tinge.

Then I saw the limp arms and legs stiffen and the face tighten into a sardonic mask.

"Touch him!"

Unwillingly, only to get the thing over with as swiftly as possible, I obeyed. Fearing's arm felt as stiff as a board and, if anything, colder than before.

Rigor mortis.

But that faint odor of putrescence — I knew that could only be my imagination.

"For God's sake, Max," I pleaded, "you've got to get him out of it." Then, throwing aside reserve, "I don't know what you're trying to do, but you can't. Velda — "

Max jerked as I spoke the name. Instantly the terrifying shell that had gathered around him seemed to drop away. It was as if that one word had roused him from a dream. "Of course," he said, in his natural voice. He smiled reassuringly and rapped.

Eagerly I watched Fearing.

Max rapped again: three — one.

It takes time, I told myself. Now the muscles were beginning to relax, weren't they?

But Max was rapping again. The signal printed itself indelibly on my brain: three — one.

And yet again. Three — one. Three — one. THREE — ONE.

I looked at Max. In his tortured expression I read a ghastly certainty.

I wouldn't ever want to relive the next few hours. I imagine that in all history there was never a trick conceived for reviving the dying that Max didn't employ, along with all the modern methods — injections, even into the heart itself, electrical stimulation, use of a new lightweight plastic version of the iron lung, surgical entry into the chest and direct massage of the heart.

Whatever suspicions I had of Max vanished utterly during those hours. The frantic genuineness and inspired ingenuity of his efforts to revive Fearing couldn't possibly have been faked. No more could his tragic, rigidly suppressed grief have been simulated. I saw Max's emotions stripped to the raw during those hours, and they were all good.

One of the first things he did was call in several of the other faculty doctors. They helped him, though I could tell that from the first they looked upon the case as hopeless, and would have considered the whole business definitely irregular, if it hadn't been for their extreme loyalty to Max, far beyond any consideration of professional solidarity. Their attitude showed me, as nothing else ever had, Max's stature as a medical man.

Max was completely frank with them and everyone else. He made no effort whatsoever to suppress the slightest detail of the events leading up to the tragedy. He was bitter in his self-accusations, insisting that his judgment had been unforgivably at fault in the final experiment. He would have gone even further than that if it hadn't been for his colleagues. It was they who dissuaded him from resigning from the faculty and describing his experiments in such inaccurately harsh terms as to invite criminal prosecution.

And then there was Max's praiseworthy behavior toward Fearing's mother. While they were still working on Fearing, though without any real hope, she burst in. Whatever reforms the psychiatrist may have achieved in her personality, were washed out now. I still can close my eyes and visualize that hateful, overdressed woman stamping around like an angry parrot, screaming the vilest accusations at Max at the top of her voice and talking about her son and herself in the most disgusting terms. But although he was near the breaking point, Max was never anything but compassionate toward her, accepting all the blame she heaped on his head.

A little later Velda joined Ma. If I'd still had any of my early suspicions, her manner would have dissipated them. She was completely practical and self-possessed, betraying no personal concern whatsoever in Fearing's death. If anything, she was too cool and unmoved. But that may have been what Max needed at the time.

The next days were understandably difficult. While most of the newspapers were admirably reserved and judicious in reporting the case, one of the tabloids played up Max as "The Doctor Who Ordered a Man to Die," featuring an exclusive interview with Fearing's mother.

The chorus of wild bleats from various anti-science cults was of course to be expected. It led to a number of stories that crept into the fringe of print and would have been more unpleasant if they hadn't been so ridiculous. One man, evidently drawing on Poe's story "The Facts in the Case of M. Valdemar," demanded that a "death watch" be maintained on Fearing and, on the morning of the funeral, hinted darkly that they were interring a man who was somehow still alive.

Even the medical profession was by no means wholly behind Max. A number of local doctors, unconnected with the medical school, were severe in their criticisms of him. Such sensational experiments reflected on the profession, were of doubtful value in any case, and so forth. Though none of these criticisms were released to the public.

The funeral was held on the third day. I attended it out of friendship for Max, who felt it his duty to be present. Fearing's mother was there, of course, dressed in a black outfit that somehow managed to look loud and common. Since the tabloid interview there had been a complete break between her and our group, so that her wailing tirades and nauseous sobbing endearments could only be directed at the empty air and the bronze-fitted casket.

Max looked old. Velda stood beside him, holding his arm. She was as impassive as on the day of Fearing's death.

There was only one odd thing about her behavior. She insisted that we remain at the cemetery until the casket had been placed in the tomb and the workman had fixed in place the marble slab that closed it. She watched the whole process with a dispassionate intentness.

I thought that perhaps she did it on Max's account, to impress on him that the whole affair was over and done with. Or she may conceivably have feared some unlikely final demonstration or foray on the part of the wilder anti-science groups and felt that the presence of a few intelligent witnesses was advisable to prevent some final garish news item from erupting into print.

And there may actually have been justification for such a fear. Despite the efforts of the cemetery authorities, a number of the morbidly curious managed to view the interment and as I accompanied Max and Velda the few blocks to their home, there were altogether too many people roaming the quiet, rather ill-kempt streets of the scantily populated suburb. Undoubtedly we were being followed and pointed at. When with feelings of considerable relief, we finally got inside, there was a sharp, loud knock on the door we had just closed.

Someone had thrown a stone at the house.

For the next six months I saw nothing of Max. Actually this was as much due to my friendship for him as to the press of my work, which did keep me unusually busy at the time. I felt that Max didn't want to be reminded in any way, even by the presence of a friend, of the tragic accident that had clouded his life.

I think, you see, that only I, and perhaps a few of Max's most imaginative colleagues, had any inkling of how hard Max had been hit by the experience and, especially, *why* it had hit him so hard. It wasn't so much that he had caused the death of a man through a perhaps injudicious experiment. That was the smaller part. It was that, in so doing, he had wrecked a line of research that promised tremendous benefits to mankind. Fearing, you see, was irreplaceable. As Max had said, he was probably unique. And their work had been barely begun. Max had obtained almost no results of a measured scientific nature and he hadn't as yet any ideas whatever of the crucial thing: how to impart Fearing's ability to other people, if that were possible. Max was a realist. To his clear, unsuperstitious mind, the death of one man was not nearly so important as the loss of possible benefits to millions. That he had played fast and loose with humanity's future — yes, he'd have put it that way — was, I knew, what hurt him most. It would be a long time before he regained his old enthusiasm.

One morning I ran across a news item stating that Fearing's mother had sold her house and gone for a European tour.

Of Velda I had no information.

Naturally I recalled the affair from time to time, turning it over in my mind. I reviewed the suspicions I'd had at the time, seeking some clue that might have escaped me, but always coming to the conclusion that the suspicions were more than wiped out my Max's tragic sincerity and Velda's composure after the event.

I tried to visualize the weird and miraculous transformations I had witnessed in Max's office. Somehow, try as I might, they began to seem more and more unreal. I had beeen excited that morning, I told myself, and my mind had exaggerated what I had seen. This unwillingness to trust my own memory filled me at times with a strange poignant grief, perhaps similar to what Max must have felt at the breakdown of his research, as if some marvelous imaginative vision had faded from the world.

And occasionally I pictured Fearing as I'd seen him that morning, so radiantly healthy, his mind and body so unshakably knit. It was very hard to think of a man like that being dead.

Then, after six months, I received a brief message from Max. If I were free, would I visit him at his home that evening? Nothing more.

I felt a thrill of elation. Perhaps the period of thralldom to the past was over and the brilliant old mind was getting to work again. I had to break an engagement, but of course I went.

It had just stopped raining when I swung down from the interurban. Remnants of daylight showed a panorama of dripping trees, weed-bordered sidewalks, and gloom-infested houses. Max had happened to build in one of those sub-divisions that doesn't quite make the grade, while the unpredictable pulse of suburban life begins to beat more strongly farther out.

I passed the cemetery in which Fearing had been interred. The branches of unpruned trees brushed the wall, making sections of the sidewalk a leafy tunnel. I was glad I had a flashlight in my pocket for the walk back. It occurred to me that it was unfortunate Max had this unnecessary reminder almost on his doorstep.

I walked rapidly past houses that were more and more frequently separated by empty lots, and along a sidewalk that became progressively more cracked and weed-grown. There popped into my mind a conversation I had with Max a couple of years ago. I had asked him if Velda didn't find it lonely out here, and he had laughingly assured me that both he and Velda had a passion for being alone and like to be as far away as possible from spying neighbors.

I wondered if one of the houses I had passed had been that belonging to the Fearings.

Eventually I arrived at Max's place, a compact two-story dwelling. There were only a few more houses beyond it on the street. Beyond those, I knew, the weeds reigned supreme, the once hopeful sidewalks were completely silted and grown over, and the lamp-poles rusted lightlessly. Unsuccessful subdivisions are dismal spots.

In my nostrils, all the way had been the smell of wet cold earth and stone.

The living room lights were on, but I saw no one through the French window where I had once glimpsed Velda and Fearing. The hall was dark. I rapped on the door. It opened instantly. I faced Velda.

I haven't described Velda. She was one of those very beautiful, dignified, almost forbidding, yet quite sexy girls that a successful, cultured man is apt to marry if he waits until he's middle-aged. Tall. Slim. Small head. Blonde hair drawn tightly across it. Blue eyes. Compact, distinguished features. Sloping shoulders, and then a body that a cynic would call the main attraction. And perhaps with partial inaccuracy, because an alert, well-informed, quite courageous mind went with it. Exquisite manners, but not much apparent warmth.

That was Velda as I remembered her.

The Velda I faced now was different. She was wearing a gray silk dressing gown. In the dim light from the street lamp behind me, the tight-drawn hair looked, not gray, but brittle. The tall beautiful body somehow seemed sterile, weed-like. She crouched like an old woman. The distinguished features in the face she lifted toward mine were pinched. The blue eyes, white circled, were much too staring.

She touched a finger to her thinned lips, and with the other hand timidly took hold of the lapel of my coat, as if to draw me away to some place where we could talk secretly.

Max stepped out of the darkness behind her and put his hand on her shoulders. She didn't stiffen. In fact, she hardly reacted except to softly drop her hand from my coat. She may have winked at me, as if to say, "Later, perhaps," but I can't be sure.

"You'd better be getting upstairs, dear," he said gently. "It's time you took a little rest."

At the foot of the stairs he switched on the light. We watched her as she went up, slowly holding on to the rail.

When she was out of sight Max shook his head and said rather lightly, "Too bad about Velda. I'm afraid that in a little while — However, I didn't ask you out here to talk about that."

I was shocked at his seeming callousness. A moment later, however, he said something which gave me a hint of the philosophy that underlay it.

"We're so mysteriously fragile, Fred. Some slight change in a gland's function, some faint shadow falling on a knot of nerve tissue, and — pouf. And there's nothing we can do about it, because we don't know, Fred, we simply don't know. If we could trace the thoughts in their courses, if we could set their healing magic radiating through the brain — but that's not to be for awhile yet. Meanwhile, there's nothing we can do about it, except to face it cheerfully. Though it is hard when the person whose mind goes develops a murderous hatred of you at the same time. However, as I said, I don't want to talk about that, and you'll please me if you don't either."

We were still standing at the bottom of the stairs. Abruptly he changed his manner, clapped me on the shoulder, steered me into the living room, insisted that I have a drink, and busied himself starting a fire in the open grate, all the while chatting loudly about recent doings at the medical school and pressing me for details of my latest articles.

Then, giving me no time whatever to think, he settled himself in the opposite chair, the fire blazing between us, and launched into a description of a new research project he was getting started on. It concerned the enzymes and the mechanisms of temperature-control of insects, and seemed to have far-reaching implications in fields as diverse as insecticide manufacture and the glandular physiology of human beings.

There were times when he got so caught up in his subject that it almost seemed to me it was the old Max before me, as if all the events of the past year had been a bad dream.

Once he broke off momentarily, to lay his hand on a bulky typescript on the table beside him.

"This is what I've been keeping myself busy with these last few months, Fred," he said quickly. "A complete account of my experiments with Fearing, along with the underlying theories, as well as I can present them, and all pertinent material from other fields. I can't touch the thing again, of course, but I hope someone else will, and I want him to have the benefit of my mistakes. I'm rather doubtful if any of the journals will accept it, but if they don't I'll publish it at my own expense."

It really gave me a pang to think of how much he must have suffered pounding out that typescript, meticulously, of course, knowing that it was the account of a failure and a personal tragedy, knowing that it wouldn't be at all well received by his profession, but feeling duty-bound to pass on information that might some day kindle another mind and prove scientific value to mankind.

And then the tragedy of Velda, which I hadn't yet been able to properly assimilate, with its faint, last-twist-of-the-screw suggestion that if Max had continued his research with Fearing, he might conceivably have learned enough to be able to avert the cloud shadowing her mind.

Yes, I thought then, and I still think, that Max's behavior that night, especially his enthusiasm about his new research project, into which he'd obviously thrown himself wholeheartedly, was an inspiring and at the same time heartrending example of the sort of unsentimental courage you find in the best scientists.

Yet at the same time I had the feeling that his new project wasn't the real reason for his summoning me. He had something very different on his mind, I felt, and as an unhappy person will, was taking himself out on other subjects as a preliminary to getting around to it. After a while he did.

The fire had died down somewhat. We had temporarily exhausted the topic of his new project. I was conscious of having smoked too many cigarettes. I asked Max some inconsequential question about a new advance in aviation medicine.

He frowned at the crawling flames, as if he were carefully weighing his answer. Then abruptly he said, without looking towards me, "Fred, there's something I want to tell you, something I felt I must tell you, but something I haven't been able to bring myself to tell you until now. I hated John Fearing, because I knew he was having a love affair with my wife."

I looked down at my hands. After a moment I heard Max's voice again. It wasn't loud, but it was rough with emotion.

"Oh come on, Fred, don't pretend you didn't know. You saw them through the window that night. You'll be surprised to know, Fred, how hard it was for me not to avoid you, or pick some quarrel with you, after that happened. Just the thought that you knew . . ."

"That's all I did see or know," I assured him. "Just that one glimpse." I turned and looked at him. His eyes were bright with tears.

"And yet you know, Fred," he went on, "that's the real reason I picked you to sit in on our experiments. I felt that knowing what you did, you would be better able than anyone else to check on my relationship with John."

There was one thing I had to say. "You are quite certain, Max, that your suspicions of Velda and Fearing were justified?"

One look at his face told me I needn't press that line of questioning any further. Max sat for a while with his head bowed. It was very quiet. The wind had died which earlier had splattered a few drops from nearby branches against the windowpanes.

Finally he said, "You know, Fred, it's very difficult to recapture lost emotions, either jealousy or scientific zeal. And yet those were the two main ones in this drama. For of course it wasn't until I had begun my experiments with Fearing that I found out about him and Velda." He paused, then went on with difficulty. "I'm afraid I'm not a very broad-minded man, Fred, when it comes to sex and possession. I think that if John had been some ordinary person, or if I had found out earlier, I would have behaved differently. Rather brutally, perhaps, I don't know. But the fact that our experiments had begun, and that they promised so much, changed everything.

"You know, I really try to be a scientist, Fred," he went on with the ghost, or cadaver rather, of a rueful smile. "And as a scientist, or just as a rational man, I had to admit that the possible benefits of our experiments infinitely out-weighed any hurt to my vanity or manhood. It may sound grotesque, but as a scientist I even had to consider whether this love affair wasn't necessary to keep my subject cooperative and in a proper state of mind, and whether I shouldn't go out of my way to further it. As it was, I didn't have to vary my routine in order to give them plenty of opportunities, though I think that if that had been necessary, I might even have done it."

He clenched his fist. "You see, so very much depended on those experiments of ours. Though it's awfully hard for me to remember that now. The feeling's all gone . . . The tremendous vision . . . this typescript here is just dead stuff . . . an obligation . . .

"I feel differently about a lot of things now. About Velda and John, too. Velda wasn't exactly the girl I thought I was marrying. I've realized lately that she had a tremendous need to be adored, a kind of cold lust for beauty and ecstacy, like some pagan priestess. And I cooped her up here — the old story — and tried to feed her on my enthusiasms. Not exactly the right diet. And yet, you know, Fred, my life's work was inspired by Velda to an extent that you might find hard to believe. Even before I'd met Velda. The expectancy of her.

"And John? I don't think anyone will ever know the truth about John. I was only beginning to understand him, and there were sides to his nature I couldn't touch. A remarkable creature. In one sense, a true superman. In another, a mindless animal. Astonishing weaknesses, or blind spots. The influence of his mother. And then the way his instincts and conscience went hand in hand. I feel that John may have been completely sincere both about his desire for Velda and his desire to help me aid mankind. It may never have occurred to him that the two desires didn't exactly go together. It's quite possible he felt that he was being very nice to both of us.

"Yes, and if John and Velda's affair were something that could happen now, I think I would feel very differently about it.

"But then — ? God, Fred, it's so hard to think truthfully about *them!* Then there existed in me, side by side, every moment of the day and night, the highest pinnacles of scientific excitement and the deepest pits of jealous rage. The one strictly subordinated!" A note of passionate anger came into his voice. "For don't think I was weak, Fred. Don't think I ever deviated so much as a hair's-breadth from the course that was scientifically and humanistically right. I kept my hatred for John in absolute check. And when I say that, I mean that. I'm no ignoramus, Fred. I know that when one tries to suppress feelings, they have a way of bursting out through unsuspected channels, due to the trickery of the subconscious mind. Well, I was on the watch for that. I provided every conceivable safeguard. I was fantastically cautious about each experiment. I know it may not have looked that way to you, but even that last one — heavens, we had often done experiments twice as dangerous, or as seemingly dangerous, testing every step of the way. Why,

Soviet scientists have had people technically dead for over five minutes. With John it couldn't have been one!

"And yet . . .

"That's what tormented me so, don't you see, Fred, when I couldn't revive him. The thought that my unconscious mind had somehow tricked me and opened a channel for my all-too-conscious hatred, found a chink in the wall that I'd neglected to stop up, a doorway unguarded for a second. As he lay there dead before my eyes, I was tortured by the conviction that there was some little thing that would revive him at once if only I could remember what it was.

"Some little mistake or omission I'd made, which only had to be thought of to be corrected, but which my subconscious mind wouldn't let me remember. I felt that if only I could have relaxed my mind completely — but of course that was the one thing I couldn't do.

"I tried every way I knew to revive John, I reviewed every step I'd taken without finding a flaw, and yet that feeling of guilt persisted.

"Everything seemed to intensify it. Velda's frozen, suicidal calm, worse than the bitterest and most tempestuous accusations. The most childish things — even that silly occultist with his talk of a deathwatch on John.

"How John must hate me, I'd tell myself irrationally. Commanded to be dead, tricked into dying, not given the faintest hint of what was intended.

"And Velda. Never a reproachful word to me. Just freezing up, more and more, until her mind began to whither.

"And John. That miraculous body rotting in the tomb. Those magnificently knit muscles and nerves, falling apart cell by cell."

Max slumped in his chair exhausted. The last flame in the grate flickered out and the embers began to smoke. The silence was deadly.

And then I began to talk. Quietly. Nothing brilliant. I merely reviewed what I knew and what Max had told me. Pointed out how, being the scientist he was, he couldn't have done anything but what he did. Reminded him of how he'd checked and double-checked his every action. Showed him that he hadn't the shred of reason for feeling guilty any longer.

And finally my talk began to take effect, though, as Max said, "I don't think it's anything you've said. I've been all over that. It's that at last I've unburdened myself to someone. But I do feel better."

And I'm sure he did. For the first time I truly sensed the old Max in him. Battered and exhausted of course, and deeply seared by a new wisdom, but something of the old Max, nevertheless.

"You know," he said, sinking back in his chair, "I think I can really relax now for the first time in six months."

Immediately the silence settled down again. I remember thinking, queerly, that it was dreadful that a place could be so silent.

The fire had stopped smoking. Its odor had been replaced by that seeping in from the outside — the smell of cold wet earth and stone.

My taut muscles jerked spasmodically at the sudden grating of Max's chair against the floor. His face was ghastly. His lips formed words, but only choking sounds came out. Then he managed to get control of his voice.

"The cue! The cue for him to come alive again! I forgot I changed the signals. I thought it was still — "

He tore a pencil from his pocket and rapped on the arm of the chair: three — one.

"But it should have been — " and he rapped: three — two.

It is hard for me to describe the feeling that went through me as he rapped that second signal.

The intense quiet had something to do with it. I remember wishing that some other sound would break in — the patter of raindrops, the creaking of a beam, the hollow surge of the interurban.

Just five little raps, unevenly spaced, but imbued with a quality, force, and rhythm that was Max's and nobody else's in the world — as individual as his fingerprint, as inimitable as his signature.

Just five little raps — you'd think they'd be lost in the walls, gone in a second. But they say that no sound, however faint, ever dies. It becomes weaker and weaker as it dissipates, the agitations of the molecules less and less, but still it goes on to the end of the world and back, to the end of eternity.

I pictured that sound struggling through the walls, bursting into the night air with an eager upward sweep, like a black insect, darting through the wet tangled leaves, soaring crazily into the moist tattered clouds, perhaps dipping inquisitively to circle one of the rusted lamppoles, before it streaked purposefully off along the dark street, up, up, over the trees, over the wall, and then swooped down toward wet cold earth and stone.

And I thought of Fearing, not yet quite rotted in his tomb.

Max and I looked at each other.

There came a piercing, blood-chilling scream from over our heads.

A moment of paralyzed silence. Then the wild clatter of footsteps down the stairs in the hall. As we sprang up together, the outside door slammed.

We didn't exchange a word. I stopped in the hall to snatch up my flashlight.

When we got outside we couldn't see Velda. But we didn't ask each other any questions as to which direction she'd taken.

We started to run. I caught sight of Velda almost a block ahead.

I'm not in too bad physical condition. I slowly drew ahead of Max as we ran. But I couldn't lessen the distance between myself and Velda. I could see her quite plainly as she passed through the pools of light cast by the street lamps. With the gray silk dressing gown flying out behind her, she sometimes looked like a skimming bat.

I kept repeating to myself, "But she couldn't have heard what we were saying. She couldn't have heard those raps."

Or could she?

I reached the cemetery. I shone my flashlight down the dark, leafy tunnel. There was no one in sight, but almost halfway down the block I noticed branches shaking where they dipped to the wall.

I ran to that point. The wall wasn't very high. I could lay my hand on its top. But I felt broken glass. I stripped off my coat, laid it over the top, and pulled myself up.

My flashlight showed a rag of gray silk snagged on a wicked barb of glass near my coat.

Max came up gasping. I helped him up the wall. We both dropped down inside. The grass was very wet. My flashlight wandered over wet, pale stones. I tried to remember where Fearing's tomb was. It couldn't.

We started to hunt. Max began to call, "Velda! Velda!"

I suddenly thought I remembered the layout of the place. I pushed on hurriedly. Max lagged behind, calling.

There was a muffled crash. It sounded some distance away. I couldn't tell the direction. I looked around uncertainly.

I saw that Max had turned back and was running. He vanished around a tomb.

I hurried after him as fast as I could, but I must have taken the wrong turning. I lost him.

I raced futilely up and down two aisles of tombstones and tomb. I kept flashing my light around, now near, now far. It showed pale stone, dark trees, wet grass, gravel path.

I heard a horrible, deep, gasping scream — Max's.

I ran wildly. I tripped over a headstone and sprawled flat on my face.

I heard another scream — Velda's. It went on and on.

I raced down another aisle.

I thought I would go on for ever, and forever hearing that scream, which hardly seemed to pause for inhalation.

Then I came around a tangled clump of trees and saw them.

My flashlight wavered back and forth across the scene twice before I dropped it.

They were there, all three of them.

I know that the police have a very reasonable explanation for what I saw, and I know that explanation must be right, if there is any truth in what we have been taught to believe about mind and body and death. Of course there are always those who will not quite believe, who will advance other theories. Like Max, with his experiments.

The only thing the police can't decide for certain is whether Velda managed to break into the tomb and open the casket unaided — they did find a rusty old screwdriver nearby — or whether tomb and casket hadn't been broken into at an earlier date by some sort of cultists or, more likely, pranksters inspired by cultists. They have managed to explain away almost completely, all evidence that tomb and casket were burst from the inside.

Velda can't tell them. Her mind is beyond reach.

The police have no doubts whatsoever about Velda's ability to strangle Max to death. After all, it took three strong men to get her out of the cemetery. And it is from my own testimony that the police picked up Max's statement that Velda hated him murderously.

The odd position of Fearing's remains they attribute to some insane whim on Velda's part.

And of course, as I say, the police must be right. The only thing against their theory is the raps. And of course I can't make them understand just how tremendously significant those raps of Max's, that diabolic three — two, seemed to me at the time.

I can only tell what I saw, in the flashlight's wavering gleam.

The marble slab closing Fearing's tomb had fallen forward. The tomb was open.

Velda was backed against the tombstone opposite it. Her gray silk dressing gown was wet and torn to ribbons. Blood dribbled from a gash above her knee. Her blond hair streamed down tangledly. Her features were contorted. She was staring down at the space between herself and Fearing's tomb. She was still screaming.

There before her, in the wet grass, Max lay on his back. His head was twisted backward.

And across the lower part of Max's body, the half-fleshed fingers stretching toward his throat, the graveclothes clinging in tatters to the blackened, shrunken body, was all that was left of Fearing.

The Thirteenth Step

The leader cut short the last chuckles of laughter by measuredly spanking the rostrum with the flat of his hand. He grinned broadly at the forty-or-so people occupying, along with their ashtrays and coffee cups, the half dozen rows of folding chairs facing him.

He said, "If anyone came here tonight thinking that the life story of an alcoholic couldn't be hilariously funny as well as heart-breakingly tragic, I imagine he changed his mind after the pitch we just heard. Any way you slice it, it's a Happy Program — sometimes even slaphappy."

His face grew serious. He said, "Our last speaker is a gal. She's surprisingly young, just out of her teens. Some of the old timers used to think you couldn't make the Program until you'd drunk your way through a dozen jobs and four or five wives and light housekeepers — or husbands! — but they've had to change their minds in recent years. This gal's only been on the Program a short time — two months — but I heard her make a great pitch at the open meetings last week. She'd so new she still gets a little emotionally disturbed from time to time — " (He paused for a brief warning frown, his eyes roving) "but I asked her about it and she told me that as long as she knows we're all pulling for her everything'll be all right. So without more ado— "

A pucker-mouthed woman with hennaed hair in the second row whispered loudly to her neighbor, "If she's that disturbed, she ought to be in a mental hospital, not an A.A. meeting."

Faces turned. The room grew very still. The leader glared steadily at the woman with the hennaed hair. She tilted her chin at him and said loudly, "I was speaking of someone else." He frowned at her skeptically, nodded once more, then put on the big grin and said, "So without more ado I'll turn the meeting over to Sue! I'm sure she's got a great message for us. Let's give her a big hand."

Forty-or-so people pounded their palms together — some enthusiastically, some dutifully, but only the woman with hennaed hair abstaining completely — as a thin ash-blonde in a dark green dress rose from the last row and made her way to the rostrum with the abstracted deliberateness of a sleepwalker. As the leader stepped back and aside for her, he simultaneously smiled warmly, sketched a bow and gave her elbow a reassuring squeeze. She nodded her thanks without looking at him. He seated himself in an empty chair at the end of the front row, switching around enough so that he had the hennaed woman within view.

Looking straight in front of her, just over the heads of her audience, the ash-blonde said in a low but somewhat harsh voice, "My name is Sue and I'm an alcoholic."

"Hi, Sue," a score-or-so voices responded, some brightly, some dully.

Sue did not immediately start her pitch. Instead she slowly swung her face from side to side, her gaze still just brushing the tops of her audience's heads with the suggestion of a heavy machine gun ranging over an enemy crouched in foxholes. Never smiling, she looked back and forth — from the inappropriate "Come Dressed as Beatniks" party poster of some other organization on the right hand wall across the leader's and the other assorted heads to the left hand wall where a row of open doors let in the balmy night and the occasional low growl of a passing car beyond the wide lawn and shrubbery. Then just as the pause was becoming unbearable —

"I accepted you people and your Twelve Steps only because I was frightened to death," Sue said with measured, almost mannered intensity. "Every day I dwelt with fear. Every hour I knew terror. Every night I slept — blacked out, that is — with horror! Believe me I know what it means to drink with desperation because the Fifth Horseman is waiting outside for me in the big black car with the two faceless drivers."

"Oh, one of those," the hennaed woman could be heard to say. She tossed her head as the leader scowled at her sharply from his seat by the inner wall.

Sue did not react except that the knuckles of her hands grasping the side of the rostrum grew white. She continued, "I had my first snort of hard liquor at the age of seven — brandy for a toothache. I liked it. I liked what it did for me. From that day on I snitched liquor whenever and wherever I could get it. The way was made easy for me because both of my parents were practicing alcoholics. By the age of thirteen I had passed over the invisible line and I was a confirmed alcoholic myself, shakes, morning drink, blackouts, hidden bottles, sleeping pills and all."

A gaunt-faced man in the third row folded his arms across his chest, creaked his metal chair and snorted skeptically. The hennaed woman quickly looked back to him with an emphatic triple nod, then smiled triumphantly at the anxious-eyed leader as she faced front again.

Sue did not take direct note of either of her hecklers, but she sent her next remarks skimming just above the silvery thatch of the gaunt-faced man.

"Why is it that even you people find difficulty in accepting the child alcoholic?" she said. "Children can do everything bad that adults can do. Children can formulate dark evil plots. Children can suffer obsessions and compulsions. Children can go insane. Children can commit suicide. Children can torture. Children can commit . . . yes! my dear friends . . . murder!"

" — self-dramatizing little . . . herself."

Ignoring the mostly indistinct whisper, Sue took a slow deep breath and continued, "I emphasize murder because soon after my thirteenth year I was to be subjected, again and again, to that hideous temptation. You see, by the time I was fifteen the big black car had begun to draw up and park in front of my home every afternoon at four thirty — or so soon as I had managed to snitch my first four or five drinks of the day."

" — just can't stand the scare-you-to-death school!" The last part of the hennaed woman's whisper to her neighbor came across very clearly. The neighbor, a white-haired woman with rimless glasses, went so far as to nod briefly and cover the other's hand reassuringly yet warningly.

The knuckles of Sue's hands grasping the sides of the rostrum grew white again. She went on, "I knew who was waiting in that car, invisible between the two faceless drivers. You people often speak of the Four Horsemen of Fear, Frustration, Disillusionment, and Despair. You seldom mention the Fifth Horseman, but you know that he's always there."

" — can't stand the let's-share-my-aberration school either!"

"And I knew whom he was waiting for! I knew that some afternoon, or some evening, or very late some night — for the big black car stayed there at the curb until the first gray ray of morning — I knew that I would have to walk out to it and get inside and drive away with him to his dark land. But I also knew that it would not be that easy for me, not nearly that easy."

For the first time Sue smiled at her audience — a lingering half-tranced smile. "You see, my dear friends, I knew that if I ever went out to the car, before we could drive away I would first have to bring *him* and the two faceless drivers back into the house and take away with us my mother, my father, my brothers, my sister and whomever else happened to be inside on however innocent a pretext."

"Look, I came here to an A. A. meeting, not to listen to ghost stories." All of the hennaed woman's whisper was quite audible this time. There was a general disapproving murmur, possibly shot here and there with approval.

Sue seemed to have difficulty going on. She took three deep, heaving breaths, not quite looking at the hennaed woman. The leader started to get up, but just then —

"*That* is why I had to drink," Sue resumed strongly. "That is why I had to keep my brain numbed with alcohol, day after day, month after month. Yet that is also why I feared to drink, for if I blacked out at the wrong time I might walk out to the car unknowing. That is why I drank, fearing to!

"Let me tell you, my friends, that big black car became the realest thing in my life. Hour after hour I'd sit at the window, watching it, getting up only to sneak a drink. Sometimes it would change into a big black tiger with glossy fur lying by the curb with his jaw on his folded paws, occupying all the space a parked car would and a little more, looking almost like a black Continental except that every hour or so he'd swing his great green eyes up toward me. At those times the two faceless drivers would turn black as ebony, with silver turbans and silver loin-cloths — "

"Purple, if you ask me!"

"But whether I saw it as a black tiger or a black car, it regularly drew up at my curb every evening or night. It got so that by the time I was seventeen, it came even on the rare days when I couldn't get a drink or hold one down."

Just at that moment a passing car, growling more softly than others, became silent, as if its motor had been switched off, followed by the faintest dying whisper of rubber on asphalt, as if it had parked just outside, beyond the dark lawn and shrubs.

"She's got confederates!" the hennaed woman whispered with a flash of sour humor. Two or three people giggled nervously.

At last Sue looked straight into her adversary's eyes. "I prayed to a god I didn't believe in that *I* wouldn't become a confederate! — that *he* wouldn't trick me into leading him and the two faceless drivers inside." Her gaze left the hennaed woman and ranged just over their heads again. "The Fifth Horseman is tricky, you know, he's endlessly subtle. I talked with him in my mind for hours at a time as I sat at the window watching him invisible in the car. When I first learned to tell time and found there was twelve hours, he told me he was the thirteenth. Later, when I learned that some people count twenty-four hours, he told me he was the twenty-fifth. When they instructed me at church that there were three persons in the godhead, he told me he was the fourth — "

"I don't think I can stand much more of this. And flouting religion — " The hennaed woman half rose from her chair, her neighbor clinging to her arm, trying to draw her down again.

Three more heaving breaths and Sue continued, though seeming to speak with the greatest difficulty, "The Fifth Horseman *still* talks to me. You know our Twelve Steps, from the First where we admit we are powerless over alcohol, to the Twelfth, where we try to carry the Message to others. We sometimes joke about a Thirteenth Step — where we carry the Message to someone because we've got a crush on them, or for some other illegitimate reason — but *he* tells me that *he* is the Thirteenth Step, which I will someday be forced to take no matter how earnestly I try to avoid it!"

"No, I cannot stand any more of this! I refuse to!" The hennaed woman spoke out loud at last, shaking off her neighbor's hand and standing up straight. She made no move to leave, just faced the rostrum.

The leader stood up too, angry-browed, and started toward her, but just then —

"I'm sorry," Sue said quickly, looking at them all, "I really am," and she walked rapidly to the door opposite the rostrum and into the night.

For three or four seconds nobody did a thing. Then the leader started after her past the rostrum, taking long strides, but when he got a few feet short of the open doors, he suddenly checked and turned around.

"Where's her sponsor?" he called toward the back of the room. "She said her sponsor was bringing her to the meeting. It would be a lot better if her sponsor went out and talked to her now, rather than me."

No one stepped forward. The hennaed woman chuckled knowingly, "I wouldn't admit to being her sponsor after *that* performance. If you ask me, it'll be a lot better if she just keeps on walking until the police pick her up and throw her in the psycho ward!"

"Nobody's asking you!" the leader rasped. "Look, everybody, I suppose the next best thing would be if a couple of you ladies would go out after her and quietly talk to her . . ."

The half dozen or so other women in the room looked around at each other, but none of them moved.

"If you're . . . well . . . nervous," the leader said, "I suppose a couple of the guys could go out with you . . ."

The thirty-odd men in the room looked at each other. None of them moved either.

"Oh my God," the leader said disgustedly and himself started to turn, though somewhat slowly, toward the huge rectangle of darkness just behind him.

"You'll just be making a big fool of yourself, Charlie Pierce," the hennaed woman said stingingly.

"Look here," he retorted angrily, whirling back toward her a bit eagerly, "you're the one who's been making fools and worse of us all and of the Program. You're — "

He got no further. The hennaed woman, staring mad-eyed and mouth a-grimace over his shoulder, had started to scream. The others in the room, following her gaze, took it up.

The leader looked around.

Then he screamed too.

The Repair People

Ann looked at the mutilated big gray clay figure bedded in pale yellow excelsior in the coffin-size shipping crate that came jerking in and bumped to a stop before Jack and her. Its crude man-shape, its tortured muteness, and in particular the signs stenciled on its partly-dismembered sections — FOOT, KNEE, GENITALS, BELLY — squeezed tears from her eyes.

"The poor guy, what he must have been through," she managed to get out.

Jack kicked the crate.

He said, "Whatever shape he's in, he brought it on himself. First lesson for apprentices down here: you can't be sympathetic."

Ann fought back outrage. Jack didn't seem to have just the professional unfeeling of a journeyman, but personal vindictiveness too. She wished she's never seen that ad: HELP THE POOR BLOBS, THEY NEED YOU, BECOME A REPAIR PERSON. She wished she'd strangled the surge of idealism it had roused in her. Besides, the remembered advertisement kept blurring and changing words and spellings in her mind.

"Those stencils now," Jack was saying, "they just show what the guy was thinking of when he fouled up. I'll give you a clue: it wasn't other people."

He squatted by the hacked gray shoulders and ran his eye from end to clay end.

"God has it easy, He only has to create 'em." He looked sideways down the line of crates. "Gotta get started!"

Stiffening two fingers and bracing them with a thumb, he suddenly drove them down in an obscene karate blow knuckle-deep in the clay forehead two inches above the blind eyes. Wet grayness splashed like mud. He swiftly jerked his fingers out.

"Stung me," he mumbled, sucking the tips. He eyed Ann. "That's a good sign."

The clay head vibrated. Something small and dark and round and heavy-looking like a musket ball came buzzing out of the hole and hovered like a horsefly. Ann shrank away. Barely glancing at its zig-zag path, Jack snatched up a close-meshed butterfly net and snagged it at arm's stretch, instantly flipping the metal hoop to confine it. Then he laid the net down beside him. From time to time the dark thing hummed enraged and humped the netting as it tunneled about under the net, seeking escape.

"The psyche? The consciousness?" Ann quavered. Then, more soft-ly still, "His soul? A bit of God?"

"You name it, kid," Jack quipped. "Here, smooth these out."

He was handing her swiftly, one by one, brightly colored gossamer films he was drawing out of the widening hole in the clay head, like a stage magician taking silk handkerchiefs out of a fishbowl.

They rippled and tugged irrationally as she smoothed and tried to flatten them — a mischievous spectrum, blue as Heaven, red as Hell, all colors. As she spread them out on the surgically gleaming table, she got the impression that there were fantastically detailed pictures lined on them, but she was unable to study them, it was all she could do to keep up with Jack. (Straighten out there! Lie down, damn you!) Journeymen seemed to have one working speed, apprentices another. Soon there were enough square films for a rainbow chessboard.

"Dreams," Jack told her. "Crumpled spectral planes inside the skull. Angel dreams. Devil dreams. Wrapping the core — " he touched with his elbow the bump in the buzzing net —"to soothe it. Comfiest blan-keting. No wonder when it got away from them and snagged in the black unconsciousness it bezerked!" He shoved his hand wrist-deep in the clay, swivelled his fingers around all the way, paused, then with-drew a wet-looking black silk bag. "There! — that's the lot! Get ready a three by five inch one-way frontal window."

"What color? — on the opaque side?" she asked, shuffling through the frontal blanks in her bin.

"Flesh, what'd you think?" he told her with heavy patience. "Now lemme see." As she trimmed the blank to size by eye, he swiftly selected four films from the rainbow field, then dove his other hand into the humping net and captured the dark thing there. The buzzing grew louder. He winced but didn't let go as he wrapped it up orderly in the films, like a bumblebee in silk handkerchiefs, changing his hold on it at every moment.

"Gotta keep it well wrapped and comforted," he explained. "The power of illusion." (Ann noted the angry buzz had sunk almost to a purring) "Yellow for sunlight and kicks," he said of the first and outmost film as he checked them off. Then, "Blue for the sky and God. Green for the forest and deeps. Red for blood and danger. There, that's the bunch." He carefully replaced the four-times-wrapped packet, as if setting it on a central needlepoint inside the clay skull. To Ann's surprise it stayed there, humming softly. Then with a sweep of his long arm Jack gathered together all the other films and crumpled them swiftly into the wet black silk bag and tossed it after the packet. It hung in the hole a moment, a puffy cushion, then fell — or was sucked — out of sight.

"You gotta put back every least thing you take out," he told Ann. "There's another basic for you. And you gotta leave 'em unconscious. We'll hope that this time the surplus dreams stay there. Now gimme that window."

As Jack fitted the flexible pane into the clay, Ann said, grieving at the uncouth gray, "He'll never be able to hide his mind from the outside now. Not for the tiniest time."

Jack said, "Nope."

The advert flared in Ann's memory: BE A HELP PERSON, REPAIR THE SLOBS, THEY HURT. Oh, why, why had she . . .? She asked, "How'll he ever be able to sleep with the light always coming in his forehead?"

Jack said, "He can go in the real dark if he has to. Not everything's a motel with pale curtains."

Ann said, "But in the day with the sunlight or bright glows always pouring down it'll be so hot."

Jack shrugged. "Better to burn than go bats, kid."

He got the flesh-colored window flush in the gray clay and pressed that flat, making a seal. He touched a button and blue light pulsed on the gray clay. Then he leaned back and said, "Arba da Carba."

Ann asked, "Who's that?"

Jack said, "Not who, what, kid. Say it backwards. God doesn't use words at all, just breath."

The hacked clay worked rhythmically and grew smooth — and pink as the window in its forehead. Its eyes opened and rolled blindly from side to side. Its mouth gaped and it began to breath noisily. The left corner of its mouth started to convulse in a two-second tic. Ann watched with wonder, then her expression became one of staring hopelessness and distaste.

"Oh why," she asked, "oh why did they ever decide to replace most regular people with these miserable globs?"

"Because they're cheaper," Jack told her. "They don't cause trouble, they don't rebel, they just suffer. And they never die, they only break down."

The crate slid away and was replaced by another. Ann continued to stare.

"Break's over, let's get going," Jack barked, placing his fisted hand, thumb turned down, over the new shape's livid brow. What's a matter, kid, you got something better to do?"

Black Has Its Charms

Hello, dear, I've got something I want to tell you, a really brilliant idea. No, don't get out of bed, I'm unused to such courtesies and it's too late for you to start them now. Just stay tucked in there like a cozy little infant and I'll sit here on the edge. You wouldn't deny me the edge of your bed, would you?

Yes, I've been wandering around the house in the dark, creeping around it noiselessly like a maniac. I know you didn't say "maniac" but you thought it, I know everything you think. Well, it simply happens that I enjoy silence and darkness, like any sensitive person, and I can't stand the bright lights you surround yourself with like a boulevard. I know that to preserve your mental health you have to read in bed, but — that's better, dear, thank you, that's almost soothing, though I'm sure you didn't mean to be considerate. The world should end first!

No, I'm not drinking. I'm just taking a little wine, a tiny sip now and then, for my raw throat. You wouldn't deny me a little wine, would you, the beverage of civilization? You wouldn't deny me a little gaiety and laughter? Of course you would. You stamp on every spark of gaiety that ever comes to a feeble glow in me. The whole twenty years of our marriage you've done nothing but deny me things. You lie awake nights figuring them out. I could be dying of pneumonia and you wouldn't give me the corner of your blanket. No, I wouldn't get in bed with you if you were the last man on earth. And don't plead, it ill becomes you.

Cold? Of course it's cold and of course I'm chilly! That's why I put on this coat — haven't you any brains in your head at all? Though why I should expect this miserable, worn, ink-dabbed rab-

185

bit skin to keep me warm I don't know — you've got a point there, you really have.

Another man might find me attractive, of course. Black lace night-gown (ripped a little in front — you once had some spirit), black-feathered high-heeled mules, and a black panther coat (another man might-n't know it was lapin) — why, it's the high school boy's dream. They wouldn't mind that I was older than some of their mothers. I've learned a lot about their tastes from your son's friends.

So I look like the vampire lady in the Charles Addams cartoons? Thank you dear, it shows there's at least some romance left in you, I mean imagination — romance died in you long ago, you're an old man before your time. No, don't start making approaches designed to soothe me and to square your own guilty conscience. I'm on to those and they mean less to me than a leer from a fat dirty janitor. Besides, I have this brilliant idea I want to tell you about, though I can sense already that you don't want to hear it. But you're going to, so dig the wax out of your ears (I won't be shocked, I have to watch you pick your nose) and listen very carefully because I'm only going to tell you once, I don't like having to cast my pearls before swine.

This is it: why don't you kill me? Why don't you murder me in some subtle way that the police will never suspect? It's really the best solution for you, dear — at one stroke you'll be rid of your biggest problem and able to marry a younger, more attractive woman, a high school girl if you like, some elfin child. And I'd appreciate it, I truly would, I'd be eternally grateful.

No, I'm being purely logical and coldly rational about it, the way you always pretend to be but never are. You and Bertrand Russell. You hate me, to you I'm an ugly old witch, you want to get rid of me. And I want to die, it would be the most wonderful thing that could ever happen to me now. You forever prate about logic, why not practice it for once?

So you won't even kill me, you won't even do that one little thing for me?

It isn't practical? How like you to return me such a cold answer, how like your frightened, gutless, old-maid mind. The scientist — excuse me, dear, I mean the technical editor, I forgot your modesty and your worship of accuracy. You kill all romance but you're scared to kill me. Yet you always know exactly what to say to kill my soul. You know how to quench every good idea I get, every least little inspiration.

I'm crazy, am I? No, you didn't, but your lips started to form the word. Or am I merely disgustingly drunk, is that the explanation of my behavior you've picked for tonight? Or drunk *and* crazy?

Yes, I'm pouring myself some brandy, it's nothing but simmered-down wine. Watch your tongue and your looks too or I'll pour myself a tumblerful and drink it straight down and then your blood will be on your own head. I have to give myself a little brandy, you won't give me anything.

Yet when I think of the things I've given you, the love, the devotion, the loyalty, the backing-up, the opportunities (that you muffed or passed up) for better jobs and money and advancement —

You didn't know that I was responsible for those, that they were my doing? Who else but me brought into your life and our home those men who tried to help you and whom you scorned? Your sainted mother? The scummy friends you had before I knew you? It is to laugh. Listen, dear, I've got more news for you: it was your ego that got flattered, but it wasn't you those men were interested in, it was me — I was the reason they came so eagerly — I, the skinny old witch in a black lace nightgown, the high school boy's dream of a whore. Now I wish I'd slept with them all, like they wanted me to. But no, I guarded your honor in those days, how well you'll never know. I might have had to sleep with a couple of them if you'd accepted their generous offers, but you didn't. You saved my virtue, dear; isn't your smug little Midwestern conscience pleased with itself to discover that after all these years?

Just the same I should have slept with them, it would have been little enough recompense for the women I've got for you. That's right, hit me! Or threaten to hit me — you've lost courage for the act itself.

But whether you hit me or just threaten to hit me (you make a brave sight, you know, you only outweigh me by a hundred and forty pounds) you can't change the facts. I got you women. I surrounded you with lots of young beautiful women. My best friends told me I was crazy, but I did. And why? — go ahead, hit me, I dare you! — simply because you came to me and in so many words asked me to get them for you so your ego would be built up and you wouldn't go crazy or kill yourself at your own lack of courage and virility and success. Well, I "made life more interesting" for you, all right. I got you dozens of women and then you didn't have the courage to take most of them after I'd got them for you. (Be very careful when you hit me, be careful to kill me, make sure in your own mind first that you're going through with it to the bitter end, because if you hit me and don't kill me I'll scream the house down.) What did you want me to do about those women you couldn't take for the asking, undress them for you? As it was, I practically pushed them into your bed.

I was too crude about it, was I, too obvious? Well, that's a big laugh. What do you think sex is, a tea party, a breathless jolly little reception for the new minister? I got you the women, that was enough, I left you to furnish the music — and the manhood. It was disgusting enough having to do it without having to paint the whole thing over with a lot of glossy nobility and pink salve for your guilt — no, in all conscience you couldn't have expected me to do that.

I misunderstood you? You actually never wanted me to get you other women? How you have the nerve to even fumble with such a lie after all these years I'll never know. Brother, you should have seen yourself in the old days pleading with me for "excitement" (you called it), I really wished I had some way of making you see it. I knew your every thought then, expressed or unexpressed, as well as I do now. You wanted other women. You wanted me to get them for you.

But you don't want them anymore, eh? You'd like me to "change" and "get nice" again? You've reformed so why don't I? Brother, you can't force a woman to become a procuress and then turn her back into a wife again just by wishing. There are some changes in human nature that even a sainted rationalist like you can't reverse. Did you know — you, who know everything — that once a man's been made a priest, even the Pope can't take it away from him, that no matter what sins he commits, what enormous crimes, he's a priest for life? Well, it's the same with a woman after she's been made a whore and procuress, a scrawny old madam in feathered black mules and a ratty old black fur coat. What's done cannot be undone. It's too late for me to get nice, much too late.

Still, I suppose I should have gone ahead and done it, I did everything else. I suppose I should have stayed at your side after I got you into bed with them, sat on the edge of your bed and patted your wrist as you made love to them and told you every five minutes that it was "all right." Or maybe I should have made love to them for you, maybe I should have crawled into the bed and made love to them while you watched, maybe that's what you wanted.

No, I won't lower my voice and I won't stop pacing either! I've listened attentively to your ranting and watched you pacing night after endless night — now you can put up with mine for a change. Don't try to stop me or I'll shout it from the housetops and I'll stamp on the roof!

Yes, that's what I should have done, I can see it now. I saved you from mental breakdown in a thousand other ways, shoring up your ego so you wouldn't take a knife and cut your throat (I wish I'd let you), so I should have gone on saving your sanity even when you were in the act of fouling your nest. Here's a girl, dear. It's all right. Put your arms around her. It's all right. Kiss her, no really kiss her. It's all right. Climb into bed. It's all right — I'll tuck you both in. It's all right, it's all right, it's all right!

Chanting and pacing are signs of insanity? Only maniacs make with sing-song? Be careful, be very careful, or I'll start telling people a few of the symptoms of insanity I've observed in you. No, I won't tell you what they are, that's my secret, one of my secrets, but wouldn't your best friends agree that you were insane, evilly insane, if I told them half of what I've been telling you now about your past behavior? Sing-song, eh? Why . . . Pour me a drink, my throat's raw.

Pour me a drink, I say, or I'll throw this glass through the window! I don't care if you and your scummy friends call me a wino behind my back — wine and brandy are the drinks of civilized people and what ignorant reformers say doesn't alter it. That's better.

Sing-song, eh? What would your best friends think if I went on to tell them about all your sing-song girls, especially the one who actually did go crazy because you wouldn't make love to her enough after I got her for you? That's right, kill me!

So you won't kill me? You won't even do me a little favor like that? I always knew you were selfish, a cheapskate and a miser, but I never realized how much until tonight. Why I can think of any number of ways you could murder me quite safely — because that's the real reason you won't kill me, isn't it? — you're afraid you'd be found out and punished — hanged or gassed or fried. Why, you could poison me tonight after getting me drunk (there's arsenic in the basement) and blame it on stomach trouble and my alcoholism — half the people who murder with arsenic get away with it. Or you could take me on a mountain vacation and find a lonely cliff and push me off —

there'd be no one but yourself to say I didn't slip. Or rent a canoe and drown me in some mountain lake — I think I could even conquer my fear of water if I were sure I was going to be given the peace of death. Or just smash my skull now and throw me down the stairs — if I'm as big an alcoholic as you say I am and if as many people know it as you say do, you'll have no trouble convincing the police that I got drunk and fell. Remember to snag the torn lining of this raggedy coat around the heel of my slipper and tear off one of my fingernails in the split of the railing.

But you won't, will you, although I've lined it out for you as I wouldn't need to for a two-year old? You'd like to, but you haven't the nerve. You're afraid your courage would break at the sticking point. You're afraid you'd blush or babble when it came to telling a simple lie to the police afterwards and sticking to it. You know you wouldn't have the simple guts to bravely play the part of the murderer *after* the murder. Why? Hah! *I* wouldn't be there to bolster your ego.

No, I don't want a cigarette. You can't shut me up that way. I'll say and drink and wear what I want. I'll go out and scream in the street if I want. I'll lay down in front of the first man who comes along — he'll be better than you.

He'd be revolted at the way I look? Well, I can't say I'd blame him if he turned up his nose at these rags — torn nightdress, moth-eaten mules, black rabbit fur. Pity the poor woman whose husband can't buy her decent clothes to whore in.

Still, I wouldn't be too sure. Other men aren't as dead below the belt as you are and black has its charms. Some day I'm going to have everything black, I'll have a black room with black mirrors, I'll drink black velvet and eat caviare on pumpernickel (that'll be exotic, that'll get the high school boys) and black currant jam with really burnt steak, and I'll black myself all over with shoe polish. Black blood will come out of my throat when you cut it — that'll be a surprise for you. There'll be lots of surprises for you, you'll find out then, surprises that I've been preparing for you for years. You aren't by any chance getting a little afraid of me now, are you, dear? No, I won't tell you what the surprises are, you'll have to kill me to find out. I will tell you one thing: I've left certain letters with certain people, to be opened when I die. I won't tell you what's in them — maybe good advice for you, the best high schools to find exotic girls in, things like that.

I do hope you marry another woman, I really do. I'd like to be around to watch. Here's a warning: another woman won't put up with one twentieth of the things I have. And a younger woman will want even more of what you won't be able to give at all, because I won't be there to sit on the edge of the bed and pat your wrists and tell you it's all right.

But you won't, I know. You'll never marry again. You'll just be a pansy, a mother's boy, and live with other pansies. I wish you joy of it.

Oh, darling, what's happened to us? What's happened to the other times that were so good or seemed so good, why can't we go back to them, why can't we have them any more? Pour me another drink — no, don't come any closer, reach with the bottle. Thank you.

What's happened to you? You used to be so gay and romantic. Now you won't even crack a joke, you're always gloomy, always serious, priding yourself that you won't take a drink. Couldn't you lighten up for one minute, one second? Couldn't you do that little thing for me? No, don't try! I forbid you to try! — it would just be pretense and I hate your pretense worst of all. Sooner than having you pretend to be gay (like a Sunday school teacher trying to say a dirty word) I'd have you sitting there like a lump on a log (a big greasy lump) reveling in the fact that you don't drink any more. Let me tell you that your friends, your real friends, have only contempt for you because you won't drink, the deepest contempt. They're bored to death with your reformation and so am I.

You've become idealistic? Hah! I've news for you, dear, you've always been idealistic, as you call it, and your idealism has been the smelliest part of you because you've never had the courage to live up to it. Remember the War and how you didn't have the courage to be either a pacifist *or* a soldier? — you crawled out of that pretty neatly with your defense job and your idea of preserving another sane man for the future. But was it a sane man that you preserved, dear, I ask you? Remember how you refused to hitch up with the socialists and fight for equality and the underdog? — and then blamed it on me, said you were catering to my prejudices? Why, you were so idealistic that even the church wasn't good enough for you. And when you finally got up the nerve to admit to yourself that you wanted to go to bed with other women, you had to butter it up with a lot of idealism about how we were all bright big beautiful people who made their own rules and about how everyone should love everyone else.

Well, I happen to know how deep your love for some of those other women actually went, because as soon as they started to leave their husbands for you, or have nervous breakdowns, or make demands that any normal woman would, you dropped them like hot potatoes (they were too hot for you, weren't they, in a whole lot of ways?) and left them in the messes you'd made.

Well, make up your mind, dear. Either hit me over the head with that bottle or pour me a drink from it.

Thank you, dear, I knew you'd take the easier way. I always know how you're going to react long before you do. You see, I know all your secrets, dear. You've told me everything for twenty years, everything. You've poured out all your miserable moods and rages, you've whispered in my ear your every last dirty little fear and desire. So that now I know exactly what makes you tick. I'm in a wonderful position to manipulate you exactly as I want to, it gets better every year, even when I'm dead I'll be able to do it. Aren't you afraid of me, dear, just a little afraid? Remember, I'm crazy too, I have DT's just for the fun of it.

Why do I hate you so? That's a laugh, a very big laugh. Just ask yourself and you'll get more answers than you can stomach.

You've taken everything away from me — my home and my friends. I gave up all my friends for you, but did you give up even one of yours?

I drove my friends away? Now I've heard everything! It was you they were disgusted with, they couldn't stand your egotism and your preaching and your snide digs, they didn't like the way you eyed their preschool daughters. You drove them away.

You even drove my son away, you made him hate me. I never did anything but build you up to him and in return you did everything you could to break down his belief in me from the start. You contradicted everything I said in his presence, you scoffed at every fine idea I tried to plant in him, you laughed when I tried to teach him manners, you wouldn't even let me make him wash his hands when he came to dinner.

Shut up! It's time you heard some home truths. Now our son won't see us or write to us, he says we're sick, but whose fault is it? Yours! — who didn't have the guts to be the strong father every boy wants.

Yours! — who couldn't think of anything to do for him but to make him think his mother a fool.

Even before my son was born, you took my pride away from me. You robbed me of my self-confidence, and that's something that can never be forgiven. You sneered at my mind, you let me know from the start that other women were better looking and more desirable, you even destroyed my little efforts at self-expression while pretending to encourage them. I tried to act, I tried to be something in a pitiful little amateur theater, you took that away from me, you wrecked that although you've done nothing yourself but act all the time. And from the very beginning you plotted, under cover of your constant acting, how to destroy me.

I'm only asking you not to take twenty more years, but get it over tonight.

Shut up, I'm not interested in your denials. I always thought that marriage was supposed to be a partnership of two against the world. I was true to that vision — nothing counted with me but what you wanted and seeing to it that other people gave you the respect I believed you deserved. But I counted for nothing with you, the most miserable evil bum won more of your respect, you cringe and grovel and crawl on the floor and bump your head to everyone but me. No, don't!

Oh, but I'm forgetting how Christlike you are, aren't I? Excuse it, God. *You love me, but you love other people too, though you do me the honor of rating me a hair's breadth ahead of them?* Thanks for nothing! I don't believe in such pawky love. I scorn it. When I love I love, when I hate I hate. I don't believe in the kind of love that can be sliced and passed around, the kind of love that undermines and destroys while it pretends to caress.

And yet (shut up!) although you've done nothing but try to destroy me for twenty years, you refuse to make a clean end of it and kill me tonight. Other men would get a kick out of it, they'd jump at the chance, they'd be grateful to me. Every man wants to kill a woman, a woman in a black lace nightgown and a fur coat — it's his dream. But you haven't enough life in you even for that.

Shut up! I know everything you're going to say, about my insanity and insatiability and everything. I've heard it all over and over again for twenty years and it means less to me than the chatter of birds.

Shut up, I've got the floor! I'm a drunk and a failure, I know that, you've told me often enough, sticking the little knife behind the ear and twisting it. I'm ugly, so ugly it's a torment to sleep with me, I know that too. I remember every one of the million insults you've given me. (Don't say you're sorry, if you say you're sorry I'll scream.) And I know that you'd like to get rid of me, you'd really like to murder me, but that you daren't because you know you couldn't do one little thing without me, you couldn't get one girl to go to bed with you one single night.

Now talk. You have the floor. I yield it to you. Talk.

So you can't talk? You haven't a word to say? That's a surprise — most of the time you have diarrhea of the mouth. If what I say is so stupid and illogical and crazy as you claim, now's the time to prove it.

I'll tell you why you can't talk. Because I'm right about everything. I know you like a book, I know myself too, and I don't lie, I never lie.

Well, if you won't talk, at least look at me. Don't flinch your eyes away from me as if you were a scared child. Look, baby, at the skinny old witch in black. My arms are like pipestems, aren't they? — you never tire of reminding me of that. You can count my ribs, my breasts are old buttons. I knew you always liked boyish girls with tiny breasts, so I starved myself for years, and my reward is that you tell me it's alcoholism, I look like a concentration-camp corpse, face like a skull, I need vitamins, I should eat. Well, I won't eat, I'll never eat again, but I do need to black out. Where are the sleeping pills? Where have you hidden them? Don't worry about me taking too many — I'd never kill myself, I'm leaving that for you, it's my present to you, dear.

Thanks for nothing! No, I only took four, count and see.

You really are frightened of me, aren't you? You really do think I'm crazy or a witch. Well, that's a little something for my pride, at least I can get that much of a rise out of you. Not as good as being killed, but something. What should I do to improve my score? Should I turn black? Should I turn into a black panther, a skinny, moth-eaten, half bald black panther? Or a fourteen-year-old existentialist girl stripped to the waist — in black Levi's and with a black pony tail? Should I jump into your brain and sit there gently squeezing the gray jelly and saying "It's all right?" Is that what it takes before you'll kill me? Oh, what is the word I should say to make you do it? What is the word that will get under your thick hide?

I seem like another person, a demon? That's wonderful, dear, go on. *A black furred beast?* Better and better. *An irrational intrusion?* Brother, that's fancy language for it!

Like something out of your unconscious mind? Brother, I'm more than that, I'm straight out of your body, flesh of your flesh. Man and wife are one flesh, and that's more than poetry. You've waited too long, the graft has taken, it's too late now. You can never divorce me, you can't even get rid of me by killing me — I'll come back, I'll still be in your body after I'm dead. If you'd killed me earlier tonight, when I asked you, I'd have done you the courtesy of not coming back, I'd have stayed quiet in your body to the end of your days and never let you know I was there — torture wouldn't have made me speak. But now I'll come back from whatever hell you send me to, I'll sit forever on the edge of your bed, I'll clamor inside you skull like a thousand bells until you butt your head against the wall and scream for death.

Don't run away. It won't do you any good. I'll be with you wherever you go. Stay and kill me.

You feel sorry for me? Sorry? Brother, I'll make you pay for that.

Something will save me? In spite of everything something will still save me in the end? Brother, I've got a surprise for you, listen close. No, closer than that, closer.

Nothing will ever save *you*. Nothing. Ever.

All right . . . run away if you must. But another time put your socks on first. They look funny over your shoes . . . as if you had elephantiasis . . .

I feel tired . . . Thanks, dear, you vacated the bed just in time, your virtue is intact . . . No, I won't sleep, I never sleep, but I'll close my eyes and think . . . maybe I'll think of the word that will turn you into a murderer . . .

I'll find it some day, you know . . . the word that will get under the elephant hide you use for skin so that in spite of all your cowardice you'll rush ahead and kill me . . . You'll know that you're putting a rope around your neck and smearing the gray jelly on your temples and stripping the last cover off your squealing pink ego, but you won't be able to stop (although you'll pray to) because I'll have found the word . . . the word . . . If I can think for a minute more I may be able to find it now . . .

No, I'm going to sleep . . . I never really sleep . . . I hear every-thing . . . I know everything . . . I hear your every thought while you sleep . . . We're always together, darling . . .

Another time, darling . . . Another time . . .

Schizo Jimmie

Today witch-hunting is an unpopular occupation. Unless the witch happens to be a red, the hunter gets a very bad press. Just the same, today as in the Middle Ages, when a decent man recognizes a real witch — the modern equivalent of a witch by the best scientific standards — then he must instantly strike down the monster for the sake of the community without counting the cost to himself.

That is why I killed my friend Jamie Bingham Walsh, the portrait painter and interior designer. He didn't commit suicide, nor did he accidentally tumble off that scenic high point of the Latigo Canyon Road in the Santa Monica Mountains. I pushed him off with my little MG.

Oh, the car never touched him though it very well might have — that was one of the necessary chances I took. But in the end he reacted just as I'd been banking on it that he would — in a senseless panic, avoiding the closest threat to himself, the closest pain.

I stopped the car an extra dozen feet from the verge and he got out and walked around in front to the very edge, to take one of those Godlike looks at things below that he always had to take. He remarked, "The old sculptor poked his finger pretty deep here into the stone, didn't he." Then, as he was staring down at the twisting rocks like robed monsters, I silently eased the stick into low gear. Then I softly called his name and as he turned I smiled at him and gunned the car forward an exact dozen feet, thinking of my sister Alice and looking straight at his damned green necktie. I was very precise about it. Two inches more and my front wheels would have been over the edge.

He could have frozen, in which case I'd have knocked him off and he'd have been found with some extra injuries that might have been difficult to explain, or all too easy. Or, if he had reacted instantly, he could have jumped out of the way to either side or even onto the hood of the car — a man as much of a romantic daredevil as Jamie *looked* might have done just that, taking his chance that I didn't intend going over with him.

But he did none of those things. Instead he sprang backward into the great soft sweep of space above the toy valley, away from the nearest hurt. As he did so, as his nerve cracked under that final testing, it seemed to me that he instantly lost all of his black power over me, so that it was a cardboard man, a phantom, who stared wildly at me for an instant from the floorless air across the creamy hood of the MG before gravity snatched him out of sight.

The mind is a funny thing and has curious self-willed blind spots. Mine was so full of the thought that I had destroyed Jamie *utterly* that it never registered at all the thud of his body hitting, though I distinctly heard the distant tinkle of a couple of pebbles as they bounced against the bulges of the rocky wall on their way down.

I sat there calm and cold, thinking of Jamie's two wives and my sister Alice and the five other women I knew about and the half dozen of his close male friends and all his other victims whose names I would never know. I wondered if they'd have given me a round of applause from their various state mental hospitals and private sanitariums if I'd been able to tell them I had just avenged them on the man who sent them there. I couldn't answer that question — some people always love their destroyer — but I knew that now at least there wouldn't be any more unfortunates going to join them and they wouldn't have to endure any more kindly useless visits from Jamie with his vivid neckties and his patter about a person's color. That necktie jazz, you know, was one of the first things that put me on to Jamie — I remembered that he'd told Alice that green was "her color" and then he'd worn a green necktie when he went to visit her at the asylum. Later I noticed the same tie-in (ha!) with others of his victims, except the color would be different in each case. Everybody had a color, according to Jamie — something to do with what he called the atmosphere of your mind. Mine, I now remembered he'd often told me, was blue. Blue, like the cloudless sky over Latigo.

I shivered and smiled and wiped the cold sweat off my forehead and then I backed up my MG and drove off down the canyon. That was the end of it. I never had to exchange a single word with the police. I simply wasn't connected with the affair.

And so Jamie Walsh departed from this life without putting up any resistance whatever. He went away from us like the man who follows the user without asking any questions when the light tap comes on his shoulder.

But perhaps Jamie didn't expect any attack. Perhaps he never knew how blackly evil he was. Perhaps he never realized he was a witch. This is a possibility I must face.

To me a witch — a modern witch, a *real* witch — is a person who is *a carrier of insanity,* one who infects others with this or that deadly psychosis without showing any of the symptoms himself, one who may be brilliantly sane by all psychiatric tests but who nevertheless carries in his mind-stream the germs of madness.

It's obviously true when you think it over. Medical science recognizes that there are such carriers of physical disease — outwardly untainted persons who spread the germs of TB, say, or typhoid fever. They're immune, they have built up a resistance, but most of those with whom they come in contact are defenseless. Typhoid Mary was a famous instance — a cook who over and over again infected hundreds of people.

By the same reasoning, Jamie Bingham Walsh should have been known as Schizo Jimmie. People with whom he came in really close contact had their minds split and started to live in dream worlds. I secretly thought of him as Schizo Jimmie for years before I gained the courage and complete certainty that let me wipe him out. The immune carrier of insanity is just as real a scientific phenomenon as the immune carrier of tuberculosis.

Most of us are willing to recognize the carrier of insanity when he operates at the national or international level. No one would deny that Hitler was such a carrier, spreading madness among his followers until he grew so powerful that there was no asylum strong enough to hold him. Lenin was a subtler and therefore better example, a seemingly sane man whose madness appeared full-grown only among his successors. And there was surely such a carrier abroad at the time of our own Civil War, there was so much madness then in high places — but I believe I have made my point.

While we generally agree on these top-of-the-heap historic cases, many of us refuse to recognize that there are Schizo Jimmies and

Manic Marys and Paranoid Petes operating at all levels of society, including our own. But just think a minute about your friends and relatives and acquaintances. Don't you know at least one person who seems to be a focus for trouble without being an obvious troublemaker? A jinxy sort of guy or gal whose close friends show a remarkable tendency to crack up, to suicide perhaps, to call the head-shrinkers a bit too late, to take long vacations in the looney bin — or vacations that are longer than long. More likely than not he's brilliant and charming and seems to have the best intentions in the world (Jamie Walsh was all those things and more) but he's just not good for people.

At first you think he's merely unlucky in his choice of friends and maybe you feel sorry for him, and then you begin to wonder if he doesn't have a special talent or compulsion for seeking out and taking up with unstable people, and finally, if circumstances force you as deep into the thing as they did me, you begin to suspect that there's more to it than that. A lot more.

Alice and I got to know Jamie Walsh when Father hired him to do an interior design job on our new home in Malibu and also, it had already been arranged two days later, to paint Mother with the Afghan hounds. Jamie was in his late thirties then, energetic as hell, a real cosmopolite, impudent, flamingly charming, and he hit our soberly intelligent household like a whirlwind. He was a terrific salesman, as you have to be in that sort of job, and every one in the vicinity got an absolutely painless bonus course in general culture — Modigliani, Swedish Modern, the works.

With the price he was getting, we certainly had a bonus coming, but we didn't think about it that way. He'd come in, waving a devil mask, or a sari, or a hunk of period wrought iron or a gaudy old chamberpot, and the day's show would be on. For three months he was a non-resident member of the family. It was exactly like being visited by a pleasantly wicked young uncle you've never seen before because he's been completely occupied having exciting adventures in strange corners of the world and also, quite incidentally, happens to be a genius.

Within two weeks Jamie was painting Alice and myself as a matter of course and in the end he even sculptured a head of Father — cast in aluminum for some abstruse reason — and that was something I'd have given odds against ever happening. But in the end, as I say, even Father was bit by the art bug and for perhaps a month his old airplane factory took second place in his interests — the only time I'm sure, before or since, that ever happened in Father's life.

There was something feverish and distorted and unreal about the interest we all took in art and in Jamie at that time. He was like a hypnotist or some master magician weaving spells, creating wonderful dream worlds.

I dropped my forced interest in Father's business and my vaguer secret ambitions to do something in psychiatry, and determined to devote my life to marine painting, at which I'd earlier shown some talent. I let the others think it was a passing kick, which made things easier, especially with Father, but it was a lot more than that.

As for Alice, she seemed on the surface to be the least affected of all of us — she didn't sprout an artistic talent — but really she was the hardest hit. For she fell in love with Jamie. And he, in his peculiar way, encouraged her.

It wasn't anything obvious, mind you. I'm sure I was the only other person who realized what was happening and at the time I didn't care. In fact it seemed to me to be a fine thing that I should be able to offer up a beautiful sister to Jamie and that he should be interested. Since then I've noticed that many men have the urge, usually unconscious or so they'd claim, to furnish the services of their wives, sisters, and daughters to friends. It seems to be about as common as the opposite urge to clobber any male who so much as looks at their womenfolk, and is probably equally primitive in origin.

Mother may have guessed that Alice had developed a crush on Jamie, but I'm sure that was as far as her guesses went. She was herself too much under Jamie's spell to think unsympathetically of him. You see, by this time we'd learned about Jamie's unhappy marriage — he'd tried or seemed to try, to conceal it, but it had come out all the same — how his wife Jane was a hopeless alcoholic who spent most of her time touring the sanitariums and that one reason Jamie had to work so furiously was to pay the bills. Even I didn't dream at the time that Jane was just another of his victims and that what kept her alcoholism flaring was his ambiguous behavior toward her — his wanting her and not wanting her at the same time, his simultaneous caring for her and getting rid of her via the asylum route. She'd caught the infection he carried and in her case it was alcohol that was nursing the infection along.

But at the time even I knew nothing of this and we were all sympathy for Jamie and his troubles, we were all living in his bright dream worlds. Alice, I'm certain, was existing for the day when Jamie would carry her off — to marriage or a fierce selfish love-affair, I don't imagine she cared which. Just as I didn't care, deep in my old subconscious, whether I became a famous marine painter or merely Jamie's assistant. Alice and I were both of us building up to a big thing happening.

What happened was exactly nothing. Jamie finished the jobs Father had hired him to do and took off for Mexico all by himself. Mother went back to playing bridge. I threw my paint boxes into the ocean I'd been trying to catch on canvas. And Alice flipped, signalizing the event by shooting the two Afghan hounds.

Mother and Father were stoned, of course, but they still didn't connect up the tragedy in any way with Jamie. And I must admit that, if you didn't want to dig, there were enough old reasons around for Alice flipping — she'd always been a shy difficult child with a mass of personality problems, she'd a terrific problem fighting overweight, later she'd dropped out of college twice, dithered around with different career dreams, been mixed up with some kids who were on dope, and so on.

No, I was the only one who saw the real part that Jamie played in the business. Mother and Father actually took the attitude that Jamie had been a *good* influence on Alice, that she'd have flipped sooner if it hadn't been for his stimulating presence and the general air of activity and excitement he brought into our otherwise stolid lives. In fact they took this attitude so deeply that when Jamie came bustling back from Venezuela six months later, all shocked sympathy at Alice's tragedy but at the same time yarning of his new adventures — he had a jaguar skin for Mother — they fell in eagerly with his idea of visiting Alice at the mental hospital. They thought it might have a good effect on her, wake her up and all that.

And I was the one who had to drive him there. I, who had begun to shrink from him because I sensed that he was dripping — honestly, that's the way it felt to me — with the invisible germs of madness. I, who remembered how he'd told Alice that green was "her color" and realized now the significance of the green necktie he was wearing.

I don't know, mind you, if *he* realized its significance. All through this, as I've said, I've been uncertain of the degree to which Jamie realized that he was creating the tragedies around him, the extent to which he knew that he was a carrier.

It was a long lonely drive under cloudless skies, prefiguring in a way the final drive I took with Jamie. As we had got in the car he had looked up at the sky and recalled that blue was *my* color. It gave me the shudders, but I didn't let on. I remember thinking, though, of the odd sensitivities painters are supposed to have. Sargent once painted a woman, and a doctor who'd never met her diagnosed incipient insanity from the portrait, and the diagnosis was confirmed shortly.

Then after a bit Jamie fell into an odd wistful mood of faintly humorous self-pity and he told me about the dismal end his wife had come to in a New York hospital and about the numbers of his close friends who had flipped or suicided.

I'm sure he didn't realize that he was giving me research materials that were to occupy my real thinking for the next several years.

At the same time I began to see in a shadowy way the mechanism by which Jamie operated as a carrier of insanity — something I understand very well now.

You see, there has to be a mechanism, or else this transmission of insanity I'm talking about would be nothing but witchcraft — just as the transmission of physical disease was once thought by most people to be a matter of witchcraft.

Then the microscope came and *germs* were discovered to be the cause of infectious disease.

What causes insanity, at least the schizoid kind, what transmits it and carries it, is *dreams* — waking dreams, daytime dreams, the most powerful and virulent of all.

Jamie awakened and fostered dreams of romance in every woman he met. They looked at him, they listened to him, they lost themselves in the golden dream of a love affair that would dazzle the ages, they made the big decibands, families, careers, suasion to abandon their security, position all of that. And then . . . Jamie did nothing at all about it. Nothing brave, nothing reckless, not even anything cruel or merely male-hungry. I'm sure he and Alice never went to bed. Like the others, Jamie just left her hanging there.

In men it was dreams of glory that Jamie roused, dreams of adventures and artistic achievements quite beyond their real capabilities. It was their jobs that the men abandoned — their schooling, their common sense. Just as it happened to me, except that I saw Jamie's trap in time and threw my paints away.

But in one sense I was trapped more completely by Jamie than any of the others, because it was given to me to sense the menace of the man and to realize that I must study this thing and then do something about it, no matter how long it took or how much it hurt me.

Yes, I became aware of all those things in a shadowy way on that first drive from Malibu to the mental hospital — and I also got one piece of very concrete evidence against Jamie, though it was years before I realized its full significance.

After Jamie tired of talking he closed his eyes and went into a sort of uneasy drowse beside me. After a while he twisted on his narrow seat and he began to mutter and murmur in a rhythmic way as if, half asleep, he were making up or repeating a jingle to the spin of the wheels and the buzz of the motor. I still don't know what sort of mental process in Jamie was responsible for it — creativity takes strange twists. I listened carefully and after a while I began to catch words and then more words. He kept repeating the same thing. These are the words I caught:

Beth is sand-brown, Brenda's gray,
Dottier was mauve and faded away.
Hans was scarlet, Dave was black,
Keith was cobalt and off the track.

Ridiculous words. And then I thought, "I'm blue."

Jamie woke up and asked what had been happening. "Nothing," I told him and that seemed to satisfy him. We were practically at the asylum.

Jamie's visit to Alice was no help to her that I could see — on her next trip home she was just as out-of-touch and even more disgustingly fat — but that was how I became Jamie's Boswell, interested in every person he'd known, every place he'd been, anything he'd ever done or said. I talked with him a lot and with his friends more. One way or another, I managed to visit most of the places he'd been. Father was alternately furious and depressed at the way I was "wasting my life." He'd have tried to stop me, except that what had happened to Alice had put the fear into him of tampering with his children. We were queer eggs and might crack and smell. Of course he hadn't the faintest idea of what I was doing. I don't think that even Jamie guessed. Jamie responded to my interest with half-amused tolerance, though from time to time I caught an odd look in his eyes.

In the course of five years I accumulated enough evidence to convict James Bingham Walsh a dozen times of being a carrier of insanity. I found out about his younger brother, who had hero-worshiped him, tried to imitate him, done a bad job of it and aberrated before he was twenty . . . about his first wife, who'd only managed to stay a year this side of the asylum walls . . about Hans Godbold, who ditched his family and an executive job in a big chemical firm to become a poet and who six months later blew out his brains in Panama. About David Willis, Keith Ellander, Elizabeth Hunter, Brenda Silverstein, Dorothy Williamson . . . "colored people" — scarlet, black, cobalt, sand-brown, gray, mauve, — for now I remembered the jingle he'd muttered in my car. . .

It wasn't just a matter of individuals. Statistics contributed their quota. Wherever Jamie went, if it was a small enough place for it to show up and if I could get the figures, there was a rise, small but undeniable, in the incidence of insanity. Make no mistake, Jamie Bingham Walsh deserved the name of Schizo Jimmie.

And then as I've told you, when my evidence was complete, when it wholly satisfied *me*, I acted. I was prosecutor, judge, jury, and executioner all rolled into one. Sometimes when you're a little ahead of the science of your day, it has to be that way. I marched the prisoner up Latigo Canyon — by chance wearing a green tie, Alice's color, which made me happy — and he made the big drop.

The only thing that really bothers me about it all now is my unshaken conviction that Jamie was a genius. A master manipulator of colors, and, whether he knew it or not, of people. It is too bad that he was too dangerous to be let live. I sometimes think that the same is true of all so-called "great men" — they create dreams that infect and rot or crumble the minds of the rest of us. They are carriers, even the most seemingly noble and compassionate of them. At the time of our own Civil War the chief carrier was that sufferer from involutional melancholia, that tormented man from whom knives once had to be hidden, Abraham Lincoln. Oh, why can't such men leave us little people to our own kinds of safety and happiness, our small plans and small successes, our security firmly based on our mediocrity? Why must they keep spreading the deadly big dreams?

Naturally enough, I haven't escaped from this affair scot-free, though as I've told you I've been in no trouble with the police or the law. But just the same it was too tough a job for one man, too much responsibility for one person to shoulder. It left its mark on me, all right. By the time I'd finished, my nerves were like crackle glass. That's why I'm in this . . . well . . . rest home now, why I may be here for a long time. I concentrated so much on the one big problem that when it was solved I just couldn't seem to attend to life any more.

I'm not asking for pity, understand. I did what I had to, I did what any decent man would do, and I'm glad I was brave enough. I'm not complaining about any of the consequences I'm suffering now, the inevitable consequences of my frazzled nerves. I don't care if I have to spend the rest of my life here — I'm not complaining about the dreams . . . the mental hurting . . . the flow of ideas too fast for thought or comment . . . the voices I hear . . . . the hallucinations. . .

Except that I *am* bothered, I admit it, by the hallucinations I have of Jamie coming to visit me here. They are so real that some days they make me wonder whether they aren't the real live Jamie and whether it wasn't just the hallucination of Jamie that I sent hurtling down to his death in Latigo Canyon. After all, he never said a word, he looked like a phantom hanging in the air, and I never heard the sound of his body hitting.

Those are the days when I wish the police *would* come and question me about his death — question me, try me, condemn me, and send me to the gas chamber and out of this life that is no more than a torrent of tortured dreams. The days when Jamie comes to visit me, smiling tenderly and wearing a blue necktie.

The Creature from Cleveland Depths

"Come on, Gussy," Fay prodded quietly, "quit stalking around like a neurotic bear and suggest something for my invention team to work on. I enjoy visiting you and Daisy, but I can't stay aboveground all night."

"If being outside the shelters makes you nervous, don't come around any more," Gusterson told him, continuing to stalk. "Why doesn't your invention team think of something to invent? Why don't you? Hah!" In the "Hah!" lay triumphant condemnation of a whole way of life.

"We do," Fay responded imperturbably, "but a fresh viewpoint sometimes helps."

"I'll say it does! Fay, you burglar, I'll bet you've got twenty people like myself you milk for free ideas. First you irritate their bark, and then you make the rounds every so often to draw off the latex or the maple gloop."

Fay smiled. "It ought to please you that society still has a use for you outré inner-directed types. It takes something to make a junior executive stay aboveground after dark, when the missiles are on the prowl."

"Society can't have much use for us or it'd pay us something." Gusterson sourly asserted, staring blankly at the tankless TV and kicking it lightly as he passed on. TVs with viewing tanks showed shows in three dimensions.

"No, you're wrong about that, Gussy. Money's not the key goad with you inner-directeds. I got that straight from our Motivations chief."

"Did he tell you what we should use instead to pay the grocer? A deep inner sense of achievement, maybe? Fay, why should I do any free thinking for Micro Systems?"

"I'll tell you why, Gussy. Simply because you get a kick out of insulting us with sardonic ideas. If we take one of them seriously, you think we're degrading ourselves, and that pleases you even more. Like making someone laugh at a lousy pun."

Gusterson held still in his roaming and grinned. "That's the reason, huh? I suppose my suggestions would have to be something in the line of ultra-subminiaturized computers, where one sinister fine-etched molecule does the work of three big bumbling brain cells?"

"Not necessarily. Micro Systems is branching out. Wheel as free as a rogue star. But I'll pass along to Promotion your one molecule-three brain cell sparkler. It's a slight exaggeration, but it's catchy."

"I'll have my kids watch your ads to see if you use it, and then I'll sue the whole underworld." Gusterson frowned as he resumed his stalking. He stared puzzledly at the antique TV. "How about inventing a plutonium termite?" he said suddenly. "It would get rid of those stockpiles that are worrying you moles to death."

Fay grimaced noncommitally and cocked his head.

"Well, then, how about a beauty mask? How about that, hey? I don't mean one to repair a woman's complexion, but one she'd wear all the time that'd make her look like a seventeen-year-old sexpot. That'd end *her* worries."

"Hey, that's for me," Daisy called from the kitchen. "I'll make Gusterson suffer. I'll make him crawl around on his hands and knees begging my immature favors."

"No, you won't," Gusterson called back. "You having a face like that would scare the kids. Better cancel that one, Fay. Half the adult race looking like Vina Vidarsson is too awful a thought."

"Yah, you're just scared of making a million dollars," Daisy jeered.

"I sure am," Gusterson said solemnly, scanning the fuzzy floor from one murky glass wall to the other, hesitating at the TV. "How about something homey now, like a flock of little prickly cylinders that roll around the floor collecting lint and flub? They'd work by electricity, or at a pinch cats could bat 'em around. Every so often they'd be automatically herded together and the lint cleaned off the bristles."

"No good," Fay said. "There's no lint underground and cats are *verboten*. And the aboveground market doesn't amount to more money-wise than the state of Southern Illinois. Keep it grander, Gussy, and more impractical — you can't sell people merely useful ideas." From his hassock in the center of the room he looked uneasily around. "Say, did that violet tone in the glass come from the high Cleveland hydrogen bomb, or is it just age and ultraviolet, like desert glass?"

"No, somebody's grandfather liked it that color," Gusterson informed him with happy bitterness. "I like it too — the glass, I mean, not the lint. People who live in glass houses can see the stars — especially when there's a window-washing streak in their germ-plasm."

"Gussy, why don't you move underground?" Fay asked, his voice taking on a missionary note. "It's a lot easier living in one room, believe me. You don't have to tramp from room to room hunting things."

"I like the exercise," Gusterson said stoutly.

"But I bet Daisy'd prefer it underground. And your kids wouldn't have to explain why their father lives like a Red Indian. Not to mention the safety factor and insurance savings and a crypt church within easy slidewalk distance. Incidentally, we see the stars all the time, better than you do — by repeater."

"Stars by repeater," Gusterson murmured to the ceiling, pausing for God to comment. Then, "No, Fay, even if I could afford it — and stand it — I'm such a bad-luck Harry that just when I got us all safely stowed at the N minus one sublevel, the Soviets would discover an earthquake bomb that struck from below, and I'd have to follow everybody back to the treetops. *Hey! How about bubble homes in orbit around earth?* Micro System could subdivide the world's most spacious suburb, and all you moles could go ellipsing. Space is as safe as there is: no air, no shock waves. Free Fall's the ultimate in restfulness — great health benefits. Commute by rocket — or better yet, stay home and do all your business by TV-telephone, or by waldo if it were that sort of thing. Even pet your girl by remote control — she in her bubble, you in yours, whizzing through vacuum. Oh, damn — damn — *damn* — *damn* — DAMN!"

He was glaring at the blank screen of the TV, his big hands clenching and unclenching.

"Don't let Fay give you apoplexy — he's not worth it," Daisy said, sticking her trim head in from the kitchen, while Fay inquired anxiously, "Gussy, what's the matter?"

"Nothing, you worm!" Gusterson roared. "Except that an hour ago I forgot to tune in on the only TV program I've wanted to hear this year — *Finnegans Wake* scored for English, Gaelic and brogue. Oh, damn — *damn* — DAMN!"

"Too bad," Fay said lightly. "I didn't know they were releasing it on flat TV too."

"Well, they were! Some things are too damn big to keep completely underground. And I had to forget! I'm always doing it — I miss everything! Look here, you rat," he blatted suddenly at Fay, shaking his finger under the latter's chin, "I'll tell you what you can have that ignorant team of yours invent. They can fix me up a mechanical secretary that I can feed orders into and that'll remind me when the exact moment comes to listen to TV or phone somebody or mail in a story or write a letter or pick up a magazine or look at an eclipse or a new orbiting station or fetch the kids from school or buy Daisy a bunch of flowers or whatever it is. It's got to be something that's always with me, not something I have to go and consult or that I can get sick of and put down somewhere. And it's got to remind me forcibly enough so that I take notice and don't just shrug it aside, like I sometimes do even when Daisy reminds me of things. That's what your stupid team can invent for me! If they do a good job, I'll pay them as much as fifty dollars!"

"That doesn't sound like anything so very original to me," Fay commented cooly, leaning back from the wagging finger. "I think all senior executives have something of that sort. At least, their secretary keeps some kind of file . . ."

"I'm not looking for something with spiked falsies and nylons up to the neck," interjected Gusterson, whose ideas about secretaries were a trifle lurid. "I just want a mech reminder — that's all!"

"Well, I'll keep the idea in mind," Fay assured him, "along with the bubble homes and beauty masks. If we ever develop anything along those lines, I'll let you know. If it's a beauty mask, I'll bring Daisy a pilot model — to use to scare strange kids." He put his watch to his ear. "Good lord, I'm going to have to cut to make it underground before the main doors close. Just ten minutes to Second Curfew! 'Bye, Gus. 'Bye, Daze."

Two minutes later, living room lights out, they watched Fay's foreshortened antlike figure scurrying across the balding ill-lit park toward the nearest escalator.

Gusterson said, "Weird to think of that big bright space-poor glamor basement stretching around everywhere underneath. Did you remind Smitty to put a new bulb in the elevator?"

"The Smiths moved out this morning," Daisy said tonelessly. "They went underneath."

"Like cockroaches," Gusterson said. "Cockroaches leavin' a sinkin' apartment building. Next the ghosts'll be retreatin' to the shelters."

"Anyhow, from now on we're our own janitors," Daisy said.

He nodded. "Just leaves three families besides us loyal to this glass death trap. Not countin' ghosts." He sighed. Then, "You like to move below, Daisy?" he asked softly, putting his arm lightly across her shoulders. "Get a woozy eyeful of the bright lights and all for a change? Be a rat for a while? Maybe we're getting too old to be bats. I could scrounge me a company job and have a thinking closet all to myself and two secretaries with stainless steel breasts. Life'd be easier for you and a lot cleaner. And you'd sleep safer."

"That's true," she answered and paused. She ran her fingertip slowly across the murky glass, its violet tint barely perceptible against a cold dim light across the park. "But somehow," she said, snaking her arm around his waist, "I don't think I'd sleep happier — or one bit excited."

II

Three weeks later Fay, dropping in again, handed to Daisy the larger of two rather small packages he was carrying.

"It's a so-called beauty mask," he told her, "complete with wig, eyelashes, and wettable velvet lips. It even breathes — pinholed elastiskin with a static adherence-charge. But Micro Systems had nothing to do with it, thank God. Beauty Trix put it on the market ten days ago and it's already started a teen-age craze. Some boys are wearing them too, and the police are yipping at Trix for encouraging transvestism with psychic repercussions."

"Didn't I hear somewhere that Trix is a secret subsidiary of Micro?" Gusterson demanded, rearing up from his ancient electric typewriter. "No, you're not stopping me writing, Fay — it's the gut of evening. If I do any more I won't have any juice to start with tomorrow. I got another of my insanity thrillers moving. A real id-teaser. In this one not only all the characters are crazy but the robot psychiatrist too."

"The vending machines are jumping with insanity novels," Fay commented. "Odd they're so popular."

Gusterson chortled. "The only way you outer-directed moles will accept individuality any more even in a fictional character, without your superegos getting seasick, is for them to be crazy. Hey, Daisy! Lemme see that beauty mask!"

But his wife, backing out of the room, hugged the package to her bosom and solemnly shook her head.

"A hell of a thing," Gusterson complained, "not even to be able to see what my stolen ideas look like."

"I got a present for you too," Fay said. "Something you might think of as a royalty on all the inventions someone thought of a little ahead of you. Fifty dollars by your own evaluation." He held out the smaller package. "Your tickler."

"My *what?*" Gusterson demanded suspiciously.

"Your tickler. The mech reminder you wanted. It turns out that the file a secretary keeps to remind her boss to do certain things at certain times is called a tickler file. So we named this a tickler. Here."

Gusterson still didn't touch the package. "You mean you actually put your invention team to work on that nonsense?"

"Well, what do you think? Don't be scared of it. Here, I'll show you."

As he unwrapped the package, Fay said, "It hasn't been decided yet whether we'll manufacture it commercially. If we do, I'll put through a voucher for you — for 'development consultation' or something like that. Sorry no royalty's possible. Davidson's squad had started to work up the identical idea three years ago, but it got shelved. I found it on a snoop through the closets. There! Looks Georgian-silver rich, doesn't it?"

On the scarred black tabletop was a dully gleaming object about the size and shape of a cupped hand with fingers merging. A tiny pellet on a short near-invisible wire led off from it. On the back was a punctured area suggesting the face of a microphone; there was also a window with a date and time in hours and minutes showing through, and next to that four little buttons in a row. The concave underside of the silvery "hand" was smooth except for a central area where what looked like two rollers came through.

"It goes on your shoulder under your shirt," Fay explained, "and you tuck the pellet in your ear. We might work up bone conduction on a commercial model. Inside is an ultra-slow fine-wire recorder holding a spool that runs for a week. The clock lets you go to any place on the seven-day wire and record a message. The buttons give you variable speed in going there, so you don't waste too much time making a setting. There's a knack in fingering them efficiently, but it's easily acquired."

Fay picked up the tickler. "For instance, suppose there's a TV show you want to catch tomorrow night at twenty-two hundred." He touched the buttons. There was the faintest whirring. The clock face blurred briefly three times before showing the setting he'd mentioned. Then Fay spoke into the punctured area: "Turn on TV channel two, you big dummy!" He grinned over at Gusterson. "When you've got all your instructions to yourself loaded in, you synchronize with the present moment and let her roll. Fit it on your shoulder and forget it. Oh, yes, and it literally does tickle you every time it delivers an instruction. That's what the little rollers are for. Believe me, you can't ignore it. Come on, Gussy, take off your shirt and try it out. We'll feed in some instructions for the next ten minutes so you get the feel of how it works."

"I don't want to," Gusterson said. "Not right now. I want to sniff around it first. My God, it's small! Besides everything else it does, does it think?"

"Don't pretend to be an idiot, Gussy! You know very well that even with ultra-sub-micro nothing quite this small can possibly have enough elements to do any thinking."

Gusterson shrugged. "I don't know about that. I think bugs think."

Fay groaned faintly. "Bugs operate by instinct, Gussy," he said. "A patterned routine. They do not scan situations and consequences and then make decisions."

"I don't expect bugs to make decisions," Gusterson said. "For that matter, I don't like people who go around alla time making decisions."

"Well, you can take it from me, Gussy, that this tickler is just a miniaturized wire recorder and clock . . . and a tickler. It doesn't do anything else."

"Not yet, maybe," Gusterson said darkly. "Not this model. Fay, I'm serious about bugs thinking. Or if they don't exactly think, they feel. They've got an interior drama. An inner glow. They're conscious. For that matter, Fay, I think all your really complex electronic computers are conscious too."

"Quit kidding, Gussy."

"Who's kidding?"

"You are. Computers simply aren't alive."

"What's alive? A word. I think computers are conscious, at least while they're operating. They've got that inner glow of awareness. They sort of . . . well . . . meditate."

"Gussy, computers haven't got any circuits for meditating. They're not programmed for mystical lucubrations. They've just got circuits for solving the problems they're on."

"Okay, you admit they've got problem-solving circuits — like a man has. I say if they've got the equipment for being conscious, they're conscious. What has wings, flies."

"Including stuffed owls and gilt eagles and dodoes — and wood-burning airplanes?"

"Maybe, under some circumstances. There *was* a wood-burning airplane, Fay," Gusterson continued, wagging his wrists for emphasis, "I really think computers are conscious. They just don't have any way of telling us that they are. Or maybe they don't have any *reason* to tell us, like the little Scotch boy who didn't say a word until he was fifteen and was supposed to be deaf and dumb."

"Why didn't he say a word?"

"Because he'd never had anything to say. Or take those Hindu fakirs, Fay, who sit still and don't say a word for thirty years or until their fingernails grow to the next village. If Hindu fakirs can do that, computers can!"

Looking as if he were masticating a lemon, Fay asked quietly, "Gussy, did you say you're working on an insanity novel?"

Gusterson frowned fiercely.

"Now you're kidding," he accused Fay. "The dirty kind of kidding, too."

"I'm sorry," Fay said with light contrition. "Well, now you've sniffed at it, how about trying on Tickler?" He picked up the gleaming blunted crescent and jogged it temptingly under Gusterson's chin.

"Why should I?" Gusterson asked, stepping back. "Fay, I'm up to my ears writing a book. The last thing I want is something interrupting me to make me listen to a lot of junk and do a lot of useless things. *Finnegans Wake* — who wants to listen to that swollen-ego mishmash?"

"But, dammit, Gussy! It was all your idea in the first place!" Fay blatted. Then, catching himself, he added, "I mean, you were one of the first people to think of this particular sort of instrument."

"Maybe so, but I've done some more thinking since then." Gusterson's voice grew a trifle solemn. "Inner-directed worthwhile thinkin'. Fay, when a man forgets to do something, it's because he really doesn't want to do it or because he's all roiled up down in his unconscious. He ought to take it as a danger signal and investigate the roiling, not hire himself a human or mech reminder."

"Bushwa," Fay retorted. "In that case you shouldn't write memorandums or even take notes."

"Maybe I shouldn't," Gusterson agree lamely. "I'd have to think that over too."

"Ha!" Fay jeered. "No, I'll tell you what your trouble is, Gussy. You're simply scared of this contraption. You've loaded your skull with horror-story nonsense about machines sprouting minds and taking over the world — until you're even scared of a simple miniaturized and clocked recorder." He thrust it out.

"Maybe I am," Gusterson admitted, controlling a flinch. "Honestly, Fay, that thing's got a gleam in its eye as if it had ideas of its own. Nasty ideas."

"Gussy, you nut, it hasn't *got* an eye."

"Not now, no, but it's got the gleam — the eye may come. It's the Cheshire Cat in reverse. Remember, Fay, how in *Alice in Wonderland* the Cheshire Cat faded until even its teeth were gone and only the smile was left? This thing'll start with a nasty gleam and get an eye and then go on from there. If you'd step over here and look at yourself holding it, you could see what I mean. But I don't think computers *sprout* minds, Fay. I just think they've *got* minds, because they've got the mind elements."

"Ho, ho!" Fay mocked. "Everything that has a material side has a mental side," he chanted. "Everything that's a body is also a spirit. Gussy, that dubious old metaphysical dualism went out centuries ago."

"Maybe so," Gusterson said, "but we still haven't anything but that dubious dualism to explain the human mind, have we? It's a jelly of nerve cells and it's a vision of the cosmos. If that isn't dualism, what is?"

"I give up. Gussy, are you going to try out this tickler?"

"No!"

"But dammit, Gussy, we made it just for you! — practically."

"Sorry, but I'm not going near the thing."

" 'Zen come near me," a husky voice intoned behind them. "Tonight I vant a man."

Standing in the door was something slim in a short silver sheath. It had golden bangs and the haughtiest snub-nosed face in the world. It slunk toward them.

"My God, Vina Vidarsson!" Gusterson yelled.

"Daisy, that's terrific," Fay applauded, going up to her.

She bumped him aside with a swing of her hips, continuing to advance. "Not you, Ratty," she said throatily. "I vant a real man."

"Fay, I suggested Vina Vidarsson's face for the beauty mask," Gusterson said, walking around his wife and shaking a finger. "Don't tell me Trix just happened to think of that too."

"What else could they think of?" Fay laughed. "This season sex means VV and nobody else — the girl with the spiky voom-voom bazoom." An odd little grin flicked his lips, a tic traveled up his face and his body twitched slightly. "Say, folks, I'm going to have to be leaving. It's exactly fifteen minutes to Second Curfew. Last time I had to run and I got heartburn. When are you people going to move downstairs? I'll leave Tickler, Gussy. Play around with it and get used to it. 'Bye now."

"Hey, Fay," Gusterson called curiously, "have you developed absolute time sense?"

Fay grinned a big grin from the doorway — almost too big a grin for so small a man. "I didn't need to," he said softly, patting his right shoulder. "My tickler told me."

He closed the door behind him.

As side-by-side they watched him strut sedately across the murky chilly-looking park, Gusterson mused, "So the little devil had one of those nonsense-gadgets on all the time and I never noticed. Can you beat that?" Something drew across the violet-tinged stars a short bright line that quickly faded. "What's that?" Gusterson asked gloomily. "Next to last stage of missile-here?"

"Won't you settle for an old-fashioned shooting star?" Daisy asked softly. The (wettable) velvet lips of the mask made even her natural voice sound different. She reached a hand back of her neck to pull the thing off.

"Hey, don't do that," Gusterson protested in a hurt voice. "Not for a while anyway."

"Hokay!" she said harshly, turning on him. "Zen down on your knees, dog!"

III

It was a fortnight and Gusterson was loping down the home stretch on his 40,000-word insanity novel before Fay dropped in again, this time promptly at high noon.

Normally Fay cringed his shoulders a trifle and was inclined to slither, but now he strode aggressively, his legs scissoring in a fast, low goose step. He whipped off the sunglasses that all moles wore topside by day and began to pound Gusterson on the back while calling boisterously, "How are you, Gussy Old Boy, Old Boy?"

Daisy came in from the kitchen to see why Gusterson was choking. She was instantly grabbed and violently bussed to the accompaniment of, "Hiya, Gorgeous! Yum-yum! How about ad-libbing that some weekend?"

She stared at Fay dazedly, rasping the back of her hand across her mouth, while Gusterson yelled, "Quit that! What's got into you, Fay? Have they transferred you out of R and D to Company Morale? Do they line up all the secretaries at roll call and make you give them an eight-hour energizing kiss?"

"Ha, wouldn't you like to know?" Fay retorted. He grinned, twitched jumpingly, held still a moment, then hustled over to the far wall. "Look out there," he rapped, pointing through the violet glass at a gap between the two nearest old skyscraper apartments. "In thirty seconds you'll see them test the new needle bomb at the other end of Lake Erie. It's educational." He began to count off seconds, vigorously semaphoring his arm. " . . . Two . . . three . ... Gussy, I've put through a voucher for two yards for you. Budgeting squawked, but I pressured 'em."

Daisy squealed, "Yards! — are those dollar thousand?" while Gusterson was asking, "Then you're marketing the tickler?"

"Yes. Yes," Fay replied to them in turn. " . . . Nine . . . ten . . ." Again he grinned and twitched. "Time for noon Comstaff," he announced staccato. "Pardon the hush box." He whipped a pancake phone from under his coat, clapped it over his face and spoke fiercely but inaudibly into it, continuing to semaphore. Suddenly he thrust the phone away. "Twenty-nine. . . thirty . . . Thar she blows!"

An incandescent streak shot up the sky from a little above the far horizon and a doubly dazzling point of light appeared just above the top of it, with the effect of God dotting an "i."

"Ha, that'll skewer espionage satellites like swatting flies!" Fay proclaimed as the portent faded. "Bracing! Gussy, where's your tickler? I've got a new spool for it that'll razzle-dazzle you."

"I'll bet," Gusterson said drily. "Daisy?"

"You gave it to the kids and they got to fooling with it and broke it."

"No matter," Fay told them with a large sidewise sweep of his hand. "Better you wait for the new model. It's a six-way improvement."

"So I gather," Gusterson said, eyeing him speculatively. "Does it automatically inject you with cocaine? A fix every hour on the second?"

"Ha-ha, joke. Gussy, it achieves the same effect without using any dope at all. Listen: a tickler reminds you of your duties and opportunities — your chances for happiness and success! What's the obvious next step?"

"Throw it out the window. By the way, how do you do that when you're underground?"

"We have high-speed garbage boosts. The obvious next step is you give the tickler a heart. It not only tells you, it warmly persuades you. It doesn't just say, 'Turn on the TV channel two, Joyce program,' it *brills* at you, 'Kid, Old Kid, race for the TV and flip that two switch! There's a great show coming through the pipes this second plus ten — you'll enjoy the hell out of yourself! Grab a ticket to ecstasy!'"

"My God," Gusterson gasped, "are those the kind of jolts it's giving you now?"

"Don't you get it, Gussy? You never load your tickler except when you're feeling buoyantly enthusiastic. You don't just tell yourself what to do hour by hour next week, you sell yourself on it. That way you not only make doubly sure you'll obey instructions but you constantly reinoculate yourself with your own enthusiasm."

"I can't stand myself when I'm that enthusiastic," Gusterson said. "I feel ashamed for hours afterward."

"You're warped — all this lonely sky-life. What's more, Gussy, think how still more persuasive some of those instructions would be if they came to a man in his best girl's most bedroomy voice, or his doctor's or psycher's if it's that sort of thing — or Vina Vidarsson's! By the way, Daze, don't wear that beauty mask outside. It's a grand misdemeanor ever since ten thousand teenagers rioted through Tunnel-Mart wearing them. And VV's suing Trix."

"No chance of that," Daisy said. "Gusterson got excited and bit off the nose." She pinched her own delicately.

"I'd no more obey my enthusiastic self," Gusterson was brooding, "than I'd obey a Napoleon drunk on his own brandy or a hopped-up St. Francis. Reinoculated with my own enthusiasm? I'd die just like from snake-bite!"

"Warped, I said," Fay dogmatized, stamping around. "Gussy, having the instructions persuasive instead of neutral turned out to be only the opening wedge. The next step wasn't so obvious, but I saw it. Using subliminal verbal stimuli in his tickler, a man can be given constant supportive euphoric therapy 24 hours a day! And it makes use of all that empty wire. We've revived the ideas of a pioneer dynamic psycher named Dr. Coué. For instance, right now my tickler is saying to me — in tones too soft to reach my conscious mind, but do they stab into the unconscious! — 'day by day in every way I'm getting sharper and sharper.' It alternates that with 'gutsier and gutsier' and . . . well, forget that. Coué mostly used 'better and better,' but that seems too general. And every hundredth time it says them out loud — inside my ear — and the tickler gives me a brush — just a faint cootch — to make sure I'm keeping in touch."

"That third word-pair," Daisy wondered, feeling her mouth reminiscently. "Ballsier and ballsier?"

Gusterson's eyes had been growing wider and wider. "Fay," he said, "I could no more use my mind for anything if I knew all that was going on in my inner ear than if I were being brushed down with brooms by three witches. Look here," he said with loud authority, "you've got to stop all this — it's crazy. Fay, if Micro'll junk the tickler, I'll think you up something else to invent — something real good."

"Your inventing days are over," Fay brilled gleefully. "I mean, you'll never equal your masterpiece."

"How about," Gusterson bellowed, "an anti-individual guided missile? The physicists have got small-scale antigravity good enough to float and fly something the size of a hand grenade. I can smell that even though it's a back-of-the-safe military secret. Well, how about keying such a missile to a man's fingerprints — or brain waves, maybe, or his unique smell! — so it can spot and follow him around and target in on him, without harming anyone else? Long-distance assassination — and the stinkingest gets it! Or you could simply load it with some disgusting goo and key it to teenagers as a group — that'd take care of them. Fay, doesn't it give you a rich warm kick to think of my midget missiles buzzing around in your tunnels, seeking out evildoers, like a swarm of angry wasps or angelic bumblebees?"

"You're not luring me down any side trails," Fay said laughingly. He grinned and twitched, then hurried toward the opposite wall, motioning them to follow. Outside, about a hundred yards beyond the purple glass, rose another ancient glass-walled apartment skyscraper. Beyond, Lake Erie rippled glintingly.

"Another bomb test?" Gusterson asked.

Fay pointed at the building. "Tomorrow," he announced, "a modern factory, devoted solely to the manufacture of ticklers, will be erected on that site."

"You mean one of those windowless phallic eyesores?" Gusterson demanded. "Fay, you people aren't even consistent. You've got all your homes underground. Why not your factories?"

"Sh! Not enough room. It's okay to come topside daytimes. But night missiles are scarier. And then there are the wild animals from the Wastes. No kidding, Gussy, don't you hear wolf-howls at night?"

"Only the groans of the deer dying from hunger and lack of hunters," the latter assured him.

Daisy brought them back to the topic at hand.

"I know that building's been empty for a year," she said uneasily, "but how — ?"

"Sh! Watch! *Now!*"

The looming building seemed to blur or fuzz for a moment. Then it was as if the lake's bright ripples had invaded the old glass a hundred yards away. Wavelets chased themselves up and down the gleaming walls, became higher, higher . . . and then suddenly the glass cracked all over to tiny fragmented concrete and plastic and plastic piping, until all that was left was the nude steel framework, vibrating so rapidly as to be almost invisible against the gleaming lake.

Daisy covered her ears, but there was no explosion, only a long-drawn-out low crash as the fragments hit twenty floors below and dust whooshed out sideways.

"Spectacular!" Fay summed up. "Knew you'd enjoy it. That little trick was first conceived by the great Tesla during his last fruity years. Research discovered it in his biog — we just made the dream come true. A tiny resonance device you could carry in your belt-bag attunes itself to the natural harmonic of a structure and then increases amplitude by tiny pulses exactly in time. Just like soldiers marching in step can break down a bridge, only this is as if it were being done by one marching ant." He pointed at the naked framework appearing out of its own blur and said, "We'll be able to hang the factory on that. If not, we'll whip a mega-current through it and vaporize it. No question the micro-resonator is the neatest sweetest wrecking device going. You can expect a lot more of this sort of efficiency now that mankind has the tickler to enable him to use his full potential. What's the matter, folks?"

Daisy was staring around the violet-walled room with dumb mistrust. Her hands were trembling.

"You don't have to worry," Fay assured her with an understanding laugh. "This building's safe for a month more at least." Suddenly he grimaced and leaped a foot in the air. He raised a clawed hand to scratch his shoulder but managed to check the movement. "Got to beat it, folks," he announced tersely. "My tickler gave me the grand cootch."

"Don't go yet," Gusterson called, rousing himself with a shudder which he immediately explained: "I just had the illusion that if I shook myself all my flesh and guts would fall off my shimmying skeleton. Brr! Fay, before you and Micro go off half-cocked, I want you to know there's one insuperable objection to the tickler as a mass-market item. The average man or woman won't go to the considerable time and trouble it must take to load a tickler. He simply hasn't got the compulsive orderliness and willingness to plan that it requires."

"We thought of that weeks ago," Fay rapped, his hand on the door. "Every tickler spool that goes to market is patterned like wallpaper with one of five designs of suitable subliminal supportive euphoric material. "Ittier and ittier,' 'viriler and viriler' — you know. The buyer is robot-interviewed for an hour, his personalized daily routine laid out and thereafter templated on his weekly spool. He's strongly urged next to take his tickler to his doctor and psycher for further instruction-imposition. We've been working with the medical profession from the start. They love the tickler because it'll remind people to take their medicines on the dot . . . and rest and eat and go to sleep just when and how doc says. This is a big operation, Gussy, — a biiiiiig operation! 'Bye!"

Daisy hurried to the wall to watch him cross the park. Deep down she was a wee bit worried that he might linger to attach a micro-resonator to *this* building and she wanted to time him. But Gusterson settled down to his typewriter and began to bat away.

"I want to have another novel started," he explained to her, "before the ant marches across this building in about four and a half weeks . . . or a million sharp little gutsy, ballsy guys come swarming out of the ground and heave it into Lake Erie."

IV

Early next morning windowless walls began to crawl up the stripped skyscraper between them and the lake. Daisy pulled the black-out curtains on that side. For a day or two longer their thoughts and conversations were haunted by Gusterson's vague sardonic visions of a horde of tickler-energized moles pouring up out of the tunnels to tear down the remaining trees, tank the atmosphere, and perhaps somehow dismantle the stars — at least on this side of the world — but then they both settled back into their customary easygoing routines. Gusterson typed. Daisy made her daily shopping trip to a little topside daytime store and started painting a mural on the floor of the empty apartment next theirs but one.

"We ought to lasso some neighbors," she suggested once. "I need somebody to hold my brushes and admire. How about you making a trip below at the cocktail hours, Gusterson, and picking up a couple of girls for a starter? Flash the old viriler charm, cootch them up a bit, emphasize the delights of high living, but make sure they're compatible roommates. You could pick up that two-yard check from Micro at the same time."

"You're an immoral money-ravenous wench," Gusterson said absently, trying to dream of an insanity beyond insanity that would make his next novel a real id-rousing best-vender.

"If that's your vision of me, you shouldn't have chewed up the VV mask."

"I'd really prefer you with green stripes," he told her. "But stripes, spots, or sunbathing, you're better than those cocktail moles."

Actually both of them acutely disliked going below. They much preferred to perch in their eyrie and watch the people of Cleveland Depths, as they privately called th local sub-suburb, rush up out of the shelters at dawn to work in the concrete fields and windowless factories, make their daytime jet trips and freeway jaunts, do their noon-hour and coffee-break guerilla practice, and then go scurrying back at twilight to the atomic-proof, brightly lit, vastly exciting, claustrophobic caves.

Fay and his projects began once more to seem dreamlike, though Gusterson did run across a cryptic advertisement for ticklers in *The Manchester Guardian*, which he got daily by facsimile. Their three children reported similar ads, of no interest to young fry, on the TV, and one afternoon they came home with the startling news that the monitors at their subsurface school had been issued ticklers. On sharp interrogation by Gusterson, however, it appeared that these last were not ticklers but merely two-way radios linked to the school police station.

"Which is bad enough," Gusterson commented later to Daisy. "But it'd be even dirtier to think of those clock-watching superegos being strapped to kids' shoulders. Can you imagine Huck Finn with a tickler, tellin' him when to tie up the raft to a towhead and when to take a swim?"

"I bet Fay could," Daisy countered. "When's he going to bring you that check, anyhow? Iago wants a jetcycle and I promised Imogene a Vina Kit, and then Claudius'll have to have something."

Gusterson scowled thoughtfully. "You know, Daze," he said, "I got the feeling Fay's in the hospital, all narcotized up and being fed intravenously. The way he was jumping around last time, that tickler was going to cootch him to pieces in a week."

As if to refute this intuition, Fay turned up that very evening. The lights were dim. Something had gone wrong with the building's old transformer and , pending repairs, the two remaining occupied apartments were making do with batteries, which turned bright globes to mysterious amber candles and made Gusterson's ancient typewriter operate sluggishly.

Fay's manner was subdued or at least closely controlled and for a moment Gusterson though he'd shed his tickler. Then the little man came out of the shadows and Gusterson saw the large bulge on his right shoulder.

"Yes, we had to up it a bit sizewise," Fay explained in clipped tones. "Additional superfeatures. While brilliantly successful on the whole, the subliminal euphorics were a shade too effective. Several hundred users went hoppity manic. We gentled the cootch and qualified the subliminals — you know, 'day by day in every way I'm getting sharper *and more serene'* — but a stabilizing influence was still needed, so after a top-level conference we decided to combine Tickler with Moodmaster."

"My God," Gusterson interjected, "do they have a machine now that does that?"

"Of course. They've been using them on ex-mental patients for years."

"I just don't keep up with progress," Gusterson said, shaking his head bleakly. "I'm falling behind on all fronts."

"You ought to have your tickler remind you to read Science Service releases," Fay told him. "Or simply instruct it to scan the releases and — no, that's still in research." He looked at Gusterson's shoulder and his eyes widened. "You're not wearing the new-model tickler I sent you," he said accusingly.

"I never got it," Gusterson assured him. "Postmen deliver topside mail and parcels by throwing them on the high-speed garbage boosts and hoping a tornado will blow them to the right addresses." Then he added helpfully, "Maybe the Russians stole it while it was riding the whirlwinds."

"That's not a suitable topic for jesting," Fay frowned. "We're hoping that Tickler will mobilize the full potential of the Free World for the first time in history. Gusterson, you are going to have to wear a ticky-tick. It's becoming impossible for a man to get through modern life without one."

"Maybe I will," Gusterson said appeasingly, "but right now tell me about Moodmaster. I want to put it in my new insanity novel."

Fay shook his head. "Your readers will just think you're behind the times. If you use it, underplay it. But anyhow, Moodmaster is a simple physiotherapy engine that monitors bloodstream chemicals and body electricity. It ties directly into the bloodstream, keeping blood sugar, et cetera, at optimum levels and injecting euphrin or depressin as necessary — and occasionally a touch of extra adrenaline, as during work emergencies."

"Is it painful?" Daisy called from the bedroom.

"Excruciating," Gusterson called back, "Excuse it, please," he grinned at Fay. "Hey, didn't I suggest cocaine injections last time I saw you?"

"So you did," Fay agreed flatly. "Oh, by the way, Gussy, here's that check for a yard I promised you. Micro doesn't muzzle the ox."

"Hooray!" Daisy cheered faintly.

"I thought you said it was going to be for two," Gusterson complained.

"Budgeting always forced a last-minute compromise," Fay shrugged. "You have to learn to accept those things."

"I love accepting money and I'm glad any time for three feet," Daisy called agreeable. "Six feet might make me wonder if I weren't an insect, but getting a yard just makes me feel like a gangster's moll."

"Want to come out and gloat over the yard paper, Toots, and stuff it in your diamond-embroidered net stocking top?" Gusterson called back.

"No, I'm doing something to that portion of me just now. But hang onto the yard, Gusterson."

"Aye-aye, Cap'n," he assured her. Then, turning back to Fay, "So you've taken the Dr. Coué repeating out of the tickler?"

"On, no. Just balanced it off with depression. The subliminals are still a prime sales-point. All the tickler features are cumulative, Gussy. You're still underestimating the scope of the device."

"I guess I am. What's this 'work-emergencies' business? If you're using the tickler to inject drugs into workers to keep them going, that's really just my cocaine suggestion modernized and I'm putting in for another thou. Hundreds of years ago the South American Indians chewed coca leaves to kill fatigue sensations."

"That so? Interesting — and it proves priority for the Indians, doesn't it? I'll make a try for you, Gussy, but don't expect anything." He cleared his throat, his eyes grew distant and, turning his head a little to the right, he enunciated sharply, "Pooh-Bah. Time: Inst oh five. One oh five seven. Oh oh Record: Gussy coca thou budget. Cut." He explained, "We got a voice-cued setter now on the deluxe models. You can record a memo to yourself without taking off your shirt. Incidentally, I use the ends of the hours for trifle-memos. I've already used up the fifty-nines and eights for tomorrow and started on the fifty-sevens."

"I understood most of your memo," Gusterson told him gruffly. "The last 'Oh oh' was for seconds, wasn't it? Now I call that crude — why not microseconds too? But how do you remember where you've made a memo so you don't record over it? After all, you're rerecording over the wallpaper all the time."

"Tickler beeps and then hunts for the nearest information-free space."

"I see. And what's the 'Pooh-Bah' for?"

Fay smiled. "Cut. My password for activating the setter, so it won't respond to chance numerals it overhears."

"But why 'Pooh-Bah'?"

Fay grinned. "Cut. And you a writer. It's a literary reference, Gussy. Pooh-Bah (cut!) was Lord High Everything Else in *The Mikado*. He had a little list, and nothing on it would ever be missed."

"Oh, yeah," Gusterson remembered, glowering. "As I recall it, all that went on that list were the names of people who were slated to have their heads chopped off by Ko-Ko. Better watch your step, Shorty. It may be a backhanded omen. Maybe all those workers you're puttin' ticklers on to pump them full of adrenaline so they'll overwork without noticin' it will revolt and come out someday choppin' for your head."

"Spare me the Marxist mythology," Fay protested. "Gussy, you've got a completely wrong slant on Tickler. It's true that most of our mass sales so far, bar government and army, have been to large companies purchasing for their employees — ."

"Ah-ha!"

" — but that's because there's nothing like a tickler for teaching a new man his job. It tells him from instant to instant what he must do

— while he's already on the job and without disturbing other workers. Magnetizing a wire with a job pattern is the easiest thing going. And you'd be astonished what the subliminals do for employee morale. It's this way, Gussy: most people are too improvident and unimaginative to see in advance the advantages of ticklers. They buy one because the company strongly suggests it and payment is on easy installments withheld from salary. They find a tickler makes the workday go easier. The little fellow perched on your shoulder is a friend exuding comfort and good advice. The first thing he's set to say is 'Take it easy, pal.'

"Within a week they're wearing their tickler 24 hours a day — and buying a tickler for the wife, so she'll remember to comb her hair and smile real pretty and cook favorite dishes."

"I get it, Fay," Gusterson cut in. "The tickler is the newest fad for increasing worker efficiency. Once, I read somewheres, it was salt tablets. They had salt-tablet dispensers everywhere, even in air-conditioned offices where there wasn't a moist armpit twice a year and the gals sweat only champagne. A decade later people wondered what all those dusty white pills were for. Sometimes they were mistook for tranquilizers. It'll be the same way with ticklers. Somebody'll open a musty closet and see jumbled heaps of these gripping-hand silvery gadgets gathering dust curls and — "

"They will not!" Fay protested vehemently. "Ticklers are not a fad — they're history-changers, they're Free-World revolutionary! Why, before Micro Systems put a single one on the market, we'd made it a rule that every Micro employee had to wear one! If that's not having supreme confidence in a product — "

"Every employee except the top executives, of course," Gusterson interrupted jeeringly. "And that's not demoting you, Fay. As the R and D chief most closely involved, you'd naturally have to show special enthusiasm."

"But you're wrong there, Gussy," Fay crowed. "Man for man, our top executives have been more enthusiastic about their personal ticklers than any other class of worker in the whole outfit."

Gusterson slumped and shook his head. "If that's the case," he said darkly, "maybe mankind deserves the tickler."

"I'll say it does!" Fay agreed loudly without thinking. Then, "Oh, can the carping, Gussy. Tickler's a great invention. Don't deprecate it just because you had something to do with its genesis. You're going to have to get in the swim and wear one."

"Maybe I'd rather drown horrible."

"Can the gloom-talk too! Gussy, I said it before and I say it again, you're just scared of this new thing. Why, you've even got the drapes pulled so you won't have to look at the tickler factory."

"Yes, I am scared," Gusterson said. "Really sca . . . AWP!"

Fay whirled around. Daisy was standing in the bedroom doorway, wearing the short silver sheath. This time there was no mask, but her bobbed hair was glitteringly silvered, while her legs, arms, hands, neck, face — every bit of her exposed skin — was painted with beautifully even vertical green stripes.

"I did it as a surprise for Gusterson," she explained to Fay. "He says he likes me this way. The green glop's supposed to be smudge proof."

Gusterson said, "It better be." Then his face got a rapt expression. "I'll tell you why your tickler's so popular, Fay," he said softly. "It's not because it backstops the memory or because it boosts the ego with subliminals. It's because it takes the hook out of a guy, it takes over the job of withstanding the pressure of living. See, Fay, here are all these little guys in this subterranean rat race with atomic-death squares and chromium-plated reward squares and enough money if you pass Go almost to get to Go again — and a million million rules of the game to keep in mind. Well, here's this one little guy and every morning he wakes up there's all these things he's got to keep in mind to do or he'll lose his turn three times in a row and maybe a terrible black rook in iron armor'll loom up and bang him off the chessboard. But now, look, now he's got his tickler, and he tells his sweet silver tickler all these things and the tickler's got to remember them. Of course he'll have to do them eventually, but meanwhile the pressure's off him, the hook's out of his short hairs. He's shifted the responsibility . . ."

"Well, what's so bad about that?" Fay broke in loudly. "What's wrong with taking the pressure off little guys? Why shouldn't Tickler be a superego surrogate? Micro's Motivations chief noticed that positive feature straight off and scored it three pluses. Besides, it's nothing but a gaudy way of saying that Tickler backstops the memory. Seriously, Gussy, what's so bad about it?"

"I don't know," Gusterson said slowly, his eyes still far away. "I just know it feels bad to me." He crinkled his big forehead. "Well for one thing," he said, "it means that a man's taking orders from something else. He's got a kind of master. He's sinking back into a slave psychology."

"He's only taking orders from himself," Fay countered disgustedly. "Tickler's just a mech reminder, a notebook, in essence no more than the back of an old envelope. It's no master."

"Are you absolutely sure of that?" Gusterson asked quietly.

"Why, Gussy, you big oaf — " Fay began heatedly. Suddenly his features quirked and he twitched. " 'Scuse me, folks," he said rapidly, heading for the door, "but my tickler told me I gotta go."

"Hey, Fay, don't you mean you told your tickler to tell you when it was time to go?" Gusterson called after him.

Fay looked back in the doorway. He wet his lips, his eyes moved from side to side. "I'm not quite sure," he said in an off strained voice and darted out.

Gusterson stared for some seconds at the pattern of emptiness Fay had left. Then he shivered. Then he shrugged, "I must be slipping," he muttered. "I never even suggested something for him to invent." Then he looked around at Daisy, who was still standing poker-faced in her doorway.

"Hey, you look like something out of the Arabian Nights," he told her. "Are you supposed to be anything special? How far do those stripes go, anyway?"

"You could probably find out," she told him coolly. "All you have to do is kill me a dragon or two first."

He studied her. "My God," he said reverently, "I really have all the fun in life. What do I do to deserve this?"

"You've got a big gun," she told him, "and you go out in the world with it and hold up big companies and take yards and yards of money away from them in rolls like ribbon and bring it all home to me."

"Don't say that about the gun again," he said. "Don't whisper it, don't even think it. I've got one, dammit — thirty-eight caliber, yet — and I don't want some psionic monitor with two-way clairaudience they haven't told me about catching the whisper and coming to take the gun away from us. It's one of the few individuality symbols we've got left."

Suddenly Daisy whirled away from the door, spun three times so that her silvered hair stood out like a metal coolie hat, and sank to a curtsey in the middle of the room.

"I've just thought of what I am," she announced, fluttering her eyelashes at him. "I'm a sweet silver tickler with green stripes."

V

Next day Daisy cashed the Micro check for ten hundred aluminum-bronze pseudo-silver smackers, which she hid in a broken radionic coffee urn. Gusterson sold his insanity novel and started a new one about a mad medic with a hiccupy hysterical chuckle, who gimmicked Moodmasters to turn mental patients into nymphomaniacs, mass murderers and compulsive saints. But this time he couldn't get Fay out of his mind, or the last chilling words the nervous little man had spoken.

For that matter, he couldn't blank the underground out of his mind as effectively as usually. He had the feeling that a new kind of mole was loose in the burrows and that the ground at the foot of their skyscraper might start humping up any minute.

Toward the end of one afternoon he tucked a half-dozen newly typed sheets in his pocket, shrouded his typer, went to the hatrack and took down his prize: a miner's hard-top cap with electric headlamp.

"Goin' below, Cap'n," he shouted toward the kitchen.

"Be back for second dog watch," Daisy replied. "Remember what I told you about lassoing me some art-conscious girl neighbors."

"Only if I meet a piebald one with a taste for Scotch — or maybe a pearl-gray biped jaguar with violet spots," Gusterson told her, clapping on the cap with a We-Who-Are-About-To-Die gesture."

Halfway across the park to the escalator bunker Gusterson's heart began to tick. He resolutely switched on his headlamp.

As he'd known it would, the hatch robot whirred an extra and higher-pitched ten seconds when it came to his topside address, but it ultimately dilated the hatch for him, first handing him a claim check for his ID card.

Gusterson's heart was ticking like a sledgehammer by now. He hopped clumsily onto the escalator, clutched the moving guard rail to either side, then shut his eyes as the steps went over the edge and became what felt like vertical. An instant later he forced his eyes open, he unclipped a hand from the rail and touched the second switch beside his headlamp, which instantly began to blink white, as if he were a civilian plane flying into a nest of military jobs.

With a further effort, he kept his eyes open and flinchingly surveyed the scene around him. After zigging through a bombproof furlong of roof, he was dropping into a large twilit cave. The blue-black ceiling twinkled with stars. The walls were pierced at floor level by a dozen archways with busy niche stores and glowing advertisements crowded between them. From the archways some three dozen slidewalks curved out, tangenting off each other in a bewildering multiple cloverleaf. The slidewalks were packed with people, traveling motionless, like purposeful statues, or pivoting with practiced grace, from one slidewalk to another, like a thousand toreros doing veronicas.

The slidewalks were moving faster than he recalled from his last venture underground, and at the same time the whole pedestrian concourse was quieter than he remembered. It was as if the five thousand or so moles in view were all listening — for what? But there was something else that had changed about them — a change that he couldn't for a moment define, or unconsciously didn't want to. Clothing style? No . . . My God, they weren't all wearing identical monster masks? No . . . hair color? . . . Well . . .

He was studying them so intently that he forgot his escalator was landing. He came off it with a heel-jarring stumble and bumped into a knot of four men on the tiny triangular hold-still. These four at least sported a new style-wrinkle: ribbed gray shoulder-capes that made them look as if their heads were poling up out of the center of bulgy umbrellas or giant mushrooms.

One of them grabbed hold of Gusterson and saved him from staggering onto a slidewalk that might have carried him to Toledo.

"Gussy, you dog, you must have espied I wanted to see you," Fay cried, patting him on the elbows. "Meet Davidson and Kester and Hazen, colleagues of mine. We're all Micro-men." Fay's companions were staring strangely at Gusterson's blinking headlamp. Fay explained rapidly, "Mr. Gusterson is an insanity novelist. You know, I-D."

"Inner-directed spell *id*," Gusterson said absently, still staring at the interweaving crowd beyond them, trying to figure out what made them different from the last trip. "Creativity fuel. Cranky. Explodes through the parietal fissure if you look at it cross-eyed. Been known to kill knot-heads, open minds, and other people with holes in their heads."

"Ha-ha," Fay laughed. "Well, boys, I've found my man. How's the new novel perking, Gussy?"

"Got my climax, I think," Gusterson mumbled, still peering puzzledly around Fay at the slidestanders. "Moodmaster's going to come alive. Ever occur to you that 'mood' is 'doom' spelled backward? And then . . ." He let his voice trail off as he realized that Kester and Davidson and Hazen had made their farewells and were sliding into the distance. He reminded himself wryly that nobody ever wants to hear an author talk — he's much too good a listener to be wasted that way. Let's see, was it that everybody in the crowd had the same facial expression . . .? Or showed symptoms of the same disease . . .?

"I was coming to visit you, but now you can pay me a call," Fay was saying. "There are two matters I want to — ."

Gusterson stiffened. "*My God, they're all hunchbacked!*" he yelled.

"Shh! Of course they are," Fay whispered reprovingly. "They're all wearing their ticklers. But you don't need to be insulting about it."

"*I'm gettin' out o' here.*" Gusterson turned to flee as if from five thousand Richard the Thirds.

"Oh no you're not," Fay amended, drawing him back with one hand. Somehow, underground, the little man seemed to carry more weight. "You're having cocktails in my thinking box. Besides, climbing down escaladder will give you a heart attack."

In his home habitat Gusterson was about as easy to handle as a rogue rhinoceros, but away from it — and especially if underground — he became more like a pliable elephant. All his bones dropped out through his feet, as he described it to Daisy. So now he submitted miserably as Fay surveyed him up and down, switched off his blinking headlamp ("That coalminer caper is corny, Gussy.") and then, surprisingly, rapidly stuffed his belt-bag under the right shoulder of Gusterson's coat and buttoned the latter to hold it in place.

"So you won't stand out," he explained. Another swift survey. "You'll do. Come on, Gussy. I got lots to brief you on." Three rapid paces and then Gusterson's feet would have gone out from under him except that Fay gave him a mighty shove. The small man sprang onto the slidewalk after him and then they were skimming effortlessly side by side. "Think of it as underground surfing," Fay said. "It's exhilarating . . . if you view it the right way," he trailed off wanly.

Gusterson felt frightened and twice as hunchbacked as the slide-standers around him — morally as well as physically.

Nevertheless he countered bravely, "I got things to brief *you* on. I got six pages of cautions on ti — "

"Shh!" Fay stopped him. "Let's use my hushbox."

He drew out his pancake phone and stretched it so that it covered both their lower faces, like a double yashmak. Gusterson, his neck pushing into the ribbed bulge of the shoulder cape so he could be cheek to cheek with Fay, felt horribly conspicuous, but then he noticed that none of the slidestanders were paying them the least attention. The reason for their abstraction occurred to him. They were listening to their ticklers! He shuddered.

"I got six pages of caution on ticklers," he repeated into the hot, moist quiet of the pancake phone. "I typed 'em so I wouldn't forget 'em in the heat of polemicking. I want you to read every word. Fay, I've had it on my mind ever since I started wondering whether it was you or your tickler made you duck out of our place last time you were there. I want you to — "

"Ha-ha! All in good time." In the pancake phone Fay's laugh was brassy. "But I'm glad you've decided to lend a hand, Gussy. This thing if moving faaaassst. Nationwise, adult underground ticklerization is ninety per cent complete."

"I don't believe that," Gusterson protested while glaring at the hunchbacks around them. The slidewalk was gliding down a low glow-ceiling tunnel lined with doors and advertisements. Rapt-eyed people were pirouetting on and off. "A thing just can't develop that fast, Fay. It's against nature."

"Ha, but we're not in nature, we're in culture. The progress of an industrial scientific culture is geometric. It goes n-times as many jumps as it takes. More then geometric — exponential. Confidentially, Micro's Math chief tells me we're currently on a fourth-power progress curve trending into a fifth."

"You mean we're goin' so fast we got to watch out we don't bump ourselves in the rear when we come around again?" Gusterson asked, scanning the tunnel ahead for curves. "Or just shoot straight up to infinity?"

"Exactly! Of course most of the last power and a half is due to Tickler itself. Gussy, the tickler's already eliminated absenteeism, alco-

holism, and aboulia in numerous urban areas — and that's just one letter of the alphabet! If Tickler doesn't turn us into a nation of photo-
memory constant-creative-flow geniuses in six months, I'll come live
topside."

"You mean because a lot of people are standing around glassy-eyed
listening to something mumbling in their ear that it's a good thing?"

"Gussy, you don't know progress when you see it. Tickler is the
greatest invention since language. Bar none, it's the greatest instrument ever devised for integrating a man into all phases of his environment. Under the present routine a newly purchased tickler first
goes to government and civilian defense for primary patterning,
then to the purchaser's employer, then to his doctor-psycher, then to
his local bunker captain, then to *him*. *Everything* that's needful for a
man's welfare gets on the spools. Efficiency cubed! Incidentally,
Russia's got the tickler now. Our dip-satellites have photographed it.
It's like ours except the Commies wear it on the left shoulder . . . but
they're two weeks behind us developmentwise and they'll never
close the gap!"

Gusterson reared up out of the pancake phone to take a deep
breath. A sulky-lipped sylph-figured girl two feet from him twitched
— medium cootch, he judged — then fumbled in her belt-bag for a pill
and popped it in her mouth.

"Hell, the tickler's not even efficient yet about little things,"
Gusterson blatted, diving back into the privacy-yashmak he was shar-
ing with Fay. "Whyn't that girl's doctor have the Moodmaster compo-
nent of her tickler inject her with medicine?"

"Her doctor probably wants her to have the discipline of pill-taking
— or the exercise," Fay answered glibly. "Look sharp now. Here's
where we fork. I'm taking you through Micro's postern." A ribbon of
slidewalk split itself from the main band and angled off into a short
alley. Gusterson hardly felt the constant-speed juncture as they
crossed it. Then the secondary ribbon speeded up, carrying them at
about thirty feet a second toward the black concrete wall in which the
alley ended. Gusterson prepared to jump, but Fay grabbed him with
one hand and with the other held up toward the wall a badge and a
button. When they were about ten feet away the wall whipped aside,
then whipped shut behind them so fast that Gusterson wondered
momentarily if he still had his heels and the seat of his pants.

Fay, tucking away his badge and pancake phone, dropped the button in Gusterson's vest pocket. "Use it when you leave," he said casually. "That is, if you leave."

Gusterson, who was trying to read the Do and Don't posters papering the walls they were passing, started to probe that last sinister supposition, but just then the ribbon slowed, a swinging door opened and closed behind them, and they found themselves in a luxuriously furnished thinking box measuring at least eight feet by five.

"Hey, this is something," Gusterson said appreciatively to show he wasn't an utter yokel. Then, drawing on research he'd done for period novels, "Why, it's as big as a Pullman car compartment, or a first mate's cabin in the War of 1812. You really must rate."

Fay nodded, smiled wanly and sat down with a sigh on a compact overstuffed swivel chair. He let his arms dangle and his head sink into his puffed shoulder cape. Gusterson stared at him. It was the first time he could ever recall the little man showing fatigue.

"Tickler currently does have one serious drawback," Fay volunteered. "It weighs twenty-eight pounds. You feel it when you've been on your feet a couple of hours. No question we're going to give the next model that antigravity feature you mentioned for pursuit grenades. We'd have had it in this model except there were so many other things to be incorporated." He sighed again. "Why, the scanning and decision-making elements alone tripled the mass."

"Hey," Gusterson protested, thinking especially of the sulky-lipped girl, "do you mean to tell me all those other people were toting two stone?"

Fay shook his head heavily. "They were all wearing Mark Three or Four. I'm wearing Mark Six," he said, as one might say, "I'm carrying the genuine Cross, not one of the balsa ones."

But then his face brightened a little and he went on. "Of course the new improved features make it more than worth it . . . and you hardly feel it at all at night when you're lying down . . . and if you remember to talcum under it twice a day, no sores develop . . . at least not very big ones . . ."

Backing away involuntarily, Gusterson felt something prod his right shoulder blade. Ripping open his coat, he convulsively plunged his hand under it and tore out Fay's belt-bag . . . and then set it down very gently on the top of a shallow cabinet and relaxed with the sigh of one who has escaped a great, if symbolic, danger. Then he remembered something Fay had mentioned. He straightened again.

"Hey, you said it's got scanning and decision-making elements. That means your tickler thinks, even by your fancy standards. And if it thinks, it's conscious — except maybe at robotic gut-level."

"Gussy," Fay said wearily, frowning, "all sorts of things nowadays have S and DM elements. Mail sorters, missiles, robot medics, high-style mannequins, just to name some of the Ms. They 'think' to use that archaic word, but it's neither here nor there. And they're certainly not conscious."

"Your tickler thinks," Gusterson repeated stubbornly, "just like I warned you it would. It sits on your shoulder, ridin' you like you was a pony or a starved St. Bernard, and now it thinks."

"Suppose it does?" Fay yawned. "What of it?" He gave a rapid sinuous one-sided shrug that made it look for a moment as if his left arm had three elbows. It stuck in Gusterson's mind, for he had never seen Fay use such a gesture, and he wondered where he'd picked it up. Maybe imitating a double-jointed Micro Finance chief? Fay yawned again and said, "Please, Gussy, don't disturb me for a minute or so." His eyes half closed.

Gusterson studied Fay's sunken-cheeked face and the great puff of his shoulder cape.

"Say, Fay," he asked in a soft voice after about five minutes, "are you meditating?"

"Why, no," Fay responded, starting up and then stifling another yawn. "Just resting a bit. I seem to get more tired these days, somehow. You'll have to excuse me, Gussy. But what made you think of meditation?"

"Oh, I just got to wonderin' in that direction," Gusterson said. "You see, when you first started to develop Tickler, it occurred to me that there was one thing about it that might be real good even if you did give it S and DM elements. It's this: having a mech secretary to take charge of his obligations and routine in the real world might allow a man to slide into the other world, the world of thoughts and feelings and intuitions, and sort of ooze around in there and accomplish things. Know any of the people using Tickler that way, hey?"

"Of course not," Fay denied with a bright incredulous laugh. "Who'd want to loaf around in an imaginary world and take a chance of *missing out on what his tickler's doing?* — I mean, on what his tickler has in store for him — what he's *told* his tickler to have in store for him."

Ignoring Gusterson' shiver, Fay straightened up and seemed to brisken himself. "Ha, that little slump did me good. A tickler *makes* you rest, you know — it's one of the great things about it. Pooh-Bah's kinder to me than I ever was to myself." He buttoned open a tiny refrigerator and took out two waxed cardboard cubes and handed one to Gusterson. "Martini? Hope you don't mind drinking from the carton. Cheers. Now, Gussy old pal, there are two matters I want to take up with you — "

"Hold it," Gusterson said with something of his old authority. "There's something I got to get off my mind first." He pulled the type pages out of his inside pocket and straightened them. "I told you about these," he said. "I want you to read them before you do anything else. Here."

Fay looked toward the pages and nodded, but did not take them yet. He lifted his hands to his throat and unhooked the clasp of his cape, then hesitated.

"You wear that thing to hide the hump your tickler makes?' Gusterson filled in. "You got better taste than those other moles."

"Not to hide it, exactly," Fay protested, "but just so the others won't be jealous. I wouldn't feel comfortable parading a free-scanning decision-capable Mark Six tickler in front of people who can't buy it — until it goes on open sale at twenty-two fifteen tonight. Lot of shelter-folk won't be sleeping tonight. They'll be queued up to trade in their old tickler for a Mark Six almost as good as Pooh-Bah."

He started to jerk his hands apart, hesitated again with an oddly apprehensive look at the big man, then whirled off the cape.

VI

Gusterson sucked in such a big gasp that he hiccuped. The right shoulder of Fay's jacket and shirt had been cut away. Thrusting up through the neatly hemmed hole was a silvery gray hump with a one-eyed turret atop it and two multi-jointed metal arms ending in little claws.

It looked like the top half of a psedu-science robot — a squat evil child robot, Gusterson told himself, which had lost its legs in a railway accident — and it seemed to him that a red fleck was moving around in the huge single eye.

"I'll take that memo now," Fay said cooly, reaching out his hand. He caught the rustling sheets as they slipped from Gusterson's fingers, evened them up very precisely by tapping them on his knee . . . and then handed them over his shoulder to his tickler, which clicked its claws around either margin and then began rather swiftly to lift the top sheet past its single eye at a distance of about six inches.

"The first matter I want to take up with you, Gussy," Fay began, paying no attention whatsoever to the little scene on his shoulder, " — or warn you about, rather — is the imminent ticklerization of schoolchildren, geriatrics, convicts and topsiders. At three zero zero tomorrow, ticklers become mandatory for all adult shelterfolk. The mop-up operations won't be long in coming — in fact, these days we find that the square root of the estimated time of a new development is generally the best time estimate. Gussy, I strongly advise you to start wearing a tickler now. And Daisy and your moppets. If you heed my advice, your kids will have the jump on their class. Transition and conditioning are easy, since Tickler itself sees to it."

Pooh-Bah leafed the first page to the back of the packet and began lifting the second past his eye — a little more swiftly than the first.

"I've got a Mark Six tickler all warmed up for you," Fay pressed, "*and* a shoulder cape. You won't feel one bit conspicuous." He noticed the direction of Gusterson's gaze and remarked, "Fascinating mechanism, isn't it? Of course twenty-eight pounds are a bit oppressive, but then you have to remember it's only a way-station to free-floating Mark Seven or Eight."

Pooh-Bah finished page two and began to race through page three.

"But I wanted *you* to read it," Gusterson said bemusedly, staring.

"Pooh-Bah will do a better job than I could," Fay assured him. "Get the gist without losing the chaff."

"But dammit, it's all about *him*," Gusterson said a little more strongly. "He won't be objective about it."

"A better job," Fay reiterated, "*and* more fully objective. Pooh-Bah's set for full précis. Stop worrying about it. He's a dispassionate machine, not a fallible, emotionally disturbed human misled by the will-o'-the-wisp of consciousness. Second matter: Micro Systems is impressed by your contributions to Tickler and will recruit you as a senior consultant with a salary and thinking box as big as my own, family quarters to match. It's an unheard-of high start. Gussy, I think you'd be a fool — "

He broke off, held up a hand for silence, and his eyes got a listening look. Pooh-Bah had finished page six and was holding the packet motionless. After about ten seconds Fay's face broke into a big fake smile. He stood up, suppressing a wince, and held out his hand. "Gussy," he said loudly, "I am so happy to inform you that all your fears about Tickler are so much thistledown. My word on it. There's nothing to them at all. Pooh-Bah's précis, which he's just given to me, proves it."

"Look," Gusterson said solemnly, "there's one thing I want you to do. Purely to humor an old friend. But I want you to do it. *Read that memo yourself.*"

"Certainly I will, Gussy," Fay continued in the same ebullient tones. "I'll read it — " he twitched and his smile disappeared, "a little later."

"Sure," Gusterson said dully, holding his hand to his stomach. "And now if you don't mind, Fay, I'm goin' home. I feel just a bit sick. Maybe the ozone and the other additives in your shelter air are too heady for me. It's been years since I tramped through a pine forest."

"But, Gussy! You've hardly got here. You haven't even sat down. Have another martini. Have a seltzer pill. Have a whiff of oxy. Have a — "

"No, Fay, I'm going home right away. I'll think about the job offer. *Remember to read that memo.*"

"I will, Gussy, I certainly will. You know your way? The button takes you through the wall. 'Bye, now."

He sat down abruptly and looked away. Gusterson pushed through the swinging door. He tensed himself for the step onto the slowly moving reverse ribbon. Then on an impulse he pushed ajar the swinging door and looked back inside.

Fay was sitting as he'd left him, apparently lost in listless brooding. On his shoulder Pooh-Bah was rapidly crossing and uncrossing its little metal arms, tearing the memo to smaller and smaller shreds. It let the scraps drift slowly toward the floor and oddly writhed its three-elbowed left arm . . . and then Gusterson knew from whom, or rather from what, Fay had copied his new shrug.

VII

When Gusterson got home toward the end of the second dog watch, he slipped aside from Daisy's questions and set the children laughing with a graphic enactment of his slidestanding technique and a story about getting his head caught in a thinking box build for a midget physicist. After supper he played with Imogene, Iago, and Claudius until it was their bedtime, and thereafter was unusually attentive to Daisy, admiring her fading green stripes, though he did spend a while in the next apartment, where they stored their outdoor camping equipment.

But the next morning he announced to the children that it was a holiday — the Feast of St. Gusterson — and then took Daisy into the bedroom and told her everything.

When he'd finished she said, "This is something I've got to see for myself."

Gusterson shrugged. "If you think you've got to. I say we should head for the hills right now. One thing I'm standing on: the kids aren't going back to school."

"Agreed," Daisy said, "But, Gusterson, we've lived through a lot of things without leaving home altogether. We lived through the Everybody-Six-Feet-Underground-by-Christmas campaign and all the Robot Watchdog craze, when you got your left foot half chewed off. We lived through the Venomous Bats and Indoctrinated Saboteur Rats and the Hypnotized Monkey Paratrooper scares. We lived through the voice of Safety and Anti-Communist Somno-Instruction and Rightest Pills and Jet-Propelled Vigilantes. We lived through the Cold-Out, when you weren't supposed to turn on a toaster for fear its heat would be a target for prowl missiles and when people with fevers were unpopular. We lived through — "

Gusterson patted her hand. "You go below," he said. "Come back when you've decided this is different. Come back as soon as you can anyway. I'll be worried about you every minute you're down there."

When she was gone — in a green suit and hat to minimize or at least justify the effect of the faded stripes — Gusterson doled out to the children provender and equipment for a camping expedition to the next floor. Iago led them off in stealthy Indian file. Leaving the hall door open Gusterson got out his .38 and cleaned and loaded it, meanwhile concentrating on a chess problem with the idea of confusing a hypothetical psionic monitor. By the time he had hid the revolver again he heard the elevator creaking back up.

Daisy came dragging in without her hat, looking as if she'd been concentrating on a chess problem for hours herself and just now given up. Her stripes seemed to have vanished; then Gusterson decided this was because her whole complexion was a touch green.

She sat down on the edge of the couch and said without looking at him, "Did you tell me, Gusterson, that everybody was quiet and abstracted and orderly down below, especially the ones wearing ticklers, meaning pretty much everybody?"

"I did," he said. "I take it that's no longer the case. What are the new symptoms?"

She gave no indication. After some time she said, "Gusterson, do you remember the Doré illustrations of the *Inferno*? Can you visualize the paintings of Hieronymous Bosch with the hordes of proto-Freudian devils tormenting people all over the farmyard and city square? Did you ever see the Disney animations of Moussorgsky's witches' Sabbath music? Back in the foolish days before you married me, did that drug-addict girl friend of yours ever take you to a genuine orgy?"

"As bad as that, hey?"

She nodded emphatically and all of a sudden shivered violently. "Several shades worse," she said. "If they decide to come topside — " She shot up. "Where are the kids?"

"Upstairs campin' in the mysterious wilderness of the twenty-first floor," Gusterson reassured her. "Let's leave 'em there until we're ready to — "

He broke off. They both heard the faint sound of thudding footsteps.

"They're on the stairs," Daisy whispered, starting to move toward the open door. "But are they coming from up or down?"

"It's just one person," judged Gusterson, moving after his wife. "Too heavy for one of the kids."

The footsteps doubled in volume and came rapidly closer. Along with them there was an agonized gasping. Daisy stopped, staring fearfully at the open doorway. Gusterson moved past her. Then he stopped too.

Fay stumbled into view and would have fallen on his face except he clutched both sides of the doorway halfway up. He was stripped to the waist. There was a little blood on his shoulder. His narrow chest was arching convulsively, the ribs standing out starkly, as he sucked in oxygen to replace what he'd burned up running up twenty flights. His eyes were wild.

"They've taken over," he panted. Another gobbling breath. "Gone crazy." Two more gasps. "Gotta stop em."

His eyes filmed. He swayed forward. Then Gusterson's big arms were around him and he was carrying him to the couch.

Daisy came running from the kitchen with a damp cool towel. Gusterson took it from her and began to mop Fay off. He sucked in his own breath as he saw that Fay's right ear was raw and torn. He whispered to Daisy, "Look at where the thing savaged him."

The blood on Fay's shoulder came from his ear. Some of it stained a flush-skin gum-pink plastic fitting that had two small valved holes in it, and that puzzled Gusterson until he remembered that Moodmaster tied into the bloodstream. For a second he thought he was going to vomit.

The dazed look slid aside from Fay's eyes. He was gasping less painfully now. He sat up, pushing the towel away, buried his face in his hands for a few seconds, then looked over his fingers at the two of them.

"I've been living in a nightmare for the last week," he said in a taut small voice, "knowing the thing had come alive and trying to pretend to myself that it hadn't. Knowing it was taking charge of me more and more. Having it whisper in my ear, over and over again, in a cracked little rhyme that I could only hear every hundredth time, 'day by day, in every way, you're learning to listen . . . and *obey*. Day by day — ' "

His voice started to go high. He pulled it down and continued harshly, "I ditched it this morning when I showered. It let me break contact to do that. It must have figured it had complete control of me, mounted or dismounted. I think it's telepathic, and then it did some well, rather unpleasant things to me late last night. But I pulled together my fears and my will and I ran for it. The slidewalks were chaos. The Mark Six ticklers showed some purpose, though I couldn't tell you what, but as far as I could see the Mark Threes and Fours were just cootching their mounts to death — Chinese feather torture. Giggling, gasping, choking . . . gales of mirth. People are dying of laughter . . . ticklers! . . . the irony of it! It was the complete lack of order and sanity that let me get topside. There were things I saw — " Once again his voice went shrill. He clapped his hand to his mouth and rocked back and forth on the couch.

Gusterson gently but firmly laid a hand on his good shoulder. "Steady," he said. "Here, swallow this."

Fay shoved aside the short brown drink. "We've got to stop them," he cried. "Mobilize the topsiders — contact the wilderness patrols and manned satellites — pour ether in the tunnel air pumps — invent and crash-manufacture missiles that will home on ticklers without harming humans — SOS Mars and Venus — dope the shelter water supply — do something! Gussy, you don't realize what people are going through down there every second."

"I think they're experiencing the ultimate in outer-directedness," Gusterson said gruffly.

"Have you no heart?" Fay demanded. His eyes widened as if he were seeing Gusterson for the first time. Then, accusingly, pointing a shaking finger: *"You invented the tickler, George Gusterson! It's all your fault! You've got to do something about it!"*

Before Gusterson could retort to that, or begin to think of a reply, or even assimilate the full enormity of Fay's statement, he was grabbed from behind and frog-marched away from Fay. Something that felt remarkably like the muzzle of a large-caliber gun was shoved in the small of his back.

Under cover of Fay's outburst a huge crowd of people had entered the room from the hall — eight, to be exact. But the weirdest thing about them to Gusterson was that from the first instant he had the impression that only one mind had entered the room and that it did not reside in any of the eight persons, even though he recognized three of them, but in something that they were carrying.

Several things contributed to this impression. The eight people all had the same blank expression — watchful yet empty-eyed. They all moved in the same slithery crouch. And they had all taken off their shoes. Perhaps, Gusterson thought wildly, they believed he and Daisy ran a Japanese flat.

Gusterson was being held by two burly women, one of them quite pimply. He considered stamping on her toes, but just at that moment the gun dug in his back with a corkscrew movement.

The man holding the gun on him was Fay's colleague, Davidson. Some yards beyond Fay's couch, Kester was holding a gun on Daisy, without digging it into her, while the single strange man holding Daisy herself was doing so quite decorously — a circumstance which afforded Gusterson minor relief, since it made him feel less guilty about not going berserk.

Two more strange men, one of them in purple lounging pajamas, the other in the gray uniform of a slidewalk inspector, had grabbed Fay's skinny upper arms, one on either side, and were lifting him to this feet, while Fay was struggling with such desperate futility and gibbering so pitifully that Gusterson momentarily had second thoughts about the moral imperative to go berserk when menaced by hostile force, or seeing a friend so menaced. But again the gun dug into him with a twist.

Approaching Fay face-on was the third Micro-man Gusterson had met yesterday — Hazen. It was Hazen who was carrying — quite reverently or solemnly — or at any rate very carefully the object that seemed to Gusterson to be the mind of the little storm troop presently desecrating the sanctity of his own individual home.

All of them were wearing ticklers, of course — the three Micro-men the heavy emergent Mark 6s with their clawed and jointed arms and monocular cephalic turrets, the rest lower-numbered Marks of the sort that merely made Richard-the-Third humps under clothing.

The object that Hazen was carrying was the Mark 6 tickler Gusterson had seen Fay wearing yesterday. Gusterson was sure it was Pooh-Bah because of its air of command, and because he would have sworn on a mountain of Bibles that he recognized the red fleck lurking in the back of its single eye. And Pooh-Bah alone had the aura of full conscious thought. Pooh-Bah alone had mana.

It is not good to see an evil legless child robot with dangling straps bossing — apparently by telepathic power — not only three objects of its own kind and five close primitive relatives, but also eight human beings . . . and in addition throwing into a state of twitching terror one miserable, thin-chested, half-crazy research-and-development director.

Pooh-Bah pointed a claw at Fay. Fay's handlers dragged him forward, still resisting but more feebly now, as if half hypnotized or at least cowed.

Gusterson grunted an outraged, "Hey!" and automatically struggled a bit, but once more the gun dug in. Daisy shut her eyes, then firmed her mouth and opened them again to look.

Seating the tickler on Fay's shoulder took a little time because two blunt spikes in its bottom had to be fitted into the valved holes in the flush-skin plastic disk. When at last they plunged home, Gusterson felt very sick indeed — and then even more so, as the tickler itself poked a tiny pellet on a fine wire into Fay's ear.

The next moment Fay had straightened up and motioned his handlers aside. He tightened the straps of his tickler around his chest and under his armpits. He held out a hand and someone gave him a shoulderless shirt and coat. He slipped into them smoothly, Pooh-Bah dexterously using little claws to help put its turret and body through the neatly hemmed holes. The small storm troop looked at Fay with deferential expectation. He held still for a moment, as if thinking, and then walked over to Gusterson and looked him in the face and again held still.

Fay's expression was jaunty on the surface, agonized underneath. Gusterson knew that he wasn't thinking at all, but listening for instructions from something that was whispering on the very threshold of his inner ear.

"Gussy, old boy," Fay said, twitching a depthless grin, "I'd be very much obliged if you'd answer a few simple questions." His voice was hoarse at first, but he swallowed twice and corrected that. "What exactly did you have in mind when you invented ticklers? What exactly are they supposed to be?"

"Why, you miserable — " Gusterson began in a kind of confused horror, then got hold of himself and said curtly, "They were supposed to be mech reminders. They were supposed to record memoranda and — "

Fay held up a palm and shook his head and again listened for a space. Then, "That's how ticklers were supposed to be of use to humans," he said. "I don't mean that at all. I mean how ticklers were supposed to be of use to themselves. Surely you had some notion." Fay wet his lips. "If it's any help," he added, "keep in mind that it's not Fay who's asking this question, but Pooh-Bah."

Gusterson hesitated. He had the feeling that every one of the eight dual beings in the room was hanging on his answer and that something was boring into his mind and turning over his next thoughts and peering at and under them before he had a chance to scan them himself. Pooh-Bah's eye was like a red searchlight.

"Go on," Fay prompted. "What were ticklers supposed to be — for themselves?"

"Nothin'," Gusterson said softly. "Nothin' at all."

He could feel the disappointment well up in the room — and with it a touch of something like panic.

This time Fay listened for quite a long while. "I hope you don't mean that, Gussy," he said at last very earnestly. "I mean, I hope you hunt deep and find some ideas you forgot, or maybe never realized you had at the time. Let me put it to you differently. What's the place of ticklers in the natural scheme of things? What's their aim in life? Their special reason? Their genius? Their final cause? What gods should ticklers worship?"

But Gusterson was already shaking his head. He said, "I don't know anything about that at all."

Fay sighed and gave simultaneously with Pooh-Bah the now-familiar triple-jointed shrug. Then the man briskened himself. "I guess that's as far as we can get right now," he said. "Keep thinking, Gussy. Try to remember something. You won't be able to leave your apartment — I'm setting guards. If you want to see me, tell them. Or just think. In due course you'll be questioned further in any case. Perhaps by special methods. Perhaps you'll be ticklerized. That's all. Come on, everybody, let's get going."

The pimply woman and her pal let go of Gusterson, Daisy's man loosed his decorous hold, Davidson and Kester sidled away with an eye behind them, and the little storm troop trudged out.

Fay looked back in the doorway. "I'm sorry, Gussy," he said, and for a moment his old self looked out of his eyes. "I wish I could — " A claw reached for his ear, a spasm of pain crossed his face, he stiffened and marched out. The door shut.

Gusterson took two deep breaths that were close to angry sobs. Then, still breathing stertorously, he stamped into the bedroom.

"What — ?" Daisy asked, looking after him.

He came back carrying his .38 and headed for the door.

"What are you up to?" she demanded, knowing very well.

"I'm going to blast that iron monkey off Fay's back if it's the last thing I do!"

She threw her arms around him.

"Now lemme go," Gusterson growled. "I gotta be a man one time anyway."

As they struggled for the gun, the door opened noiselessly, Davidson slipped in and deftly snatched the weapon out of their hands before they realized he was there. He said nothing, only smiled at them and shook his head in sad reproof as he went out.

Gusterson slumped. "I *knew* they were all psionic," he said softly. "I just got out of control now — that last look Fay gave us." He touched Daisy's arm. "Thanks, kid."

He walked to the glass wall and looked out desultorily. After a while he turned and said, "Maybe you better be with the kids, hey? I imagine the guards'll let you through."

Daisy shook her head. "The kids never come home until supper. For the next few hours they'll be safer without me."

Gusterson nodded vaguely, sat down on the couch and propped his chin on the base of his palm. After a while his brow smoothed and Daisy knew that the wheels had started to turn inside and the electrons to jump around — except that she reminded herself to permanently cross out those particular figures of speech from her vocabulary.

After about half an hour Gusterson said softly, "I think the ticklers are so psionic that it's as if they just had one mind. If I were with them very long I'd start to be part of that mind. Say something to one of them and you say it to all."

Fifteen minutes later: "They're not crazy, they're just newborn. The ones that were creating a cootching chaos downstairs were like babies kickin' their legs and wavin' their arms, tryin' to see what their bodies could do. Too bad their bodies are us."

Ten minutes more: "I gotta do something about it. Fay's right. It's all my fault. He's just the apprentice; I'm the old sorcerer himself."

Five minutes more, gloomily: "Maybe it's man's destiny to build live machines and then bow out of the cosmic picture. Except the ticklers need us, dammit, just like nomads need horses."

Another five minutes: "Maybe somebody could dream up a purpose in life for tickers. Even a religion — the First Church of Pooh-Bah

Tickler. But I hate selling other people spiritual ideas, and that'd still leave ticklers parasitic on humans . . ."

As he murmured those last words Gusterson's eyes got wide as a maniac's and a big smile reached for his ears. He stood up and faced himself toward the door.

"What are you intending to do now?" Daisy asked flatly.

"I'm merely goin' out an' save the world," he told her. "I may be back for supper and I may not."

VIII

Davidson pushed out from the wall against which he'd been resting himself and his two-stone tickler and moved to block the hall. But Gusterson simply walked up to him. He shook his hand warmly and looked his tickler full in the eye and said in a ringing voice, "Ticklers should have bodies of their own!" He paused and then added casually, "Come on, let's visit your boss."

Davidson listened for instructions and then nodded. But he watched Gusterson warily as they walked down the hall.

In the elevator Gusterson repeated his message to the second guard, who turned out to be the pimply woman now wearing shoes. This time he added, "Ticklers shouldn't be tied to the frail bodies of humans, which need a lot of thoughtful supervision and drug-injecting and can't even fly."

Crossing the park, Gusterson stopped a hump-backed soldier and informed him, "Ticklers gotta cut the apron string and snap the silver cord and go out in the universe and find their own purposes." Davidson and the pimply woman didn't interfere. They merely waited and watched and then led Gusterson on.

On the escaladder he told someone, "It's cruel to tie ticklers to slow-witted snaily humans when ticklers can think and live . . . ten thousand times as fast," he finished, plucking the figure from the murk of his unconscious.

By the time they got to the bottom, the message had become, "Ticklers should have a planet of their own!"

They never did catch up with Fay, although they spent two hours skimming around on slidewalks under the subterranean stars, pursuing rumors of his presence. Clearly the boss tickler (which was how they thought of Pooh-Bah) led an energetic life. Gusterson continued to deliver his message to all and sundry at thirty-second intervals. Toward the end he found himself doing it in a dreamy and forgetful way. His mind, he decided, was becoming assimilated to the communal telepathic mind of the ticklers. It did not seem to matter at the time.

After two hours Gusterson realized that he and his guides were becoming part of a general movement of people, a flow as mindless as that of blood corpuscles through the veins, yet at the same time dimly purposeful — at least there was the feeling that it was at the behest of a mind far above.

The flow was topside. All the slidewalks seemed to lead to the concourses and the escaladders. Gusterson found himself part of a human stream moving into the tickler factory adjacent to his apartment — or another factory very much like it.

Thereafter Gusterson's awareness was dimmed. It was as if a bigger mind were doing the remembering for him and it were permissible and even mandatory for him to dream his way along. He knew vaguely that days were passing. He knew he had work of a sort: at one time he was bringing food to gaunt-eyed tickler-mounted humans working feverishly in a production line — human hands and tickler claws working together in a blur of rapidity on silvery mechanisms that moved along jumpily on a great belt; at another he was sweeping piles of metal scraps and garbage down a gray corridor.

Two scenes stood out a little more vividly.

A windowless wall had been knocked out for twenty feet. There was blue sky outside, its light almost hurtful, and a drop of many stories. A file of humans were being processed. When one of them got to the head of the file his (or her) tickler was ceremoniously unstrapped from his shoulder and welded onto a silvery cask with smoothly pointed ends. The welding sparks were red stars. The result was something that looked — at least in the case of the Mark 6 ticklers — like a stubby silver submarine, child size. It would hum gently, lift off the floor and then fly slowly out through the big blue gap. Then the next tickler-ridden human would step forward for processing.

The second scene was in a park, the sky again blue, but big and high with an argosy of white clouds. Gusterson was lined up in a crowd of humans that stretched as far as he could see, row on irregular row.

Martial music was playing. Overhead hovered a flock of little silver submarines lined up rather more orderly in the air than the humans were on the ground. The music rose to a heart-quickening climax. The tickler nearest above Gusterson gave (as if to say, "And now — who knows?") a triple-jointed shrug that stung his memory. Then the ticklers took off straight up on their new and shining bodies. They became a flight of silver geese . . . of silver midges . . . and the humans around Gusterson lifted a ragged cheer . . .

That scene marked the beginning of the return of Gusterson's mind and memory. He shuffled around for a bit, spoke vaguely to three or four people he recalled from the dream days, and then headed for home and supper — three weeks late, and as disoriented and emaciated as a bear coming out of hibernation.

IX

Six months later Fay was having dinner with Daisy and Gusterson. The cocktails had been poured and the children were playing in the next apartment. The transparent violent walls brightened, then gloomed, as the sun dipped below the horizon.

Gusterson said, "I see where a spaceship out beyond the orbit of Mars was holed by a tickler. I wonder where the little guys are headed now?"

Fay started to give a writhing left-armed shrug, but stopped himself with a grimace.

"Maybe out of the solar system altogether," suggested Daisy, who'd recently dyed her hair fire-engine red and was wearing red leotards.

"They got a weary trip ahead of them," Gusterson said, "unless they work out a hyper-Einsteinian drive on the way."

Fay grimaced again. He was still looking rather peaked. He said plaintively, "Haven't we heard enough about ticklers for a while?"

"I guess so," Gusterson agreed, "but I get to wondering about the little guys. They were so serious and intense about everything. I never did solve their problem, you know. I just shifted it onto other shoulders than ours. No joke intended," he hurried to add.

Fay forbore to comment. "By the way, Gussy," he said, "have you heard anything from the Red Cross about that world-saving medal I nominated you for? I know you think the whole concept of world-saving medals is ridiculous, especially when they started giving them to all heads of state who didn't start atomic wars while in office, but — "

"Nary a peep," Gusterson told him. "I'm not proud, Fay. I could use a few world-savin' medals. I'd start a flurry in the old-gold market. But I don't worry about those things. I don't have time to. I'm busy these days thinkin' up a bunch of new inventions."

"Gussy!" Fay said sharply, his face tightening in alarm, "Have you forgotten your promise?"

" 'Course not, Fay. My new inventions aren't for Micro or any other firm. They're just a legitimate part of my literary endeavors. Happens my next insanity novel is goin' to be about a mad inventor."

The Casket-Demon

"There's nothing left for it — I've got to open the casket," said Vividy Sheer, glaring at the ugly thing on its square of jeweled and gold-worked altar cloth. The most photogenic face in the world was grim as a Valkyrie's this Malibu morning.

"No," shuddered Miss Bricker, her secretary. "Vividy, you once let me peek in through the little window and I didn't sleep for a week."

"It would make the wrong sort of publicity," said Maury Gender, the Nordic film-queen's press chief. "Besides that, I value my life." His gaze roved uneasily across the gray "Pains of the Damned" tapestries lining three walls of the conference room up to its black-beamed 20-foot ceiling.

"You forget, baroness, the runic rhymes of the Prussian Nostradamus," said Dr. Rumanescue, Vividy's astrologer and family magician. '*Wenn der Kassette-Teufel . . .*' — or, to translate roughly, 'When the casket-demon is let out, the life of the Von Sheer is in doubt.'"

"My triple-great grandfather held out against the casket-demon for months," Vividy Sheer countered.

"Yes, with a demi-regiment of hussars for bodyguard, and in spite of their sabers and horse pistols he was found dead in bed at his Silesian hunting lodge within a year. Dead in bed and black as a beetle — and the eight hussars in the room with him as night-guard permanently out of their wits with fear."

"I'm stronger than he was — I've conquered Hollywood," Vividy said, her blue eyes sparking and her face all Valkyrie. "But in any case if I'm to live weeks, let alone months, I *must* keep my name in the papers, as all three of you very well know."

"Hey, hey, what goes on here?" demanded Max Rath, Vividy Sheer's producer, for whom the medieval torture-tapestries had noise-lessly parted and closed at the bidding of electric eyes. His own little shrewd ones scanned the casket, no bigger than a cigar box, with its tiny peep-hole of cloudy glass set in the top, and finally came to rest on the only really incongruous object in the monastically-appointed hall — a lavender-tinted bathroom scale.

Vividy glared at him, Dr. Rumanescue shrugged eloquently, Miss Bricker pressed her lips together, Maury Gender licked his own ner-vously and at last said, "Well, Vividy thinks she ought to have more publicity — every-day-without-skips publicity in the biggest papers and on the networks. Also, she's got a weight problem."

Max Rath surveyed in its flimsy dress of silk jersey the most volup-tuous figure on six continents and any number of islands, including Ireland and Bali. "You got no weight problem, Viv," he pronounced. "An ounce either way would be 480 grains away from pneumatic per-fection." Vividy flicked at her bosom contemptuously. Rath's voice changed. "Now as for your name not being in the papers lately, that's a very wise idea — my own, in fact — and must be kept up. *Bride of God* is due to premiere in four months — the first picture about the life of a nun not to be thumbs-downed by any religious or non-religious group, even in the sticks. We want to keep it that way. When you toured the Florence nightclubs with Biff Parowan and took the gon-dola ride with that what's-his-name bellhop, the Pope slapped your wrist, but that's all he did — *Bride's* still not on the Index. But the wrist-slap was a hint — and one more reason why for the next year there mustn't be one tiny smidgin of personal scandal or even so-called harmless notoriety linked to the name of Vividy Sheer."

"Besides that, Viv," he added more familiarly, "the reporters and the reading public were on the verge of getting very sick of the way your name was turning up on the front page every day — and mostly because of chasing, at that. Film stars are like goddesses — they can't be seen too often, there's got to be a little reserve, a little mystery.

"Aw, cheer up Viv. I know it's tough, but Liz and Jayne and Marilyn all learned to do without the daily headline and so can you. Believe an old timer: euphoric pills are a safer and more lasting kick."

Vividy, who had been working her face angrily throughout Rath's lecture, now filled her cheeks and spat out her breath contemptuously, as her thrice-removed grandfather might have at the maunderings of an aged major domo.

"You're a fool, Max," she said harshly. "Kicks are for nervous virgins, the vanity of a spoilt child. *For me, being in the headlines every day is a matter of life or death.*"

Rath frowned uncomprehendingly.

"That's the literal truth she's telling you, Max," Maury Gender put in earnestly. "You see, this business happens to be tied up with what you might call the darker side of Vividy's aristocratic East Prussian heritage."

Miss Bricker stubbed out a cigarette and said, "Max, remember the trouble you had with that Spanish star, Marta Martinez, who turned out to be a *bruja* — a witch? Well, you picked something a little bit more out of the ordinary, Max, when you picked a Junker."

The highlights shifted on Dr. Rumanescue's thick glasses and shiny head as he nodded solemnly. He said, "There is a rune in the Doomsbook of the Von Sheers. I will translate." He paused. Then: "'When the world has nothing more to say, The last of the Sheers will fade away.'"

As if thinking aloud, Rath said softly, "Funny, I'd forgotten totally about that East Prussian background. We always played it way down out of sight because of the Nazi association — and the Russian too." He chuckled, just a touch nervously. " '. . . fade away,'" he quoted. "Now why not just 'die'? Oh, to make the translation rhyme, I suppose." He shook himself, as if to come awake. "Hey," he demanded, "what is it actually? Is somebody blackmailing Vividy? Some fascist or East German commie group? Maybe with the dope on her addictions and private cures, or her affair with Geri Wilson?"

"Repeat: a fool!" Vividy's chest was heaving but her voice was icy. "For your information, Dr. 'Escue's translation was literal. *Day by day, ever since you first killed my news stories, I have been losing weight.*"

"It's a fact, Max," Maury Gender put in hurriedly. "The news decline and the weight loss are matching curves. Believe it or not, she's down to a quarter normal."

Miss Bricker nodded with a shiver, disturbing the smoke wreathes around her. She said, "It's the business of an actress fading out from lack of publicity. But this time, so help me, *it's literal.*"

"I have been losing both *weight and mass*," Vividy continued sharply. "Not by getting thinner, but *less substantial*. If I had my back to the window you'd notice it."

Rath stared at her, then looked penetratingly at the other three, as if to discover confirmation that it was all a gag. But they only looked back at him with uniformly solemn and unhappy — and vaguely frightened — expressions. "I don't get it," he said.

"The scales, Vividy," Miss Bricker suggested.

The film star stood up with an exaggerated carefulness and stepped onto the small rubber-topped violet platform. The white disk whirled under the glass window and came to rest at 37.

She said crisply, "I believe the word you used, Max, was 'pneumatic.' Did you happen to mean I'm inflated with hydrogen?"

"You've still got on your slippers," Miss Bricker pointed out.

With even greater carefulness, steadying herself a moment by the darkly gleaming table-edge, Vividy stepped out of her slippers and again onto the scales. This time the disk stopped at 27.

"The soles and heels are lead, fabric-covered," she rapped out to Rath. "I wear them so I won't blow over the edge when I take a walk on the terrace. Perhaps you now think I ought to be able to jump and touch the ceiling. Convincing, wouldn't it be? I rather wish I could, but my strength has decreased proportionately with my weight and mass."

"Those scales are gimmicked," Rath asserted with conviction. He stooped and grabbed at one of the slippers. His fingers slipped off it at the first try. Then he slowly raised and hefted it. "What sort of gag is this?" he demanded of Vividy. "Dammit, it does weigh five pounds."

She didn't look at him. "Maury, get the flashlight," she directed.

While the press chief rummaged in a tall Spanish cabinet, Miss Bricker moved to the view window that was the room's fourth wall and flicked an invisible beam. Rapidly the tapestry-lined drapes crawled together from either end, blotting out the steep, burnt-over, barely regrown Malibu hillside and briefly revealing in changing folds "The Torments of Beauty" until the drapes met, blotting out all light whatever.

Maury snapped on a flashlight long as his forearm. It lit their faces weirdly from below and dimly showed the lovely gray ladies in pain beyond them. Then he put it behind Vividy, who facing Rath, and moved it up and down.

As if no thicker anywhere than fingers, the lovely form of the German film star became a twin-stemmed flower in shades of dark pink. The arteries were a barely visible twining, the organs blue-edged, the skeleton deep cherry.

"That some kind of X-ray?" Rath asked, the words coming out in a breathy rush.

"You think they got technicolor, hand-size, screenless X-ray sets?" Maury retorted.

"I think they must have," Rath told him in a voice quiet but quite desperate.

"That's enough, Maury," Vividy directed. "Bricker, the drapes." Then as the harsh rectangle of daylight swiftly reopened, she looked coldly at Rath and said, "You may take me by the shoulders and shake me. I give you permission."

The producer complied. Two seconds after he had grasped her he was shrinking back, his hands and arms violently trembling. It had been like shaking a woman stuffed with eiderdown. A woman warm and silky-skinned to the touch, but light almost as feathers. A pillow woman.

"I believe, Vividy," he gasped out. "I believe it all now." Then his voice went far away. "And to think I first cottoned to you because of that name Sheer. It sounded like silk-stockings — luxurious, delicate . . . *insubstantial*. Oh my God!" His voice came part way back. "And you say this is all happening because of some old European witchcraft? Some crazy rhymes out of the past? How do you really think about it, how do you explain it?"

"Much of the past has no explanation at all," Dr. Rumanescue answered him. "And the further in the past, the less. The Von Sheers are a very old family, tracing back to pre-Roman times. The runes themselves — "

Vividy held up her palm to the astrologist to stop.

"Very well, you believe. Good," she said curtly to Rath, carefully sitting down at the table again behind the ugly black casket on its square of altar cloth. She continued in the same tones. "The question now is: how do I get the publicity I need to keep me from fading out altogether, the front-page publicity that will perhaps even restore me, build me up?"

Like a man in a dream Rath let himself down into a chair across the table from her and looked out the window over her shoulder. The three others watched them with mingled calculation and anxiety.

Vividy said sharply, "First, can the release date on *Bride of God* be advanced — to next Sunday week, say? I think I can last that long."

"Impossible, quite impossible," Rath muttered, still seeming to study something on the pale green hillside scrawled here and there with black.

"Then hear another plan. There is an unfrocked Irish clergyman named Kerrigan who is infatuated with me. A maniac but rather sweet. He's something of a poet — he'd like me light as a feather, find nothing horrible in it. Kerrigan and I will travel together to Monaco — "

"No, no!" Rath cried out in sudden anguish, looking at her at last. "No matter the other business, witchcraft or whatever, we can't have anything like that! It would ruin the picture, kill it dead. It would mean my money and all our jobs. Vividy, I haven't told you, but a majority committee of stockholders wants me to get rid of you and reshoot *Bride*, starring Alicia Killian. They're deathly afraid of a last-minute Sheer scandal. Vividy, you've always played square with me, even at your craziest. You wouldn't . . ."

"No, I wouldn't, even to save my life," she told him, her voice mixing pride and contempt with an exactitude that broke through Maury Gender's miseries and thrilled him with her genuine dramatic talent. He said, "Max, we've been trying to convince Vividy that it might help to use some routine non-scandalous publicity."

"Yes," Miss Bricker chimed eagerly, "we have a jewel robbery planned for tonight, a kitchen fire for tomorrow."

Vividy laughed scornfully. "And I suppose the day after that I get lost in Griffith Park for three hours, next I rededicate an orphanage, autograph a Nike missile, and finally I have a pool side press interview and bust a brassiere strap. That's cheap stuff, the last resort of has-beens. Besides, I don't think it would work."

Rath, his eyes again on the hillside, said absently, "To be honest, I don't think it would either. After the hot stuff you've always shot them, the papers wouldn't play."

"Very well," Vividy said crisply, "that brings us back to where we started. There's nothing left for it — I've got to . . ."

"Hey wait a second!" Rath burst out with a roar of happy excitement. "We've got your physical condition to capitalize on! Your loss of weight is a scientific enigma, a miracle — and absolutely non-scandalous! It'll mean headlines for months, for years. Every woman will want to know your secret. So will the spacemen. We'll reveal you first to UCLA or USC, then the Mayo Clinic and maybe John Hopkins . . . Hey, what's the matter, why aren't you all enthusiastic about this?"

Maury Gender and Miss Bricker looked toward Dr. Rumanescue, who coughed and said gently, "Unfortunately, there is a runic couplet in the Von Sheer Doomsbook that seems almost certainly to bear on that very point. Translated: 'If a Sheer be weighed in the market place, He'll vanish away without a trace.'"

"In any case, I refuse to exhibit myself as a freak," Vividy added hotly. "I don't mind how much publicity I get because of my individuality, my desires, *my will* — no matter how much it shocks and titillates the little people, the law-abiders, the virgins and eunuchs and moms — but to be confined to a hospital and pried over by doctors and physiologists . . . No!"

She fiercely brought her fist down on the table with a soft, insubstantial thud that made Rath draw back and set Miss Bricker shuddering once more. Then Vividy Sheer said, "For the last time: there's nothing left for it — I've got to open the casket!"

"Now what's in the casket?" Rath asked with apprehension.

There was another uncomfortable silence. Then Dr. Rumanescue said softly, with a little shrug, "The casket-demon. The Doom of the Von Sheers." He hesitated. "Think of the genie in a bottle. A genie with black fangs."

Rath asked, "How's that going to give Vividy publicity?"

Vividy answered him. "It will attack me, try to destroy me. Every night, as long as I last. No scandal, only horror. But there will be headlines — oh yes, there will be headlines. And I'll stop fading."

She pushed out a hand toward the little wrought-iron box. All their eyes were on it. With its craggy, tortured surface, it looked as if it had been baked in Hell, the peep-hole of milky glass an eye blinded by heat.

Miss Bricker said, "Vividy, don't."

Dr. Rumanescue breathed, "I advise against it."

Maury Gender said, "Vividy, I don't think this is going to work out the way you think it will. Publicity's a tricky thing. I think — "

He broke off as Vividy clutched her hand back to her bosom. Her eyes stared as if she felt something happening inside her. Then, groping along the table, hanging onto its edge clumsily as though her fingers were numbed, she made her way to the scale and maneuvered herself onto it. This time the disk stopped at 19.

With a furious yet strengthless haste, like a scarecrow come alive and floating as much as walking, the beautiful woman fought her way back to the box and clutched it with both hands and jerked it towards her. It moved not at all at first, then a bare inch as she heaved. She gave up trying to pull it closer and leaned over it, her sharply bent waist against the table edge, and tugged and pried at the casket's top, pressing rough projections as if they were parts of an antique combination-lock.

Maury Gender took a stop toward her, then stopped. None of the others moved even that far to help. They watched her as if she were themselves strengthless in a nightmare — a ghost woman as much tugged by the tiny box as she was tugging at it. A ghost woman in full life colors — except that Max Rath, sitting just opposite, saw the hillside glowing very faintly through her.

With a whir and a clash the top of the box shot up on its hinges, there was a smoky puff and a stench that paled faces and set Miss Bricker gagging, then something small and intensely black and very fast dove out of the box and scuttled across the altar cloth and down a leg of the table and across the floor and under the tapestry and was gone.

Maury Gender had thrown himself out of its course, Miss Bricker had jerked her feet up under her, as if from a mouse, and so had Max Rath. But Vividy Sheer stood up straight and tall, no longer strengthless-seeming. There was icy sky in her blue eyes and a smile on her face — a smile of self-satisfaction that became tinged with scorn as she said, "You needn't be frightened. We won't see it again until after dark. Then — well, at least it will be interesting. Doubtless his hussars saw many interesting things during the seven months my military ancestor lasted."

"You mean you'll be attacked by a black rat?" Max Rath faltered.

"It will grow," said Dr. Rumanescue quietly.

Scanning the hillside again, Max Rath winced, as if it had occurred to him that one of the black flecks out there might now be *it*. He looked at his watch. "Eight hours to sunset," he said dully. "We got to get through eight hours."

Vividy laughed ripplingly. "We'll all jet to New York," she said with decision. "That way there'll be three hours' less agony for Max. Besides, I think Times Square would be a good spot for the first . . . appearance. Or maybe Radio City. Maury, call the airport! Bricker, pour me a brandy!"

Next day the New York tabloids carried half-column stories telling how the tempestuous film star Vividy Sheer had been attacked or at least menaced in front of the United Nations Building at 11:59 P.M. by a large black dog, whose teeth had bruised her without drawing blood, and which had disappeared, perhaps in company with a boy who had thrown a stink bomb, before the first police arrived. The *Times* and the *Herald Tribune* carried no stories whatever. The item got on Associate Press but was not used by many papers.

The day after that *The News of the World* and *The London Daily Mirror* reported on inside pages that the German-American film actress Vividy Sheer had been momentarily mauled in the lobby of Claridge's Hotel by a black-cloaked and black-masked man who moved with a stoop and very quickly — as if, in fact, he were more interested in getting away fast than in doing any real damage to the Nordic beauty, who had made no appreciable effort to resist the attacker, whirling in his brief grip as if she were a weightless clay figure. *The News of the World* also reproduced in one-and-a-half columns a photograph of Vividy in a low-cut dress showing just below her neck an odd black clutch-mark left there by the attacker, or perhaps drawn beforehand in India ink, the caption suggested. In *The London Times* was a curt angry editorial crying shame at notoriety-mad actresses and conscienceless press agents who staged disgusting scenes in respectable places to win publicity for questionable films — even to the point of setting off stench bombs — and suggesting that the best way for all papers to handle such nauseous hoaxes was to ignore them utterly — and cooperate enthusiastically but privately with the police and the deportation authorities.

On the third day, as a few eyewitnesses noted but were quite unwilling to testify, (what Frenchman wants to be laughed at?), Vividy Sheer was snatched off the top of the Eiffel Tower by a great ghostly black paw, or by a sinuous whirlwind laden with coal dust and then deposited under the Arc de Triomphe — or she and her confederates somehow created the illusion that this enormity had occurred. But when the Sheer woman, along with four of her film cohorts, reported the event to the Surete, the French police refused to do anything more than smile knowingly and shrug, though one inspector was privately puzzled by something about the Boche film-bitch's movements — she seemed to be drawn along by her companions rather than walking on her own two feet. Perhaps drugs were involved, Inspector Gibaud decided — cocain or mescalin. What an indecency though, that the woman should smear herself with shoeblacking to bolster her lewd fantasy!

Not one paper in the world would touch the story, not even one of the Paris dailies carried a humorous item about *Le bete noir et enorme* — some breeds of nonsense are unworthy even of humorous reporting. They are too silly (and perhaps in some silly way a shade too disturbing) for even silly-season items.

During the late afternoon of the fourth day, the air was very quiet in Rome — the quiet that betokens a coming storm — and Vividy insisted on taking a walk with Max Rath. She wore a coif and dress of white silk jersey, the only material her insubstantial body could tolerate. Panchromatic make-up covered her black splotches. She had recruited her strength by sniffing brandy — the only way in which her semi-porous flesh could now absorb the fierce liquid. Max was fretful, worried that a passerby would see through his companion, and he was continually maneuvering so that she would not be between them and the lowering sky. Vividy was tranquil, speculating without excitement about what the night might bring and whether a person who fades away dies doubly or not at all and what casket-demons do in the end to their victims and whether the Gods themselves depend for their existence on publicity.

As they were crossing a children's park somewhere near the Piazza dell' Esquilino, there was a breath of wind, Vividy moaned very quietly, her form grew faint, and she blew off Max's arm and down the path, traveling a few inches above it, indistinct as a camera image projected on dust motes. Children cried out softly and pointed. An eddy caught her, whirled her up, then back toward Max a little, then she was gone.

Immediately afterward mothers and priests came running and seven children swore they had been granted a vision of the Holy Virgin, while four children maintained they had seen the ghost or double of the film star Vividy Sheer. Certainly nothing material remained of the courageous East Prussian except a pair of lead slippers — size four-and-one-half — covered with white brocade.

Returning to the hotel suite and recounting his story, Max Rath was surprised to find that the news did not dispel his companions' nervous depression.

Miss Bricker, after merely shrugging at Max's story, was saying, "Maury, what do you suppose really happened to those eight hussars?" and Maury was replying, "I don't want to imagine, only you got to remember that at that time the casket-demon wasn't balked of his victim."

Max interrupted loudly, "Look, cut the morbidity. It's too bad about Vividy, but what a break for *Bride of God*! Those kids' stories are perfect publicity — and absolutely non-scandalous. Brady gross forty million! Hey! Wake up! I know it's been a rough time, but now it's over."

Maury Gender and Miss Bricker slowly shook their heads. Dr. Romanesque motioned Max to approach the window. While he came on with slow steps, the astrologist said, "Unfortunately, there is still another pertinent couplet. Roughly: 'If the demon be balked of a Von Sheer kill, On henchmen and vassals he'll work his will!' He glanced at his wrist. "It is three minutes to sunset." He pointed out the window. "Do you see, coming up the Appian Way, that tall black cloud with blue lightning streaking through it?"

"You mean the cloud with a head like a wolf?" Max faltered.

"Precisely," Dr. Romanesque nodded. "Only, for us, it is not a cloud," he added resignedly and returned to his book.

Mr. Adam's Garden of Evil

TAGGART ADAMS — Tag to a few other millionaires in the magazine world and to the top echelon of his staff — glared across the jade parquetry of his desk and ten yards of tiger-skin carpeted publisher's office at the jasper-inlaid pneumatically-snubbed door which Erica Slyker had nevertheless just now managed to slam on her exit.

From twelve frosted neon-illuminated glass panels in the walls, eleven superb Kittens-of-the-Month in penultimate stages of undress ogled down at him eagerly, but they might as well have been in neck-to-toe Mother Hubbards or black shrouds and executioners' masks for all the notice they got from Tag.

A deep flush of rage and shame suffused his normally leering stout-Satan's face as his memory replayed the last side of his conversation with Erica:

ERICA SLYKER: Being Kitten-of-the-Month ruined my sister! I would no more consider —

TAG ADAMS: Ruined? Ridiculous! No one laid a hand on Alice while she was here. I still offer you —

ERICA: (fiercely!) Perhaps it would have been better if they had! This six-story pad of yours is plastered with sex, but there's not an ounce left of the genuine man-woman article. Power-drive and fear-drive have driven it all out.

TAG: I'll overlook those bad-tempered remarks. Miss Slyker, I'm as sorry as you are that several weeks after she was resident here, your sister suffered some sort of illness that —

ERICA: Alice went into a five-day coma! She awakened from it with an empty child-mind, eaten with vanity, all talents lost, fodder for the mental hospital! Lobotomized mind! Vegetable mind! (Rises from leopard-upholstered chair and points at a Kitten resembling herself) And you still dare flaunt her picture? (Seizes a silver ashtray and hurls it at the offending panel, which shatters, the flesh-pink shards clinking softly down on the wall-to-wall tiger-skin and inside the illumination recess) Ha! Witch Queen's curses on you!

TAG: (cooly) I trust you've entirely discharged your infantile angers and will now hear wisdom. Your criminally, destructive action I pardon — I like my Kittens to have a little tiger in them. I still offer you —

ERICA: Pah! Sooner than be photographed for Kittens magazine with one shoulder strap slipped, I'd make love to you! Ah! That frightens you, doesn't it? I rather thought it would. Good day , Mr. Adams! (Exits, slamming jasper door)

Tag Adams took a very deep breath, slowly let it out, then looked down at the seven large glossy color prints neatly spread on the finely-morticed jade of his desk. Each showed Erica Slyker in a pearl-worked pearl-gray suit that beautifully set off her long lustrous blue-black hair. Each was posed against a background of jungle-leafed indoor greenery. In each the long pale face bore an expression of infuriating haughtiness, the short, bee-stung lips puckered in smiling contempt, the high-arched brows lightly pinching between them a queenly frown.

He selected the photo that seemed haughtiest, then methodically crushed the other six in his big gardener's left hand, as a first-beard adolescent crushes beer cans, and tossed the jagged balls into a tiger-skin wastebasket inset around its rim with genuine tiger teeth.

Then he hurried to the chair Erica Slyker had occupied, scanned its fabric at close range, and finally with a grunt of satisfaction picked up something from the leopard skin between his middle finger and thumb.

Returning to his desk, he deposited in a small white envelope a single long lustrous blue-black hair, closed the envelope and clipped it to the uncrumpled color print.

"She prate of witchcraft?" he breathed softly. "Ho!"

He rummaged rapidly through a couple of drawers until he found the color print of a rising red-headed young female off-Broadway dramatic talent who had recently refused to become America's Crown Princess of Sex Kittens for thirty days and he checked the envelope clipped to it to make sure three green nail clippings were still there. Next he thrust both prints in a large manila envelope, tucked it under his left elbow, and himself hurried through the jasper door and past a luscious graveyard-shift receptionist, of whom he noticed only the faint odor of the carbon tet used to clean the shoe-soles of all visitors before they were permitted to tread the tiger-skin.

Then he was hastening along the deluxe vari-colored corridors of what one recklessly irreverent columnist called "Kitten Kastle" and, eschewing the gilded openwork antique elevator, down the rainbow flights of stairs with their shadowed kiss-niches and half curtained woo-booths, which were strictly off limits to both visitors and personnel except for publicity photographs.

It was 7 a.m. and tonight's party was approaching its aseptically orgiastic climax. Two widely placed jazz bands racketed Dixie and twisted towards each other. The corridors were filled with hordes of beautiful girls with daring decolletages and other carefully-calculated anatomic exposures and with hosts of sharply-dressed, worried, watchful men.

Yet, despite the rapid writhings of the dancers and the posturings of the comedians and the chattering rushes of the self-appointed party-energizers, no members of one sex ever touched a member of the other except for the minimum permitted contacts of the dance and the fleetingest finger-touches and shoulder-pats of soap pure fellowship.

Ever present was the fear that someone would do something the papers or the police could seize on, something gauche, like becoming naively romantic or drunkenly ribald or substituting for Kitten the forbidden word Pussy.

All looked dreadfully tired but masking it with grinning resolution.

As the Lord and Master of Kitten Kastle came trotting along, manila envelope under elbow, each man drew aside respectfully, with a fawning manly smile ready to pop if the ruddy, bald, sharp-bearded Satan's face should glance his way, while each girl assumed her melting ready-to-please-milord expression and thrust forward invitingly, but not at all pushingly, her lips, throat, bosom, hip, dimpled knee or whatever other portion of her anatomy she considered her chef-d'oeuvre and main strength.

But Taggart Adams looked neither to the right or to the left. Men irritated him, and as for girls his hypnotist had been trying for the past three years to revive his aggressive male interest in them, with little success. He was hardly the bold lusty wastrel indicated by his beard and tiny mustache, which were merely his variant of G.I. standard for publishers and editors of "magazines for men."

At the moment the only girl who interested him in any way was one with blue-black tresses draping a pale mask of contempt, and she would soon be taken care of in a rather special fashion.

As for the stuff crowding the corridors . . .well, the jeweled sex-puppets — poupes de l'amour — were jigging around the well-disciplined dark-suited male marionettes, the tombstones were jumping at an hour when squares went to work . . . it was sufficient.

Downward and ever downward trotted Taggart Adams. Past the turquoise swimming pool with its bevy of bikinied beauties, each with her invisible guard rail. Past the pool's 25-foot-deep "basement," where a lone girl with aqualung and with silver blue hair streaming like the beautiful long iridescent deadly filaments of a Portuguese man-of-war, glided among the living corals behind the 2-inch-thick view window — and in front of which a boy and girl in passionate embrace jumped apart tremblingly at Tag's approach, blanching at the merciless frown he shot them. Until he was alone in the somber oak-paneled male-tapestry-shrouded corridor below even the watery basement.

A quick glance either way to make certain of privacy, tapping of an oaken rosette in a quick three-one rhythm, then a silvery-tawny panel had silently slid aside, moist warmth and flower odors and a kind of tangible night had billowed out, and Tag had slipped inside. The panel closed swiftly behind him.

He was in an extensive room that was in deep darkness except for a dab of bluish light forty feet away dimly illuminating four photos on a wall and silhouetting just in front of it a table set with a few small earthenware pots, a phone, and hand-size gardening tools.

But although the rest of the room was black-dark at first sight, there pressed from it an intense aura of femininity, a faint musky sweet various sleeping-woman-scent coming in wave on wave.

And as one's eyes got fully adjusted, there was the barest suggestion of ranks on ranks of thick-stemmed, leaf-hooded flowers — flowers giving ghostly disturbing gleams of russet and gold and auburn and ivory and rosier hues . . . or perhaps the suggestion was more of rows of slim living sleeping dolls hung by their hair deep amid greenery . . . or . . . at any rate, most tantalizing and strange and disturbing.

With a confidence born of perfect knowledge of the room's contents, Tag walked briskly to the potting table and went to work. He set the phone aside. From a tiny shelf below the photographs and their bluish night-light he took a brownish bulging envelope labeled in spidery hand and brown-faded ink "Mimics" (after quickly setting back one labeled "Vamps" which he'd first picked up.)

From the almost crumbly old envelope he carefully withdrew a round black gleaming seed a little larger than a plum's, wrapped around it eleven times Erica Slyker's hair, thrust it two inches deep into the moist grainy soil of one of the pots, and patted the surface flat.

"Requiescat," he said solemnly as he dusted the gritty loam off his fingers above the pot, "but not in peace."

He carefully leaned the color print of Erica face-inward against the pot and drew a second seed from the envelope, but then he grew lazily pensive and his stern expression softened as his gaze went to the four large old photos affixed to the wall. The one figure common to them all was that of a tall elderly lady in the chin-high, wrist-and-floor long dress of the last century, with a piercing-visaged aristocratic face, the thin beaky nose and narrow jutting chin pointing a little toward each other like those of a story book witch.

A genuine soft affectionate smile came to Tag's lips, instead of the tight Satan's grimace he invariably showed the world. It was always so nice and relaxing to be, even fancy-wise or photo-wise, with truly elderly women — sprightly, gossipy, thankful old girls, wittily waspish at times, even vastly malicious, but totally devoid of the insolence of the sex-urge. And then Tag had so many reasons, including the supreme one, for feeling friendly and grateful toward his brilliant Great-aunt Veronica, world-famous as a biologist in certain mystical and un-stuffy scientific circles, who ten years ago had bequeathed him much more than her monetary riches.

He gently rubbed the second seed between his fingertips and touched the still-bulging envelope with a miser's tenderness as he rested his eyes and his feelings on the four photographs.

The first showed his Great-aunt, not quite so elderly, standing with Luther Burbank in a cactus garden.

In the second, very elderly indeed, she was accepting in Tiflis the reverent handclasp of Trofim Lysenko, Soviet proponent of the theory that environment shapes genetic heredity, at some time before that rogue-scientist's nominally voluntary resignation as head of the All-Union Academy of Agricultural Science.

In the third she stood alone and grimly smiling in front of the shut doors of what a brass plate identified as the head-quarters of the American Botanical Society. That was the one signed "Veronica Adams, D.S." in the same large spidery script as that on the old brown envelopes.

The last showed her in a Parisian dining room together with a group of quaintly bearded men in full evening dress — all the faces almost flat white from an overly powerful magnesium flash. She was receiving from them the Meta-Lamarckian Medal for her paper, "Seventeen Verified Instances of the Shaping of Plant Development by Thoughts, Symbols, Pictures, and Exodermal Tokens."

Tag's expression grew more pensive still and he began to tug gently and rhythmically with the hand holding the seed at his wide-based sharp-pointed chin-beard. His eyes closed and his face grew tranquil. He began to snore very softly.

His hands did not fall asleep, however. After a bit, although his face did not change at all, they went busily to work, planting the second seed without more ado in the second pot, over which he was leaning closely, extracting from its envelope and planting a "Vamps" seed in a third pot just beside the second, finally replacing both envelopes on their shelf.

Then his hands grew still and his face woke up with a shake and a start. For a moment he was frightened, then he realized he'd simply been dozing standing up — he'd been driving himself lately and Great-aunt Veronica was such a pleasantly soporific topic for reverie. Strange, though, he thought, the dazed abstraction he'd felt for a moment had been very like the state of mind he used to experience when his hypnotist had implanted some particularly strong suggestion — but he hadn't summoned the man for the last three months.

He'd had a flash of the same sort of feeling sometime earlier today, he recalled. Yes, it had occurred during the first part of his interview with the abominable Erica Slyker.

But she was well taken care of now. In fact all his work here was done, he decided after the quickest of glances, and it would come to fruition in due course.

Meanwhile he had no business loitering away a moment more at this time of the month, he reminded himself as he spun around and trotted through the dark toward the secret panel.

There was a sharp bzzz behind him. It made him jump — for an instant it activated his old fear of bees, a fear most unsuitable in a gardener, but so deep that even his hypnotist had never been able to counteract it.

Then he realized it was only the phone. . . and he kept on toward the secret panel. In a flash of intuition he'd know it had to be his Executive Managing Editor and that for once the bumbler had a thoroughly adequate reason for calling him at his secret number.

There was grueling work to be done for the next five days, and not one moment to delay.

Specifically, Kittens had to be put to bed — not stupid pushy cuddle-crazy girls, but something really important . . . the next issue of a stunningly successful national magazine!

For the next five hectic days Taggart Adams hardly thought once of his secret garden or of the incidents leading up to his last visit there, though he did remember to fire the staff boy and girl he'd caught embracing.

During these periods when he couldn't spare time for himself, the garden was cared for by an elderly Sicilian deaf-mute of submoronic intelligence but absolute trustworthiness with growing things — his ancestors had trained vines and coaxed hedges for the ancient Romans.

But now at least the next Kittens was abed on its whirring ink-acrid presses, the first run mercilessly checked and rechecked, and Tag had a full recovery-week to do exactly what he wanted — no parties to appear at, no avidly hopeful new girls to check over, no boringly abstract undress photography sessions, no new geniuses to give a grudging hearing, no V.I.P.'s to bully and charm . . . and only one or two members, if that many, of his house-or-magazine staff knowing what he really was up to or even where he really was.

He could canoe — copt through Canada's hidden-most lakes, submarine the West Indies in this technically illegal private submersible, dig London, take a whirl through the Continental capitals, shoot Africa with the seventh wealthiest man in the world, study the Swiss banking system from the inside, or simply tend his secret garden . . . quietly vegetate . . .

Well, in any case he would start off with a look-see at the last, he decided.

This time when the panel closed behind him, it was "day" inside. Great glowing checkerboards of window-simulating sunshine-shedding panels in ceiling and walls made him squint. He patiently let his eyes accommodate and after a minute he saw his garden in its full glory.

To either side of the aisle between him and the potting table, row on row of potted plants went back in rising banks to the walls of the huge room. Each plant was like a large jack-in-the-pulpit or love-in-a-mist or fever-tree flower, in that each thick stemmed bloom was canopied and bowered by great dark green leaves of the sort botanists called spathes and bracts.

But these must be jill-in-the-pulpit, for each green alcove enshrined a flowering slip girl about twelve inches high. Many showed only their faces, though with swellings in the stem indicating where bosoms and hips were developing.

The less developed showed just a tassel of blonde, brown, reddish, or other-colored hair above a green head-bulge, or perhaps the green husk opening enough to reveal pale forehead and tiny darting eyes.

In the more developed the sheath of the stem had split down the front and peeled back, like a bolero jacket or green dressing robe, half revealing a delectable torso, baby pink yet an anatomically perfect replica of some celebrated figure.

For as one studied these flower-girls, it became apparent that they were not some exotic genus unlinked to individual humanity. One began to recognize faces and forms.

Here were the opulent or sweetly up-tilted breasts of some reigning screen star. There was the profile of a celebrated society beauty, or winsome junior member of a royal family. A few of the more memorable Kittens-of-the-month were represented, but on the whole the social trend was upward.

There is a rather crude joke in which one Thames barman asks another, "Bill, which 'ave you enjoyed the most — the women you've 'ad in real life, or the ones you've 'ad only in the realms of your imagination?" And Bill replies, "The latter, Jim — for there you meets a better class of women."

The same was true of Taggart Adams and his garden.

Not every plant was unique, however. There were several groups of identicals, including three full blooms in a front row which resembled Erica Slyker just enough to make one realize they or their plant-ancestor must have been grown with the help of photos and exodermal tokens of her sister Alice.

A very few of the long-stemmed girls bulged with seeds. These had their eyes closed, but most of the rest were peering about, chiefly toward Tag.

And although they were armless they clearly had more than ocular powers of movement, for a small rustling went through the ranked flowers now, as if a tiny breeze were sifting through the subterranean hothouse, troubling the canopy leaves; stems twisted just a little toward Tag; minute lips parted and there was the faintest shrill sibilance in the air, as of voices almost too high to be sensed even as noise.

Tag took deep languorous breaths of the varied girl-scent, feeling utterly content.

This was the place where the world was perfect for him, he decided for the thousandth time: the place where girls were not big troublesome bounding meaty things with rights and ideas and desires, but fragile blooms with just enough consciousness and limited life to make them interesting; fragile blossoms, blooms to be potted and repotted, tenderly nurtured, watered and fertilized and sprayed, brought to the acme of perfection, and then carefully hand-pollinated and set to seed, or ruthlessly snapped off and extirpated forever as the whim took him.

Pinning up girls in a million-copy magazine was pretty good, admittedly. But potting them in a garden . . . oh, how much he owed to his Great-aunt Veronica and her patient largely-unappreciated research and her mimic-seeds! What stretches of bliss he'd enjoyed during the seven years since he'd chanced on the black spheroids in her effects and stumbled on their purpose!

Here was the secret of his power in the real world, the sweetly-flowering earth from which like Antaeus he periodically renewed his strength.

Almost his sole regret was that he couldn't regrow his Great-aunt herself. He'd tried — he had a daguerreotype of her as a 17-year-old and a lock of her girl hair — but it had turned out that the process wouldn't work for dead women. Else he'd have had not only his perpetually blooming row of "Veronica's" but his Cleopatras, Madam Dubarry's, Nell Gwyns, Lola Montezes, and Jean Harlows — granting he could locate authentic pictures and/or genuine exodermal tokens, even if only a pinch of ashes.

But apparently for a girl plant to develop properly it needed to "draw on" the living original girl in some obscure vampirish way, telepathic or sub-etheric, who could say? — since even his Great-aunt had no wholly satisfactory theory.

The effect on the girl whose seed had been planted with proper picture and token varied greatly. Frequently there was none at all, so far as Tag could discover. Sometimes she would be reported as confined to bed or sent to hospital with a mild undiagnosed fever or in a light (or occasionally heavy) coma, especially during the period of blooming. Such symptoms generally terminated, and the girl returned to her normal life, with the withering and/or seeding of her plant. If Tag continued to re-seed her, as in the case of Alice Slyker, there might be rumors of protracted depressions together with periods of retreat in some mental hospital.

Once a Swedish beauty queen he'd terminated (with hedge shears) had died the same night (decapitated in a traffic accident), but Tag was inclined to attribute that to coincidence. What the devil, he wasn't trying to work black magic or hurt anyone, he was only satisfying an aesthetic impulse, using tools supplied by a very high-minded old lady. No, he wasn't trying to hurt a soul.

Of course condign punishment, as now of the abominable Erica Slyker, was something else again! That thought stirred him from his delightful lethargy and he trotted to the potting table, past rows of Alices and Bridgettes and Margarets and Sonias and a single Jacquelin.

He started grinning before he got there. His "Erica" had developed with commendable rapidity. Clearly Anselmo had remembered the vitamin and hormone supplements. Already the face was in full bloom and the bosom had begun to bulge nicely. The haughty arch-ings of the minuscule eyebrows as she glared at him and the petulant poutings of the tiny lips were balm to his injured psyche — and as much so was the thought of her twisting and moaning now on some hard couch or hospital bed while doctors went over her baffledly; he'd asked one of his earlier victims about her coma and she'd unsuspect-ingly told him it had been filled with horrid half-formed dreams of being buried alive and bound to a stake and subjected to nameless indignities.

"And serves you right, Slyker," he said now to the flower, lightly flicking one pale cheek with a fingernail.

The resemblance was perfect. The eleven-looped hair and the inward-facing color print had done their work well.

But something was wrong: the second pot he'd planted had no photo tilted against it. Automatically he glanced to the floor and there was the manila envelope, where it must have slipped from under his elbow five days back. He stooped and drew from it the print of the off-Broadway redhead talent with the small white envelope still clipped to it containing the three green nail clippings.

What the devil had he buried with the second mimic seed?

His eyes came up over the edge of the potting table and he looked for the first time at the plant rising sturdy-stemmed from the second pot.

It was topped by a walnut-size replica of his own head, leaf-ruffed. The face, in full bloom even to the wide-based pointy beard, was star-ing at him anxiously and gaping its mouth, as if shouting an inaudi-bly shrill message.

His first impulse, an instant one, was to rip it out by the roots and stamp on it.

His second impulse, which was so violent it rocked him back on his heels and sent his clutching hands flying up into the air, was to nurse and protect and watch over the thing as if it were a hundred-thousand gulden Dutch black tulips — at least!

Veils fell from his mind's eye. He suddenly saw that only a blind idiot would have blithely attributed to coincidence the Swede's grisly traffic death on the same night he'd snipped her stem at the neck. No, he must cherish the Taggart-plant in every way! My God, what if a blight suddenly struck the garden? — some horrid creep-ing purple mold . . .

Or what if he went into a coma now? He'd no sooner thought that than he was blinking his eyes, taking deep breaths, slapping his cheeks hard, and rapidly stamping his right foot on the concrete. Clearly he'd almost gone into a coma a minute before, back at the secret panel. Probably only the high pitch of tension involved in putting Kittens to bed had saved him from blackout during the past several days.

The atmosphere of this damned place was soporific! Maybe he should flee to the Canadian North Woods with its clean bracing air? — yes, but it puts you to sleep, they say . . .

And if he were away, people could get at the garden — get at the Taggart-plant! Kidnap it, hold it for ransom, torture it, take great big shears and . . . He'd never really trusted Anselmo!

Gradually sanity returned, especially when it struck him that his deep breathing, hyperventilating his lungs, was all by itself about to throw him into a faint.

He shifted his mind into gear and set it to work under a careful throttle. Dimly he could recall now tugging his beard in the moon-blue dark while the second mimic seed had still been in his fingers. Evidently he'd loosened a hair or two and then buried them along with the seed. His body bending over the pot and thereafter its close presence in the same building had been the equivalent of a picture or more. In any case, Great-aunt Veronica herself, according to her papers and notes, had never been certain whether the pictures or the exodermal tokens were the most important factors.

Thinking about the thing this way, scientifically, began to put it into perspective for him and he grew calmer, though it remained most disturbing to realize that he had been absent-minded enough (or conceivably hypnotically influenced?) to pull such a trick.

Still, the thing was done, and nothing now remained but to see the Taggart-plant through its relatively brief flowering span (that thought elicited from him a residual shiver) and then just let it whiter away normally. Reasonable care should easily do the job. After all, who in the world now Great-aunt Veronica was dead knew more about mimic-plants than he? He would be his own best caretaker. As for coma, many girls never seemed to suffer it, even during the blooming period. Why should a strong man?

And, what the devil, didn't all truly great research doctors and physiologists try their serums on themselves? He was one of their lion breed now!

He looked down at the Taggart-plant, which — all shouting anxiety gone — returned him such a brash Satan's grin that he felt greatly bucked up, positively exhilarated . . . to such a degree that for an instant, but an instant only, he imagined himself down there smirking up at his own moon-big face.

What the dickens, if that brave little guy could keep up his spirits, so could he!

Whistling, he fetched a small red can and carefully watered himself — and as an afterthought, Erica. It occurred to him that he might try an experiment in cross-pollenization when the stems were fully opened. Normally he self-pollenized all his flowers to keep strains true — girl-girl crosses tended toward mediocrity beauty-wise, he'd discovered by repeated experiments. And of course he wouldn't want to produce any true seeds of himself — he'd never feel safe if any such were in existence, no matter how tightly locked up. But his pollen on Erica's gynoecium — it was a tantalizingly attractive thought!

In his bemused high spirits he even watered the nameless little plant growing in the pot between his and Erica's, but nearer his own.

There was a sharp bzzz! It was evidence of the amount of nervous apprehension still floating around in him under the camouflage of his high spirits, that he dropped the red watering can.

Damn that phone, he thought as he stooped and righted the trickling can. It had no right to sound so much like a bee coming in for the kill. He must have the tone altered at once — would have had it altered before, except he'd been reluctant to admit his fear of bees was so great.

But that was silly. Bees were his great ineradicable dread, and he might as well face up to it, just as he'd faced up now to the existence of the Taggart-plant. Why, if it weren't for his dread of bees, he'd have long ago tried experiments in insect pollenization. It was titillating to think of bees crawling all over his flower-girls, buzzing lazily from one to the next — except that he was himself so terrified of the six-legged monsters with the built-in torture hypodermic.

But who the devil could be calling him here? — he asked himself as he reached for the phone. Better not any of his magazine-flunkies now Kittens was abed — he'd chew their ears off, or rather say them one poisonously sweet word and fire them tomorrow. Not more than a dozen people knew this number — the last person he'd given it to had been the President.

A charming voice said, "Erica Slyker here. Hello, Taggart-blaggart-waggert-haggert-sleep-sleep-sleep! Now that I've given you the cue we agreed on, you will answer any questions I put to you. You will do whatever I tell you. Can you hear me clearly?"

In his imagination Taggart slammed down the phone, rushed upstairs, called another secret number, and — using the latest underworld code — hired two reliable, conscienceless mobsters to beat up Erica Slyker, being sure to black both eyes and kick her in the stomach.

In actuality he said in a sing-song voice, "Yes, I can."

"Good. You're in the garden?"

"Yes, I am."

"Excellent. Place a chair by the table so you can watch both our plants. Then sit down in it."

He managed to face the chair away from the table, but it turned out this only meant he had to straddle it, resting his forearms and the phone on its back.

"You're sitting in the chair watching our plants? How's the vamp doing?"

Obediently Tag focused on the little plant next to his own, only now learning what it was. He'd planted two of those horrors six years ago and decided never again — the tendrils of the one of them had strangled a promising Gina, while those of the other had whipped out and caught a little finger he'd brought incautiously close, inflicting tiny but nasty wounds with their microscopic suckers. Even Great-aunt Veronica had been a little doubtful about the benefit to humanity of her vampire plants. She had suggested their use to protect tropical dwellers from scorpions, centipedes, giant spiders, and the like and — tentatively — in the conquest of Mars.

"It is doing quite well," he reported into the phone. "The forehead is showing and I can count six . . . no, seventeen pale red tendrils. They are about an inch long and have begun to wave a little."

"Bravo! Keep watching that plant too. Now hang up the phone and await further instructions."

Taggart Adams obeyed and then eternity set in for him. An eternity the passing of whose centuries were marked by calls from Erica only to repeat the "blag-wag-hag" formula, whose millennia were each signalized by an additional inch growth of the red tendrils of the vamp.

After about thirty-five hundred years the face of the vamp became fully visible. As he'd long since guessed from the color of the tendrils, it was that of the off-Broadway red head talent — evidently the picture and the three green nail parings had been able to do their work from the floor, as being the nearest picture-and-token available and otherwise unoccupied.

She had a great talent for the evil eye, Tag decided after a thousand years of being glared at. And for writhing her lips back from her tiny white fangs. And for waving suggestively close to the Taggart-plant those wire-worm tendrils that arched around her face like the hair of Medusa.

Meanwhile the Erica and the Taggart were developing their proper bulges and finally splitting their green stem-sheaths down the front: the slowest and least titillating strip-tease in the universe.

The Erica looked back at him with a contempt that only became more smiling as the ages passed.

The Taggart, on the other hand, grimaced and grinned and winked its left eye at him unceasingly. Tag became dully infuriated with the little idiot's irrationally high spirits — and bored, horribly bored. If that was the way he'd looked all his life to other people . . .

He felt the ache of thirst and the sickness of hunger, but they were dulled by a titanic listlessness.

A million times he told himself that a man couldn't be held hypnotized like this against his will, surely not after a one-session indoctrination into which he'd somehow been tricked by a mere abominable girl. Not one of the most powerful men in the world, not the sex-puppet master, not the publisher of Kittens, not Veronica's Grand-nephew, not the Lord of Kitten Kastle, not the girl-gardener . . .

A million times a little voice from a dark high corner of his mind replied only, "Blag-wag-hag."

Thrice there were "nights" lasting for many centuries.

After twelve thousand years he heard the secret panel open and footsteps drag up the aisle. Someone stopped and retrieved the red watering can. It was Anselmo, he could tell from the corner of his eye — no mistaking that hand like a bleached ham, that face big as that of a white horse, for in addition to being a submoronic deaf-mute, the ancient Sicilian had acromegaly.

Tag tried to shout, to whisper, to beckon with a finger, just to lift one — to no avail. Without even a single curious glance toward his employer, so far as Tag could tell, Anselmo went about his chores.

For decades and scores of years his big shoes scrapped the concrete and there came the periodic gush of the tap as he patiently watered and fertilized and sprayed. Twice the phone bzzd for a repetition of the inevitable formula, but there was no alteration in the sound of Anselmo's movements. Both times Tag tried to drop the phone on the floor — and only set it the more carefully back.

A third time the phone bzzd — much sooner than the once-a-century rhythm called for. A brisk grating voice said, "Tag George. All ready to pop those lions, boy? Rhodesia's waiting for us." To Tag's horror all he could say was, "No, thanks," and all he could do was hang up.

Finally Anselmo arrived at the potting table and began methodically to care for the three plants there, insensible to Tag's mental screams, even when Anselmo's sprinkling reawakened Tag's searing thirst and they became the inward shriek, "For the love of God, pour some of that in my mouth!"

Anselmo finished with the Erica, the vamp (a bit cautious with his huge hands there as they moved around the foot-long tendrils), and finally the Taggart. Only then did his behavior alter. He stood ox-still and stared an interminable time at the smirking walnut-head of the Taggart. Hope rekindled in Tag.

Then Anselmo turned and stared for almost an equally long period at his life-size employer. Tag's hope flamed. If only there were some readable expression in that white face big as a washbowl . . .

Then Anselmo looked back at the walnut-head, puzzledly shook his own in three wide horse-like swings, shrugged his sloping shoulders, and dragged off down the aisle. The secret door opened, then closed behind him.

A trapdoor opened in the corridor and Anselmo plummeted into the hottest room in hell — in Tag's imagination.

A mere thousand years and ten phone-calls later, Erica added, "I know the garden's under the pool. How do I get in?"

Tag focused his will and thought, "Sooner than tell you, I'd see myself in Hell. I'd become a pauper. You're the evil woman my Great-aunt Veronica always warned me about. You're the Witch Queen. No."

What he said into the phone was, "Turn right at the foot of the main staircase. The seventh vertical molding to your right. The seventh rosette from the floor. Press three-one."

"Thanks. I won't be long. Incidentally, you are in Hell and there is no pauper alternative. Oh, by the way, it's about time you were getting out of your body — it won't live much longer, even with you in it. Don't look at my plant any more, don't look at the vamp, just look at the you-plant . . . and project . . . project . . . project . . ."

Tag complied. After a century the walnut-head began to bob and smirk in exact time with his own blinking. Then suddenly it grew moon-huge. Looking down, Tag saw that he had grown a large green full ruff around his neck.

His first reaction to the realization that he was now in the Taggart-plant was to try and project himself back into his rightful body.

One glance at it changed his mind. That gray-faced elephantine hulk, that moon-tongued mountain, looked dead.

This tentative information didn't depress him perhaps as much as it should have. He felt a vivification, an unreasoning cockiness, a confidence in his own powers, although he could only move his head and wriggle his torso a bit. Perhaps it was because he was no longer thirsty — Anselmo had watered well and cool moisture pervaded his every tissue.

Also, time had speeded up for him again — minutes no longer dragged like years.

Or perhaps his exhilaration was due to his increased sensitivity. Air-eddies intangible before now rippled against his bare flesh like brook water. A drifting bit of lint bumped him like a paper boat. Colors were brighter — he could see with the fresh-washed vision of a child. Odors were a symphony, chiefly of girl-accents, which he realized he had never properly appreciated before; now he could pick out each instrument in the orchestra.

And he could hear with exquisite precision and clarity. Why, he could even hear what the flower-girls were saying!

"We hate you, Tag Adams, we loathe and despise you," they were chanting, occasionally varying it with obscenities in several languages.

His chest swelled. Why, it was a kind of hymn. No wonder the little guy had acted so happy. Where was that little guy now anyhow? Absorbed in his own larger consciousness? No matter, just listen . . . now what was that French girl calling him . . .?

"Enjoy it while you can," the Erica-plant cut in sweetly.

"Shut up!" he snapped, swiveling his head toward her. My, my, she certainly was as handsomely constructed as he'd guessed she'd be when she first entered his office — he decided with an appreciative, quite involuntary whistle.

"How gallant," the Erica-plant replied with a shrug. "Give him a hug for me, Red."

The vamp, far more supple-stemmed than the mimics, thrust forward between them. The Medusa-face mopped and mowed. The eyes glared white-circled. The white fangs clicked and shirred. And then the inch-thick living tendrils whipped around him until they were like a red-barred cage, their tips not quite touching him, until one slowly dipped and drew itself stingingly across his chest . . .

"Cut it short, Red," the Erica-plant commanded.

There was a distant grating noise. The red tendrils whipped away. The grating noise continued.

The secret panel was opening. Then the tramp of giant footsteps — Tag could feel their almost painful vibrations coming up from the concrete through the table and his pot and his earth.

Erica Slyker had entered the room: a girl as tall as a pine tree, bigger than a dinosaur to Tag, a colossal Witch Queen.

She was wearing a platinum mink coat over her pearl-worked pearl-gray suit. To the left shoulder of her coat was pinned a big spray of white funeral lilies.

Under her left elbow she carried a small cubical white box, big as a piano crate to Tag. It hummed, as though there were several electric motors running inside it.

Halfway down the aisle she stopped to look at the three Alices.

"Save us, save us!" all the flower-girls called to her.

She slowly and rather sadly shook her head. Then she jerked the three Alices screaming out of their pots.

"Kill or cure, my dear," she said in a voice that to Tag was like thunder. "Anything's better than the state you're in."

She stooped, swinging the three still-screaming Alices high in the air and smashed them against the concrete with a heavy thud, the vibrations from which made Tag wince, and left them there.

All the flower-girls grew alert. The pot-jarring footsteps resumed. Erica sat down the white box on the potting table and the electric motors added their different but painful vibrations to the others. Tag writhed. He was discovering why his flower-girls had never liked hi-fi the nights he'd played it to them hour after hour, full blast.

Erica bent toward him. It was like a face leaning down out of Mt. Rushmore. He could look down her pores, see the powder grains, retch at her overpowering odors.

"It's not so much fun being a sensitive plant, is it, Mr. Adams?" she rumbled slowly.

"May my Great-aunt torture you in Hell!" Tag squeaked.

"You'll find Erica in Veronica," she replied cryptically. Then she slowly unwound a long blue-black hair from around the ear of his corpse. She dangled it in front of him and said, "There are many variants of the hair formula, Mr. Adams — and more than one way of applying an exodermal token."

Then she dug her fingers into the pot of her own plant, carefully loosened its roots, gently shook them out and wrapped them in a wet handkerchief, then tucked and fastened the she-flower in the center of her spray of lilies.

Then she looked at Tag across the white box.

"The Witch Gods do not love you, Mr. Adams," she whispered in a voice like distant thunder.

She took the cover off the box. A black bee, yellow-striped and big as a half-grown kitten, crawled up on the rim.

"You signed your will and your death-warrant, you know, Mr. Adams," she continued, "within an hour of our meeting in your office. Signed them in more senses than one."

With the bzzz of a power lawn mower the bees took off and came circling widely around Tag.

"After all, you've had a long life," Erica went on. "About fourteen thousand years, wouldn't you say? — even if most of them were spent here during the last few days."

Tiny tears of horror trickled down Tag's face as he craned and craned his neck. He'd often wondered exactly what the drops of dew on the flower-girl's checks had meant.

"I'll be leaving soon, Mr. Adams," Erica said. "You'll have the place to yourself. The lock will be jammed. Anselmo will assume you've set it against him. I'm going to leave the sunlight turned on full — it's the kindest thing I can do for the others."

The bee lit on Tag's shoulder like a six-legged live helicopter. It stank acidly. Of the million screams inside him he dared not utter one.

"Don't be frightened," Erica rumbled. "Bees don't sting flowers — if they're quiet. And the scent of a male plant, such as you, happens to be irresistible to these."

Two more bees climbed to the rim and took off and came circling.

"It's really an honor to you, Mr. Adams," she continued. "Judging from your magazine, it's what you've always wanted to have happen. It should be an exquisite fate, from your point of view."

More bees took off. A second landed on Tag's neck. The first walked slowly down his chest, its sticky hair-fringed feet pricking and tickling almost unbearably, its stinger wagging in his face.

"Yes," she explained, standing up, "the bees are merely going to carry your pollen to all these beautiful girls." She spread her arms wide, then leaned forward and finished. "But before they can carry your pollen, Mr. Adams, they have to collect it."

Detectives Morris and O'Brien stayed for a last ruminative look around the stuffy, dried-out garden, after the rest of Homicide had come, sniffed and sniffed, finally shrugged and departed.

"There's something real mysterious here," O'Brien declared, staring at the rows of shriveled brown plants. "For instance, why do I keep thinking of mummies?"

Morris shrugged. "The coroner says Adams died of simple inanition. That means nothing but lack of water and food. Now why should a guy with all that dough and all those beautiful babes lock himself in a secret hot house and starve? There's your mystery."

"He couldn't have been such a bad joe," O'Brien observed absently. "Look at all that money he left to the girl fresh out of the mental hospital — Alice something-or-other." He moved to the potting table. The intent note came back into his voice. "But there's still a mystery here. Take those dead bees all in and around that one pot — that pot with the dried-up plant that's got dead vines around it from the next pot and that still looks to me — "(he shivered) "a little like him."

Morris chucked uneasily. "The real mystery," he said to O'Brien, "is where you get your morbid imagination."

Afterword: or my own thank you to Fritz Leiber

How on earth do you sum up the lifetime achievement of someone like Fritz Leiber? In truth, I don't believe you can, at least not to any great satisfaction. Leiber's influence on the horror, fantasy and science fiction genres is incomparable. You only have to look at the slew of modern fantasists and fabulists out there with their urban take on horror and the lurking evils of stone and slate to see the paranoid nightmares of Smoke Ghost creeping across the rooftops all over again.

Fritz Leiber was special. Not only was he a genuine literary titan, there's no question of that, he was a gentleman known for getting into long correspondences with fans, an actor and a scholar. Still the question remains, where do you begin? Obviously one angle would be to focus on the critical acclaim and the shelves laden with Hugo's, Nebula's, and World Fantasy Awards but the truth is awards only tell so much of the story. Equally, one could attempt to dissect the body of work left behind, picking out the highlights from a career of highlights, offering thoughts on just why Conjure Wife and Our Lady of Darkness are two of the most chilling occult novels of all time, or on what makes Fafhrd and the Grey Mouser such a captivating – and lasting – pair of rogues but that has been done so wonderfully by writers much more accomplished than I. A brief biography perhaps? Illuminating the dry spells which interestingly enough seemed to almost always end with a change in writing direction might be interesting.

Or one could simply say thank you for the chance to share such a precious gift.

I can still remember the scene quite vividly. I was nine and my father was working away from home a lot. On one of his rare returns he came into my bedroom clutching a very battered copy of Fritz Leiber's Night's Black Agents he had found on the train. He thought it might be my cup of tea because the blurb promised "Worlds of fantasy and adventure!" coupled with "Nightmare stories of the oily-clawed beings that lurk in the coal-sack shadows of the city!" He was going through a stage of absent parent guilt, I think. It was just after the divorce and both he and my mother were very worried as to how I would take it, after all, divorce was a relatively new phenomenon back then. About the only thing he knew for sure about me was that I loved 'strange' stuff like Star Wars, so over the last few homecomings he had brought copies of Tolkien's The Two Towers (another novel rescued from a train) and one of Brian Daley's Han Solo spin-offs. All of these were terrific introductions to the literature of the fantastic and in their own way shaped my childhood into one of awe and wonder where nothing was ever quite as it seemed and shadows existed for no other purpose than to cloak a deeper and more sinister darkness. I was hooked.

That copy of Night's Black Agents travelled with me to school for about three months with me reading each of the stories over and over. My favourites differed from week to week, depending on my mood. One week I might be haunted by The Dreams of Albert Moorland, the next I would be unable to escape the lure of The Girl With The Hungry Eyes. Thanks to Fritz Leiber, I know one truism for sure: you never forget a good story.

When I was fourteen – and had devoured the entire stock of Lankhmar novels shelved in the local library, as well as Silver Eggheads and Green Millennium – I went back to Night's Black Agents, to read again The Sunken Land and Adept's Gambit. It was a hot summer day and England were doing fairly well in the Test Match so my English teacher, Mr. Knock, was in a benevolent mood. Free reading was the order of the day. Whilst my classmates lifted out battered copies of Henry IV Part One and Cold Comfort Farm I took refuge at the back of the class and lost myself in Simorgya once again. While Fafhrd and Mouser were in danger of being sucked down by the sinking island Mr. Knock plucked the book out of my hands and began thumbing through the yellow-edged pages, perhaps looking for some adolescent sex scenes, after all, I was utterly engrossed and that never happened with school work. Holding front and back cover delicately, he opened the book like a bird taking flight, the breaks in the spine showing which pages I kept returning to most frequently or lingering on longest. Smiling to himself, Mr. Knock began to read aloud:

"I think of the autumn of 1939, not as the beginning of the Second World War, but as the period in which Albert Moreland dreamed the dream. The two events — the war and the dream — are not, however, divorced in my mind. Indeed, I sometimes fear that there is a connection between them, but it is a connection which no sane person will consider seriously, if he is wise."

He ended up spending the next thirty minutes reading The Dreams of Albert Moorland to the class. About a week later, I noticed a copy of The Book of Fritz Leiber on his desk. Coincidence?

Apart from in itself being a dream come true, putting together The Black Gondolier And Other Stories has been a gift more precious than I can begin to express. I had actually forgotten just how wonderful some of these stories are. The language is crisp, the dialogue rich, the imagery vibrant. It is an incredible thing when you think about it, but The Casket Demon's media savvy heroine would be equally at home in today's Hollywood, her jet-setting lifestyle a match for an army of modern starlets, her command of the paparazzi sharp enough to rival the glamour of even the boldest and the most beautiful. And it's not just that story. The Black Gondolier with its prescient oil is more even more vital now than it was in 1964. Think United Nations edict 666, think Kuwait and Sadam, think of the x-million cars a day that roll over the bridges into our major cities, think of the failure of so called green power and the fallout of Chernobyl. Who can say for sure that the black stuff isn't working to its own agenda?

I think this longevity of not just story but the actual writing as well is the ultimate tribute I can offer to Fritz Leiber as a writer. That, coupled with the honest admission that there are eighteen stories gathered here and I dearly wish that I had written all of them, they are quite simply that good. As a writer, Leiber transcended the natural scope of genre, creating equally brilliant stories in the fields of fantasy, science fiction and horror, something a good many of the self-professed literati still claim is impossible despite the evidence laid before them.

All I want to say then is a simple thank you, Fritz, wherever you are.

Steve Savile
Stockholm, June 5th 2000

Biography

Fritz Leiber

Fritz Leiber is considered one of science fiction's legends. Author of a prodigious number of stories and novels, many of which were made into films, he is best known as creator of the classic Lankhmar fantasy series. Fritz Leiber has won awards too numerous to count including the coveted Hugo and Nebula, and was honored as a lifetime Grand Master by the Science Fiction Writers of America. He died in 1992.

OPEN ROAD
INTEGRATED MEDIA

Open Road Integrated Media is a digital publisher and multimedia content company. Open Road creates connections between authors and their audiences by marketing its ebooks through a new proprietary online platform, which uses premium video content and social media.

Printed in Great Britain
by Amazon.co.uk, Ltd.,
Marston Gate.